THE
RECKONING

BOOK THREE: ALL THE DEVILS ARE HERE

JEFFREY
PIERCE

Black Rose Writing | Texas

ISBN: 978-1-68513-055-8
PUBLISHED BY BLACK ROSE WRITING
www.blackrosewriting.com

Printed in the United States of America
Suggested Retail Price (SRP) $22.95

The Reckoning: All The Devils Are Here is printed in Garamond

*As a planet-friendly publisher, Black Rose Writing does its best to eliminate unnecessary waste to reduce paper usage and energy costs, while never compromising the reading experience. As a result, the final word count vs. page count may not meet common expectations.

For Betty Jane.

If you are so inclined, kiddo, you can read these when you're seventeen-ish, but you are 100% not required to. Just know, you are my favorite human being and the primary reason I get out of bed in the morning. (Yes, I do have to feed the dogs and take them out, but you know what I mean.)

ACKNOWLEDGEMENTS

Special thanks to Brian and Susan. Again, I am grateful for your friendship, candor, support, and enthusiasm. Thanks to Jai Mitchell who has again blessed me with his artwork. Thank you to those who have read books one and two. Two more to go after this one, then the story will have been told. Thank you for your readership. Some days, you folks are the only reason I am able to force myself to the keyboard.

THE RECKONING

BOOK THREE: ALL THE DEVILS ARE HERE

DRAMATIS PERSONAE

David Durant—A lieutenant in the Canadian Army.

Matthew Durant—David's older brother.

Isaiah Taylor—A black American ex-pat, son of a sharecropper, a decorated corporal in the French Foreign Legion.

Caitlin O'Leary—An Irish VAD nurse in the British Army.

Jonah Unger—A young Jewish machine-gunner in the German Army.

The Red Maiden/Gunnhildr—A long dead woman. A Viking raider chieftain.

Francois Annuniké—A Senegal warrior serving in the French Foreign Legion.

Alexandre Renoir—A Belgian sergeant in the French Foreign Legion.

Wolfgang Strathmann—A captain in the German Army.

Richard 'James' Cox—An American dispatch rider serving in the British Army.

Harlan Cox—James's elder brother.

Richard Cox—James's father.

Donnie McMaster—James and Harlan Cox's pal.

Big Don McMaster—Donnie McMaster's father.

Finbarr Kelly—An Irish Fusilier, former lover of Caitlin O'Leary, secretly serving the Fenian cause.

Rupert Fuchs—A German sapper.

Adolf Hitler—A psychologically blinded Austrian boy in the German Army.

Major Edward Danforth—A British cavalryman.

Lieutenant Brian Hugh—Major Danforth's subordinate.

Sergeant Darren Tremaine—A British cavalry NCO.

Shen Su—A member of the Chinese Labour Corps.

Zi Chang—Shen Su's friend, also in the CLC

Sergeant Li Peng—NCO in charge of Shen Su and Zi Chang's company.

Juddha Jai Pandit—A Nepali corporal in the Ghurka Rifles.

Oberon Junius—A Centurion in the Roman Army. In possession of the body of a one-eyed Scotsman.

Publius Quinctilius Varus—A long dead Roman General.

"Hell is empty. And all the Devils are here."

–Wm. Shakespeare *The Tempest*

PROLOGUE

—

HOPE

Isaiah Taylor stumbled through snowfall. He stopped and bent over, resting his hands on his knees, willing his heart and lungs to calm and recover. His uniform still held a heavy perfume of kerosene and petrol. The poisonous cocktail wafted up into his nose. Isaiah gagged and spat. He knelt, listening to the wind whipping the trees, gusting and spinning snow into drifts against the trunks. While his breath evened out and his pulse steadied, he looked back at the black and grey world the night brought on. His footprints were diminishing as tumbling snow filled them; he could not say for certain if the coming monsters' methods of tracking were the same he would use to hunt down prey, but he could hope.

"*Hope in one hand, shit in the other. See which one fills up first.*"

Mama had looked on Papa with reproof when he said it. As the visual dawned on Isaiah's baby sister, she began bawling with laughter.

Papa smiled. "*I ain't suggesting against hopin'. Hope all you want. But know it's a hollow word if you don't fill it up. You best put some fierce deeds behind hopin' and prayin' because without action, neither-a-those sentiments gonna get you a damn thing.*"

A keening howl ripped the night and sent a shiver through Isaiah. If whatever beast had sounded off was hunting him, maybe it did not need to see tracks in snow to run down prey. Scent alone might turn him out. He stood, then

I

froze when a black shape exploded out of the snow-capped evergreens, racing full speed, careening straight toward him.

As Isaiah tried to dodge, he tripped. The Red Maiden's saber slipped from his grasp and vanished in the snow. Isaiah spun onto his back, too late to stop the assault.

Then Black Betty stood over him, straddling his chest with her forepaws, breath heaving in and out, pink tongue finding his face and smothering him with wet kisses. Isaiah tried to fight her off, but she ducked her forehead and found his, pressing gently but insistently into him until he relaxed enough to push back into her warmth and accept her greeting. She licked him again, then stood and looked into the night, tongue lolling.

Isaiah wiped his face and scratched her broad chest roughly.

"Goddamn, girl. Missed you, too."

Black Betty's hot breath steamed out of her mouth. As he stood, she bowed her chest and wagged her tail, inviting him to play. She quickly saw that he was, perhaps, not in the mood. She circled him, sniffing at his ankle. He looked down as he rubbed her ears and realized she had caught the scent of fresh blood when he saw the dark stain beside his boot.

"Aw, fuck."

Isaiah bent and felt around for the cold steel of the German saber. He picked it up and stood gingerly on the bad leg.

"Fuckin' lion mighta saved me once, but them scratches still likely to be the death of me."

He looked up at Betty. She walked a few steps and glanced at him over her shoulder. She looked into the night, then turned again to see if he intended to follow.

Isaiah gritted his teeth and pressed on after her. Whatever was howling for blood out there in the storm would not catch him sitting and waiting to be taken, lacerated ankle, or no.

Francois led Caitlin and Adolf from the woods onto a snow-covered road. He had honed his sense of direction on the savannah of Senegal, mapping routes for French canals, then helping chart a course for the railway from Dakar to the Niger River in French Sudan. Even in this foreign land, he trusted his way-finding ability. Francois looked back, past Adolf and Caitlin, searching for pursuit. Nothing. If anything was out there, it hunted in silence.

"Come. It should not be far now," Francois said.

Caitlin was too spent to reply with words. She nodded and followed in his quickening steps.

Adolf Hitler understood 'Come'. It was close enough to German for there to be little trouble translating what the big African meant. He trailed Caitlin, close on her heels. Her head was bent against the falling snow, her shoulders hunched tightly, arms folding Isaiah's shotgun to her chest in a death grip. Adolf looked beyond her to Francois, leading the way, cutlass in hand. He found himself fervently wishing he had a weapon of any sort. The fact he failed to take a Mauser from the rifle rack in the Riqueval Tunnel when he had the opportunity gnawed at him, but then he recalled he had still been happy to be blind then; it would have struck the others as odd if the 'blind boy' grabbed a rifle when the time came to run.

Adolf pondered again the things that the demon in the barbed wire imparted to him in their brief, bizarre exchange. It could not have been more than a few seconds before Wolfgang Strathmann shut the thing up with the butt of his rifle, but in Adolf's recall of the moment, it seemed the dead man's whispers transported him.

They were seated together in the dark of a sleek, modern cinema in Berlin. His hands, resting on the red velvet arm rests, were his hands, but older—the lines and wrinkles accentuated by time. The scrawniness of war in their past, they were now soft, pink, plump, and manicured. Adolf realized he was wearing a perfectly tailored black suit-and-tie affair, nicer than anything he had ever owned in his life. It fit like a glove, and as he inhaled, he felt his posture rise to meet the fit of the suit. The clothes made the man.

The demon sat beside him, but now he was a smiling Fat Man, not a drowned German foot soldier. On the screen before them, tens of thousands of soldiers stood in rank and file. And *there*, there he was. Adolf shuddered with a burst of pride when he saw himself on the screen, three stories tall, stern and strong-seeming, watching his vast cavalcade of warrior-sheep in grey wool march past in rigid goosestep, all, all, all of them fervently saluting, arms held out, straight and erect, like a field of stiff grey cocks, and Adolf filled with joy. His mother and papa would be so proud. Papa would never smack around a man that all-powerful and mighty.

The Fat Man squeezed his arm. He raised a hand, snapped pudgy fingers, and the film froze on an image of Adolf, fists on hips, looking particularly imposing.

Adolf shot a sharp look at the demon. He was having a grand time. He very much wanted the film to keep playing. The fiction it created was as wonderful a thing as he could imagine.

"Our time is short, friend. I want you to know three things," said the Fat Man.

Adolf nodded, impatient. *"Yes? What?"*

The Fat Man patted Adolf's arm, patronizing.

"Number one—you must get away from Captain Strathmann. If you do not, he'll be the end of you, and we can't have that."

Adolf swallowed. The big captain definitely cut an imposing figure.

"Two, when you get past the wire, run straight for the woods. The Senegal and that comely little Irish nurse'll find you there. Go with 'em. Leave a trail if you can. If we don't find you before morning, when the time is right, I sure would appreciate it if you killed 'em in their sleep." The Fat Man smiled and drew a finger slowly across his neck. *"Kill 'em both dead."*

Adolf bit back fear. As much as Wolfgang Strathmann intimidated him, the big African was twice as terrifying. But he thought he might be able to summon the courage to slit his throat while he slept.

"Number Three—if you do those two simple things, all the glory you see on this screen will be yours for eternity, friend."

The Fat Man snapped his fingers again, and the film jumped and played on, and Adolf was a pig in shit as his infantry and cavalry stamped past the grand viewing stand, rigid and automaton, all individualism stripped, ready to commit every crime Adolf could think of, willing to let every crime of cowardice and weakness Adolf ever committed be forgotten, as he wrote a new myth with himself at the heart of its tortured fiction.

Then Wolfgang Strathmann cut it all violently short, caving in the demon's skull with his Mauser's steel butt plate.

Adolf had roused and followed the demon's advice, escaping the barbed wire and Wolfgang, then finding himself 'found' by the African and the Irish girl. Now he just needed to find a way past the cutlass and the shotgun to kill them with his bare hands. The odds seemed bleak, but if the Fat Man was to be believed, their deaths would earn him a kingdom, crown, and scepter to wield in any ways he saw fit. A bit of Irish and Senegalese blood spattered on his hands seemed a small price to pay.

♠   ♠   ♠   ♠   ♠

Donnie McMaster was fucking lost. He had the whole of the French frontier before him to escape into, but he could not for the life of him decide which path he ought to take. All roads seemed to run straight to Hell.

He saw movement, and his rifle flew up, taking aim. His index finger brushed the steel trigger, settling against it instinctively, pressure applied, a squeeze began, smooth and practised, just like his uncles showed him in the Mississippi woodland, but before he triggered the explosion, he stopped.

Finbarr Kelly's hands, the right one still wrapped in bloody cotton, shot up in surrender. "No! It's me! It's Fin!"

Donnie lowered the rifle and took a step toward the Irishman.

Then, the same howl that cut Isaiah's courage vibrated through the hollow.

"Oh, Lord... Where do we go?" whispered Donnie, a frenzy of terror building in him as he pictured a wolf at the head of the thousands of men coming after them.

Finbarr bit his lip, torn. He was not sure he wanted company. He had lost Caitlin and Francois' trail and abandoned hope of finding it before the hunters caught him. Donnie McMaster would either be an asset or a liability. A liability would get him killed. An asset, at this point, meant maybe gimpy Donnie and his rifle would sacrifice themselves in a rearguard action, allowing Finbarr to escape.

Fin was not proud of his gift for cold calculation, but he was not ashamed enough to pretend it was not who he was. He was finding he could forgive himself for a lot of sins, even if he never professed them in the confines of a confessional to some moldy priest.

"This way," Finbarr said.

Without looking back, Fin charged into the woods, running southwest. He knew Donnie would accept the invitation. He had pegged Donnie from the jump as a follower. Finbarr Kelly was a keen judge of character.

♠ ♠ ♠ ♠ ♠

The Little Boy sat on the stoop with his wolf's empty rope leash, gazing out at the shimmering dunes.

The Old Woman came out on the porch and wiped her hands on her apron. She stood behind the little boy and set her fists on her hips.

"Dog ain't come back yet?" she asked.

The boy stared down at the raw wooden steps, sullen.

"You lookin' worried," she said.

"Ain't." The boy fiddled with the leash. "Goin' to get her," he mumbled.

"What's that you say? 'Goin to get 'er'? No, you ain't. Get your little butt back inside."

He shot her a contemptuous glare.

"Child, you best mind y'self. Don't invite no trouble in that you don't want keepin' you company. You hear?"

He stood without looking at her and brushed past her into the diner.

"Hoo. 'Bout ready to put that leash on you, boy. Can't get no good help these days."

♠ ♠ ♠ ♠ ♠

The little boy stalked through the roadhouse. At the bar, the Fat Man contentedly devoured his meal. The boy stopped in the middle of the room, face flushed with impotent rage. He squeezed the rope leash in his hands, feeling the prickly hemp stab his palms. He wondered where his lupine friend was now. Having more fun than he was, certainly.

The crone had not come back inside and was no longer on the front porch. The Fat Man seemed lost in consumption. The little boy glanced at the back door. The old maxim, *Forgiveness is easier granted than permission'* rung in the boy's ears. He quietly headed for the exit.

The Fat Man heard the boy leaving but did not look back. He was pleased. He knew who was coming through the desert toward him now. With the boy and crone absent, he was just as happy to make his next move in private.

The back door shut silently. When the Fat Man finally turned and looked over his shoulder, no sign of the boy remained.

♠   ♠   ♠   ♠   ♠

The little boy awoke, covered in snow. The body creaked and groaned into motion as he bent it to his will. This was the second corpse he had ventured into since he went from the French child into the chaplain to kill that meddlesome Russian bastard in the Talmas church. His failure to stop the others there, while they were still in disarray, earned him mockery and punishment. He was back in the game now, determined to make the most of it. Redemption awaited.

He stood and stretched, then looked down at his naked, petroleum-charred flesh. He found himself quite pleased by the horror of it all. Anyone whose last sight was this burnt monster coming out of the dark to savage them would die in terror. He picked up the broken, charred lance that struck down good Doctor Halstead and tested the weight of it. Still sufficient for throwing. Outstanding for thrusting and stabbing, killing and maiming.

He stretched his chest again and smiled as he took in the black flow of the St. Quentin Canal, which had so recently been a firestorm. The Red Maiden's failure was twice as ignominious as his; at least the Russian was out of the way. Now a true competition was afoot.

The Little Boy turned Doctor Philip Halstead's corpse away from the canal and scrambled it up the steep slope, guiding it on a southerly bearing, privately hoping to find his pet on the way. The thrill of the hunt thrummed inside him.

♠   ♠   ♠   ♠   ♠

Isaiah Taylor had been correct. Had he stayed in the barn where the bastards tried to hang him and awaited nightfall, he would have nearly busted a gut watching Harlan Cox, Sheriff Coombs, Daddy Cox, and Donnie McMaster's father—beefy bully 'Big Don' McMaster—trying to stand and walk on the shattered leg bones of the bodies they exited at dawn and were hoping to re-enter.

Harlan was the first to give up the unfortunate attempts at walking and submerge, flowing out through Siggy's nostrils and mouth. With no empty vessel awaiting him, the mist of beingness—the 'soul', for lack of a better term—evaporated, seeming to wink out of existence.

♠   ♠   ♠   ♠   ♠

Harlan awoke in the desert. He leaned up, closing his eyes against the blinding sun. When he opened them again, Daddy Cox, Big Don McMaster, and Sheriff Coombs were with him. The four of them stood. The white-hot sun was already pinking the bare skin of their necks and arms. No one spoke. Richard Cox saw the roadhouse looming in the hazy distance. He headed that direction. The others came after, Harlan last.

Harlan hurried his pace and caught his father.

"Daddy… Do you know what's going on?" Harlan asked.

Richard smiled at his eldest. "Dreaming, son. Having a dream's all. Go back to sleep."

"Daddy… this doesn't feel like any dream I ever had."

Daddy Cox smiled, tight-lipped. "How do you know?"

"What?"

"You remember every dream you ever had?" Daddy Cox asked.

"Yes… I mean, no, not always… Sometimes I don't think I've dreamt at all. Sometimes I remember a dream when I wake up and forget it before I'm done with breakfast."

"Yes, son. That's the picture. Maybe this dream is the kind you don't think you've had. Maybe it's the kind you wake up from and forget… All I know is, this can't be real."

"… Why?" asked Harlan.

Richard Cox patted his oldest boy's shoulder. "'Cause you been dead and gone for a good handful of years now, son. Put you in the ground myself. Laid that first shovel of dirt on your casket. 'Ashes to ashes' and all that mess. If this ain't a dream, I don't know what it could be."

Harlan was silent for a long time as his own memory of the event washed through him.

"I… I wasn't, Daddy," said Harlan.

"Wasn't what?" his father asked.

8

"... Dead, Daddy... I was still living and breathing when that first shovelful hit."

Daddy Cox stopped. He looked at his son and swallowed hard. He reached out for him, but stumbled and fell to his knees. "Oh, Lord... Oh, Lord... Oh, Lord..."

Sheriff Coombs and Big Don looked on, hiding their discomfort—they understood the emotional response, but could not condone it.

Harlan knelt by his father and grasped his hands. "It's okay, Daddy. What's done is done. We're here now, ain't we?"

Daddy Cox nodded, wiping tears from his cheeks, ashamed. He looked ahead, across the desert to the diner.

"I thought I'd been having nightmares all this time..." said Daddy Cox.

A tremor of guilt flushed through Harlan as he remembered the nightmare events that led up to his collapse in the church.

The black girl in the rooming house.

The things he and Donnie McMaster had tried to do to her.

Then Donnie tried to erase their shame by choking her until she died, while Harlan stood back and watched.

Harlan reached out and took his father's hands, helping him to standing. "Daddy... I thought this was all a dream at first, too... But now I think it's something else... I believe we may be doing the Lord's work." The quote came to his mind, almost unbidden, then tumbled out of him, all that Bible study finding its purpose. "For Behold, the Lord will come with fire and with His chariots, like a whirlwind, to render His anger with fury and His rebuke with flames"..."

Sheriff Coombs and Big Don were listening now. The idea that they were being loosed on the world for divine reasons was appealing. Sheriff Coombs had used the star on his chest to justify his questionable deeds in life. Big Don had hidden behind his flowing Klan robes. To think that they would now be free to do as they pleased under the banner of a righteous God was thrilling. King Richard the Lionheart slaughtering Muslims on his Crusade, Spain's 'Hammer of Heretics' Tomás de Torquemada, and bloody Cardinal Richelieu embarking upon his Inquisition must have all experienced the same lightheaded joy when they decided Jesus would literally forgive them for ANYTHING.

Harlan recalled his rebirth, when he murdered and strung up the German scout at the train depot. It had indeed been like a living nightmare. But not a nightmare he was dreaming; a nightmare he was *delivering*. He, Harlan Cox, *was* the nightmare itself. The things he had done to Siggy had been a Grand Guignol horror show. When he took over Siggy's body and opened the dead man's eyes, the first thing he saw was his baby brother, James, and a young black man who seemed awfully familiar, though he could not place him at first.

After the fracas in the train depot, they chased the black man down on the railroad tracks and beat him senseless. It was then that he remembered Isaiah from Donnie McMaster's rotten cotton field. Stringing him up in the barn seemed the best way to bring Isaiah's nightmare to its fullest realization. But he had underestimated the young man's resourcefulness. They were back in the desert because of it. He would not make that mistake again.

"Yes, Daddy... I believe we're doing the Lord God's work," Harlan said. He took Daddy Cox's hands and helped him to his feet.

Richard Cox took out his handkerchief and blew his nose. He stashed it away and squeezed Harlan's hand. "Alrighty then, that being the case, let's go see where that old lady'd like us to go from here. Mayhap there's more to be done, or maybe our earthly work is over, and the Lord is ready to bring us to His bosom," Daddy Cox said. "Either way, standing out in this heat with our thumbs up our butts isn't gonna cut it."

Daddy led them, pressing on through the heat toward the distant roadhouse. Harlan, Big Don, and Sheriff Coombs followed.

♠   ♠   ♠   ♠   ♠

The three cavalrymen charged along the creek bed through the falling snow. The sounds of the horses' breath, their hooves breaking the thin layer of ice, the rhythmic slap of sabers against hips, were the only things Sergeant Darren Tremaine could hear. But he did not need to hear it to know what was behind them. He witnessed the men pouring through the barbed wire in slobbering pursuit of Isaiah and gladly turned his horse to follow Major Danforth and Lieutenant Hugh as they galloped away. Death was coming.

When Major Danforth reined in, Tremaine had to yank his horse's head sharply to match him.

"Split off! Sergeant Tremaine, go south. Lieutenant Hugh, ride north. I'll continue west as long as I can. Rally at the barge in St. Quentin by dawn; but for God's sake, don't turn for it until you've evaded pursuit."

"Yes, sir!" said Tremaine.

Major Danforth wheeled his mount and galloped west along the stream. Lieutenant Brian Hugh turned north. Sergeant Darren Tremaine kicked flanks and headed into the snowy woodlands in the opposite direction.

♠   ♠   ♠   ♠   ♠

Tremaine rode hard through the snow for a mile, then eased to a walk. Killing his horse would avail no one, most of all, himself.

He patted Bathsheba's neck and brushed snow from her mane. "Good girl. Good girl."

He looked back, wondering if perhaps the hunters had missed the moment when the three had ridden their separate ways. As lucky as he had been throughout all his life, he doubted he was that fortunate.

Darren was the youngest of the three Tremaine boys. A surplus baby, a surprise arrival, perhaps one child more than his parents were prepared to govern.

Gavin Tremaine was the eldest. The well-groomed apple of his father's eye. His actions and opinions were meticulously structured. He was the future of the Tremaine family name. Making certain he survived and thrived, that he burnished the family honor and appreciated its value, was vital. He rose to become a rigid statesman, a Member-of-Parliament, staid and regal in bearing, his upper lip as stiff as they come beneath its handsome moustache. Gavin expressed envy when his younger brothers both went off to war, but Darren knew the military would not have suited his eldest brother. Even though his father could have purchased him a lieutenant's commission, Gavin's strict upbringing left him relishing and requiring control. Following orders from men he considered his inferiors would have driven him mad.

Second-born Cyrus came into the world quiet and demur. He was sickly as a babe and his parents lost years of their lives fretting over his ability to survive infancy, but the boy's genes were strong, and although he would not have lived to see his first birthday in any century prior, the physicians of London kept the baby breathing until he could grow and thrive on his own. By the time Cyrus turned one, he was out of imminent danger, to his parents' great, sweeping, weeping relief. Suffering through that first year only to lose the boy to pneumonia or the like would probably have killed both of them.

There was a brief reprieve when all seemed right with the world. Then Darren surprised them by showing up in his mother's womb, and all the fatigue they had accumulated hit at once. Between managing the eldest, trying to make certain of his future as the face of the family, and unable to shake the habit of worry over sickly Cyrus, Darren was left to his own counsel, for when he came screaming into the world, they were too tired to make any attempt at governance. The youngest Tremaine would have to seek life's boundaries on his own.

For most of his youth, it worked out wonderfully for him. He did as he pleased when he pleased, and damn the consequences, for there usually were none for a wealthy, white, child of the upper class. That is, until he discovered the army.

In 1908, just out of school and staring down the road at a life of ease and leisure that had been handed to him on a platter, something inside Darren snapped. He stood up, walked to the stables, and had his gelding, Sampson, saddled. He rode Sampson from the manor into town and signed on with the newly formed British Territorial Force.

When the recruiting sergeant asked if he wanted to purchase a lieutenant's rank, Darren demurred. The last thing he wanted was command. He wanted boundaries. He wanted discipline. He wanted to be rewarded for good behavior and punished for bad. What his family and his society could not provide him, he hoped the military might.

Darren was reborn as Private Tremaine and finally discovered the strict discipline he had spent his entire youth yearning for. He excelled within that framework and made his way quickly from Private Tremaine to Lance Corporal Tremaine. He was proud of the accomplishment. He earned his stripes through action, while the Officer Class paid for theirs with birthright and cold, hard cash.

By 5 August 1914, when The Times' headline screamed "BRITAIN AT WAR", Darren had risen to become Corporal Tremaine with command of his own section of cavalrymen. They deployed to Belgium with the first wave of the British Expeditionary Force to head off the brutish Hun assault.

The morning of their first engagement, long, lean Captain Edwards stood before his officers and non-commissioned other ranks while the enlisted men finished feeding and watering the horses.

"Alright, lads. Now we're in it. On the Colonel's command, the bugles will sound the charge. Ride like the devil at them. If we can catch them in awe, we'll get one pass through before they've a chance to form squares. That should break their line. We shall wheel then and come through for a second pass. After the second charge, those Huns will be running for Berlin. We shall turn one last time and run down every bloody one of them who does not throw down arms and surrender. Understood?"

There was a chorus of, "YES, SIR."

"Rally the company. And may God be with you. Death or Glory, lads. Death or Glory!"

'Death or Glory' had been the way for centuries of mounted warriors, forcing their horses to charge into hailstorms of arrows at Crécy and forests of bayonet points at Waterloo. As Darren readied his section for the charge, he realized that while 'Death' seemed fairly clear-cut, he had no earthly idea what 'Glory' actually meant. He intended to find a dictionary and look it up as soon as possible, though he never did.

The Lancers formed their line. The Colonel gave the order. The bugle made its clarion call. Every man kicked flanks and yelled their battle cry. Sabers flashing, long bamboo lances couched, their steeds thundered forward, charging into the breach.

One moment, Darren's section was tearing through the field at full gallop, toward a distant line of men in field grey with long, serrated bayonets fixed to their Mausers and antiquated spiked helmets atop their heads. The next, there was a terrific roar and clatter and Darren was shooting through the air, up and over his dead horse's neck, his saber flying from his hand, his lance nearly breaking his spine as he somersaulted and landed on top of it.

He slid to a stop and lay on his back, stunned. He heard horses and men screaming. He heard what sounded like a hundred machine guns clattering away, and the CRACK of bullets as they zipped invisibly fast through the cyan sky he was staring up into.

As the shock subsided and the pain in his back escalated, Darren rolled over onto his belly. He pulled his broken lance off his back and threw it aside. He crawled through the field to his horse. Sampson was already dead when he reached him.

Darren pulled his rifle out of its scabbard and gathered the few men from his section who were still living. They fought a rearguard action, using their dead horses as cover, keeping up steady fire while the surviving men of the company escaped. Darren earned the Distinguished Conduct Medal and was given a Sergeant's stripes for his efforts.

It was the final British Cavalry charge of all time, and it had been a spectacular failure, but an excellent lesson. Darren had finally found the true boundaries he sought. Actual war came with immediate, life-and-death consequences. Where his parents, teachers, siblings, and society failed him, War succeeded. It finished the job of turning him from a boy—unbridled, carefree, immortal, and foolish—into someone who realized that life was short, bullets did not mind who your parents or your God were, and death was insatiable, uncaring, and constantly ready for you, whether you were ready for it, or not. In one morning, war turned him into a man.

♠   ♠   ♠   ♠   ♠

Darren reined Bathsheba in, swung his leg over the saddle, and dismounted. He opened his saddlebag and grabbed a handful of oats. He watched the path behind him, listening intently while Bathsheba ate from his gloved hand. He gave her two more helpings while he sieved through his options.

He knew the city of St. Quentin was less than five miles south. The barge they had painstakingly provisioned from abandoned German stores awaited them in the canal. He was certain he could trace the route to the boat once he came to the canal, or even from the Somme River that the canal flowed into, but he knew if he turned that way too soon, if he led an army of the dead there while night still had its hold, all the effort to prepare the barge would be for naught.

A bone-chilling howl echoed in the wilderness.

"Christ…" murmured out of him.

He mounted and let Bathsheba walk while he checked his compass. He was headed south. A direct ride to St. Quentin would take less than an hour. If his horse did not collapse, if he did not run headfirst into an unexpected band of the dead, he could reach the city and make course corrections then. For now, putting distance between himself and the dead men he felt coming was all that mattered. He urged Bathsheba to a trot and pressed on.

♠   ♠   ♠   ♠   ♠

CHAPTER ONE

—

HC SVNT DRACONES

Shen Su's thick shoulders and arms ached, but he pressed on. His feet slipped in the freshly fallen snow, but he pressed on. The four petrol cans, with their full loads, sloshed back-and-forth. The pairs of fifty pounders, barely balanced on the ends of the metal ramrod resting across the back of his neck, were torturous, stifling circulation to his arms, which tingled painfully in response, but he kept on, numbing himself to the pain. He knew the others were counting on him. As long as he stayed on the road, he would reach them. He believed if he could remain numb and place one foot in front of the other, he might beat the setting sun and save them. Shen Su did not realize that behind the storming clouds, the sun had set half an hour back.

He froze when he heard them coming. Su bent his exhausted knees and dumped the gas cans off his aching neck, then stumbled and fell into the cover of the snowy trees.

One hundred yards below him, three British riders tore out of the darkness, rounding the bend at a gallop and racing their frothing horses along the frozen bed of a small creek. They pulled up sharply, their mounts huffing and stamping as the men shouted in English between them; then the three horsemen split in different directions, galloping into the night.

Shen Su waited until he was certain they had gone before he began to stand. Halfway to his feet, he heard a rumbling in the distance.

An army was coming.

Su saw the first ranks of thousands of the dead emerge from the darkness. He ducked back. His face quivered and his hands clutched involuntarily as he watched the massive horde slow, then split into three parts, each group chasing a different rider's hoofprints.

Ten minutes passed, and the flow of dead men finally trickled away. Su nearly sobbed with relief.

When he peeked out and saw *her* coming in their wake, he nearly bit through his lower lip to stay silent.

The Red Maiden rode her magnificent white and black Andalusian along the track her army had left. The stallion paused and bent its neck, slaking his thirst from the stream the army's boots had revealed below the fresh layer of ice and snow topping its flow.

She looked back. A trio of dead men came running through the trees to the west. As they approached her, Su heard them talking, but it was not a language he recognized. When the lead man finished, he saw her nod in agreement. She directed the three of them south. Without hesitation, they turned and ran across the stream into the tree line.

The Red Maiden, in Léonie's body, pulled her reins, bringing Joshua's head up from the water. Before she spurred his flanks, she stopped. She looked into the woods in Shen Su's direction.

Su's breath caught, and a new flush of terror washed through him. He tucked back, willing himself to be part of the tree and no longer a man. He squeezed his eyes shut; certain she had seen him. He fought through his terror. He forced himself to open them. He peered around the trunk. She was gone. The swath torn in the stream bed was the only sign she, or her army of dead men, existed anywhere but in his head.

But Shen Su knew he had not gone lunatic. This was not something crafted by a broken brain and psyche—both might be badly injured right now, but he knew he was not insane. All this horror had a clarity to it insanity could not create. He had observed that clockwork order playing out in real time on Good Friday.

When the Canadian soldiers came to Shandong Province and offered contracts, Shen Su was the first in his village to sign. Su was not an eager beaver volunteer. He was not in search of adventure or war. He was a peasant blacksmith from a long line of peasant blacksmiths with no aspiration beyond his trade. He loved his family and his work at the forge and in the shop. He had less than zero understanding of what the Canadian Major was trying to tell them about 'Standing up to the Germans', nor would he have particularly cared. He felt no fealty to the flags of Great Britain or Canada. If anything, he owed them disdain. Memory did not have to reach far to recall the heartbreaking day word of his uncle's penniless death while laying track for the Canadian Transcontinental Railroad arrived. What differed here and now, tempting him to walk away from the comfort of his home and life's work was the sacrosanct paper the Canadian set before him.

A Contract.

On the table was an opportunity, an enticement, to put his strength to use with real, long-term purpose. Ink your mark on the line and for three years, regardless of your circumstance, the Canadians would send your honored mother and father bi-weekly payments. With his own salary included, it was more than enough to stead the family for a decade, even under the worst circumstances.

A contract was a fascinating thing. An agreement on parchment that might as well be etched in stone, violently binding two parties together, putting the entirety of their beings at risk if either violated the compact. Su had the magistrate read it through to him a second time, then, before all the other young men in the village, he stepped forward and solemnly made his mark.

He did not regret it until he was on the ship, stuffed into its belly, riding steerage, cramped in with thirteen-hundred other men who had signed their lives away to join the Chinese Labour Corps.

It took eighteen days to cross from Beijing to Vancouver. The ship docked in the dead of night and the cargo bay doors flung open, letting out the stench and thick air, replacing it with the crisp cut of Canadian spring. The taste of clean air was pure intoxicant. Su reveled in it as they were hustled and force-marched to the railhead under cover of night.

Disgusted Canadian soldiers processed them through a cattle yard, stripping and washing them down, coating them with delousing powder, then handing them ill-fitting blue uniforms and straw hats with 'CLC' stitched on the brim. Before dawn came, they were fed gruel and bacon, then the same Canadian soldiers shoved them along, up into cattle cars behind a locomotive, whose steam whistles screamed as the train car doors were padlocked shut. Then the steel wheels shrieked against the rails and the engine was grinding them east via tracks built on the bones of these same Chinamen's forefathers. The irony that he was riding roughshod over his favorite uncle's graveyard was not lost on Su.

On the trip east, rumors in the boxcar began to swell that perhaps things were not what they seemed. Perhaps they had not been brought to Canada to serve as labourers and mechanics. Perhaps they had been brought for something far more sinister. Perhaps they were to be live target practice for the Canadian Armed Forces. Perhaps they were to be slaughtered and fed to the soldiers in some barbaric rite that would stimulate lust for German blood. A mild panic in the exhausted men began to spread. It was then that Shen Su stood up in the packed boxcar and reminded them all why they were there.

"Stop."

The mutterings ceased. Su was not a towering man, but his strength of presence was felt in any room he walked into. Perhaps it was inheritance from the Huns who raided and raped their way through his ancestors, for when he stood tall, he was immediately recognized as a force to be reckoned with. He stood firmly in the center of the swaying train. All eyes in the cattle car turned to him.

"I cannot tell you what comes next any more than you can tell me. But just as you, I have a contract. We have given them three years, and in exchange, our families will be paid and fed, regardless of what becomes of us. If you have regrets now, keep them to yourselves. For me, I will live as if I have already given my life for my family. If you signed your life away with any other expectation, then you did not understand why you were making your mark and your ignorance is your own failing. Do not break the will of the rest of us with idle talk, with rumor-mongering. For my own self, I know why I signed, and I accept that they are bound to this contract as surely and inextricably as I am. I accept it, even as a death sentence, because my family will be cared for regardless what comes of me. I signed that contract with honor. Unless the Canadians break faith, I will sacrifice myself with honor if need be. This is the Tao before *us. This is the Way we have chosen. If we live, it is as it is. If we die, it is no different. So, let it be.*"

Shen Su was raised in the Taoist creed. He embraced its truths and lessons as well as he could. He could be like water—effortless in action, flowing with calm force, pressing on, relentless, through any twist or turn until it reached the sea.

And so, one month later, all the steel trains and riveted ships released them from their depths and cast them up onto the docks at Le Havre, into the waiting arms of the Canadian and British Armies.

Then Good Friday came and ended things.

As the world fell apart, Shen Su was fairly certain that the contract he signed in Shandong had suddenly and unceremoniously been abrogated. All the Canadians he might have thought to hold to account for breach were dead before Easter Monday, and now he found himself flowing along a snowy track, carrying the liquid means of survival for his trapped companions across his shoulders. If he could reach them, they might live. If he could not, they would die. Now, unlike when he stood in the train and made his speech, dying seemed an entirely different outcome than staying alive.

He had seen that in no uncertain terms at sunset on Good Friday.

Su pushed away the thoughts and memories. He ignored the 'ifs' for the time-being. He could not change the past or control the future. The best he could do was his best in the now. He took a breath, then he slogged on through the snowstorm.

♠   ♠   ♠   ♠   ♠

The screen door slammed shut behind Big Don McMaster. He trailed Sheriff Roy, Harlan, and Daddy Cox through the diner toward the counter.

The Fat Man wiped his mouth and spun around on his stool. A broad smile cut across his wide face. He laughed aloud when he saw the stern, sunburnt faces of the Klan members. "Hoo-whee. Ain't you boys a sight. Heard there was some trouble with a, heh-heh, sixteen-pound fence maul…" The Fat Man chortled.

Daddy Cox grunted, unamused. "Is the proprietor on hand?"

The Fat Man shrugged and grinned. "Afraid she's currently indisposed. Something I can help you with?"

Daddy was not quite sure how to answer that question.

The Fat Man wiped his chin. "You know what they say? They say ten percent of folks are good, ten percent are evil, and eighty percent will gladly follow whoever is strongest. Ain't that something?"

Daddy Cox was unsure how to respond.

"I s'pose you're a might confused, good sir," the Fat Man continued. "Mayhap a bit disoriented by this entire turn of events. Why, you had just settled into bed with the missus, hadn't you, Master Cox? When you woke up and smelled the smoke? Burnt your hand on the doorknob, but then you went and opened it anyway. I bet the draft of fire flying in to eat all the oxygen in your bedroom caught you and the missus by surprise a tad, didn't it? Sucked the oxygen right out of your lungs, burnt off all your eyelashes and eyebrows, turnt that silver mane into a Roman candle. Your fine bedclothes lit up, all that silkworm spit just fused right to your skin. Last thing you heard, the Missus shrieking and diving headfirst out the window in flames. Glass caught her jugular vein, or she might've survived the fall. Shame. What's the last thing you recall? On the floor, choking on cinders when your heart went and popped in your chest?"

Daddy's sun burn was the only red in his skin, the rest of him was ashen.

"The only thing you can be sure of in the end is that the end ain't gonna be pretty. And your end was ugly as sin, wasn't it?" The Fat Man looked past Daddy to Big Don McMaster and laughed hard. "Don, Don, Don, Don, Don! Speaking of ugly as sin. They got you good, too, didn't they?"

Big Don remembered sitting bolt upright in bed when the boiling hot tar poured onto his chest, burning through the skin, sticky and searing. Then they had beaten him with axe handles and cut open his down comforter, coating the hot tar with smothering goose feathers. They dragged him across his own porch, down the front steps, through the dirt yard and lynched him up on the ancient oak that his ancestors had used as a whipping post for their slaves, many, many times.

"Tarred, feathered, *and* strung up. Mm, mm, mm. The trifecta! What a way to go. HA!" The Fat Man laughed and wiped his chin with his napkin. He looked past Big Don at Roy Coombs. "And you, Sheriff Coombs. Hoo-boy. They kep' it simple, didn't they? Held you down, shackled you in your own cuffs, sat on your neck and let the life leave you breath by breath. Made sure you saw it coming and had time to think it all through. They let you beg for your life with the only breath you had until you finally let go of hope, 'cause you knew there was not a goddamn thing you could do about it. Then, *poof*, the candle finally snuffed out. Wasn't the first time you experienced that, was it? Was just the first time you was on the receivin' end and not the givin'.'"

He looked over at Harlan. "And lastly, Young Master Cox. Your ending happened a good while back, but Miss Jean's work was impressive as Hell, too."

"What business is that of yours, sir?" asked Daddy Cox.

"What business? HA! In short, *you boys* are my business. And business is a-boomin'. You fellas and your kind have bought and sold some kind of idea that there's a Lucifer out there in the wilds of some vicious, burning Hell that comes and whispers in your ear, tempting you to sin. Mighty convenient, that. When you do wrong, it wasn't you, it was Satan! Well, I'm here to tell you this; the only Satan there is lives right inside there." The Fat Man poked Daddy square in the middle of his forehead, leaving a white indentation in the pink. "And what I'm here to do is to help you dance with that devil, instead of pretending that's NOT. WHO. YOU. ARE. Everything in you wants to do wrong. When given the choice, you almost always choose to do wrong, or do nothing. And every choice you people have made has bent the world toward the end it's at. And I'm of the opinion that will not change. So, my 'business' is to offer you what you pray for every Sunday—Divine Forgiveness. And the opportunity to wake up 'Monday morning' and do it all over again, with even more zeal than you did it the week before."

The four men were silent. This was not entirely the 'Righteous Divine Mission', as they had defined it for themselves.

The Fat Man shoved a piece of bacon in his mouth and chewed it down. He followed it with a swallow of coffee and grinned. "Now, let's get to brass tacks. You boys ready to be cut loose? All forgiven-and-forgotten, slate of sins wiped clean so you can chalk up as many fresh ones as you can handle?"

They were silent.

"I'll take that silence as consent, then. Time to get your 'hanging party' back under way. Close your eyes."

He saw hesitation. "Boys, I'm about to cut you off the leash. Just asking you to do what comes natural to your kind. Or, I can send you on to receive some more punishment, if that's what you'd prefer."

The threat hung in the air.

"Let's try this, fellas. Whyn't you just imagine that you are all indeed dreaming, and let your pure, natural instincts lead you where they may? I believe that if you can just relax and realise that you ain't actually 'Good Men' you'll do just fine in the trial set before you."

He let that sink in, making sure they understood what he was offering. They did not appear to be swallowing it entirely. "Or... OR, we can decide that I'm sending you forth to do God's righteous work, if you all would prefer it in those terms."

He could tell that the simplicity of that was more to their liking. "Fine. We'll call it that. Now—Close. Your. Eyes."

The four, following Daddy Cox's lead, submitted.

"Hip, hip, hooray," said the Fat Man. "Now go forth, 'Children of God', Conquering and to Conquer."

♠   ♠   ♠   ♠   ♠

When Harlan opened his eyes, he was in a dark pine box. Memories of his death in Cox County flooded him and he shrieked through the dead German Major's dry throat. He punched up and the lid of the casket loosened. He kicked and punched again, pummeling upward until the thin pine shattered and he was free.

He sat up in a white-washed cellar in St. Quentin and found himself with three other coffins in a makeshift morgue. He helped Daddy, Big Don and Roy Coombs out of their own wooden resting places. They stood there looking at each other.

"Daddy?" asked Harlan.

A black-haired Bavarian Captain nodded. "Yes, son. I'm here."

"Sheriff Coombs?"

A Sapper Lieutenant with a thick blond mustache nodded in response. "Yes, Harlan."

The last of them was a big, square-shouldered Sergeant.

"Big Don?..." Harlan asked.

Big Don McMaster nodded.

"Alright then," said Harlan, "I believe that fat fella said we were to continue with our 'hanging party'?"

"Indeed, he did," said Daddy. "In Jesus' name."

♠   ♠   ♠   ♠   ♠

Waiting for them at the top of the cellar stairs were three German Shepherds. Daddy Cox knew hunting dogs. He saw that these were prime beasts.

As they ventured into the empty streets of St. Quentin, they followed the dogs, collecting rope and a long spool of telephone wire along the way. When the dogs caught the scent of living men hiding in the ruins of the city, they drove them out into the open where Harlan and his fellows captured, tortured, and hung them, reveling in the gift of freedom and righteousness the Fat Man had bestowed upon them. Amen. Hallelujah.

♠   ♠   ♠   ♠   ♠

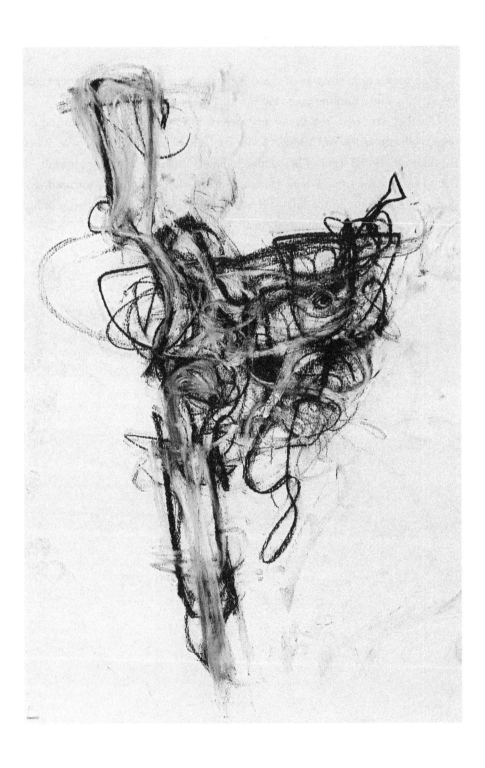

Chapter Two

—

Little Jim Nantuck

Jonah Unger wanted the end. He saw the grey shape of Rupert Fuchs running through the snow ahead of him. He knew Lieutenant Durant and Sergeant Renoir were just beyond Rupert, charting the course. He sensed James Cox and saw his arms pumping in his peripheral vision. He heard Captain Strathmann coming just behind them, his presence urging Jonah to keep pressing forward. The pressure his peers were applying was all that kept him from laying down and succumbing.

It was the horses that had done it. The sight of them sapped his will to live. That early morning in 1915… the re-visitation of the sights, sounds, and smells of the day were triggered by the brave British cavalrymen. He had managed to suppress the memory for two years, crushing it into a tight ball and shoving it into the corner of a deep hall closet in his mind, slamming the door shut and bolting it, nailing sturdy beams across the threshold to keep it interred. The mental exercise had been a success. It held the memory at bay, or at least kept it out of the sunlight, but it seemed now that all the effort was in vain. In the dark closet of memory, the thing his actions birthed must have continued to grow and flourish, feeding on the darkness; and now, it seemed to have found a key and escaped, a fully-matured black mass inside of him.

The wheat field had been prime. Green and still growing, the spears thick, the stems and stalks seeming longer by the second. Unfortunately, the men who should have been champing at the bit to reap the harvest of their laborious planting were dead, or on their way to it.

The patriarch, Thiéry, died of a heart attack when the family fled the German invasion. The eldest son, Michel, was killed on the battlefield two weeks after he graduated from infantry school. The youngest son, Henri, too young to join the French Army, currently lay in hospital, dying of influenza he contracted as he and his mother moved from refuge to refuge, seeking shelter in Paris. But the sum total of the men's labors had outlived them all and was in a gorgeous state. Had they lived to see their field, pride and avarice would have moved through all of them. The harvest would have been spectacular, the cash return, huge.

Jonah walked through the winter wheat, stunned. Wolfgang Strathmann was near at hand; Lieutenant Diestle, too, whose quiet gallows' laughter was the only thing Jonah heard over the tinny ring in his ears. The green wheat brushed his knees, and he wished he could smell it, but his nose was filled by the stench of machine-gun oil, burnt lead, and ignited white powder.

The sun caught the bright, shining horse hides perfectly. Their brushed coats and braided manes gleamed in brown, honey, and gold tones. The blacks of fetlocks and forelegs shone like pitch, the white diamonds on their foreheads and chests gleamed like fresh paint. Their riding tack was immaculate; polished saddles and reins, shining brass, and silvery steel bits between their teeth. The blood was the brightest shade of red Jonah had ever seen.

Jonah staggered.

His acne-pocked loader, Ernst Steiner, grabbed him and helped him stay standing.

"*Chin up, Jonah, chin up,*" Ernst said.

Jonah nodded. He did not want to look like a weakling, especially in the presence of Lieutenant Diestle, who never let up with the ridicule and name-calling of his 'Little Jew Gunner'. Looking as though he had lost his appetite for war would lead to no end of abuse, and in Jonah's experience, abusive behavior spiraled at the first sign of weakness in the victim. He would walk this field as brazenly as Lieutenant Diestle, or die trying.

Jonah did not count the dead horses. Later he was told that there were one-hundred and forty-four of them. He could not help but keep count of the still-living ones he finished at close range.

Eight.

Eight magnificent beasts in various states of suffering that he, or one of the other two gunners, began killing with their machine guns and now had to summarily finish with a bullet to the head. He shut his eyes each time he fired his rifle.

There were eighty-five dead men, too, and a score of stunned survivors and wounded, but they were not put down. They were catalogued and disarmed, sent to the rear to suffer the loss of their equine companions in prison camps for the remainder of the war.

After the last dying horse was extinguished, Jonah's company moved forward. The 12th ASC Labour Battalion arrived, and before midday, had crafted a long, zig-zagging trench at the far edge of the field. The battlements would only deepen and grow from there, shooting arteries out in all directions like a living thing; a virulent, spreading cancer fed on the industrial-scale bloodletting that took place above it.

By mid-afternoon, Jonah and Ernst had finished setting up their MG '08 in its emplacement. They secured it with sandbags around the tripod, on a perfect fire-step that would keep them low enough to avoid snipers, but high enough to direct their field of fire into any British infantryman sent screaming in their direction, bayonets fixed, 'killing faces' engaged.

The wind washed a bitter scent over Jonah and Ernst. Jonah looked back at the field of green wheat. The Labour Battalion had stripped the dead horses of their riding tack and dropped it all into wagon beds. All the leather and metal would be put to good use. Nothing wasted. Then they began the butchering. The ripe blood, organs, and intestines, the stench of an open-air slaughterhouse caught by an easterly spring breeze, nearly brought Jonah to tears.

The meat and organs would end up in stew pots, the beautiful hides would become gloves, belts, boots, and black leather gaiters for German officers. The intestines would be stretched and strung into suture thread for the medical corps. The rest—the bones and cartilage, the spilled blood and brains—would stay in the field, feeding the green wheat's roots until it flourished to full growth. Then the stalks would be scythed down, ground to flour, and baked into loaves of bread for the army.

Nothing wasted.

Everything wasted.

Jonah was given the Iron Cross, First Class for gallantry. He survived two more years of war and never fought off another cavalry charge. He purposefully avoided looking at horses that entire time. Of course, he was aware when a quartet of the beasts hauled artillery past or dragged the field kitchen up for a hot breakfast, but for thirty-one months he succeeded in never looking directly at a horse again. It was a curious feat, but he managed it quite well. If he could pretend the horses were not there, he could certainly pretend that all the ones he had machine-gunned and mercy-murdered did not still reside in a dark closet in his brain.

But now, with the world at its end, the sight of the British horsemen coming to their rescue had broken that streak, and broken the door that held those memories fast, and he felt them charging out of it. The memory was alive. It felt as real as if it was all happening again. The recall of that Indian summer morning and all that came with it filled him to his toes, engulfing him, stampeding over him, revealing him as broken, trampled—his insides, his soul, his very being smashed to nothing by the things he had done and seen. Jonah prayed. He prayed for death to find him quickly and put him out of his misery so he would not have to do it himself.

No answer to his prayers came. For now, buoyed solely by his mates, he ran on.

Durant was leading the way, twenty feet ahead of Jonah, with Renoir just behind him. After them came little Rupert Fuchs, followed by Jonah Unger and James Cox, running in tandem.

Wolfgang was at the rear, alternating between looking back for pursuers and looking ahead to where his brother's murderer cut a path in the snow behind Durant. More than once, he considered accelerating and running Alexandre Renoir down right then, tackling, then bludgeoning him to death with his bare hands. Voices in his head were urging him to the deed, screaming for vengeance, but Wolfgang held back their entreaties for now. He would know for certain, and then he would act. Until then, survival was paramount. When dawn came and the monsters pursuing them fell, he would find out the truth. Then what would be, would be.

Durant stopped, and the others caught up, huddling around him. "We should be near St. Quentin soon. We'll keep to the woods and skirt it until we reach the river, then we can follow it back toward the city until we find the cavalryman's boat. Make sense?" Durant asked.

There was no conversation. Wolfgang translated for Jonah and Rupert. They nodded understanding.

"What about everybody else?" asked James.

Durant considered it. "I don't know. I don't know where they all split off to. I don't know who made it through the wire and who didn't. And I don't see any way in hell we want to head back toward what was coming after us. I think we'll have to hope the cavalrymen can round them up or lead the..." Durant had trouble summoning a fitting word for the monsters. "... The 'things' away from us. Maybe they'll be able to pick up everyone else's trail in the morning and bring them along to their boat... I don't know."

There was silence. Durant stood and led his companions on toward St. Quentin at a steady run.

♠   ♠   ♠   ♠   ♠

This was not the first time Durant had run in snow from death. When he and his brother arrived in the northernmost Canadian territories, the first snows of winter had already begun. They would grow much worse before any weak springtime reached the tundra and turned the ice to running rivulets, creeks, and rivers of pure water, but no amount of melted snow would wash away the blood that followed in their steps.

Before Matthew and David reached Vancouver, they stayed the night with an old friend of Matthew's in Kamloops, on the Thompson River. After David went to bed, Matthew stayed up into the early morning hours in deep discussion with his pal. He sold their father's wagon and team to him at a bargain rate, then they took their guns and money the rest of the way by riverboat.

In Vancouver, on the very same docks that Shen Su and his comrades would be ushered through en route to the Great European War, they booked passage on a steamer bound for the Yukon Territory. It took nearly a week in rough seas to reach Skagway, and another five days beyond that to make their way by wagon team to Carcross. They rode into town as the sun set. Even in the gloaming, Matthew knew exactly where he was headed.

When they left what little there was of Carcross's main drag behind them, David turned to Matthew. "Where are we going?"

Matthew smirked. "Belly of the beast. We're gonna pay a call on my old pal Hamish Jarmusch. See if we can't make a bargain with him."

David hesitated. "I thought you said the Mounties were after you, that you got in a gunfight with them."

Matthew laughed. "In a manner of speaking. It was more of a simple misunderstanding than anything else. And what I failed to mention, is that Captain Jarmusch doesn't know that I partook in said 'gunfight'. It'd be best if we kept it that way, you understand?"

"Yes, " David said.

Matthew continued, "If I use some of papa's money to clear my debt, I've got a feeling Captain Jarmusch can put us to use and we can earn it all back and then some, then leave here free and clear. You're not afraid of a little hard work, are you?"

"No. I'm not afraid of work," David said.

He should have been.

Smoke wafted out of the stone chimney in Hamish's log cabin.

Matthew reined in the team and pulled the wagon to a stop in front of it. "Stay where he can see you. Keep your hands high so he can tell they're empty. He might come out a little hot, but I'll manage him."

David swallowed his fear and nodded.

Matthew looped the reins and stood in the buckboard. He raised his hands and called out. "Captain Jarmusch, it's Mattie Durant out here. I know you're in there enjoying your fire, and like as not, a bit of Scotch whiskey. I feel pretty certain you've got a Winchester aimed at me right now, and I don't take that hard at all. Come on out and let's have a parley, Captain. I didn't come back to do you wrong, no, siree. I came to make things right."

The door to the cabin swung open. A big man stepped through. The hitch in his gait, remnant of his stretch killing Boers in South Africa for the British Army ten years past, did nothing to diminish him. The limp may have been distinct, but it gave no whiff of handicap in the big man. He wore the yellow-striped blue britches of the North-West Mounted Police tucked into polished knee-high boots. His red tunic hung loose and unbuttoned. A thick salt-and pepper mustache curved around the ends of a smile as he studied the two young men in the wagon. In his hands was a .404 caliber Nitro Express Elephant gun. Hamish had used it to kill seventeen Boer men, women, and children, one leopard, two lions, a Cape Buffalo, one Black Rhino, three elephants, plus a hundred-some American Buffalo back on the North American continent. He would have tried for a hundred more had the northern herds not dwindled away to nothing.

Hamish grinned. "Matthew Durant, as I live and fucken breathe. And with some kind of fucken kin, to boot; the spitting image of you. My Winchester's still in the rack, but this one here's nothing to sneeze at. Like as not, if I pull the trigger she'll cut the pair of you in half from nut-sacks on up."

Matthew smiled. "Well, I can't say as I'd like that very much, Captain. Wouldn't like it even a little. I know we parted company under circumstances beyond my control, and if it didn't weigh a little on my conscience, I'd still be in San Francisco living the life. I'm here to make amends."

"Amends? Shit, son, I'm pretty sure you're here to get your name off the Wanted List."

"Well, sir, now that you mention it…" Matthew replied with a grin.

"What you owe, plus interest."

"Wouldn't have it any other way."

"Glad of that."

"On the question of interest,-"

"Wasn't a question in that sentence. Apologize if it sounded like there were," Hamish said.

Matthew nodded. "Yes, I understand, but the thing is, I can pay you the principle in cash right now. Then we can work off the interest and go our separate ways, if that'd be alright with you."

"Ha! And how would you intend to do that?"

"Well, Captain, according to the papers, and our mutual friend down in Kamloops, I know you've got some business with the Indians."

"Hm. You spend a lot of time reading the papers, do you? You never struck me as the reading type."

"More as a pastime than anything else, but any time I see an acquaintance mentioned in print, I don't pass it by."

"They mentioned yours truly by name?" asked Hamish.

Matthew shrugged. "Well, not specifically, but I knew when they mentioned the North-West Mounties, they were talking about you for certain."

Hamish released the rifle's hammer and rested the weapon on his shoulder.

Matthew's eyes twinkled. "You know I've got good friends among the Tagish elders. I did right by them, and they did right by me, even if it did upset some friends of yours. I think I could save you a headache. I can talk them into letting go of their tots and sending them to boarding school without a fight. But not the one up here. The one near Vancouver. My brother and I'll wrangle the kids, take 'em south, and leave 'em in care of the nuns and priests. I'd be happy to take a deputization and handle it all for you."

Hamish laughed. "What's your angle here, Durant?"

"Like I said. Clear my debt. Clear my name. Go on with my life in a prosperous fashion. That's the long and short of it."

"I don't believe you for a fuckin' minute."

"There is the 'per child bounty' to think of," Matthew said.

There was a brief pause as the gears turned in Hamish's brain. "Hadn't heard about that," Hamish replied.

"Well, sir," said Matthew, "in order to keep the government checks coming, the boarding schools have to meet student quotas. If I help the Catholics meet their numbers, you can bet that some of that government money is going to come my way. And I don't see why we wouldn't give you a solid cut of it."

"Stands to reason."

"Then there's a deal to be had?"

"I'll count my cash on the barrel first, then get an exact figure of what my cut would be, an' we can go from there."

"I'd expect no less." Matthew turned to David. "Brother, grab the cashbox, would you?"

David was numb, but he nodded. He climbed into the wagon bed and rummaged for the black metal box. He hefted it by its brass handle and carried it back out.

As he entered his cabin, Hamish Jarmusch unconsciously echoed what their father had said upon Matthew's homecoming. "Come on in if you're comin'."

The brothers followed him in.

♠　♠　♠　♠　♠

After the transaction was complete, the Durant brothers rode out. They made their camp off the road a mile away. David got the fire going. It was at full blaze, settling to a steady burn when Matthew came back with more fuel. He set the bigger pieces into a pile and sat across from David. He watched his little brother turning his hands in front of the flames to warm them.

"You all right?" Matthew asked.

David looked up from the fire. "Yeah. I suppose."

"Sorry I didn't tell you the whole story before."

David nodded. He was silent for a stretch. "Is there more?"

"More what?"

"More to the story."

"Oh. Shit. Um. Not really."

"Sounds like maybe there is."

Matthew laughed.

"I'm not sure I want to do this, Matthew."

"To do what?" Matthew asked.

"Kidnap Indian kids and take them south."

Matthew laughed again and shook his head. "We're not 'kidnapping' them. We're delivering them to school. We'll be official deputies and everything. And it's not like we're taking them to prison. We're running them down to a bunch of Catholics. The kids are gonna learn reading and writing and arithmetic. They're gonna get fed and housed and have the fear of God slapped into 'em by nuns and priests, and when they're seventeen, they'll let 'em loose in the wild; learnéd Christ-y folks instead of a pack of wild savages. Civilizing them. Nothing wrong with that. We'll be doing them a good turn."

David shook his head. "Still doesn't seem right. Don't you think that if it was what they wanted, they'd deliver them to Vancouver themselves? And why's the church paying a bounty if it's all for the good?"

Matthew shrugged. "Here's the thing—the Indians don't necessarily know what's best for themselves, so the government and the Catholics aim to teach them. I know you wouldn't've gone to school unless mama made you, would you? This isn't different from that, but the Tagish mamas don't know it's for the good of their kids. And, regardless, I can tell you this—it's better than what's come before. Papa ever tell you about Cypress Hills?"

David paused at the mention of his father.

"You never heard of the Cypress Hills Massacre?" Matthew asked.

"No," David replied.

Matthew let out a long sigh. "He used to tell me about it when he was slurring drunk. Like he was bragging. Or warning me what he could do if he set his mind to it. This was after the American War. Papa had come back up to Saskatchewan, or thereabouts. Bunch of American wolf hunters—I think papa served with a couple of them in the war—crossed the border and he met 'em there. They made camp and hit the bottle. Prob'ly singing marching songs and reminiscing about killing Bluecoats. When they woke up the next morning, some of their horses had wandered off. Well, they were on Assiniboine land; not that they cared much, they had a big wolf pack on the run and weren't thinking about borders, per se, they were thinking about pelts and money. Anyway, they figured their horses got stolen by the Indians. Papa got some trappers to show them where the Assiniboine were camped, and they lucked into finding one of their horses nearby. Assumed it was confirmation of the theft, when it was probably just dumb luck. And bad luck for the Indians. As I said, Papa and those boys had been up to their snoots in the bottle the night before, and the Indian folk they ran into had likely been doing the same. Tempers ran hot, and I figure they musta all still been high as kites, because papa's pals went on a goddamn rampage. Somebody said something rash. It pissed the Assiniboine off well and good. One of the younger injuns starts stripping down for battle. Before he got his shirt over his head, one of the Americans pulled his piece and shot him in the belly. Then all hell broke loose. Before it was over, they killed a baker's dozen of the Assiniboine—all comers. Guessing there was rape and robbery, too, though papa didn't make mention of that. After it was all said and done, his pals sobered up and ran back to America. Papa headed west, ended up in Hope. Planted himself there and didn't look back unless he was far gone in the bottle."

David had not heard of it.

"It's the whole reason the North-West Mounties formed up. Gotta keep the Americans on their side of the border and the injuns on our side and out of trouble. Now, these schools we're talking about are part of the solution. It's not like they were invented yesterday. The Catholics, the Anglicans, even the Presbyterians, been taking Indian kids to their boarding schools for a long time. It's just expanding now, and we can be a part of it, and get a good return."

"It still feels wrong."

"Nah. It's progress. Less than a hundred years ago, you could collect a bounty for scalps. Now, you deliver the Indian alive-and-well, scalp still attached. The head priest in Vancouver says, 'We're killing the Indian inside the Indian instead of killing the Indian.'" Matthew laughed. "A little roundabout, but seems like progress for sure."

David nodded. Progress. Sure.

♠　　♠　　♠　　♠　　♠

David and Matthew sat inside the smoke-filled Tagish lodge. They wore the uniforms of North-West Mounted Police. The red coats and blue pants were poorly cut, as the work had been farmed out for slave wages to the Canadian Penal System. The prisoners, who may have been reasonably talented criminals, were less than gifted tailors, it seemed.

Despite the cold outside, the heat in the lodge was oppressive. They had been talking back and forth for more than an hour. It was slow-going torture. David stretched the neck to get the itchy wool off his skin. Through the open doorway he saw the island at the heart of the lake—a massive turtle's back rising out of the ice-cold water, surrounded by the snowcaps of the distant Yukon's peaks, all flowing up to a perfect, cloudless, turquoise sky that begged him to escape into it.

The Tagish elder, Frank Nantuck, sat across from Matthew and listened silently as he told of the wonders of a Catholic education. The lodge's other residents sat behind Frank, listening patiently while Matthew made his pitch with a deft, respectful charm. One of the children, who could not have been more than ten, smiled shyly at David. David smiled back. Frank raised his hand and Matthew stopped mid-sentence.

"We have the Anglican school nearby. Why send our children way down to Vancouver, a world away?" Frank asked.

Matthew shrugged. "Well, the Catholics are a cut above. If you want your children to have the best education possible, the Catholic school in Vancouver is superior in every way. Tell me the truth, are you happy with the education your children are getting from the Anglicans?"

There was silence before Frank spoke. The grim faces on the parents behind him answered the question before he did.

"No," said Frank.

"And why not?" asked Matthew.

"Hard to recognize them when they come back spouting Jesus. And I mean no offense to your Jesus. He says many wise things. But our children come back saying 'Jesus is the only way' and ashamed of themselves, ashamed of their parents, ashamed of their history."

Matthew nodded, somber. "I understand."

Frank turned to his family. He waved the nine-year-old boy forward. "This is my grandson, Jim."

"Hello, Jim," Matthew said with a smile.

"Hello," Jim replied.

Frank sat Jim next to him and hugged him around the shoulder. "There is nothing in this world more precious to me than this boy. Why should I give him up to you and the Canadian government, Matthew?"

"Well, first, you know it's the law. No one wants to see more Tagish arrested, least of all me. We've had a good business relationship, you and I, and I'll always be indebted to you for the arrangements we made that let me trap and hunt on your land. Unless you would say otherwise, I feel I always treated you fair when it came time to compensate."

Frank Nantuck bobbed his head in agreement. He had become a wealthy man by letting Matthew and his crew poach on Tagish lands.

Matthew continued, "By Canadian law, all native children have to attend residential school from the age of five to seventeen. So, you can send them to the Anglican School, which you don't seem satisfied with, or we can deliver them safe and sound down to Vancouver, then bring them back, confirmed in their relationship with Jesus, educated in the ways of the modern world, and ready to lead your people into this new century. It really is that simple."

Frank revealed nothing.

Matthew played his last card. "There's also the matter of restitution. The Canadian government is allotting a certain dollar figure per child for their schooling. But the children have to be there for it to get paid out. The government can't just go handing out money willy-nilly. There's got to be an accounting. For every Tagish child that attends the Catholic School, I can guarantee you ten Canadian pounds."

Frank mulled that over before he spoke. "So, for one-hundred children, that is one-thousand Canadian pounds."

"That's the figure, for certain."

Frank was quiet for a time. "Why don't the Anglicans pay?'

"Well, sir, I hate to tell you this; the Anglicans receive the same amount of money from the government per student, but they keep it for themselves."

A murmur played through the lodge at the revelation.

Matthew raised a hand. "I'm not saying that the Anglicans are bad men. If the Catholic school in Vancouver was filled to brimming, as the Anglican school is up here, I'm sure they'd be doing the same, but the Catholics are sorely wanting for students. They could end up shut down if they don't fill their classrooms, you understand?"

"The Canadian government will send the Catholics money every year, for every student that they have?" Frank asked.

Matthew nodded. "Yes."

"So, the Catholics will send us money every year that our children are there."

Matthew paused. "Hm... I'm fairly certain that if I talk with the Monsignor something could be arranged."

"You can guarantee ten pounds for every Tagish student, every year?"

"I don't think the Catholics will have any argument against that."

Frank tousled his grandson's hair. Little Jim smiled and leaned into his elder's embrace. Frank spoke to him in Tagish and the boy stood and returned to his mother. Frank looked back to Matthew. "We must discuss amongst ourselves, Matthew. Come back in a week's time."

Matthew nodded and smiled. "We'll be here."

♠   ♠   ♠   ♠   ♠

Ultimately, it took eight weeks of Matthew's charm, guile, bribery, threats of eternal damnation, and force of will, but he got commitments from Frank

Nantuck and the other Tagish elders. They delivered one hundred and fourteen of their children, ages four to fifteen, to Carcross on the designated day.

Matthew used nearly the last of David's inheritance to book passage to Vancouver. Little Jim Nantuck left his grandfather's side and was the first to board the ship, assisted by David.

From Vancouver, Matthew made a deal on credit to run the children via paddleboat up the Thompson River to Kamloops.

When they approached the school itself, Little Jim held tight to David's hand, awed by the priests and nuns draped in their long black cloth. David pried his fingers free and patted the little boy's shoulder as he ushered him forward.

The head priest, Monsignor Magritte, had one of the nuns reckon out all of Matthew and David's expenses, along with one-hundred Canadian pounds per child. To Monsignor Magritte's joy, all one-hundred fourteen of the children had arrived at the Kamloops Residential Indian School alive and well. They would not leave there in the same fashion.

Little Jim held a brittle, ancient nun, Sister Marian Kelly, by the hand. He waved goodbye to David as the brothers walked away from the Kamloops School. David waved, then looked to the waiting paddle boat. He could not bring himself to look back at the children they had left behind. There was a choking emotion in his throat, but he forced it down and spoke.

"Matthew… I don't want to do that again."

"Do what?"

"I don't want to run any more Indian kids down here."

"Yeah. Neither do I. And the pickings'd be slim. I think we got every last 'heathen' child the Tagish had been holding back from the fucking Anglicans."

David nodded.

"Anyway," Matthew hefted the cashbox, "in case you hadn't noticed, we're bona fide rich men. We're gonna take this money back to Carcross, pay off Hamish and the Tagish, then grow richer still, little brother."

Matthew and David went back through Vancouver and turned north again. Their cash box was brimming with money passed through the Catholics by the Canadian government. After paying Frank Nantuck and Hamish Jarmusch their cuts, Matthew knew exactly how he intended to invest the remaining financial returns. The brothers arrived back in Skagway alive and well. They would not leave there in the same fashion.

♠   ♠   ♠   ♠   ♠

CHATEAU - MARGAUX
1er VIN 1900

Pillet-Will

©jm2022

CHAPTER THREE

—

AN ELEGANT MARGAUX

Six years later, on Good Friday of 1917, Monsignor Magritte opened the first bottle of 1900 Chateau Margaux that his thoughtful older sister in France, Gertrude, had mailed him at no small expense. A second and third bottle sat in the wine cellar. He fully intended to let them gather dust until Christmas, unless the Bishop paid a call, which was certainly a possibility. Together they would toast the success of the re-education they had lain on the Indian children in his care. It was a brutal business, sure, and there were moments when Father Magritte feared they were doing more harm than good, but in the interest of trying to save these people's eternal souls, he had been promised by his superiors that no amount of force could be considered too harsh. Bishop Grandin, God rest his soul, had written, "We must instill in them a pronounced distaste for the native life so that they will be humiliated when reminded of their origin. When they graduate from our institutions, the children have lost everything Native except for their blood." And that was true. Though sometimes they lost their blood as well. When Father Magritte confessed to the Bishop that losses of that sort had occurred, he was told to say five Hail Marys and know that it was simply God's Will. Any children lost at a holy institution were either past saving— unable to renounce their heritage and already damned—or blessed by being pulled early to the bosom of The Lord. Monsignor Magritte had his doubts, but he let the Bishop salve them and continued with his mission. And now he might well become a Bishop in his own right. The thought of taking on the Pectoral Cross thrilled him.

As Monsignor Magritte sipped the deep, delicious red wine, he said a small prayer, grateful for the vintage. It was a heavenly blend, the product of a perfect year of harvest, from start to finish. It nearly brought him to tears. He began to pen his sister a long letter of thanks. As the wine seeped through his system, leaving its savor in his palate, diving down to his belly, leaving its poisons in his liver, then penetrating his blood stream and saturating his neural circuitry, his script became looser and his thoughts began pouring out onto the paper until he had a piece that flowed with warm gratitude and told of his great, secret, sinful pride at his forthcoming promotion. It climaxed with an open-hearted revealing of his doubts and fears about the mission, but culminated with the strong certainty that her loving brother was doing God's work, and doing it handily at that.

At the midpoint in his proofread, he went to refill his glass and found the bottle empty. He stood, and the heady rush of the alcohol hit him fully with a flush of ecstasy. One more glass. That was all he needed to reach the letter's conclusion. He toddled down to the wine cellar and pulled the second bottle off the shelf, then returned to his study.

He finished the draft of the letter in fine form. At least that is what his wine-sodden brain told him. He re-read it and it brought him laughter, then tears, then redemptive joy as it came to a peak of pure belief that God was guiding him, that all the sacrifices and brutalities done in Jesus's name could only be to the good, and that any doubts of that were Lucifer whispering poison in his ears. He finished the second bottle, then signed his name with a flourish.

With great affection, your loving brother, Monsignor Charles Magritte

Then he struck through *Monsignor* and wrote *Bishop* above it. It felt brazen. It felt naughty. It was thrilling and heady. When the letter reached her, he believed with all his heart that the promotion would already be complete.

He folded the letter carefully into the envelope and set it aside for the next week's post.

The second bottle was empty. How had that happened? The glass goblet's last drop was settled into a red film at the bottom of the bowl above the crystal stem.

He stood. The room spun, but settled fairly quickly, and he knew he was well and truly drunk. His bed was calling. But so was the third bottle, sitting all by its lonesome in the cellar, whispering up the stairs to him. A half glass more in the chill night air, then off to bed. The night would be officially capped.

He eased down the stairs with his lantern and made his way through the dust and filaments of ancient cobweb to the wine rack.

It was empty.

Monsignor Magritte shook his head. What in God's name? It had just been there.

Then the lost bottle struck him in the head. The heavy glass heel and punt shattered, cutting his scalp deeply and bathing him in rich, perfect Margaux. Magritte stumbled, concussed, but still conscious. He reached for his torn scalp and felt sharp shards of glass sticking out of his head. With his other hand, he stretched out, grasping for the wine rack to catch himself. His cassock robes caught up in his feet. He misjudged the rack's distance. He tripped and fell, forehead smacking off the wine rack as he went. He was unconscious before his chin struck the brick floor.

♠   ♠   ♠   ♠   ♠

Little Jim Nantuck was sixteen when he finally succumbed to his Catholic upbringing. Six years after David and Matthew left him to the tender mercies of the priests and nuns, he died. The official cause was pneumonia. The truth was that Father McKinnon, the big red-faced Irish bastard, had punched Jim in the face, then shoved his desk over. After that, he kicked him in the ribs twice. No one ever checked to see what the bruising might reveal under the skin, but the fragile ribs had broken badly. For three nights, Little Jim lay awake in bed, unable to sleep from the pain. The infection got into him then. It made its way down, down, down, all the way to the base of his lungs. A week later, the wrenching, violent coughing, the ugly tasting green phlegm, the redoubled pain of his injuries; it was all gone. He lay still on his cot, drowned in diseased mucous.

Father Magritte stood beside weeping Father McKinnon. He patted his friend's shoulder. "God's will, Father McKinnon. God's will."

McKinnon nodded, consoled.

Sister Marian covered Jim's body. She had the groundskeeper, Ewan Cooper, come for him then. Ewan had already scooped a burial plot. It was tough going in the cold ground, but Ewan was no stranger to hard labor. Over the years, he had done this many, many times. It needed doing again, so he did it.

Ewan dumped the little malnourished corpse in and buried it. He used the flat of his shovel to bring the ground smooth and level. If there was to be no headstone, there was no sense leaving any other indicator of the boy's passing.

♠ ♠ ♠ ♠ ♠

It was pitch black and biting cold when Father Magritte awoke. He could not move. His head was pounding. The remains of the Margaux, the bruising of his skull from the floor, and the deep cuts in his scalp from the shattered green glass, all fought for the attention of the pain centers in his brain, overwhelming them.

As his wits began to coalesce, he was terrified he had somehow broken his neck in the drunken fall and been paralyzed. His body did not seem to be responding to any of his commands. He tried to take a deep breath to calm himself, but even that seemed impossible; his chest and belly would not expand to allow much oxygen in. His adrenaline spiked at the sensation of suffocation. He felt his pulse accelerating, and with a sudden burst of joy he realized he could not be paralyzed if he could feel his heart beating in his chest. He indeed felt sensation, down to his fingers and toes. The issue was, he could not move them, not a millimeter. He was buried in the ground, up to the throat of his black cassock.

A match struck. The light blinded him when the sulphur exploded. The warm glow touched to a wick and a hurricane lantern settled into being as the glass chimney was lowered onto it.

Father Magritte blinked his teary eyes. The skeletal figure across from him sat calmly, watching. Little Jim Nantuck was naked. His skin was blotchy with blood that had congealed inside him. His eyes were sunken. His hair was dry and matted to the sides of his head. His left hand sat on his lap. Father Magritte saw that the nails were broken and chipped, covered in dirt from clawing his way up and out of the ground.

"Jim?..." shuddered, almost soundless, out of Father Magritte's throat.

Jim nodded.

"Help... me..."

Jim's smile was small. It vanished as quickly as it came. "I will," the dead Tagish boy replied.

46

The lantern caught the reflection of the broken bottle in Jim's right hand. Quick as thought, Jim stabbed the shards into Magritte's head, and a strangled scream burst from Magritte's mouth, unable to provide enough oxygen for a full expression of the pain.

Little Jim Nantuck stood on his skinny, malnourished legs. He picked up the large glass jar of honey he had found in the cellar stores. He undid the string holding the waxed cloth on top of it, then upended it, pouring the bee's thick, golden leavings onto the buried man, drowning him deep with it.

For a moment, as the honey covered his mouth and nose, Magritte could not breathe at all. Gravity pulled it past his lips, and he was able to suck in a taste of air. "Pl-please, Jim… Please help me… God will forgive you… Please help me…. God will have mercy on your soul."

Jim looked down at the man of the cloth, his bloody face and scalp covered in shining gold honey, the blood reminiscent of Christ's rent scalp beneath his crown of thorns, the shining honey reminiscent of the gold his Christian tribe sought and pillaged at every step in their invasion of the world, all the time carrying the words of Christ (along with sabers, whips, and muskets) to express his eternal love.

Jim took it all in for a time, then turned away. As much as he would have liked to stand witness to everything the fresh blood and raw honey would draw from the wilderness to feast, Jim knew that Father McKinnon, Sister Marian, the groundskeeper Ewan Cooper, and all the other priests and nuns in the school needed killing before the dawn came. It was a significant task, but Jim felt up to it.

He surely was.

He killed Ewan Cooper last, on Easter Saturday morning, just before the sun rose. As Jim left the twitching, shuddering body, he knew his work was done. When the sun broke the eastern plane, Jim Nantuck's body fell. Its work complete, the corpse lay still and never rose again. In time, it would return to the dust from whence it came.

♠ ♠ ♠ ♠ ♠

©jm2022

Chapter Four

—

We'll See

Lieutenant Brian Hugh looked back. The way he had come was clear. He slapped his thigh, pleased. When he separated from Major Danforth and Sergeant Tremaine at the creek, he rode directly north for a fast quarter mile. He found a road there that ran east and west. He cantered one hundred yards west on it, then cut north, again off road, making a broad half-circle, arcing east through the woods; back to where he first found the road. He paused there and listened. He heard the dead men churning toward him. He rode another hundred yards east, then cut across the road and galloped directly south.

He rode parallel to the northbound path he had made for a mile, hoping to God that the things chasing him were not organized enough to send scouts out on their flanks. He slowed his mount in a stand of snow-covered pines and halted, listening.

The steady crash of men running through the trees, chattering back-and-forth in what sounded like a thousand different tongues, was terrifying. It took long minutes for the dead army to move beyond his hiding place. Brian Hugh imagined them reaching the road and plowing along the trail he had laid to the west, following it back through the woodland, then turning south to where he stood now. He kicked his mount in the ribs and guided him west through the woods, straight to the broad swath the dead men had left behind them. He turned south and galloped through the torn snow, praying his passage was as imperceptible as it seemed.

When he reached the creek bed where he originally split from Major Danforth, he rode at a steady clip along the path on which they had come until he reached the Siegfried Line. From there, he cut south, following the edge of the barbed wire.

After an hour of steady riding, he found the St. Quentin Canal, whose cut would lead him down to St. Quentin proper and the barge's promise of hope. Brian slowed his horse to a walk. He saw burnt bodies, put to the torch by Philip Halstead, riding the canal's gentle current south. He looked through the fast-falling snow for pursuers. Nothing but swirling ice crystals and darkness. It seemed he had successfully put them off his trail, yet he did not feel too comforted. He drew his saber, resting it on his shoulder. He had seen these things move fast and silent. If they came for him while he was edged against the canal, he would not have time to draw and respond. In the distance, he heard a canine howl.

"Stay sharp, lad, stay sharp," he said to himself. He rode on, slow and steady toward St Quentin.

♠　　♠　　♠　　♠　　♠

The Little Boy wearing Philip Halstead's blistered skin paused in the snow. He heard his wolf sounding off, and he fought the urge to howl back at her. He wanted her by his side for this hunt, though he knew it was foolish. He really just ought to let her enjoy herself. Eventually, she would catch his scent and find him, or he would find her, and then they could go forward together. Patience. For now, he would track the horseman's hoofprints until he ran him down.

He checked the trail. The horse had slowed to a walk and falling snow had not yet softened the outline of the horseshoes. The cavalryman would not be far. Little Boy Halstead loosened his spear arm and lengthened his strides.

He covered several hundred yards at a steady clip. As he rounded a long bend in the canal, he caught sight of the rider ahead of him in the distance, trotting along the toe-path toward the city. When the horseman looked back to see if he was followed, Halstead ducked low. He circled up into the woods overlooking the canal bank and began to close the ground between him and his prey. Now the real game began.

♠ ♠ ♠ ♠ ♠

Shen Su tripped and fell. The metal pole struck the base of his skull where the top vertebrae connected, stunning him, sending a jolt of pain shivering through his back. The gas cans crashed into the snow.

Su pushed himself up, righting the cans quickly to save their precious cargo. Only then did he pause to recover from the pain. He knelt and carefully shifted his stiffening neck. It still had most of its range-of-motion. He worried that might not remain the case. There was a crackling noise coming from it as it turned. Although it was not brutally painful, the sensation suggested something beyond a minor bruising.

He bent down and slid the ramrod back through the gas can handles, then knelt and eased the pole behind his neck, balancing the cans as he set his front foot and pressed back up to standing. He lost balance for a second, but caught himself before he tumbled again. Su leaned in the direction he needed to go, forging ahead on legs that felt brittle, praying for the strength to reach his destination. He had never felt this weak in his entire life.

When the cargo ship carrying its load of Chinese men finally reached France from Canada, Shen Su was far from the strong young blacksmith he had been when he boarded the first ship. Midway across the Atlantic, they hit the first storms. The rest of the journey found them in a near constant gale. From the bowels of the ship, it seemed the massive waves were trying to turn and flip them at least once every half hour. Whenever the ship yawed past forty-five degrees, whimpers of terror ran through the hold, and though Su kept his whimpering silent, inside, his mind was crying out, too.

When they stepped haltingly on unsteady legs down the long wooden gangplank onto the solidity of the French docks, he was unsure he would be able to find the willpower to climb back up into the ship that would be meant to take him home, assuming he somehow survived his three years of indenture. Between poor nutrition and sea sickness, he had dropped at least twenty pounds. Most of what had vanished, he was certain had been muscle. Shen Su did not think he would ever regain the strength lost on the long journey.

After the last Chinese man disembarked from the ship, they milled on the wooden jetty and watched the bustle of men and materiél pouring out of the quay. Thousands of crates, pulled off cargo ships sent by America and England, were piled high. Cranes hefted artillery pieces from ship decks and swung them over onto the dock, narrowly missing swarms of men in olive drab and horizon blue who were running about beneath them, trying to organize the chaotic flow of incoming ordnance without getting killed by it.

A gangplank dropped off another ship, and row-upon-row of sullen British infantrymen tramped down, returning to a war they had hoped and prayed would somehow be over and done before their leave in England ended. The French concrete beneath their feet was proof the prayers had gone entirely unanswered.

Su watched Labour Battalions slaving away. It was a bizarre sight, a shock to Su's system—this world he had known bits and pieces of, but never imagined would be realized. He had, of course, heard of black men and women, not figuring he would ever see one in the flesh. Here, the docks were teeming with them. Scar-faced Senegals in French Horizon Blue, turbaned Indians in khaki (not black-skinned, but the hue of their flesh was still far from Su and his compatriot's own fair complexions.) Beside them worked stout, brown-skinned New Zealander Maoris, their faces tattooed even darker with brutal Ta Moko ink.

A flurry of Canadian non-commissioned officers began counting off platoons of fifty men, separating the Chinese into companies of two hundred, and lining them up with Warrant Officers.

Shen Su found himself in a group facing Andy Millington, a dumpy Canadian fellow with bright-blond hair and a Warrant Officer's crown on his shoulder. He smiled at the muddle of Chinese men who had survived a journey across two oceans and a continent then staggered down out of their floating tomb to be reborn on the docks under his command.

A big Chinese fellow stood beside Andy. Li Peng wore the blue tunic and pants of the Chinese Labour Corps, but his uniform had a sergeant's chevrons sewn on the sleeves. Andy gave Peng a nod and he began in Mandarin.

"I am your Sergeant. You will call me Sergeant Li. You will do as I command. Understood?" Peng asked.

Su and the others in his company listened and nodded. Li Peng's Chinese was not too badly broken, despite the Canadian accent.

Sergeant Li nodded toward Andy, *"This is Warrant Officer Millington. He don't like Chinese folks, even though he smiles a lot. But we don't care if a Canadian likes us, or hates us, so long as he pays us, yes?"*

There was a murmur of laughter amongst the CLC men. Although his second-generation Chinese was a shade less than perfect, it seemed that Sergeant Li was a truth-teller.

Li Peng continued, *"Now, Warrant Officer Millington is head man here. I know he looks like a soft-bellied fool, and he sure is that, neh? But the crown on his sleeve defines him, not the truth of him. He can't speak Chinese, and I sure don't intend to try to teach it to him, neh? Mine is bad enough. And better that we can say what we need to say amongst ourselves without a bother, yes?"*

There was a general nodding of agreement in Peng's audience.

Peng continued, *"He's got some things to speak and I'm gonna translate them, but don't get confused here. He's in charge. We're here to work at whatever he tells us. We're gonna break our backs. We're gonna break our legs. Some of you gonna break your necks and never see Shandong and your mommas and papas again. You're gonna see some things you never seen and they're gonna stay in your brain until the day you die—ugly things... But I promise you this—long as you do your work and don't cause me headaches, I'm the man who's gonna hand you your pay and make the marks that guarantee your mamas and papas get their money, too, when all is said and done. You all understand?"*

There was some quiet nodding in response.

"Don't just stand there nodding. When I ask you a question, from this moment on, I want you to say two words, loud and clear, and only two words. I ask a question; you say 'Yes, Sergeant!', understood?"

There was more nodding and a few quiet attempts at "Yes, Sergeant".

Peng bit his lip, then sighed. *"No, no, no. Ach."* He mocked them, meek and humble, quiet and unassuming, *"Not 'yes, sergeant.' Like this—"* He puffed out his chest. *"I say, 'do you understand?'. You say 'YES, SERGEANT LI!!!' Otherwise, Warrant Officer Millington is not gonna believe that you heard what you was told to do, neh?"*

There was quiet laughter.

"We gonna try again, okay?" Peng put his hands on his hips. "DO YOU UNDERSTAND?"

This time, the response shook the docks as Su and all his compatriots replied, buoyed by the fact that an ally now stood between them and their fate. *"YES, SERGEANT LI!"*

Sergeant Li smiled. He turned to Warrant Officer Millington with a slight bow. "Sir."

Andy stepped forward. He gave a long discourse about duty and serving the King and how he would not take any nonsense off his men. Li Peng dutifully translated.

Afterwards, they were marched from the docks to a fatigue camp where they were given another thorough, poisonous delousing and fresh blue uniforms, along with puttees and ill-fitting boots which wore their feet to hot, blistered mush as they were marched without cadence into France.

After a two-hour hike, they boarded a line of idling trucks and rode them over potholes and mud toward The Front, passing long lines of beleaguered French and British wounded being lorried and marched the opposite direction.

When the truck Shen Su was riding in pulled to a halt, Su got a good look at the soldiers humping east when a file of broken men, eyes open and seeing things that had nothing to do with the roadway before them, stumbled past.

Su shook his head. His scrawny neighbor, Zi Chang, saw it. *"What are you shaking your head at, Shen Su?"*

Su watched the seemingly never-ending line of half-dead men draw away from them as the trucks lurched forward and bounced on down the road. *"They may not be dead, but something's been killed in those fellows. That's for sure,"* Su said.

Chang nodded. *"That's how war does a man. My father looked like that after Yihetuan. Both his brothers shot dead in front of him in Beijing by the fucking Americans. I remember when he headed off to fight, he believed he could not be killed. I believed it, too. I'd seen the fighter he was. Strong. Fast hands. Gleam in his eye when he boxed. But that gleam disappeared in Beijing. He came home without a gleam, with no more brothers, his eyes looking just like those fellows. He sits around now, drinking rice wine, waiting for his guts to fail so he can go and box with his brothers again in the afterlife, neh?"*

Su nodded. Everyone knew someone who had taken part in the Boxer Uprising and paid the price. Every time the tax collectors visited the village, they paid the price again, as a vast portion of the proceeds the collectors subjected them to were bound to flow across the ocean as 'reparations' to the Americans, British, Germans, Austrians, Japanese, French, Russians, and Italians who linked arms to bring the proud Chinese boxers back down to their knees.

It was past midnight when they settled into camp in a vast lavender field bordering the British Army's General Headquarters. Su sat outside the canvas tent, inhaling the lush scent of lavender blooms and staring up at the vastness of space. The waxing moon was almost strong enough to vanquish the light of the Milky Way and the constellation of the White Tiger rising in the west. Beneath the tiger, the horizon lit up in strobing explosions as Germans and Britons traded Black Marias, Whizz-Bangs, and Jack Johnsons back-and-forth between them.

Su looked up with shock as a trio of French Sopwith Camels buzzed overhead. The launching biplanes cast unearthly black silhouettes against the midnight-blue sky and its veil of stars.

Zi Chang came out of the tent and saw the planes sailing away. He watched the high-explosive detonations lighting the horizon, jaw slack, in awe. *"Did you ever see such a thing?"* He sat next to Su. *"It sounds like New Year's at the Gate of Peace in Beijing."*

Su let out a low whistle. *"I bet it feels like the whole city of Beijing is being dropped on your head from a mountain top if you're sitting underneath it."*

Chang shuddered at the thought. *"Aiee. One building at a time... On the upside, we ain't gonna be the ones sleeping under it."*

"Unless the Canadians lose their war."

That possibility had not occurred to Chang. *"Aiee."*

"We'll see," said Su.

Chang laughed. *"Ha! You're the Chinaman in the parable."*

"Which one?" asked Su.

"The one where the farmer has a son. Whole village tells him how lucky he is to have a strong boy. Farmer says, 'We'll see'. Boy grows to be a strong young man, marries up the prettiest girl in the village, becomes the best horseman, too. Whole village is telling the farmer, 'looky how strong and handsome your boy has become, he's gonna be a real someone in this world!' Farmer just nods and says, 'We'll see.' Then one day, his son falls off a horse and goes lame in his leg. Can't sit a horse no more. Can't barely walk. Whole village tells the farmer how sad they are for his terrible misfortune. Farmer says, 'We'll see'. Then one day, soldiers come through, conscripting for the war. They get to the farmer's house, see the cripple young man, and they don't take the boy because he doesn't walk good anymore. They say, 'No offence, but we're not gonna take some cripple boy to war. Bad luck for your house's honor, neh?' Farmer shrugs and says, 'We'll see'. Days go by. Then word comes back that all the young men that marched off for war, so excited and ready to bring honor to their mamas and papas got killed straight away. Farmer goes and hugs his son. Kisses him on the forehead. He may be crippled, but he's alive. Whole grieving village tells the farmer, 'You the luckiest so-and-so in the town, you still got a son.' Farmer just smiles, shrugs, and says 'We'll see.' You see? The crippling turns out to be the best thing that could've happened!"

Su nodded. *"The farmer's a wise fellow."*

Chang smiled. *"Yes. You never know what event will be a blessing and what event will be a curse. Maybe the worst thing a man can do is decide for himself whether what happens to him is good or bad, neh? Got to take it all as it comes."*

Sergeant Li came striding through the dark camp. He saw Su and Chang watching the distant fireworks and paused. He looked to the horizon. A couple impressive flashes burst and echoed their way, the thunder rolling over them ten seconds after the light. Li Peng grinned. *"It's really something, neh?"*

Su and Chang looked up and nodded. *"Yes, Sergeant Li."*

Sergeant Li squatted next to them and took out a pack of cigarettes. He shook the cigarettes loose and offered them up to the boys. Su and Chang nodded gratitude as they pulled cigarettes from the pack.

"You gonna see it firsthand before you know it." Li Peng took his own cigarette out and let it dangle from his lip as he put the pack into his breast pocket and patted his trousers for matches.

Zi Chang pulled a box of matches out of his tunic. *"I have matches, Sergeant Li."*

Chang slid out a matchstick and struck it, then brought the flame to Peng's cigarette. Sergeant Li puffed it to life. Chang leaned over and lit Su's, then he brought the licking flame to the tip of his own cigarette. Before he could light it, Peng blew out the match.

Chang smiled and looked at him, quizzical.

Li Peng spat a tobacco fiber onto the grass. *"Three on a match is bad luck."*

"Huh? Never heard that before. Bad luck comes in fours," said Chang.

Sergeant Li's smile was grim. *"In the Motherland, for certain, number four is shit. But not in the world you're in now. Three seconds on a match is about the time it takes for the German version of them aeroplanes to find you in the dark and drop hell on your head. Close to the front, it's about the time it takes for German sharpshooters to get you in the bead and make your head burst open like a cantaloupe dropped on the cobblestones."*

Su noticed that Li Peng was carefully cupping his cigarette's orange ember in his hand.

Peng took out his own matchbox and carefully covered a match while he struck it. He held the flame out to Chang, who leaned forward and sucked life into his cigarette.

"One... Two..." said Li Peng.

Chang stared at Sergeant Li over the lit match, eyes wide.

Su leaned forward and blew the match out.

Peng laughed quietly. *"You're a fast learner. What's your name?"*

"Shen Su."

"Ancestor of the Gods? Your mama had some big aspirations for you, neh?"

Su looked down and quietly blushed. His grand name had always been something of a sore spot.

"You're a big boy, too. Got some strength in those arms, neh? What kind of work did you do at home?" asked Peng.

"Smith."

"Hm. You got some skill with tools?"

Su shrugged. *"Adequate."*

"Well, Shen Su, I like a fast learner with a strong back and a humble disposition. And 'Adequate' is better than most of them peasants you came here with. We gonna try you out to be a section leader in the morning and see how you do with mechanics. Might be better use of your back than digging graves and shit holes for the Canadians to aim their chubby white assholes into. How's that sound?"

Shen Su mulled it over. *"Does it pay better?"*

"Ha! And a practical man at that. If you make the grade and I put a stripe on your arm, it will. We'll see how you do and go from there."

Su nodded.

"You know five more smart boys who got some strength and know their way around a wrench?" Peng asked.

"I can find them," Shen Su replied.

"Good. After they blow the Rouse come morning, you get some breakfast in your belly, then bring me five smart, strong lads. We got a mission to do."

"Four!" said Zi Chang.

Li Peng looked at him.

"He's only got to find four. I like tools, Sergeant Li. My father repaired farm equipment and carts all his life," Zi Chang said.

"Plus, you aspire to more than digging holes for loose stool and dead men, neh?" Peng laughed.

"Yes, Sergeant, Li. One hundred percent," said Chang.

"Ha! Then I guess it's an auspicious night for me." He looked toward Su. *"But still, bring me this skinny one and five more with a little of your bulk after breakfast. We're not in China, but four is still rotten fucking luck."* With that, Sergeant Li stood and headed off into the night, cigarette ember still cupped tightly in his palm.

Su and Chang copied him, carefully covering their own orange-and-black embers.

How about that?" said Chang. *"An auspicious night for all three of us, neh?"*

Su nodded. *"We'll see."*

Chang laughed. *"Okay, 'wise farmer'. We'll see."*

They watched the fireworks display on the horizon until Sergeant Li's cigarettes were smoked to the last morsel, then they ground them out, crawled back into the tent, and shut their eyes.

Shen Su came back to the now. Even with all the snow fall, he was sure he recognized the path before him. If he was not close to The Dragon at this point, he thought he never would be. He lowered his head, plowing on, wishing he could leave the past behind him as his philosophy suggested he should, knowing that it no longer existed in a physical sense, but dully aware that it remained, its empty echo resounding, no matter what its physical limitations might be.

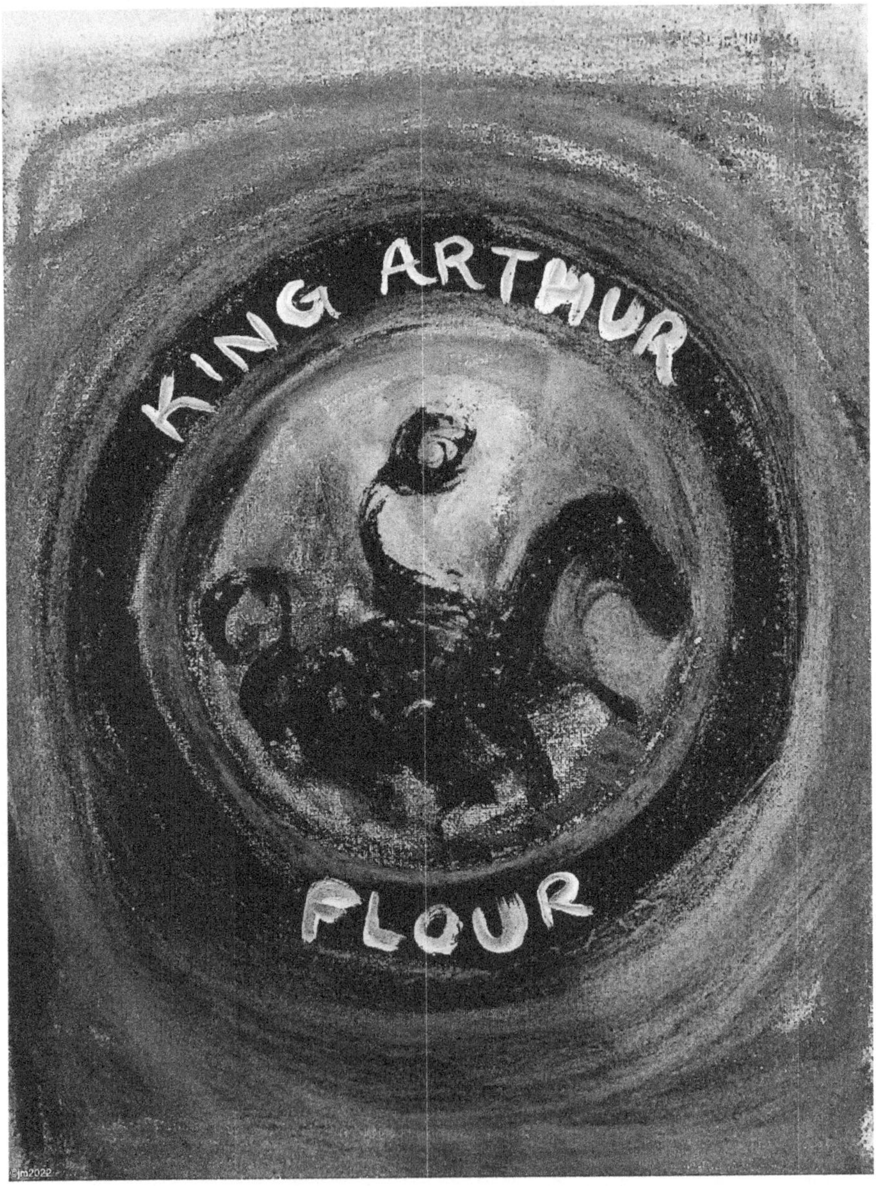
KING ARTHUR
FLOUR
©jm2022

CHAPTER FIVE

—

ADAM

Sergeant Tremaine slowed Bathsheba to a walk. The sign demarcating the northern outskirts of St. Quentin had a triangle of snow crusting in the lower corner. If the snow kept falling and the wind continued, the wet snow would stick, defying gravity, covering half the sign within an hour.

It was still too early, far too early, to head for the barge and hunker down, awaiting dawn. Darren gnawed on his lip and considered options. The hornet's nest they had kicked up at the Siegfried Line had been 'unanticipated', to say the least. Since Good Friday, they had not seen more than a few dozen of the things together, and they had been careful not to engage any groups that size. That they had accidentally charged headlong into a confrontation with a brigade-sized contingent was overwhelming to consider. A group that big could separate into platoons and scour every inch of St. Quentin and its surrounding woods, fields, and hamlets, turning out anyone hidden away in a cellar or hayloft. If they were methodical, they could traverse the entire city, inch-by-inch. He had little doubt that hiding in the hold of the lone barge in a narrow canal would be a literal dead end.

The city was directly south of him. If he turned east and circled it in that direction, he would eventually hit the Somme River. He could burn time following the river's edge back west until he reached the delta where the St. Quentin Canal joined it. From there he could take his time tracing the canal to the barge. By then the distant dawn would be closer and he would know for certain if he had been trailed or not.

Darren Tremaine turned Bathsheba's head and spurred her off-road, heading southeast into the trees.

♠   ♠   ♠   ♠   ♠

The dim outlines of the decimated village of Vermand appeared out of the snowstorm. Francois guided Caitlin and Adolf through a wide-open field, on a straight course to the steeple and cross that poked up into the dark sky above the bell tower of Ste. Marguerite church.

When they came to the wooden fence that demarcated the property of the diocese, Francois stopped. Caitlin and Adolf came to a halt beside him.

Caitlin saw the concern in his tightening jaw muscles. As they contracted, they pushed the scars on his face into deep furrows. "What is it?" she asked.

"There is… there is a body here. We must destroy it if it remains, but then we can shelter in the church tower."

"Only one?" asked Caitlin.

"Oui. At least there was only one this morning. I should have cut it to pieces while it lay dead, but I did not imagine I would return here."

Caitlin nodded.

Adolf had no idea what had halted their forward momentum. *"What? What is going on?"*

Caitlin held a finger to her lips. She mimed a throat being slit and pointed toward the church. "Dead man. There's a dead man in the church."

Adolf hoped he misunderstood.

Francois led the way, cutlass hanging naked and ready in his hand. Caitlin and Adolf followed his steps.

♠   ♠   ♠   ♠   ♠

The inside of the church was silent. As Francois opened the doors, the howl of the wind and swirling snow scattered in from the porch and onto the stone floor of the narthex. Francois stood in the portal for a protracted moment, trying to get his eyes adjusted to the gloom, but, even then, he could only see the smidge of light the stained glass filtered in.

He felt Caitlin and Adolf standing behind him. Had they not been there, he would not have entered the black depths in a million years. He would have stood in that doorway until he died.

He stepped into the church proper and they followed. If he was walking them to their death, the choice was their own.

Caitlin closed the door, entombing them in darkness. She choked down the fear that rose up as she recalled the little boy murdering Father Davies in the church in Talmas. It seemed as though that all happened in some fevered nightmare a year past.

The bright grey of the snow gone, it took a moment for their eyes to see anything but blackness. Caitlin heard Francois reach past her and slide the bolt home, locking the door behind them. He pulled off his pack and rummaged in it, then came back out with the sapper flashlight he had taken from the barge in the Riqueval Tunnel. She felt his hand find hers, then he guided her fingers to his shoulder.

Caitlin saw the shape of Adolf's pale face in the dark behind her. She held the shotgun out to him. "Here," she whispered, letting him take the butt end so he could follow closely.

Adolf's hands found the smooth walnut of the stock, and he grasped it. His fingers felt the trigger guard, and a tingle of excited adrenaline sparked in his crotch. A weapon. He now had his hands on a weapon that would certainly do the trick to dispatch Caitlin and Francois. Wrest it from the Irish bitch when the right moment came, and he could earn everything the demon said was waiting for him on the other side of their murder.

Francois' flashlight burst to life. The beam led them, slow and steady, into the nave and up the center aisle. Francois searched the darkness for any sign of movement. If Matheus Nilsen's corpse was still here, the advantage was entirely his. The light played over each line of oak pews, seeking any potential lair in the shadows. Francois' only hope was that his response to an attack was faster than the attack itself. He knew that was a 50/50 proposition at best.

They reached the bay and Francois paused, looking to the side chapel that extended out to his right, watching the dark stained glass for any silhouette that might reveal Adam lurking. For a millisecond, he saw him, kneeling there, watching them, and Francois' heart stopped. He swung the beam toward it, revealing Saint Marguerite, frozen in stained glass veneration, supplicant in prayer, silhouetted against the dark grey of the storm outside. If Saint Marguerite was risen, rampaging for her God, she was not here in the little cathedral in Vermand that bore her name.

Francois moved deeper into the church, leading them through the transept and into the alcove, to hidden stairs that circled up and away into the bell tower. As he stepped into the tower's base, his foot hit steel and sent a shrapnel helmet spinning away into pitch black. It clattered to a stop, and the three of them stood there, silent, breath caught, waiting for demons to descend upon them. But no bloody implements stabbed them in the kidneys, no sound of coming death echoed down from the steeple above, nothing appeared out of thin air to devour their souls.

Francois let himself breathe, trying to gather his wits. He closed the door, then he continued, feeling his way to the dark stairs, finding each kickboard with his toes, then stepping up gingerly, flashlight shining upward as they climbed, eyes focused on the darkness above, seeking Matheus's waiting corpse, cutlass held ready to strike.

When they stepped onto the landing at the top of the stairs, Francois' instincts were humming with terror. He searched the corners. There was no trace that Adam had been there that very morning, lying dead inside Matheus Nilsen.

A dull gray rectangle shone down from above the ladder that led to the bell tower's aery. Cold wind blew down with it. Francois took a breath in and exhaled slowly, then he grasped hold of the ladder and ascended.

The flashlight's zenith stabbed up into the trapdoor portal above, followed by the silver of the cutlass blade. Caitlin and Adolf climbed out of the pitch-black after him.

As Francois came into the tower, the white powder of swirling snow gusted past him. It had left a fine coat of icy crystals on the bell tower floor, but the angle of the sharp peaked roof above had kept most of the snow from finding a foothold.

Francois scanned the corners behind him. Nothing there. The night beyond was a whirling dervish of snow, whipped by the wind, falling from the dark clouds at a steady pace.

Francois came all the way up onto the deck and moved around the tarnished brass bell that hung in the center.

"Francois."

Francois froze. He was not certain he would have seen him first had he not heard his name spoken.

Matheus's body sat on the floor in the corner of the tower, leaning back against the snow-capped balustrade. Snow rested in the folds of his uniform, coated his shoulders, dusted across the top of his hair, turning it white, giving the impression that he had dear Adam's fair hair instead of Matheus Nilsen's black locks.

"I knew if I waited you would return," Adam said.

Francois relaxed his shoulders and readied his sword arm to strike.

♠ ♠ ♠ ♠ ♠

Isaiah Taylor stopped and tried to get his bearings. The snowfall was almost as blinding as the night. He prayed he had not somehow turned himself around and started back in the direction of the Siegfried Line's barbed-wire nightmare. Fat flakes kept sifting down, like flour onto Aunt Jean's breadboard, preparing the way for loaves of her finest wheat bread. He almost heard Aunt Jean humming in the background as she folded dough.

As a child, Isaiah sat at the old dinner table while Jean baked, working on the readers his aunt scrounged from the families she cleaned and cooked for. Isaiah was top notch at math. As soon as he knew what the shapes on the page meant, the numbers fell into place easily. The sense of where they should end up in the final sum column was clear as day to his sharp mind. He simply filled in the blanks. But what he took true delight in was the joy of disappearing into a good book. His Mama claimed he read straight off the page at three, and even if it had been four, it remained a point of immense pride.

Isaiah embraced his gift, diving headfirst into the worlds fiction created. He felt as though he gained a full second lifetime while lost inside the pages of some great work. It amazed him that multitudes of long-dead men and women could talk inside his head through squiggles, lines, and dots on a page.

The new tome before him was thick, bound in dark, worn leather with fading gold flake on the cover and spine.

"Aunt Jean?..."

Jean looked up from her work. "Yes?"

"Where is Came-Lot?"

"You mean 'CAM-eh-lot'."

"I suppose."

"Where do you imagine it to be?" Jean asked.

"Don't know."

"They don't say in the book?"

"Not far as I can tell," Isaiah replied.

"Then the writer is leaving it up to you."

"To me? That's crazy, Auntie. I didn't write no books."

"You didn't write 'any books'," she corrected.

"I suppose."

"Well, 'Saiah, if the writer didn't specify, and you don't know the answer, then it's up to your mind to fill in the blanks."

He pondered that. "They say it's on a big island..."

"Do they?"

Isaiah nodded. "... And Grandmama was from an island."

"Indeed."

"Haiti?" Isaiah queried.

"Yes."

"Then maybe Camelot is on Haiti a long, long time ago."

"Fair enough," replied Aunt Jean.

That solved, Isaiah dove back into the hole the open pages laid before him. In his mind, these black-skinned Haitian men—in shining silver armor, fighting giants, wicked sorcery, and dragons, battling in tournaments for the love of beautiful black-skinned women—came to life in a Camelot on the Caribbean isle of Haiti. They became kin to him, and he was the heir apparent to all their lessons of virtue, grace, courage, martial power, and chivalry.

Isaiah stopped again. He sensed something in the darkness. He searched the woods for pursuers. Nothing there but trees disappearing into snow, vanishing into the night.

What he would not give for a warhorse, some silver armor, and Excalibur right about now. He supposed he would have to settle for his legs and his dog. The nicked up, dulled cavalry sword in his hand that the Red Maiden nearly cut down Caitlin with twenty-four hours prior would have to be his Excalibur.

Isaiah sighed ruefully at the image. "Saddest fuckin' knight I ever seen."

Black Betty had been circling out again, running in long circuits around him and eventually reappearing at his side. He was unsure if it was purposeful on her part, or just part of her game, but he knew it would confuse the hell out of anyone hunting them. She had been gone for some time. He began to wonder if this time she might not return. Then he heard her bark sounding out ahead of him. He picked up his pace and moved toward it.

When he crested a small ridge overlooking an open field, he dropped and ducked back into cover. Black Betty was a hundred yards ahead of him, backing away from a trio of men. She barked and growled, charging toward them, then wheeling at the last second and running away. The lead man took a swing at her with a bayonet, but she stayed just out of reach, taunting and threatening with her teeth and growl. Then the three men charged, sprinting toward her. Black Betty spun and tore into the woods, leading them away from Isaiah.

"Oh, Black Betty. Bam-ba-lam," Isaiah said quietly.

Isaiah waited for a long minute. Her bark grew further and further distant, muffled by the snow and wind until he no longer heard it at all. He scanned the woods for any other hunters. Nothing.

But where there were three, there were more. Like finding a cockroach in the cupboard, he knew there had to be a hundred that kept themselves invisible. The second the candle was out, they would swarm out of their warren, searching for repast. He did not aim to satisfy their need.

Isaiah stood and jogged down from the rise, bent low, looking both directions. He reached Betty's path and cut directly across it, heading the opposite way she had led her pursuers. If there was rhyme and reason to her game, he hoped he was comprehending its meaning.

The woods began to thicken as he churned up a long, gentle rise. He slowed, panting, and stopped to catch his breath under a large oak. As his heart calmed and his breathing came under control, he brushed snow from the oak's trunk, revealing patchy moss beneath it. North. Black Betty had led the pursuers north.

He lined up his cheek to the tree, taking a bearing directly south on another stand of trees a hundred yards away.

While Black Betty ran those fools north in circles, he would head directly and unerringly south, hoping to find any survivors from his party. That was his plan, anyway. Plans these days seemed to go directly the opposite of intention, but Isaiah was glad to have one, regardless. He would deal with everything else as it came.

Isaiah stood and continued south, filling his hopes and prayers with action.

♠　♠　♠　♠　♠

Sergeant Tremaine cantered out of the trees onto a road. He heard Bathsheba's steel shoes striking flagstones set carefully in the earth by Roman hands, fifty years before Jesus sprung forth from his mother's belly in Jerusalem town.

Darren dismounted and picked up a handful of snow. He took hold of Bathsheba's reins and led her along at a gentle walk. He took a bite of the snowball and let the powder melt to icy water in his mouth. He was surprised how thirsty he was and realized Bathsheba likely needed water far worse than he did.

"Plenty of water at the Somme, my darling. Enough to drown us both. Steady on until then, alright?"

He patted her muzzle, then led her onward along the ancient Roman road. After some five hundred yards, the woods around them began to thin, and Darren found himself looking out on furrowed fields that disappeared into the falling snow on either side of the road. He checked his compass. The road ran directly east. The Romans certainly knew how to keep their paths straight and true.

Bathsheba stopped.

Darren turned back. "Come on, girl. Don't dig your heels in. I promise I'll get you to water. If you lay down now, I'll have to leave you, and no one wants that, eh? Come on."

He gave a gentle, steady pull on the reins and she relented, following.

Another thousand yards on, out of the gloom, in the field to the south of them, a towering grain silo beside the large black rectangle of a barn rose up. It hovered on the edge of Darren's vision, like some massive, ghostly castle. Where there was a silo, there might be grain. Where there was a barn, there should be water. If the Germans had not pillaged it bare, there would be oats, or at least hay in ready supply.

Darren looked back. No pursuing army. Yet. He worried his lower lip. The monsters chasing him were apt to rise up out of the night and snow as unannounced as the barn and silo had, but without a proper feed and watering, he sensed that Bathsheba would resist if he tried to re-mount now. If the men chasing them caught him on foot, he would quickly be as dead as they were.

Darren led Bathsheba into the field toward the barn and silo. The wind whipped snow in little whirlwinds of stinging ice, striking his cheeks and forehead. As they reached the barn's leeward side, the buffeting calmed, blocked by the tall, grey, wood façade. Darren looked again for the coming horde, but still, no sign of anything coming. He held Bathsheba's lead with one hand and grabbed the right-hand door, fighting it open through drifted snow until it was wide enough to walk Bathsheba into the blackness of its interior. He led her in.

It was dark as pitch in the barn, but the respite from the biting wind and falling snow was welcome. Darren rummaged through his saddlebag for his flashlight. He found it and flicked it on, playing the beam through the empty stables until it found a waiting water trough and feed bin.

"Jackpot."

Bathsheba smelled the water and grain. She pulled ahead of Darren and ducked her head to the trough, slurping the cold water down, slaking a life-threatening thirst. Darren undid her bridle while she drank and pulled the crown over her ears. He slipped the bit out of her mouth and stood back as she moved to the feed and began gorging herself.

He scanned the barn and found a tin bucket. He edged in next to Bathsheba and filled it with grain, then dumped it into his saddlebag, replenishing the nearly empty stores. He hoped they would both live long enough to empty it a second time.

As he set the bucket down, he heard the distinct *CLI-CLACK* of a pistol hammer being cocked. Darren rose slowly and froze as he felt the steel barrel press hard against the back of his head.

"Are ya living, or are ya dead?" asked a raw-voiced Irishman.

"For the moment, friend, I'm alive and well. And hoping you've no plans on changing that situation. I've enough to worry about as it is," Tremaine replied.

"Come about slow. Give me your torch and show me you're not a walking corpse, or I'll scatter your brains to the wind, eh?"

Darren nodded. "Understood." Darren held up the flashlight, and the man took it from him.

"Come 'round. Slowly now," said the man.

The barrel eased off Darren's head as the man holding the pistol stood back.

Darren turned, hands raised. The flashlight shone over his body, revealing a stained uniform, but no wounds to speak of.

There was a grunt of relief, and Darren heard the pistol hammer release.

"I'm Darren Tremaine. Lancers."

"Patrick O'Neill. Irish Fucken Fusiliers."

"Have you been here long?" asked Darren.

"What?"

"I said, have you been here long?" Darren repeated.

"I dunno.... Maybe two, three days. What day is today?"

"Tuesday. Going on Wednesday."

"Fucken Hell... Day and a half then. They captured my company on Good Friday. Butchered us... For days, the bloody fuckers... I ran when I could."

Darren nodded. "I think we found another of your company on the road. A sergeant from the Irish Fusiliers."

"Fin? Was it Fin Kelly?"

"I'm sorry. I don't recall his name."

"I'm guessing it was him. Only other man I saw make a run for it. Couldn't do a thing for the rest, y'know... Good old Fin. A right cunt, but a funny fucker when he chooses to be." Patrick laughed. "You should've seen it. Their boss man—this big bald-headed bastard in a Scot's plaid kilt, fucker'd been shot through the eye—he puts our Captain to the cross, then sets Will Trumble on fucken fire, but this dim, one-eyed cunt has petrol all over himself, so it sets his kilt on fire, too; and while all the other Roman bastards are laughing at their burnin' boss, Fin Kelly has the last laugh; he makes a run for it. Hops the bags and the fucker is off and gone into the night. Well, sir, as you can imagine, that one-eyed twat, who's now burnt his kilt and his bollocks, he leads all his lads at a mad dash after Fin. They left me in the pit. I shook loose and fucken ran myself... Fucken Fin... Is he still alive?"

"I don't know. Last I saw him he was."

Darren patted Bathsheba and set her bit back between her teeth, then pulled the crown and bridle onto her.

"Good old fucken Fin... Didja see any of 'em fucken Romans on the road?" Patrick asked.

"Romans?"

"Ay. Fucken Romans. Talkin' back and forth in their Latin while they sliced and diced us up. They was either a bunch of fucken priests, or they was Romans. Didja see any of 'em?"

"I can't say if they were Roman or not, but I've seen plenty of them out there."

"How many, d'you think?"

"Thousands... Looked like thousands of them."

Darren heard a sharp gasp from behind the flashlight.

"What? 'Thousands'? Ya' seen 'thousands'? Fucken Hell... Are they after you?"

"I don't—I don't know. They were, but my mates and I split and rode in different directions. I don't know if they followed me or not."

"Fucken Hell..."

"You're right about that."

"You brought 'em straight to me..."

Darren heard rage and fear simmering behind the flashlight.

"YOU BROUGHT 'EM STRAIGHT FUCKEN TO ME!"

Darren eased his hands up. He heard the pistol hammer cock back again.

"Patrick... I'd no idea anyone was in here. Don't shoot. If you kill me, you know as well as I, that I'll rise up and finish you, and not of my own accord. All I wanted was to water my horse; that and the feed I've already taken. That's all. I've no wish to stay here or put you in harm's way. Put down the pistol and I'll be gone. I'll lead them away from here, you've my word. Please don't shoot me."

"You fucken English. Your fucken 'word'... You bloody fucken bastard..."

Darren could make out the Webley pointing at him over the flashlight, the pit of its barrel blacker than the surrounding dark, his ending sitting chambered on the far end of it. He felt surprisingly calm as some neurochemical flushed into his brain to ease his ending. Flashes of his too-short life zipped through his mind's eye at dizzying speed; mother, father, loving brothers, tears and laughter. First broken bone, first shave, first kiss, first breast, first climactic orgasm—its 'little death' sweet and thrilling, kinder than any 'big death' could ever be. Drudgery of school, dissolution until he found his path. Then horses and bridles, saddle soap and saber oil, rifles and parade, uniforms and first mustache. Then last kiss, last fuck, last fight, last laugh, last kill, last ride. The blur of every horror since Good Friday whipped past, and then he was there in the barn, standing before his end. And the brevity and emptiness of it all were near to overwhelming.

Then the barrel disappeared as Patrick lowered it. There was bitter laughter in the dark. "Aye... If I kill ya, you'll just rise up, and likely nail me to the wall, cut off my bollocks and watch me bleed, wouldn't you, you fucker?"

Darren kept his hands where they were. He nodded. "Yes. That's the least of what we've seen them do."

"You fucken English..." said Patrick.

Darren heard the emotion shifting from terror and rage to tears.

"... You see my fucken barn and decide you'll take it for your own, just like you see everything else in this fucken world; like your fucken God set it down here for you and your fucken King... Well, we'll see who has 'last laugh' now, eh? 'Cause I think it's gonna be *you* gets nailed to the wall, and no' me."

BANG!

Darren's ears rang with the sound. He saw Bathsheba rear up. The flashlight seemed to move in slow motion for a brief moment, then it fell fast, its yellow beam cutting through the darkness in a dizzying flash and final bounce as gravity stuck it to the hard-packed dirt floor.

Darren heard the muffled thud as Patrick's dead body hit the ground in the darkness beyond the beam.

Darren scrambled for the flashlight. He grabbed it and searched the darkness with its weak yellow light until it played across the twitching body, its boots kicking and quivering one last time as they got the news that the brains guiding them had been scattered across the barn wall next to the fresh corpse.

Darren shined the light up along the body and found the bloody mess that had been a skull. The Webley had been set to Patrick's right temple and fired straight across, taking a good portion of cranium and scalp with it on the exit. Darren dry heaved at the unanticipated scent of fresh brains and blood.

One final twitch, and Patrick stopped moving.

Darren knew what was coming. He wanted to run. Had he not known that running was a pointless act, he would have. He steeled himself. He shifted the flashlight to his left hand and drew his saber.

Patrick's body shook and arched sharply once, as if high voltage current had been pressed to his genitals, then faster than Darren could have imagined, Patrick was on his feet and running toward him.

Darren swung the saber in a low arc. In the flashlight's beam, he saw the saber strike the side of Patrick's knee and stick fast, halfway through, lodged between the femur and fibula. Then Patrick hit him, almost concurrent; hot, stinking breath shrieking into his ear, and the flashlight went flying, spinning away into the darkness.

Hands fought to get under Darren's chin as they fell, strong fingers grasping for his windpipe. Darren tried to hold the hands at bay with his left and punched up with his right. He swung as hard as he could, and after the first miss, he found Patrick's bloody head and cracked skull. He felt the sharp edges of shattered skull bone bite into his knuckles, but he kept punching, heedless of the pain.

One of Patrick's hands got under his chin and started shoving his jaw up and to the side. He felt the nakedness of his throat, its pulsing arteries revealed, and imagined teeth hitting that skin and tearing in, savaging through neck muscle and rending life-delivering arteries.

Darren heard Bathsheba whinny and buck, then a sudden storm of hooves smashed into he and Patrick. Bathsheba's forelegs knocked them both sideways. As her back legs caught them in the wash, Darren was kicked in the ribs and went tumbling away from Patrick's thrashing body. He saw Bathsheba hit the barn doors and bolt out into the snow. Darren sucked in a breath, then leapt to his feet and raced after her.

In the field, he saw her, forty yards away, stamping and calming herself. Darren ran toward her. He glanced back. Patrick was standing in the barn door, staring at Darren with dim glee out of his shattered head. He reached down and grabbed the pommel of Darren's saber, then wrenched it free. The ruined leg nearly buckled, but somehow held, and he started after Darren, dragging the broken leg behind him, building speed as he found that it would not bend, but had not broken, under his weight.

Darren covered the first thirty yards at a sprint. As he neared Bathsheba, he slowed, desperate not to spook her. If she bolted, he doubted he would catch her, and most certainly could not control whether she ran back toward the army hunting him or not.

He eased forward, all focus on her, trying to ignore the man halting across the field toward him like some reborn Richard-the-fucking-Third. She calmed. He got hold of the saddle horn with his right hand, but she bucked, tearing away from him. As she came back down, his hand closed on his lance. He grabbed the bamboo shaft and pulled it free as Bathsheba shied away.

Darren turned. Patrick was closing. Darren lowered the nine-foot spear and charged.

The lance head hit Patrick square in the chest. It shoved through the sternum and stuck in his spine. Darren held fast to the pole and spun hard to the left, twisting Patrick like some speared shark so that all his weight shifted onto his ruined right leg. Darren heard the patellar tendon's leathery pop and the other ligaments snapped like rubber bands. The leg folded the wrong direction. Patrick went down with a scream of rage. Darren shoved forward, pressing the lance down, pinning Patrick like some butterfly sadistically wall-mounted by a hideous-natured child. Then Darren twisted the lance hard the opposite direction and it tore free from the spine.

Darren backed away from Patrick, whose upper body was still jittering. The lower half, with its right leg stuck in a perfect right angle in the incorrect direction, was immobile, but Patrick still took a weak swing at Darren with the saber. Darren kept his distance. He hauled back and thrust with the lance, spearing through Patrick's neck. Once. Twice. Three times. Then he stopped counting. He thrust again and again until finally the head lolled free. Darren watched his saber fall away from Patrick's clutching fingers.

Darren caught his breath and realized he was weeping. He wiped the tears away and circled warily. There was no movement, but Darren did not care. He slid the point of the lance through the saber's guard and dragged it away from the corpse. He picked it up and wiped the gore off the blade, grateful it was not his own blood, then he sheathed it. He backed away from Patrick's body until it was just a dark patch in the snow, then crossed the field to Bathsheba.

He felt her terror. He knew it mirrored his own. He stuck the butt of the lance in the ground and mastered his emotions, then he calmly walked to her. She let him take her reins. He got one foot in the stirrup, then, as he had a thousand times, he was up and in the saddle.

She followed his lead to the lance. He pulled it from the ground and slid its loop over his shoulder, then he settled Bathsheba to stillness.

He searched his pocket and found his compass. He checked his bearings and turned Bathsheba until they were facing southeast toward The Somme. Reach the river. Find a crossing. Follow it west to the canal. Follow the canal to the barge. Wait for morning to come. Easy Peasy.

He looked again to Patrick's corpse. It had not stirred. Beyond it, he saw the light from his flashlight glowing faintly in the barn. He considered venturing in to get it. Then he laughed, bitter and ironic. No. No, no, no. No chance in Hell he was going to do that.

He gave Bathsheba's flanks a gentle kick and cantered her across the field, over a small farm road, and into the dark woods beyond, allowing his flashlight and Patrick's mutilated corpse to rest where they were, decomposing into their base atomic particles until the end of time.

♠   ♠   ♠   ♠   ♠

CHAPTER SIX

—

TRACKS & TIES

In the crenellated bell tower above the church in Vermand, overlooking a town that had been burned to the ground, leaving only piles of snow-covered brick and ash where a community thrived just a few years prior, Adam Gillét—in the body of a dead German boy whose birth name was 'Matheus'—saw the dull blue gleam of Francois' approaching cutlass in the flashlight's beams.

Adam half-smiled. *"I see you still have your 'Cutlass',"* he said.

Francois paused halfway between Caitlin and Matheus Nilsen's corpse.

"You are not Adam," Francois said, though he was nowhere near as certain as he sounded.

Adam laughed gently and looked at his hands. He did not need a looking glass to tell him this was a different body than the one he left behind, but he knew for certain he remained connected to the Adam he had lived as for twenty-nine years.

"I know. But I told you all of our story last night. How would I know those things if I was not?"

"Devilry," said Francois.

"Hm. I've seen a few of those since I awoke, that's certain… and maybe a couple while I slept. And perhaps I am become one myself."

He thought of the old woman serving him petit dejeunér and his hands trembled a little. Despite her smile and efforts to please, the fear she stoked burned coal-hot in his guts.

He recalled awakening in the burning sands, just as all who had gone before him. He felt hot breath hitting his cheek and opened his eyes to see the she-wolf's muzzle and the white spikes of her canines millimeters from his face.

His last memory from life was machine-gun fire lighting up the night from its hidden nest. He did not hear the bullets, just saw the muzzle flashing and felt the dull impacts as lead punched through the center of his being. A flash of pain, a roaring in his ears, then silence as his body began to fall. Organs eviscerated, he felt nothing by the time his body landed in the muddy crater of water and splashed into its slime, coming to rest on shell splinters that stuck up like jagged teeth from its bottom. His lungs filled with water and blood. He sunk down and stayed. Even as the corpse bloated and tried to raise him up, the shell's sharp shrapnel kept him submerged, pinned to the earth. Eventually, the skin slipped off his bones, the organs dissolved to mush, and what was once beautiful Adam Gillét rotted to mud and soil.

And then the desert sun awoke him. He heard the she-wolf growl, thunder in her chest, then a sharp yank on her leash pulled her back.

The Little Boy contemplated the Frenchman before him.

"Come and see," said the little boy.

Adam sat up and stood. He followed the grimy little boy through the desert to the roadhouse. They passed by the Ford Model A, parked askew by the front stoop. Adam tried to look through the dusty windows, but whoever sat behind the wheel was invisible through the fine dirt and grit that was stuck to it.

The mood inside the roadhouse itself was subdued. In a booth near the counter bar, a Fat Man sat across from a young man wearing a German uniform. Adolf Hitler's eyes were bound with bright, clean, white-cotton bandages. He held a light-blue pamphlet tightly in shaking hands, as if holding fast to it was the only thing keeping him tethered.

Adam heard the Fat Man say, *"… Kill 'em both dead. You understand?"* in German.

"Yes, papa. Yes. You will be so proud of me," blind Adolf replied.

The Little Boy led Adam to a seat at the counter.

The Old Woman behind it smiled, but it only reached her teeth.

"Bon matin, Monsieur Gillét. You just in time for breakfast," she said.

Then she fed him and told the story of his father's death. She laid out the case against Francois Annuniké so plainly that Adam felt as if he had been in his father's tent when Francois cut him down, beheaded him with the Portuguese cutlass, then slipped into the night unseen; revenged, but no less empty than he had been before.

"What you think about that?" said the Old Woman.

Adam was silent. She set a cup of coffee before him.

"Drink your coffee. It'll give you the gumption you need to carry on. I'm about to give you a gift, Msr. Gillét. The gift of vengeance for your father's murder. Most people would kill for that chance. I hope you will, too, Ha!"

Adam stared at the dark coffee, black with a shimmer of brown to it. It recalled the precise shade of Francois' skin.

She set a saucer of cream beside the coffee. *"You want to lighten that up?"* she asked.

Adam shook his head. *"No... It is perfect as it is."* He lifted the cup and sipped the sharp brew.

"Your breakfast is almost ready."

Adam, in the handsome body he remembered so well, sat at the counter, subdued. His mind was still muddled from the oppressive, stifling heat in the desert outside. He gazed through the front windows at the stark landscape. With the sun blasting down onto it, merciless, the white sand could have easily been mistaken for frozen tundra had the heat not been beyond any Adam had ever encountered; even in Senegal's midsummer, in the heart of the savannah. It had been brutal; sweat-through and spent, overseeing black men laying out wooden sleeper beams and ties, spiking dead wood into the soil with sledgehammers, hauling five-meter long, burning-hot steel rails and joining them with thick bolts, ratcheting them to steel fish plates, then repeating the arduous task, again and again. He thought then that the men under his charge were laboring in Hell on earth. He was not wrong. But the heat of the desert outside the diner bested that experience.

The old woman set down a glass of water before him. She smiled. *"I'll just leave the pitcher, honey. You look like you could use every drop of it and then some."*

She turned to the stove and the three eggs bubbling in the griddle's oil.

Adam drank the water. He folded his hands on the counter and rested his head on top of them.

When he awoke, he nearly went mad. He was at the bottom of the canal in the Riqueval Tunnel, in Matheus Nilsen's corpse. He kicked his way to the surface and coughed all the muck and water from his lungs. Then he fumbled along through the pitch-black canal until he reached the exit.

He walked for several hours, caught in a madness that was reflected by the violent rainstorm engulfing the land. It was as if the meal in the roadhouse brought forth a rabid nature that had been sitting just below the genteel, civilized surface of Adam Gillét. The old woman had not caused the insanity in him— she had revealed it. When he found two German survivors hiding in a blockhouse, he killed them both without a moment's hesitation.

In the woods, he came across the party of men carrying Isaiah Taylor, and just as Ganan soon would, he recognized them as brothers-in-arms.

At the train depot, he found Francois' trail. Matheus's cold heart began pounding in Adam's chest. He followed in Francois' footsteps to the very church that only remained standing because Matheus's faltering, superstitious hand failed to press the demolition plunger. A foolish notion. A church was no less holy than anything else humanity was laying certain waste to. Regardless, the haven still stood, and Adam knew that the man who murdered his father was hidden in it. He walked through the transept, passed the cold altar, and climbed the stairs in the bell tower, until only the trapdoor stood between him and his prize.

But when the moment came; when he had Francois cornered in the tower, when he might have walked outside and triggered the demolition with the explosives the men who were sent to finish Matheus's job had already placed, he did not. In recalling his journey with Francois, he accidentally touched his own vanishing humanity, and he could not force himself to finish the act he had been sent to commit.

♠　♠　♠　♠　♠

And now, in the Vermand church bell tower, Adam stared up through Matheus's eyes at Francois' scarred face. He recalled the first time he had seen him in Dakar, and the revulsion he felt at the ritual cuts Francois' people believed made him demon-proof.

78

He remembered the African heat on the savannah, broiling him on their first mission beyond the garrison at Tambacounda. Sitting in the shade of his tent's flaps gave little in the way of relief. The humid Senegalese air was an invisible, hot, wool blanket, cooking him from the inside out. Adam imagined his sweat boiling inside him and bubbling up out of his skin to parboil him. He unbuttoned the top of his uniform blouse, trying to let the heat escape, but the air seemed too thick to fight its way out of his collar. The Monsoon would come soon. As miserable as the rains were, at least the sun would not add to his misery then.

The rhythmic *clank-bang* of railroad spikes being hammered into fresh ties echoed dully through the steel rails, telling him they were nearly done with the repairs.

A month past, a train had come from Dakar on these tracks, heading east to the Mali River. There, it would fill its cars with plunder from French Sudan, intending to haul the treasure to the coast for shipment home to France. But three quarters of the way to the Mali River, the locomotive cut straight through a herd of cattle who had wandered aimlessly onto the rails. When the train halted, the cattle shepherds pulled the train engineer from his seat and beat him bloody for the loss of half their herd.

After the train pulled away, word of the cattle killing spread, and before the train completed its journey east, the offending railroad tracks had been dismantled; the rails dragged away, the wooden ties burned in pyres.

On the return trip, when the treasure-laden train reached the stretch of ruined track, it barely stopped in time. They raced back toward the Mali River in reverse until they reached the next station in the line. They swapped the caboose and engine, then returned to French Sudan, terrified the entire way that they were about to be ambushed and looted.

Word tap-tap-tapped desperately through the telegraph wires to distant Dakar. In short order, Capitan Adam Gillét was dispatched on a train with workmen and two sections of Spahi African soldiers to oversee restoration of the Republic's railroad tracks. They had been at it for three miserable days when things went south.

Adam looked up from inspecting the freshly laid tracks as a man approached, moving slow and easy in the heat. Sergeant Francois Annuniké's crisp salute was at odds with the tribal scars on his cheeks. The grace and ease with which the big black man carried himself made Adam feel more like a barbarian than a refined Frenchman in his presence.

"Captain."

Adam returned the salute. *"Good morning."*

"We are being watched," Francois said.

Adam took that in. He nodded. He stepped back into his tent and returned with his pistol belt and field glasses. *"Show me."*

♠ ♠ ♠ ♠ ♠

Francois led Adam through the camp to the armored train's locomotive compartment. They climbed up into the shade of the cabin.

Francois pointed out the right-side, due south. *"Perhaps five hundred meters. In the tall grass."*

Adam glassed the field slowly. It took a long moment to find the black men hidden in the thicket. *"Yes. I see them. What do you think?"*

"Perhaps the men who lost their cattle and destroyed the track, worried we have come to hang them. Or scouts."

"Scouts?"

"For a raiding party."

Adam looked back through the binoculars. *"Shit... They've gone."* Adam chewed his lip for a moment. *"Let's head out and give the area a sweep, see if anymore of the buggers are out there."*

♠ ♠ ♠ ♠ ♠

Adam and Francois walked a long, cautious circuit around the camp. The ring of hammer on rail spike continued to sing out as the tribe of men laying track dragged timber ties and steel rails from the nearly empty train car's flatbed onto the way, then secured them to the earth.

"I think we'll have the tracks joined by mid-day tomorrow," Francois said.

"Yes..." Adam replied. *"If all goes to plan."*

They completed the perimeter check and found no sign of hostiles. Adam breathed easier. If the men in the brush were simply shepherds worried the French imperialists had come to crush them under their boot heels, they need not be concerned; any retribution the shepherds faced for the destruction of the tracks would come from their local chieftains, who were soon-to-be brutally taxed for the damage to the railway.

It was noon when Adam and Francois found out it was something else entirely.

The three riders wore loose-flowing robes criss-crossed with bandoliers of ammunition for single-shot Snyder-Enfield rifles. At their hips were curved cutlasses and daggers. Fifty yards from the railway encampment, they reined in their horses and waited for a parley.

Adam and Francois walked out to meet them. They stopped a respectful distance away.

Francois spoke first. *"God's peace be upon you."*

"And also on you," replied the man on the right.

The big man in the middle watched it all, impassive. He looked at Adam, then past him to the train engine and the workers, who had slowed their efforts, and were watching the goings-on while trying to appear still engrossed in the rail laying. Men with more power than they had were making decisions that might impact their lives in profound ways.

"What is the matter with your train?" asked the man.

"The tracks have been destroyed. We are making repairs," Francois replied.

"Hm. Your boss, he does not speak Wolof?" asked the man.

"No. Only French. I will make any translation necessary for him. What can we do for you?" Francois asked.

"You can do nothing. But your boss can. Tell him."

Francois nodded. *"Of course."*

"Among your slaves are two of ours that have run away," the man said.

Francois translated to Adam.

"Tell him that the Europeans have outlawed slavery, as he should know. And we have no slaves. These are all free men being paid for their labor," Adam said.

After Francois translated, the big man in the center laughed. His voice rumbled out, rivaling Francois' own deep bass. *"Tell him that is the stupidest thing I have ever heard. These men dragging steel and wood in the heat, wasting their bodies in sweat and labour, trading this day and the day after, and hundreds of days at the tail end of their lives for what? For gold? For paper? And with that paper, they will trade for scraps of food and miserable shelter. And they will rise tomorrow in misery and do it again until their bodies are broken and of no more use to their masters. Then their masters will take the broken men's children and put them to the same chore. If that is not slavery, I do not know what is."* The big man continued, *"And I see those scars on your cheeks and that Portuguese cutlass at your side, brother. How many black bodies did your father's father's father trade for that blade, I wonder, back when the Europeans made their money from only our bodies, not our lands?"*

Francois translated all but the last bit, which seemed targeted at his ears only.

Adam took it in. He had never quite thought of it that way. "Tell him that his argument may have merit, but I am not the arbiter of societal debate. If two of his men are among ours and they are indeed slaves, I cannot, by rule of French law, return them to him. It would be sanctioning slavery and I cannot do that. If he has a complaint, he must petition the local magistrate and let the court settle the matter."

The big man listened to Francois' translation. He looked past them again at the men slaving on the tracks. His laugh was harsh and humorless. *"The magistrate. Yes, of course. That seems an excellent course of action. Putting ourselves in the hands of Europeans has always been the wisest of choices."*

Francois translated. He did not express the irony that dripped from the big man when he said it, but Adam felt the disdain.

The big man turned his horse.

"Farewell, sir," said Francois.

"God be with you until we meet again," replied the big man as he led his men away.

Adam and Francois watched them go until they disappeared from view.

"What do you think?" asked Adam.

"I think it best that we finish laying this track and turn for Dakar as soon as possible."

"How many men might he have out there?" asked Adam.

"As many as two-hundred if he's the local lord. But only if he has them all assembled."

Adam worried his lower lip. His twenty unhorsed Spahi soldiers paled in compare to a mounted unit of that size. *"What are the odds they are already assembled?"*

"If he is clever, he mustered them before he made himself known to us."

"Hm. He seems quite clever," Adam replied.

Francois nodded agreement. *"We can have the track finished by tomorrow if we push hard. We can be safe in French Sudan by tomorrow night. Or, we can stop work now and ride the train in reverse for a day or so, until we can swap out the locomotive and return to Dakar."*

"The Governor will not be pleased if we come back to Dakar with our tails between our legs," said Adam.

Francois laughed. *"Will he be pleased if we are all killed out here?"*

Adam's smile was rueful. *"Not necessarily 'displeased'. Perhaps 'dismayed'. We don't hold nearly as much value to him as this railway does."*

"Then perhaps we are indeed slaves," Francois replied.

"By that chieftain's logic, we're all slaves to someone, lash or no. It would make for an interesting philosophical debate, but I don't think debate is what he has in mind. Do you think two of his slaves have hidden amongst our men?"

"Perhaps it is simply pretext for him, but it would not be impossible."

Adam sighed. *"Shit... Well, let's find out for certain. Have the foreman do a head count. We'll press on with the rails as fast as we can, hopeful that he still must marshal his forces. With a bit of luck, we can be gone before they attempt anything rash."*

Francois nodded.

They walked back to the railway. On close inspection, the foreman found the pair of runaways. They were terrified Adam would turn them over, and he considered it long and hard, but put off any concrete decision for the time being, holding onto hope that it was a moot point.

While Adam and the foreman pushed the pace with the railway gang, Francois put the other Spahis on alert. They did a handful of patrols, looping out into the bush. There was no indication of the big man and his companions.

As sunset neared, Adam had Francois set sentries around the camp and ordered all the workers' canvas tents circled up around the locomotive. He and Francois did one last long circuit of the perimeter and found nothing. As the umbrella of bright stars began to take hold of the night sky, they returned to camp and settled in.

♠ ♠ ♠ ♠ ♠

It was well past midnight when the assault began. Rifle fire shocked Adam out of half-doze. He believed he had only closed his eyes for a moment, but did not have time to find his pocket watch to see for certain. He heard the shouts of his sentries and the sound of horses coming at a gallop as he kicked his feet into his boots and grabbed his rifle. The men from his garrison shouted to each other in French and Wolof and the workers cried out in terror. By the time Adam got out of his tent, the clash of battle and shrieks of the wounded were echoing all around.

The low-burning campfires in the small tent city illuminated workmen spilling from their tents and running from horsemen who ranged through the camp, scimitars arcing down, slicing through the backs of terrified men who came this way for French pennies that seemed a King's ransom. They had willingly slaved for rewards that would feed their families in the new order the French conquerors brought to their land, but now, they only wanted escape, that they might see those families again. Instead, they found themselves trampled and slaughtered by men who shared a skin complexion very close to their own.

Adam started for the battle line. Francois appeared out of the darkness, cutlass hanging from his hand. In his other, he had a bucket of water. He emptied it onto the fire in front of Adam's tent. The steam hissed and the fire's orange remnants went black.

"Report," said Adam.

"We are overrun. There are a hundred on horseback. It is no good to fight. We must go," said Francois.

Adam hesitated. *"My men…"*

"If they are smart men, they have already run. If they are stupid men, they will die. There is nothing we can do to save them. We must be smart men and run ourselves."

Adam looked around the camp. The riders bore torches soaked in pitch. They lit them from campfire embers and began setting the rows of cotton tents on fire. Francois was correct, the brave men had been killed, the smart ones had run, the men a hair-too-slow were being ended now.

"Come!" Francois extended his hand. Adam took it. Together, they ran into cover of the night.

♠   ♠   ♠   ♠   ♠

Francois led Adam on a long, loping arc south, then west. It brought them back to the train tracks well beyond the raiders' outriders. The camp burned away to nothingness behind them, all the sweat and blood and painfully laid meters of track for naught. For the moment, Adam and Francois had their lives, that was all. It would have to be enough.

Under a canopy of stars, they followed the rails toward distant Dakar, walking in silence for several hours. As the sky turned from black to purple to deep blue and the sun's first rays began to rise like a crown of fire on the eastern horizon, a quiet burst of laughter came out of Adam.

Francois looked over at him. *"What?"*

"My father… My father is going to think this is the most pitiful thing he has ever heard."

"In what way?"

"Running from those bastards," said Adam.

"Wisdom walks away from a certain death," Francois replied.

"Hm. You don't know my father."

"He would have preferred that you stand and be slaughtered?" asked Francois.

Adam laughed again. *"Ha! Most certain. It would have made a better story in the newspapers."*

"My son gave his life for a train track?"

"Oh, I'm sure he would've stretched it into something else entirely. In the end, I would've gone out in blazing glory for the good of all France. I can see him on the podium, weeping at the peak of his speech; his grand finale, a rallying cry of 'Liberté, Egalité, and Fraternité'."

"It sounds impressive," said Francois.

"If it's impressive enough to garner votes, my father will assuredly attempt it. Politicians and generals are quite something. He is both."

Francois smiled. *"In that case, Captain, you should be a good son and go back and get yourself killed."*

Adam laughed quietly. *"I have considered it."*

They continued on for a bit. Francois broke the silence. *"What else could you have done?"*

"How do you mean?"

"With twenty men on foot against one-hundred horsemen, what would your father have done differently?"

"I don't know. He'll come up with something. This will be a stain on his honor," said Adam.

"Perhaps when you tell him the truth of what occurred, he will see the logic behind it."

"In the world of politics, it is not a question of truth or logic, it is a question of what his public believes."

"I don't understand. Can the truth not simply dispel a lie?" asked Francois.

"Would it were so. I'll give you an example. Recently, in my country, an officer in our army, a Jew, was accused of trading secrets with the Germans."

"Hm. This is a great betrayal?"

"Oh, yes. The Germans are our nearest and dearest enemies. The Jew, Captain Dreyfus, was convicted and sent to prison in French Guyana. The army, the Catholics, the conservatives, they crowed that justice had been done to the evil Jew who betrayed us. La. For five years, he was imprisoned on Devil's Island. They call it the 'Dry Guillotine' because it is near certain to kill you, even if you have not been sentenced to death."

"The 'Dry Guillotine'. Apt."

"Indeed. And for three of the years that Captain Dreyfus was being 'guillotined' on the island, the army was spending considerable energy hiding the fact that the real spy had been discovered. The man was put on trial in secret, and, predictably, an invisible military tribunal acquitted him. After all, he might have been guilty of being a spy, but he was not guilty of being a Jew. He retired quietly with a full military pension."

"What? Are you not all Frenchmen? What of 'Liberté, Fraternité, Egalité'?" asked Francois.

"I don't know. But I do know that the army knew Captain Dreyfus was innocent, that he was not a Catholic, that he was decidedly Jewish, and someone had to pay in public. The Jewish part, in particular, made him easy to scapegoat. In the press, they could make the convenient case that the Germans and Jews were colluding enemies of France."

"Why?" asked Francois.

"Because without defined enemies it is very difficult to assemble the coalitions necessary to force a republic to your will. If you can make the populace fear a powerful enemy and hate a powerless minority, you can get them to sanction whatever you want."

"You have spent some time considering this," said Francois.

"All of my nation has. The Dreyfus Affair has been an ongoing saga. A revelation of who we are. It can be discomforting to look into that kind of mirror."

"And Msr. Dreyfus died in the prison?"

"No. When word spread to the people that he had been falsely convicted, he was returned to France for a second trial."

"And the court freed him? So, 'Liberty, Brotherhood, Equality' prevails in the end."

"Ha! No. I may not have made clear how much disdain our politicians, military high command, and the priests have for Jews. He was found guilty a second time and sentenced to ten more years on Devil's Island."

"Hm… Perhaps he is wishing the guillotine was the wet kind," Francois replied.

"No. Fortunately not. A small newspaper presented Dreyfus's innocence to the public in ways that could not be ignored. It united the entire opposition—no one likes to imagine what it would be like to be crushed, unjustly, by the actions of The State. No individual, regardless of their politics, likes to imagine that an all-powerful government would set their sights on them. For if there is no actual justice in the court of law, once you are in their teeth, all the individual's power is gone, guilty, or no. Ultimately, Msr, Dreyfus has been freed, but only because the population would have burned Paris to ashes had the government not finally come 'round."

"Yes. I see… But you are not Jewish, correct?" Francois asked.

"No. I'm not. But that does not mean I cannot feel empathy for their situation."

"Empathy?"

Adam considered for a moment before putting it into words. *"It means—when I see the conditions of their lives, I can imagine how it would feel if they were my own."*

Francois nodded.

Adam continued, *"But my father's real enemies are not the Jews or the left wing. His true enemies are his contemporaries. They share his politics but covet his position. And they own newspapers of their own. When we reach Dakar, there will be an investigation by the Governor's office. Word will reach Paris, and my father's enemies will catch wind of it. They will threaten him with headlines of my failure in order to bend him to their will. Failing that, they will bring it to the public via the front page, then they will hammer him in public debate, in the press, on the campaign trail. His enemies will use my failure to paint him however they see fit."*

"I see."

"And the truth is, he will not be morally offended by what has occurred, what my action or inaction brought about. He will be offended by the fact that it happened in public and I did not have the instinct to fall on my sword. My death in battle would have been a weapon he could wield. My survival is a blow he must defend himself from. What would your father say?" asked Adam.

Francois mulled it over for a long moment. *"My father is a chieftain. As long as I acquit myself with wisdom and courage he would not care."*

"Then he is a good man."

"I did not say that. He, too, might face attacks from enemies within the tribe."

"Of course."

"But my father would simply have them killed. He does not have time or energy for politics."

Adam laughed. *"Believe me, if my father could get away with it, he would certainly have his enemies within and without of our 'tribe' murdered."*

Francois raised a finger to his lips. Adam froze. They listened. Adam heard nothing. Francois grabbed his arm and led him quickly across the tracks, pulling him into the brush.

"What is it?" Adam whispered.

"Horses."

Adam slid the Berthier rifle's sling off his shoulder and thumbed the safety off.

Francois' hand found Adam's forearm and squeezed it. He leaned in and whispered, *"No. Gunfire will draw them all to us."*

Adam nodded understanding. Francois' cutlass slid out of its scabbard. They sat and watched the tracks. Out of the harsh morning light came four horsemen at a walk, two on each side of the rails, searching both sides of the path as they rode.

Francois and Adam watched silently. The horsemen passed, slowly disappearing around a long bend. After several minutes, Francois released Adam's forearm and slid the cutlass back into its sheathe.

"Come, we must stick to the brush."

Adam nodded. He followed Francois deeper into the damp woodland, and they marched on.

"You missed your chance," whispered Francois.

"How so?" Adam replied.

"You might have run charging after them, firing your rifle, sacrificing us both for your father's honor."

Adam's smile was without humor. *"I wouldn't be my father's son if I hadn't considered it."*

♠　♠　♠　♠　♠

They continued west for five hours. As mid-morning neared, they reached the brown waters of the Nieri Ko River. Both men were parched, and even with the gritty silt, the taste of the fresh flowing water was a godsend. They slurped from cupped hands until their bellies were full.

Adam walked into the trees to relieve himself. When his bladder was empty, he headed back toward the riverbank. He pulled up short before he could break out of the tree line.

Francois stood at the river's edge, his cutlass drawn. Three men on horseback stood before him. Adam quietly slid his rifle off his shoulder. He opened the bolt and checked the chamber. The brass of a fresh round shone up at him. He ran it closed silently, set the butt to his shoulder and switched the safety off, taking a bead on the chest of the man at the front of the riders.

Francois held his ground. Adam heard the lead man yell something in Wolof. When he raised his Snyder-Enfield to fire, Adam pulled the trigger.

The bullet caught the man just under the armpit, spinning through heart and lungs. His body wrenched to the side, his trigger finger spasmed, and the Snyder-Enfield fired blind, striking Francois just below the ribs.

The horses spooked at the rifle fire. The man Adam mortally wounded dropped his rifle as his horse reared and threw him backward. He landed on his head. His neck broke cleanly with an audible '*crack*'.

Francois clutched his side and ran for the woods, energy leaving his body as he ran. He made it five steps before he sagged and fell on the sandy shore.

The other two horsemen raised their rifles, but the panicking horse infected its comrades, and the men fought to rein them back in.

Adam fired again. The shot struck the nearest rider in the face. He went limp and slumped in the saddle. All tension gone from the reins, his horse bolted. The dead man tumbled free, landing face down in the water at the river's eddying edge.

The last man wheeled and charged away, following the riderless horses at a gallop.

Adam ran to Francois. He dropped to the sand beside him and lay prone, taking careful aim at the vanishing rider. He squeezed the trigger. The time the bullet took from the ignition's report to striking the man's spine was measured in milliseconds. It went straight through the center vertebrae. His back arched in spasm, his head rocked backwards, his hands lost hold of his rifle and reins. He was paralyzed from the neck down before he hit the ground.

The horseman died on the river's edge, over the course of hours, frozen in a hellish stasis, baking as the sun rose higher and higher, while his blood trickled, slow, but insistent, from the small hole in his back. He lay there, a prisoner in his own body, while his mind screamed and mourned for all he was losing and had lost. It took all day, but as the sun set, he finally, mercifully, bled to death.

Adam rose and ran to Francois. There was an exit wound just above his kidney. He rolled the big man onto his side and inspected the entry hole. Francois gasped in pain. The wound in his belly was small, but blood was flowing steadily from it, soaking his shirt.

"*Well, you've gone and gotten yourself shot, Sergeant.*"

Francois gritted his teeth and nodded.

"*Can you apply pressure to it, or are you going to pass out?*"

Francois nodded. "*Yes. I can.*"

"*I'm going to pull you into the shade. I want to make a try for a couple of those horses. If they've stopped running, I'll bring a pair back, alright? I promise I won't leave you.*"

Adam squatted behind Francois and wrapped his hands under his armpits, then he dragged him across the sand into the trees. He laid him on his side, pulled off his Kepi cap, and tore the cloth flap from the back of it. He spread it so it covered the bloody entry and exit holes.

"This is as clean a bandage as we've got. Hold it tight to the wounds."

Francois placed one hand on his belly and another on his lower back.

"I will return soon," Adam said. He ran and picked up his rifle, then followed the hoofprints north. His belly was riled by the adrenaline of the killings, and he fought an impulse that shot up out of nowhere to lay down and sleep. He knew if he expected to survive the day, much less the week or more it would take to trek to Tambacounda, he had to have a horse.

It took the better part of half an hour to find them, lazily drinking water from the river, content they had found freedom from the men who kicked their flanks and yanked their bridles and bits.

Adam slung his rifle and approached the nearest horse slowly. One big, dark-brown eye gazed at him from behind long lashes.

"Come, beauty. You and I are going to be near and dear, cherie. I will take you back to Dakar and you will live the rest of your days like a king, yes?"

Adam reached out slowly and touched the warm bristles of hair on the horse's jaw. The dappled stallion snorted through his nose but made no sudden movement. Adam caressed the jawline and face, then gently took the reins. He ran his other hand down the mane and rested it on the saddle horn.

"Now, mon ami, I am going to sit upon you, oui? And you are going to save my very life."

Adam lifted his foot into a stirrup, then mounted. He guided the stallion in a circle, then rode him at a walk to the closest charger. He leaned down and reached for its reins, but before he could grab them, the horse kicked out toward its fellow. Adam held fast to the saddle as his own stallion reared and lashed out with its own hooves. The other horses bolted, and Adam felt his mount, enraged, balking at having a rider aboard while his brethren ran free. As the horse began to drop to its knees to roll him off and crush him beneath it, Adam swung his foot free of the stirrup and yanked hard on the reins. The stallion's side hit the ground as it tried to roll. Adam's leg barely escaped being broken under the saddle, but he was an experienced horseman. He kept his right foot in the stirrup and pulled the bridle firmly. As the stallion followed his lead, he rode it back up to standing, quickly turning the horse and kicking its flanks, pressing it firmly back into service. He looked to where the other horses had vanished and cursed his luck. There was no time to waste in pursuit. The men hunting them were likely growing closer by the minute. With a kick, he drove the stallion back along the river to Francois.

Adam tied up the horse, then tore Francois' tunic into strips. He flushed the wound with river water, then bandaged the cloth tightly around Francois' belly. He helped Francois onto the saddle, then climbed on in front of him.

They forded the muddy river, pressing west, feeling their pursuers behind them, hoping to gain as much ground as possible before their trail was discovered.

On the third miserable day, the summer monsoon began. It did not cease.

Any trail they had left vanished in the downpour. The men pursuing on horseback gave up, turning back east to their tribal lands, basking in the arrogance of their victory over the French Colonials and their serfs, unaware that they had signed death warrants for every member of their tribe.

Adam fashioned a lean-to and left Francois sheltered from the downpour while he searched out the tubers and roots that Francois described to him to stave off starvation. When he returned, they choked down the raw vegetables and drank handfuls of fresh rainwater that was soaking them to the bone. Adam felt the heat of fever emanating out of Francois.

"At least we will not die of dehydration," said Adam.

Francois smiled, grim. *"Yes. But I fear my cutlass will rust into nothingness."*

His skin had taken on a decidedly grey cast as the wounding continued taking its toll, trying to end his life.

"Where did you get it?" asked Adam.

"The cutlass? My father's father's father."

"Is it French?"

"Portuguese," said Francois.

"Slavers?"

Francois patted the pommel. *"The Portuguese slaver who owned this was killed with it. And now it has passed down through the generations to me. Had my father's father's father not killed him, my own father would've been born in chains in the Americas."*

"Then it is a righteous weapon."

"The idea of it is. But a weapon is only as righteous as the man who wields it."

"That's wisdom."

Francois took another sip of water. He closed his eyes. *"I do not think I can ride on."*

Adam looked at Francois' ashen face. *"Nonsense. You've made it this far. If you're not dead yet, I don't believe you will die."*

"The wound will not close in the wet. It will weep and remain open. If it is not already infected, it will become so," Francois replied.

Adam was silent.

"You should ride on to Tambacounda," said Francois.

"No. It will take me three days to get there, and another to get back if they will send a train, three more if I return on horseback. I think you would definitely be dead by then."

"If I am not, you will have a doctor with you and food, and spare horses. Go."

Adam gathered more roots and broad leaves to catch rainwater. He gave them to Francois. Then he mounted the stallion. Before he spurred him, he looked back at Francois' muddy boots, poking out of the lean-to. He knew that in a week's time, the muddy boots would be in the same position, but the man wearing them would be bloated and rotting, likely opened and eaten in stages by the forest's predators and scavengers.

Adam dismounted. He tied the stallion to a tall Acacia, where it could graze and water at its own content, then he crawled back into the lean-to.

"What are you doing?" asked Francois. *"You must go."*

"I should. But I will not. We'll stay here until your wound closes and your fever breaks. Then we'll ride for Tambacounda together."

He left unsaid the alternative. Francois' fever would likely prove fatal and then he could leave him, his conscience clear.

As night and rain fell, Francois and Adam slept, leaning against each other in the shelter. It took two days for the fever to finally break, and another two for the wound to seal itself. It may be that those were the four days it took them to fall in love, or perhaps those four days allowed them both to accept what was, and though neither spoke of it, when they remounted the horse and continued on to Tambacounda, the relationship had been forged. It was more real than anything either man would encounter again in their lives.

After Adam's court martial, he was stripped of rank and sent back to France, his future placed in his father's hands. He wrote Francois weekly, and Francois replied as often as he could.

As Adam had supposed, his father, Field Marshal Paul Gillét, paid the price politically for his son's disgrace. But when the Germans struck their first blow in 1914, he saw an opportunity for redemption. Adam was given a command and sent to the front to stem the German tide while earning his father political currency.

When Adam was killed in the first days of trench warfare, a letter, held in trust by his commanding officer, was sent to Dakar where it reached Francois. When Francois read it, his heart broke. He deserted his post and booked passage to France. He joined the Légion Étrangère and sought a path to revenge Adam's death.

Francois served with honor, taking his first vengeance on Germany, alongside Renoir and Isaiah. It would take him two years to find Field Marshal Paul Gillét. When he did, he could not stop himself. He cut him down in his command tent, brutally, then made his escape back to The Front. On Good Friday, he traded a French Field Marshal's head along with a sandbag-full of German ones for British Strawberry Jam. Yet the vengeance had no satisfaction in it. The emptiness inside Francois remained, a vacuum created by Adam's loss, a blank, painful void.

♠   ♠   ♠   ♠   ♠

Adam opened his eyes and was back inside of Matheus Nilsen's body in the Ste. Marguerite bell tower.

Francois stared down at the man who was and was not Adam that sat before him. The Portuguese cutlass felt as heavy as one of the long steel rails he had guided toward Koulikoro and the Niger River.

"How are you here?" Francois asked.

Adam's bitter laugh tumbled out of Matheus's mouth. *"I don't know... I only know why."*

"Then why?"

Adam lingered on his memories for a breath, then he spoke. *"She sent me to kill you."*

Caitlin touched Francois' back gently. "What's happening?"

Inside, Francois wanted to burst out laughing. It was, in truth, the most obvious question in the world, but the answers it elicited were laughable at best, insanity at worst. "J' n' sais pas... I do not know," he said.

Caitlin looked at Matheus's corpse, sitting in the snow. "This is the dead man you said was here?" she whispered.

Francois nodded.

"The one you said, 'if you kill it we can shelter here'?

Francois nodded again, numb, the cutlass heavy in his hand. He did not have the strength to swing it.

For the first time, Adam/Matheus looked past Francois at Caitlin and Adolf. When he saw Adolf, his brow furrowed.

"I know you…" Adam said in French. When Adolf did not respond, he repeated it in German, *"I know you."*

"No," Adolf said. *"I don't think so. I was in the 18th Bavarians. I don't know you."*

"No. I know you from the roadhouse. In the desert. You were there. Blindfolded," Adam said.

Adolf shook his head. *"I don't know you. I've never been to any desert. You are a dead man. You don't know me."*

"Yes, I do."

Adolf ripped the shotgun out of Caitlin's hands and shoved her aside. She hit the stone parapet and fell. Adolf racked the slide and aimed Isaiah's shotgun at Adam's head. He pulled the trigger.

CLICK. The hammer fell on the empty chamber.

Francois' hand shot out and grabbed the shotgun barrel. He twisted hard, wrenching it out of Adolf's hands.

Adolf stumbled back, hands rising to ward off the strike from Francois' cutlass that he knew was coming. When it did not, Adolf opened his eyes and kept backing away.

"What is wrong with you?" Francois shouted. But Adolf did not understand.

"Stop him," said Adam.

Francois hesitated.

Adolf turned and ran to the ladder, nearly tumbling through the black rectangular hole, but he managed to set his feet in the rungs and disappear into it. They heard his boots hit the landing, then the sound of him fumbling down the stairs in the dark echoed up to them.

Adam stood as Francois turned back toward him.

"What are you doing?" Francois asked.

"I saw him. He was blindfolded, but I'm sure it was him," Adam said.

"Where?"

"I don't know where it is. Perhaps nowhere. Perhaps Hell. But I know I saw him there, and I know he must be killed. The big man sent him to murder you."

"Francois, what's happening?" Caitlin asked, lost in the flurries of French.

"He says we must kill the German," Francois replied.

"Francois... You're taking for truth the words of a man we both can say for sure is a dead man. A man you told me an hour past you were certain was aiming to kill you."

"He is not... He is not who he seems," Francois replied.

From the stairwell, they heard the door below slam open and Adolf's footfalls echoing away into the church proper.

"Francois, I'm not staying here alone with this one. And there's nothing waiting for us outside this church other than death and snow. Let the German go."

Adam saw Francois' hesitation. He approached slowly, as he had the stallion by the Nieri Ko River. Francois turned toward him. Adam reached out and touched Francois' shoulder. *"Stay here. I'll get him,"* he said.

He moved past Francois and dropped down the ladder, disappearing into the blackness, as if venturing into a deep, dark well.

Francois felt the touch on his shoulder even after Adam had gone. He handed Caitlin her shotgun. Then he knelt down and wept.

♠   ♠   ♠   ♠   ♠

CHAPTER SEVEN

—

MOLOSSOS

Black Betty stopped and looked back, panting. Her tongue hung gaily out of her mouth; a pink flag, flapping in the wind. The snow kept coming, and she shook her coat, sending a spray of white and wet exploding outward, joining the snow on the ground. She sat patiently and caught her breath.

The kernels of a long-ago memory tickled her mind. She was given these gifts from the past often, particularly as a nipping puppy, battling her litter mates for a fresh teat swollen with her mother's milk. The mock battles she fought with her brothers and sisters were informed by knowledge she had not discovered on her own. The humans called it instinct; but that just meant they could not conceive how the information might have passed to some 'dumb animal'.

Perhaps it was simple jealousy that they, too, were dumb animals; too dumb to rely on the inherent gifts of past generations to know how to survive, how to seek food, water, and shelter, to know the scent of danger and violence on the wind without being ceremoniously taught about it by their patriarchs.

Forced to take all life-saving information at face value from their so-called elders opened humanity up to all sorts of abuse, quite unlike the other animals, whose ancestors passed down their gifts without self-serving superstition, self-absorption, or any expectation of recompense. After all, their instinct's prime originators were long dead when the stored knowledge was handed down to future generations.

The animal's gift was also a curse. Had they instead owned voice boxes and run in diverse tribes, they might have passed word across species to the North American Lions or the Australian Giant Kangaroos that humans were coming and would end them entirely. Alas, with no shared knowledge that the new arrivals were cowardly assassins, the big animals simply stood and watched casually while the pitiful little invaders approached and speared them.

The animals that escaped slaughter taught their heirs, rightly, that humans carried with them death and violence, chaos and bloodshed, and if one did not care to be eaten, beheaded, and secured to a wall, or worn as an ornament, fighting was pointless and running away was best.

Black Betty's ancestors were more cunning than most. When the wolves realized what was afoot—certain extinction—they used their skills to teach humankind that they could be allies and friends, useful in any way necessary; anything, ANYTHING, to not end up nailed to a wall, impaled and spun on a fire spit, gutted and skinned, their thick, soft fur wrapping the naked humans in their corpse's warmth, their flayed and stripped flesh, cleaned and divested of all hair, fat, and other extraneous matter, soaked in dilute tannic acid, and turned into leather for armor, boots, and sundry trinkets.

No. The canines—those who could stomach bowing and scraping, begging and submitting—would endure anything not to suffer the fate of their brothers and sisters of the vanishing animal kingdom.

Over time, in the care of tribesmen of the Asian steppes, Black Betty's submissive ancestors were nurtured and bred into Molossos Mastiffs. Alexander the Great, during his pillage of ancient Asia, discovered the massive, fierce dogs and brought them home with him. When the Romans came along and gutted Greece and Macedonia, they, too, became enamored of the big dog's possibilities and brought the Mastiff breed home to Rome. On the sand of the Colosseum, Rome celebrated the violence that Romulus and Remus's mother's descendants could be coaxed to.

When Black Betty slept, the memories of that time came and consumed her. The dreams taught her history as she barked, growled, and twitched, living out her ancestors' lives, creating her 'instincts'.

When her far distant grand dame first fought in the Colosseum, it was against a slave. When the shaking man turned and ran, she ran after. His action told her he was prey. She took him by the hamstring, pulling him down as her own grandsires had taught her to take elk. She bit him under his chin and crushed his throat as they had taught her to kill caribou. The crowd's roar startled her at first, but then she realized it was adulation, and she knew that adulation meant she was not bound to become a boiled leather breastplate or dinner. There would be treats and rewards to go along with all that applause.

The next slave she fought was given a spear. He ran when she charged, and she ended him as she had the first.

Then they sent two slaves with spears. Then three. She vanquished all of them.

The Molossos was a sure-fire hit. When she went into heat in her next cycle, they pulled her out of the pits and let her breed.

She next fought a professional slave—a Gladiator. She danced well with him. When he struck her with his trident, she stayed locked to his thigh. He died a week later of sepsis. She recovered from the wound and two months later birthed a litter of rough-and-tumble brindle babies. Effortlessly, she gifted them with her knowledge of how to survive in the fighting pits.

After the pups were weaned and taken to learn their duty as fighters and guardians, she was unleashed back into the Colosseum. She fought a pair of gladiators and killed them both. But when they sent her against three armed professional killers, she could not stand and fight and win. She forced them to chase her through the sand until they ran out of breath, then one-by-one she took them apart. It took nearly forty-five minutes, and her own breath was heaving, her mouth a bloody foam, her hide slashed and cut by their weapons, but the three enslaved fighters succumbed to their wounds while hers were stitched and bound up. The crowd was bored to tears.

She would not fight again. She was retired to the kennels to breed future fighters until she passed.

Her last litter of pups inherited more knowledge than the first. They knew that three armed men were too many to stand and face. And now, two millenium later, Black Betty, whose dreams had taken her through that fight in the arena a dozen times, was facing three killers of her own.

The trio of risen dead men, enslaving the bodies they had conquered and taken, came over the rise behind her. Black Betty barked and wagged her tail.

She came back to all fours and tucked her chest toward the ground, inviting them to play.

Like Isaiah, these men were not interested in playing. Murder was all they had on their minds. The man in the center looked to his compatriots. He spoke to them in Norse.

"Spread out."

His companions eased their way out and forward, forming a flanking crescent as they made their way down toward Black Betty. She allowed the skirmish line to expand. Then she ran toward the man at her right and skidded to a stop, spraying him with snow. She turned and bolted as he dove after her, slashing with his bayonet, cutting space she had already vacated. He lost his footing, then quickly stood. The three gathered themselves, then chased after her again.

Betty charged northward, bounding through the powder, leading them away from Isaiah. The game had lost no savor yet.

When the sound of distant howling came from the west and reached her sensitive ears, she paused and sniffed at the wind. She could run from the three behind her all day, but the thing she heard and now smelled in the distance was something else altogether. A worthy enemy was out there—its howl, a direct challenge. Betty's hackles rose, unbidden. She would not shrink if she met the thing, but she would not face it and her three current pursuers at the same time. That was certain death.

She sensed the men coming behind her. She leapt forward, running downhill. The notion of a battle to the death with a worthy competitor sparked more collective unconscious memories of blood, glory, and sharp teeth on the fine white sand of Roman fighting pits. If the howling thing was hunting her, it might find her, but she would not back down from facing whatever it was one-on-one.

When she gained a hundred yards on her pursuers, she caught another scent. Death and decay, moldering wool, scabby blood. She found the path cut in the snow five minutes later. It was trampled to ice by the passage of thousands of boots. She smelled horses, too.

A third of the things were headed directly south. Toward Isaiah.

Black Betty could not help the stab of fear that brought a snarl to her mouth. Her game with the three men pursuing her staled. Isaiah's safety meant more to her than any game could.

She stepped into the pathway the legion of dead men had carved and ran with it, as Brian Hugh had before her, hiding her footprints in the path they had torn through the snow. She knew that no man could track her steps in that mass of prints. After a thousand yards, she cut abruptly south, seeking Isaiah's scent as she ran.

Lieutenant Brian Hugh felt certain he was being watched. He kept looking back, searching the snowy woods, but it was impossible to make out anything beyond the first ranks of trees. Whatever was hunting him was not ready to present itself.

He knew one of two things was the truth. The first possibility, that his imagination had overpowered his actual senses. His mind was creating false information that seemed solid and factual. There was no one in the trees hunting him. He was paranoid and losing his mind.

The second possibility was that something clever was indeed out there, moving just beyond his line-of-sight, waiting to make a perfect strike.

He was tired and beyond raw, worn to nub-ends by the war, then shattered, full stop, by Good Friday. But he did not believe that his imagination was pulling his strings. He was almost certainly being hunted. Yet the lack of proof made it feel like slowly advancing insanity.

He wanted to scream a challenge, throw down the gauntlet and demand single combat, but he quashed the impulse. It would be actual madness to give away his position by hollering into the night. But the game this thing was playing was wearing on him. He felt it in his bones. Something *was* out there watching him. And it was enjoying the torment of making Brian Hugh question his own sanity. That alone made him want to charge out and saber it to its knees. He felt sure that if whatever was out there had numerical superiority and certainty of victory, they would already have made their move, but being baited into fighting on his enemy's terms was a guarantor of defeat.

If he had not lost his mind, if there was a predator out there, he would let it show itself, then he would ride it down. Until then, he fought an internal battle to stay sharp, focused and most importantly, alive.

He kicked his mount to a canter and continued on. St. Quentin was close.

CHAPTER EIGHT

—

THE DRAGON

Shen Su paused, searching the ground before him. The goat path he was following had tightened, and with the steady falling snow, he was having a hard time discerning whether he was still on a path of any sort, or merely rambling aimlessly through the woods, no closer to his friends—perhaps further away— than he had been ten minutes ago.

He fought to stop the rapid descent into chaos his mind was inviting him to enter. He knew the first step down that path was the easiest, but like any quagmire, dragging yourself out of despair was a supreme test of will. He took a breath. He exhaled the fear. He took another deep inhale and pressed on. He was on the path. He had to be. It would not be far now.

He forced himself to appreciate the cold. He was glad the weather had turned, and that he was not attempting this feat in Good Friday's climate.

When Good Friday morning arrived, it came on hot and humid, like mid-day July in Beijing. The blue tunics of the CLC men were sweat through before they finished breakfast.

Su spent the morning scouring the food line, searching out candidates for Sergeant Li's impending mission. He picked out five of the strongest men he could find and had them follow him to Sergeant Li's tent, along with Chang, whose skinny arms and slight shoulders looked comically out of place amongst the big men.

Li Peng sized them up and nodded his approval. When he got to Chang, he smiled and wrinkled his forehead, wry. *"You sure you're up for this, little fellow?"*

"We'll see, Sergeant!" Chang smiled.

"Ah. A philosopher. I suppose we can always use one of those."

Zi Chang grinned. *"Shen Su is the philosopher, Sergeant Li, not me."*

The eight men piled into the back of a canvas-covered truck bed and bounced away over the potholes and cobblestones of an ancient Roman road, grinding gears and rolling west toward what sounded like an oncoming thunderstorm.

"Where are we going, Sergeant Li?" asked Chang.

Li Peng smiled, grim. *"You'll see."*

♠ ♠ ♠ ♠ ♠

It took most of the day to reach their destination. On the teeth-jarring ride, Su watched the world through the rectangle of stiff canvas at the back end of the truck bed. It slowly transformed from a country made of vibrant colors of oncoming springtime to muddy browns, flat blacks, and ugly, mauvish greys.

Occasionally, they saw men and vehicles headed the other direction. At one point, Su thought they passed two white men with a caged lion in their horse-drawn wagon, but he figured the vision must have been caused by fumes from the lorry engine that were pumping out of the tailpipe and floating under the canvas awning, making his stomach heave ungently as it asked to bring his breakfast back up and out. He choked it down, along with fear that was building, as the sounds of war got louder.

By the time the truck's drum brakes shrieked and pulled the conveyance to a halt, the sun was nearing the western horizon and the rattle of battle had reached a steady roar.

Su glanced across at Chang. His new friend was three or four shades too pale. He could tell that Chang was in some intestinal distress, swallowing a lot of hot, bitter saliva every couple of seconds. The thought of it made Su choke back his own gorge again. He had to look away.

Sergeant Li stood up. "Okay, labourers. Time to earn your money."

He hefted a large rucksack, then stepped through the canvas rectangle and dropped to the mud. Su, Chang, and the other five followed with the opposite amount of certainty.

When Zi Chang hit the ground, he was able to hold in his vomit for one step, then two, then it exploded out of him, projectiling into the mud.

As a loud convoy of Red Cross trucks began moving past them, Sergeant Li bent down and looked in Chang's eyes, *"You gonna be okay, Chang?"*

Chang nodded and spat viscous saliva away. *"Yes, Sergeant Li. Feeling much better now."*

Li Peng patted his shoulder. *"Lesson of the day. If you can make it to lunch, skip breakfast. A lot of days here, it's going to be a meal your body tries to make you see twice."*

Su saw a British Sergeant, stinking in the heat, his ruddy face shining with sweat, slogging through the thick mud toward them.

"You lot the Labour Corps chinks?" he asked over the roar of trucks grinding their gears.

Li Peng was the only one who spoke English. He smiled. "You the Limey twat who can't get your playthings out of the mud?"

The Limey twat was taken aback. "What'd you say, mate?"

Sergeant Li's face was newborn baby innocent. "I say, 'we here to get your tank out of the mud, boss.' What do you think I said, boss?"

"You've got some pretty good English."

"For a chink, I do just fine. Your English could use some help."

"What?"

"Your English tank could use some help, I hear."

The Sergeant was pretty sure that was not what Li Peng said the first time, but he had not slept more than an hour or two at a stretch in fourteen days and was worn thin and brittle as a stale cracker. The German barrage the night before had pushed him closer to breaking than he had thus far been, so he ignored any additional input that might flick him carelessly over the edge. "Right. Follow me. Keep your heads down if you want to keep them attached to your necks. Stay on the duckboards if you don't want to drown in the mud."

Li Peng turned to Su, Chang, and five strong Chinese men who were beginning to hate Shen Su for volunteering them for the day's labour. *"Okay, keep on the wooden tracks. Mud out here is deep enough to drown you, slow and ugly. We're gonna follow this shitbag to his broken tank. Then we're gonna get it out of its predicament. Then we're gonna get back in that truck and go home. Understood?"*

"What kind of tank? A water tank? A fuel tank?" asked Chang.

Li Peng shrugged. *"Neither. They call it a 'tank'. I don't know why. I call it a fire-breathing dragon. Stay close. Keep your heads down. He says it's dangerous up ahead."*

The British Sergeant led them through the reserves, past ranks of filthy, exhausted infantrymen trying to catch a quick nap or a cigarette on the muddy ground. As they approached a small ridge, a support trench cut from the earth opened up before them. They followed its angling descent until the sandbags rose up on both sides of them, dulling the sounds of bullets whistling overhead and the occasional whiz-bang of German artillery shells hurtling in.

The trenches quickly began zig-zagging. As they turned a sharp corner, the sound of gunfire rending the air struck them. A line of British Infantrymen was on the fire step, ranging their Enfield SMLEs over the battlements and hurling rifle rounds at an invisible enemy.

Su saw Li Peng look up at them. The lightness with which he began the day was gone. His expression had taken on a grim tone.

"E-everything okay, S-sergeant?" asked Chang. He had seen the look, too.

Sergeant Li nodded. *"More action than I thought there would be. But as the Canadians say: What cannot be cured must be endured."*

They turned the next corner. The riflemen's cause dulled away in the distance as the bark of a Hotchkiss machine-gun team at the apex of the next trench corner drowned it out. All they could see were the backs of two men working in tandem behind a steel armor plate that shrouded the business end of the gun. They swept the MG back and forth. Its staccato roar sounded like some hellish sewing machine's rattle.

"Good heavens… good heavens…" said Chang. It was something his mother used to say all the time when she came upon he and his older brothers fighting in the yard. Su patted his shoulder.

They came to a section of the trench that had been blown to bits by a direct shell hit. There were still blackened remnants of men, nearly unrecognizable, buried in likewise blackened sandbags and twists of barbed wire.

The British Sergeant stopped there. "You'll come out of the trench here. The tank's about fifty yards out. Boche been trying to get to her, too. Want to see if they can't take her home, eh? Once the bastard artillery boys start their barrage, we'll advance and form a perimeter west of the tank. You lot'll follow us, get her up and running, then fall back," he said.

Sergeant Li considered. "Where is the crew?"

The Brit shrugged. "Still in the cockpit, dead as doornails, far as I know."

Peng nodded. "Does it have petrol?"

"Ought to. It didn't get but that fifty yards before it shat the bed and died. Ain't been running since."

"Tools?"

"Should be a full set in the belly."

"Tracks intact?" asked Li Peng.

"What?" asked the Sergeant.

"Did it slip a track?"

"You mean them wheely things on the side?"

Li Peng nodded.

"No. Like I said, it just 'in't running. If I could tell you why, I could fix it myself, right?"

Sergeant Li took a small trench periscope out of his rucksack. He put the aperture over the lip of the blown trench and looked out at the battlefield beyond. He took a breath and held it a millisecond longer than was natural before putting the periscope aside.

Sergeant Li turned to Su, Chang, and the others. He pointed to them in turn, starting with Su and ending with Chang. *"One, two, three, four, five, six, seven. Those are your numbers. When the sun sets, we gonna head out and try to get this thing running. One, two, and three, you coming with me. Chang, you're my lucky number seven. You stay here with this."* He handed Zi Chang the periscope. *"If one of us gets hit, number four's gonna come join us at the tank. If two of us get hit, number five's gonna come running then. If he falls, number six is up. If four of us get hit, Chang, you're up and over those sandbags and you sure as Hell better not get hit. It takes four men to drive that tank once we've got it running and you'll be all I've got, understood?*

Chang was glad he had already thrown up. There was nothing left inside to come out. He nodded. *"Wh-what if you get hit, Sergeant Li?"*

Li Peng smiled. *"If I get hit, none of you knows how to fix a tank. I guess it'll mean you have to drag it out of there by hand, neh? She's pretty heavy. Maybe best if you say some prayers that I don't get hit."*

♠   ♠   ♠   ♠   ♠

Shen Su paused at the fork in the snowy trail. He recognized the large rock at its apex. He leaned up against it and took in a deep breath. He was on the right path. His prayers had not been answered in the affirmative on Good Friday, but it looked like his current ones had not been entirely ignored. Not far now. He pushed off the rock and carried on.

♠   ♠   ♠   ♠   ♠

Durant slowed his troop to a walk. Renoir, Rupert, Jonah, James, and Wolfgang eased up as they caught him, grateful for the chance to rest their legs.

The woods were thinning quickly, and Durant saw a wide field opening up beyond its edge. The snow, unimpeded by branchy canopy, was coming down full force, ferocious in its effort to turn the world to a blank, white canvas.

Durant stopped cold. Instinct, perhaps; his animal brain registering something it could not quite factor out. Durant raised a hand and halted the men behind him. He looked back for Wolfgang at the tail of the column.

"Wolfgang," he whispered, summoning him with a wave.

Wolfgang eased forward. Durant could make out his bullet-torn face, swathed in bloody cotton. The eyes behind the injuries gazed back, sharp and clear.

"What is it?" Wolfgang asked quietly.

"It's an open field out there, no cover," Durant replied. "I'm gonna have a look. Keep an eye out behind us while I do."

"Ja," Wolfgang said.

Durant signaled for Renoir, Rupert, James, and Jonah to stay put. He headed for the edge of the field while Wolfgang circled back behind them.

As he left the woods, Durant began to think he had come upon some orchard, akin to the ordered ranks of trees in the field behind the Chateau de Bois. He saw that there were indeed trees in the field, and their rigid, careful placement was undoubtedly manmade, but through the dark, swirling snow he could not make out any foliage that would hold leaves and fruit of any sort.

As he neared the base of the first tree, he stopped. His breath caught. He could see the naked frost-bitten feet, impaled through the ankles by a railroad spike to the dead tree. The crucified man hung from the rugged cross, limp, unmoving.

Durant looked ahead, down row-upon-row-upon-row of 'trees' vanishing away into the falling snow. This was no orchard. It was a field of ordered torture, perfectly laid out, performing lingering murder that had been the standard of excellence for the Babylonians, Assyrians, and Persians.

Alexander the Great discovered the method on his bloody trek east and was delighted to bring it home (along with mastiffs) to the Mediterranean, where the Romans, too, became fans of it and spread the brutal practice far and wide. The Roman Legion popularized it so effectively that it was visited back upon them when Germanic tribes captured Roman tax collectors and staked them up violently to sacred trees for their audacity.

Durant was not a student of history, but he had been to church enough times to recognize what he was looking at. This was Jesus of Nazareth, Gestas, and Dismas times one hundred.

Durant heard men laboring. He slipped into cover behind the base of the crucifix. He recognized the sounds of logging; distant axes striking rhythmically, a shout of warning followed by the *crack* of the pith, the slow fall of the tree, and the massive *whumpf* it made as it struck the earth. He heard jabbering, then axes again, working their way up the fallen tree quickly, stripping it of limbs.

Durant could not tell how many men were in the logging team, but by the murmurs reaching him, he knew there must be a dozen working at the task. Had Finbarr Kelly been beside him, he would have told Durant that the language was Latin, that these were the same Roman legionaries he had already escaped once, and that running fast and far was the only chance he had.

Durant ducked low and made his way back into the timber, certain at any instant he would be spotted and the alarm sounded; but knowing if he ran there was no question he would give himself away.

When he got to the men, he signaled for silence and led them quick and quiet back into the dense forest. After ten minutes, he paused, and they circled him.

"What was it?" asked Renoir, breath heaving.

"Crucifixions… A hundred. Maybe more," Durant said.

"O, Lord…" James clenched his hands into fists to stop them from shaking.

"Perhaps we must find somewhere to hide where we can wait for morning to come," said Renoir.

"I don't think so," said Durant. " I think all the ones from the canal are still back there behind us somewhere. If we can't get to the other side of St. Quentin this way, I think we could cut straight down to the river and follow it through the city."

Wolfgang translated for Rupert and Jonah.

Rupert spoke up. *"I know the city. My company did fatigue duty in St. Quentin. I can get us through."*

"What is it?" asked Durant.

"He says he knows the city well enough to guide us safely through," Wolfgang replied.

Durant took a breath. In an infinite black ocean, a jot of hope. "Alright. Let's go."

♠   ♠   ♠   ♠   ♠

Less than a half-mile from Durant's party, Finbarr Kelly was churning through the snow. Donnie McMaster, breath heaving, halted along on his bum leg, two steps behind him. They reached a small crest and started down it when Finbarr froze. Donnie came inches from crashing smack into him.

The hair on Fin's neck stood. His ears hummed. A shot of cold air gulped down into his lungs. Inside his mind, he screamed, but it came out of his mouth as an almost inaudible whimper.

He was looking at the same field Durant had stumbled into, but from straight on. Even in the dark, he clearly saw rows of twenty and thirty-foot-high crosses through the falling snow. Muffled moans and whimpers of suffering from the crucified echoed up to them.

A tall birch lay on the ground in the field. It had been cut down and fashioned into a cross. As Fin and Donnie watched, a man was dragged through the snow to the axis, hefted up, and slammed down onto it by a pack of men.

Fin and Donnie heard the victim shouting in French, then the sound of a sledgehammer hitting a metal spike punctuated his shrieks as the monsters holding him joined him to the fallen tree.

Fin ducked low and slunk back into the woods. Donnie, face pale as the snow, stumbled along behind him. When they got to the peak of the rise and the rows of crosses disappeared, Finbarr ran. He did not look back to see if Donnie was coming. He did not particularly care. The Devil was welcome to the hindmost, and Fin devoutly intended for that not to be himself.

Finbarr felt the cold air burning his lungs and the falling snow stinging his eyes, but he kept on. Being crucified had been a stubborn, recurrent nightmare from the moment his mother explained to him why good, sweet Jesus was hammered to a cross with that gaping wound speared in his side, blood dripping from that fucking crown of thorns, eyes a-gog, staring up to heaven, supposedly requesting that his dear old dad, 'forgive them, they know not what they do'.

Fin had never believed for a moment that the Romans 'knew not what they did'. They knew exactly what they were doing and had done it to the best of their abilities. In young Fin's nightmares, they did it to him, too. He could feel the railroad spikes nestle sharply into his palms. He imagined the pain of them being hammered between the delicate phalanges' bones, driving through flesh and sinew, securing him to the pliable wood below while blood poured out. The nailing of the feet would be worse. Then the raising of the cross, putting all his weight onto the black steel pins, would eclipse all of it. The long death of dehydration while carrion birds and flies feasted on him would be worse still. The finality of death when it arrived would be pure mercy.

The pain of running was nothing compared to what he had seen those same men do to his fellow Irish Fusiliers. So, Fin ran, certain that dying of heart failure would be a million times less painful and more efficient than whatever the Romans had in mind.

Fin broke free from the trees and onto a road. He bent over and listened to his pulse throbbing in his ears. His chest ached. The heart attack did not come. He caught his breath.

Then Donnie tumbled out behind him, face bright-red and splotched, likely much closer to heart failure than Fin. He dropped the Mauser and collapsed to all fours, panting, clutching his chest. Perhaps Missy's cooking had finally caught up to him.

In the long run, Fin did not particularly care if the American lived or died. He certainly hoped Donnie would die before him, but in the near term, it would be a useless death if it did not buy Fin time. Fin was struck by the realization that if Donnie did die here and now, in all likelihood, something worse would fill Donnie's flesh and become a clear and present danger immediately.

"Aye... Are you all right?" Fin whispered.

Donnie could not speak, but he nodded. It took him long moments to regain his breath.

Fin helped him up onto wobbly legs, then bent down and retrieved the Mauser with his good hand. "I'll carry this for you."

Donnie nodded. He had thought about just dropping it in the woods and was glad to cede the weight and responsibility of the weapon to Finbarr.

"This fucken snow keeps falling, it'll fill our tracks, I think... Maybe even better on this road than in the woods where the trees can get in the way of it. I say we follow this road, fast as we can, until we find some place to shack up, eh? I don't figure on getting nailed up to some fucken tree."

Donnie nodded again. "Okay... Me neither."

"Are you fit to go on?" Fin asked.

Donnie did not feel fit enough to do anything, but the alternative, simply giving up and surrendering to the demons, as James Cox had done (to his instant regret) the night before, was not something Donnie was ready to do just yet, so he nodded.

Fin shouldered the rifle, delicately slinging it past his ruined hand, running the strap diagonally across his chest. He turned to the road and ran. Donnie trucked doggedly along behind him.

♠　♠　♠　♠　♠

Darren Tremaine slowed Bathsheba. He dismounted and wrapped her reins around a low-hanging branch. He drew his saber and bent low, easing his way toward the sound of axes biting sharply, rhythmically, into living trees.

When he found the edge of the orchard, he stopped. He saw the shape of the cross rising up before him and all the ones lined up in the field beyond it, disappearing into the snow. He saw the man pinned to it, hanging limp, not twenty yards away. The man's eyes opened. He saw Darren.

"... Help me..."

Darren froze. The axes striking wood in the distance kept up their percussive exchange.

"… Help me… Help me!... HELP ME! *HELP ME!!!*"

Darren heard the chopping axes falter. He backed away, turned, and ran up the hill to Bathsheba. The crucified man's screams died away with a shriek of pain and terror, then Darren was mounted, riding, pushing Bathsheba in the opposite direction. To his great shame, he had no 'help' to give.

♠   ♠   ♠   ♠   ♠

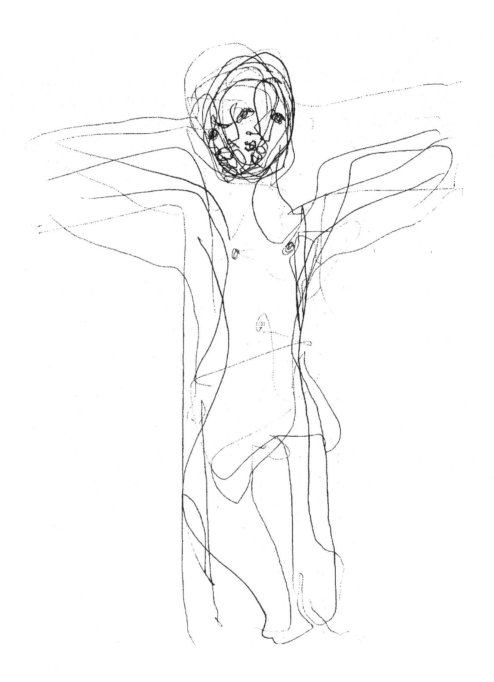

©jm2022

Chapter nine

—

ODERANT DUM METUANT

On Good Friday, when the demons came for the Ghurkas, they got more than they bargained for. The Hindu children of the Himalayas, born and raised in the shadows of their massive mountain peaks, were survivors and warriors of the first degree. One hundred years prior, their ancestors had surrendered for the last time, then joined the British Redcoats in the brutal subjugation of their own people. After the war, they continued dutifully serving the British East India Company, bringing their unruly Indian cousins into line with the Empire's aims.

Juddha Jai Pandit was barely twenty. His birthday had come and gone just the week before. His father had been a Ghurka infantryman, and the fierce young man proudly followed in his footsteps. The pathway led him from the garrison in Nepal to the battlefields of France, and a flat-seeming foreign land devoid of the towering mountains that defined the world as he knew it. He had been told of Alpine mountains that rose up to the south, but Juddha Jai felt that if you could not see the peaks from wherever you stood, they could not truly be called mountains.

Juddha Jai had been mulling that over, staring out at the flat Belgian countryside, standing watch as Good Friday's night fell. When he saw the wave of men coming out of the dark toward his fire trench, he sounded the alarm with the trigger of his Lewis Gun, sending rounds spitting into the line rushing toward him. Within half a minute, the entirety of the Ghurka Royal Rifles Company was at the lip of the trench, adding their fire to Juddha's.

When the German dead men breached the barbed wire and reached the trench, Juddha and his Nepali brothers met the charge with their heavy, boomerang-shaped Khukuri knives.

Juddha cut down seven Germans before a bayonet nearly speared him. He dodged the thrust, but tripped backward and went ass-over-tit into the trench. His arms flailed and he felt his bloody Khukuri machete slip from his grasp and spin away. Then came the impact of his skull striking the duckboards eight feet below. Then he was out.

His fellow Ghurkas fought the dead men fiercely for another ten minutes. The Khukuri was the near perfect weapon to face the dead men's onslaught. The physics of the blade, with its forward bend, made it ideal for slashing blows that cut bone as easily as it might cleave thick brush and saplings. Had their enemies been killable, the Ghurkas would have made chowder of them. Unfortunately, they were not. Killable, that is. The fighting was as good as done when the first Ghurkas were overwhelmed and murdered by the sheer numbers of German dead men. When the dead Ghurkas rose and bent their Khukuris toward violent amputation of their own brothers-in-arms, the tide quickly turned.

When Juddha Jai awoke, his head felt as though it had been struck squarely by Isaiah Taylor's 16lb fence maul. He was on the duckboards of a trench filled with remnants of men in grey and men in green whose bodies had been so utterly savaged in the battle that they were no longer ambulatory.

The Ghurkas stood their ground to the last man, and after the last man fell to the demons, those that could rise, rose, inhabited and infested by the old souls of broken men and women whose thirst for death and bloodshed was in no way sated. They ran on into the night, devouring everything in their path, collapsing at dawn, right around the time Juddha Jai came to.

Juddha was covered in tacky blood. He found a Khukuri in the mess. It was not his personal weapon, but in the pile of limbs and rent corpses, he could not tell where his had vanished off to. Whoever's Khukuri he had would not miss it, and Juddha did not propose to go forward into the unknown unarmed.

He searched the trenches for life. After an hour of walking the killing field, head pounding and back aching, he gave up hope of finding survivors. He walked the boards to his dugout. In the confines of his temporary home, he washed away all the blood and gore he could, stripping his ruined uniform. In his kit, he found neatly folded dress greens and put them on. He cleaned his acquired Khukuri of blood, then ran his Chakmak along the blade until it was shaving sharp. He fit it into its sheath, then packed the rest of his personal belongings into his rucksack and slung it on his back. He took his Enfield down from the rifle rack and headed out.

At the MG nest, he used a periscope to glass no-man's-land one last time. To the east, nothing. What had been the German front line appeared deserted. Given the toll the battle had taken on his company, Juddha had to assume that the Germans broke the Ghurka ranks and drove a salient deep into British territory. He was ashamed he and his men failed to hold the line. He did not yet know that 'holding the line' was a physical impossibility.

Juddha Jai took his kit and headed west, rifle in his left hand, Khukuri hanging ready in his right. Blood was the only thing that could wash away his shame. He swore he would not sheathe the Khukuri again until it was bathed in vengeance for the loss of his dead brothers.

At noon, he found them. The ranks of dead Ghurkas were surrounded by dead Germans, dead British cavalrymen, Black Senegals and Somalis, pale French infantrymen, and a score of dead Belgian civilians.

Juddha Jai Pandit could make no sense of the battlefield. The dead all lay as if sleeping, giving no evidence they had been fighting each other when they fell.

He said a prayer for his countrymen, and one for his sanity, then he continued on, following the Somme River's edge. He traced its curves for two days. There did not seem a better path to take. It walked him directly to his fate.

Juddha slept, unmolested, through the night on Saturday. He rose and walked all day again, then slept under the stars on Sunday night. He continued his slog on Monday, weathering the rain and lightning that came at sunset in the remains of an ancient stone cottage whose roof had tumbled in over the winter.

He slept off and on, awakened by lightning that dashed itself against the earth. When the rain subsided, he tried to get back to sleep, but the damp chill cut to the bone. It differed from the dry Himalayan cold he had been born in, and he decided that, since sleep would not embrace him, he ought to continue until the dawn came and slumber then.

The storm gone, the moon's full grace shone down, lighting his path beside the Somme's flow. He had been walking for nearly an hour when he caught the faintest odor of unwashed men and blood. The Khukuri hung ready in his hand. He saw the outlines of men moving through the dark, slow and sure, hunting.

Juddha Jai saw no sense in running. If they were his enemies, he would die on the battlefield. If they were allies, he would not. Juddha liked it when choices were refined into something simple and stark.

"Who goes there?" he challenged.

There was laughter from the dark. Juddha realized there were a lot more of them creeping through the night than he had thought.

He had long since accepted that he would die at some point. In Nepal, there were a thousand ways that death, the Goddess Kali Mata, the Dark Mother, could take a man who walked the mountains pretending she was not there, just out of sight, waiting for you. Whether it was the altitude stealing your breath or breaking your heart, a slip in the ice that sent you plummeting into a crevasse, or an avalanche that buried you deep and killed you with starvation if suffocation and bitter cold did not take you first, Kali was there. From the blue sky and the towering peaks, to the icy tundra and floes spreading from their feet, she was always there, waiting patiently. Juddha's mind told him he stood now in her presence.

Then a shiver went down his spine. He had a flash of fear, and his body trembled. Perhaps it was not Kali before him. Perhaps it was her lover, the world-ender, the sower of chaos, dancing father and mother God of the apocalypse, Shiva.

As they closed the distance with him, Juddha Jai shook away the superstitious terror, ashamed. These were men, and they were coming for him, weapons drawn and ready. He would meet them on the field and test their mettle. If death was here for him, it was not in the hands of some supernatural deity; it was in the hands of men, and he would bow to no man. He ran toward them, screaming his battle cry.

But Juddha Jai was wrong. These were not men. And perhaps the mythology of his Hindu upbringing was closer to the truth than he wanted to accept. The dead Romans who chased Finbarr Kelly through the night were overjoyed when they realized the Hindu lad would not run from them as Finbarr had. They charged forward to meet him, gleeful.

They were shocked by his efficiency with the Khukuri. He gutted and dismembered four of them before they overwhelmed and took him down, and even then, he fought and savaged his attackers with the blade.

A strong arm wrapped around his neck from behind, and despite his hacking and slashing, the dead man who held him would not let go. They hog-tied him and dragged him back through the woods, triumphant.

The one-eyed, kilt-clad man who led them, Centurion Oberon Junius, picked up Juddha's bloody Khukuri. He spun it in his hands, admiring the weapon. The damage done to the first ranks of men that captured the Ghurka was a lesson in its destructive capabilities indeed, and it had a much more promising heft to it than the British bayonets did. It reminded him of the Roman Gladius sword he had worn on his hip for two decades, two thousand years in the past. The bend in the blade was an innovation, and he could feel that this was a blade made for hammering, scything blows more than the traditional stabbing he was accustomed to. He did not mind. He was an old Roman dog, but he knew the key to survival was learning every new trick one could. Oberon Junius could not wait to try out the weapon first-hand.

He had two of his subordinates hold Juddha Jai fast. A third grabbed him by the hair and yanked his head back, exposing the strong neck and Adam's apple. Oberon saw the pulse pounding in Juddha's carotid, his heart rate revealing fear, but the man's eyes remained defiant.

"Oderint dum metuant," said a voice behind Oberon.

Oberon Junius turned to see who had interrupted him with the Roman dictum, "*Let them hate us, so long as they fear us*".

The man was on horseback. He wore the body and uniform of a French Field Marshal. His cape was thrown back over one shoulder and he sat the saddle, imperious, fist resting on his hip.

General Publius Quinctilius Varus looked past Oberon to Juddha Jai, whose defiant glare had not changed. *"Where is the joy in victory if the enemy does not know he has lost all before the final blow comes? Bind this one and bring him along. Gather your men. We must have him and two thousand more. We will teach them to hate us. Then we will teach them to fear us. Then we will put them all to the cross."*

And so, Juddha Jai Pandit was given a brief reprieve. He was the first captive taken that night, destined for crucifixion. The legion swelled its ranks as dead Romans rose and flocked out of the darkness to General Varus's reborn standard. They followed Varus west and swept up two-hundred more prisoners before settling on a wide field and getting to work.

By dawn, nearly half of the prisoners had been crucified. Juddha Jai and the remainder of the survivors were bound hand-and-foot to each other with bales of telephone wire and left to await the legion's sunset return.

They spent the day listening to the cries of the freshly crucified, and as Varus predicted, any man still holding fast to hatred, found himself embracing fear. Even Juddha Jai Pandit's appetite for defiance ebbed.

As the snow began to fall, and the sun began to set, Juddha watched the dead legions rise. Then the horror of crucifixion began again.

♠　♠　♠　♠　♠

CHAPTER TEN

———

THREE

Shen Su paused when the howling echoed through the hollow. It was distant; but if that wolf bitch was between him and his destination, this was all for nothing. He said a quick prayer to his ancestors to intercede on his behalf, then he plowed ahead, recalling again that his last round of prayers had done little to no good. By sunset on Good Friday, all seven of Sergeant Li's men had spent a fair amount of time in one form of supplication or another, and it all fell on deaf ears. Su sighed at the memory of their devout, deluded prayer circle. Surviving Good Friday, and the nights and days that followed, had nothing of the ethereal divine in it; it had all been pure, unearned luck.

♠ ♠ ♠ ♠ ♠

After Shen Su, Zi Chang, and their five fellows finished praying for survival, the rattle of gunfire from the trenches slowly diminished—almost certainly unrelated to their prayers—and only occasional random rounds cracked the air over their heads. The British riflemen on either side of them returned the anonymous animosity, firing blind, back toward the German lines.

Long after the last glow of twilight faded, the sweaty British Sergeant reappeared, struggling through the trenches. He found Sergeant Li's command where he had left them. Behind him came a line of British infantrymen, girded for battle, too exhausted at this juncture to question if wasting their lives for a piece of machinery was in their personal best interest.

Li Peng took out his flashlight and shouldered his rucksack.

"Barrage is coming," said the British Sergeant. "You lot ready?"

"As we can be," said Li Peng. He looked to Shen Su, Zi Chang, and the others. *"Okay. We're going now. Chang, you keep an eye on that periscope. If I flash my torch twice, that means you send the next man out to join us, understand?"*

Chang nodded, breathless.

Sergeant Li looked to Shen Su and his first wave. *"One, Two, Three, cinch your nutsacks tight. Remember, you're doing this for your mamas and papas."*

Shen Su nodded. He had not forgotten his purpose.

The British Sergeant turned to his infantrymen. "You cunts, once our shells start raining, we're going over the top. The Huns'll be coming for our tank and she's the property of King George, so while these chinks get her sorted, we'll be sorting out the fucking boche, understood?"

It was decidedly not the St. Crispin's Day speech, but Henry the Fifth would have been proud of the sentiment, nonetheless.

On schedule, bombardment kicked off. British batteries launched their loads from two-thousand yards back, sending their gifts in long, bright arcs through the night sky. The molten orange balls of TNT hit in front of the German lines, sending shrapnel and fire spinning out, shredding the handful of Germans not conscientious enough to be hiding in their funkholes.

The British Sergeant and his men took the cue. They elbowed past Su and his companions. The parade of clammy, sweat-through wool, steel helmets, well-worn walnut rifle stocks, and blackened sword bayonets climbed over the wrecked trench and the dead bodies half-interred in it. Once the platoon had disappeared into the battlefield, Sergeant Li, Shen Su, and Numbers Two and Three followed.

Chang raised the trench periscope and watched. At first, all he could see was the bright impact of the British shells striking barbed-wire thickets less than a hundred yards away. Chang was shocked at how close the Germans were.

Then, from the German lines, a Star Shell launched. It exploded above the battlefield, and it was as if the coldest, whitest sun in the galaxy suddenly rose above them. Chang saw the British infantrymen in a scattered line, running bent over toward the rhomboid shape of a listless Mark II Battle Tank. Sergeant Li, Shen Su, Number Two, and Number Three were behind the infantry, nearly halfway there. When the British reached the tank, they continued past its hulk, forming a prone skirmish line between the derelict machine and the German trenches.

As the British barrage began to die out, the German Star Shell faded, too. All seemed to be going to plan. A moment passed in the dark. Chang's eyes adjusted to the gloom, and he thought he could see Sergeant Li and Shen Su reach the tank. Then he heard a *pop*, and another Star Shell burst over the field, turning it again to false day, as if they lived on the smallest planet ever imagined, whose rotation turned day to night in a dizzying span of seconds.

A moment later, the German riflemen opened fire. Chang saw the man behind Shen Su collapse in a heap of blue. Su grabbed him under the armpits and dragged him toward the cover of the tank.

Chang's breath caught in his throat. As the Star Shell faded, he watched Sergeant Li kneel next to the body, then he looked back in Chang's direction and flashed a pair of bursts toward him.

Chang looked at his comrades. *"Sergeant Li says send Number Four."*

Number Four was not impressed. He was also not happy that he had been named Bad Luck Number Four, but he knew that failing his family was not an option. Stoic, he climbed up onto the parapet. When the round hit his ribs, he tumbled back, crashing on top of Chang and numbers Five and Six, knocking all three men to the muddy duckboards.

Number Four lay on top of Zi Chang for what seemed like a very long time. He felt the man's last gasps come choking in and rattling out as the warmth of blood saturated his chest, and the cold, wet mud at the trench bottom soaked his back. Then Number Four let out one last effortless sigh and went still.

Chang struggled from under him and clawed up to his feet beside Number Five, who was breathing in and out too quickly through his nose. Number Six was nowhere to be seen.

The sound of gunfire in the field and the explosion of another German Star Shell shocked Zi Chang back into the moment. He stumbled over Number Four's corpse and leaned against the parapet. He held the periscope up to his eye, but to his great dismay, he saw that the little mirrors were now coated in mud and blood. Chang took a deep breath, knowing a German bullet was definitely going to turn him into fertilizer, then he eased his head up over the battlement and looked toward the tank. No bullet found him.

At the tank's rear end, Sergeant Li had a look of consternation on his brow. He double-flashed the torch in Chang's direction again.

Chang ducked back down. *"Sergeant Li wants you to come and join them."*

Number Five nodded. He looked down at hands that were quivering. He turned and ran away through the trenches, leaving Zi Chang standing there, helpless and alone, with his useless periscope.

Chang set the periscope down. He attempted to wipe some of the trench mud and Number Four's gore off on his pants but was not terribly successful; it just made the mess more uniform in color and composition. He looked down at poor Number Four, glassy eyes reflecting the Star Shell. He looked in the direction that Number Five, and, apparently, Number Six had gone, wistful. As the night faded back to blackness, Chang took a breath, then, before thought could stop him, he grabbed a handhold and pulled himself over the battlement, running through the muddy field toward the inert Mark II battle tank.

All he heard was his breath, and his building heartbeat thumping dully in his chest. He knew bullets were going by, not necessarily beaded on him, but the feel of them cutting the air around him was motivation to keep his legs and arms grinding. As he neared the tank, a Star Shell burst and Chang dove headfirst, sliding through the wet mud, coming to rest at Sergeant Li's feet. Su and Sergeant Li grabbed him and pulled him into the protective cover of the tank's fuselage.

"What happened to Four, Five, and Six?" asked Sergeant Li.

Chang did not have the words to explain what happened to Numbers Five and Six. Bringing shame to their acts of cowardly self-preservation—which in truth was the only sane response to what Chang had asked of them—seemed like heaping insult onto injury, so his one-word response stuttered out. *"D-D-D-D-Dead…"*

Sergeant Li nodded. *"Okay. In we go."*

Li Peng led Chang around the left side of the tank. Each side had protruding sponsons which held matching sets of gun turrets. A Hotchkiss Machine-Gun barrel projected from the middle ball turret and a Six-Pound Naval Artillery Gun pointed out the front. At the rear of the left sponson was an open door into the dark interior.

Chang watched as Number Three backed out of the door, dragging a body along with him. Number Three dropped the corpse on top of five others that rested casually in the mud. The face of a dead British Major stared up into the sky, caught in the glare of a Star Shell.

Sergeant Li grabbed Chang's shoulder. *"In we go."*

Li Peng led the way, ducking his head and squeezing through the tight metal frame. Chang saw the flashlight pop on, lighting the tank's innards. Shen Su and Number Three followed Li Peng in. Zi Chang climbed up after them, slamming the door shut behind him.

The interior was cramped and ugly. Chang saw blood spattered on the steel floor decking and the curling ports of engine exhaust pipes that rose up from the central engine block and exited through the roof. The handles of the Hotchkiss machine gun and six-pound cannon on the left-hand side were mirrored by identical weaponry on the right.

Sergeant Li pointed to seats at the back of the tank beside a large steel crank. *"Shen Su, Number Three—you sit here, yes?"*

Shen Su and Number Three nodded and eased into the chairs. There were levers next to their hands.

"When the engine starts, you won't be able to hear me. I'm gonna bang on the hull with a spanner. When you hear that banging, you look up at me and whatever direction you see me pointing, the man on that side pulls their lever until they see me stop pointing. That's how we turn this thing, understood?" asked Li Peng.

Shen Su nodded.

"Repeat."

"You bang. You point. We pull the lever until you stop your pointing," said Su.

Sergeant Li clapped him on the shoulder. *"Quick study. Zi Chang, come up here with me."*

Sergeant Li pulled Chang past the gun ports to a pair of seats at the cockpit. Chang looked to his right and was shocked to see a pigeon staring back at him through the slits of a birdcage. It cooed gently as he went by.

Sergeant Li squeezed past the butt of a Lewis machine gun that looked forward, poking out of a port in front of the right-hand seat. He sat into the driver's chair on the left side. Li Peng patted the right-hand seat. *"You sit here,"* he said.

Chang sat. Outside, another Star Shell burst and lit up a long, thin view slit above the Lewis Gun. A host of bright dots appeared in the fuselage from front to back, like some formless constellation. It took a moment for Chang to realize that they were not some sort of mystical faerie lights. They were bullet holes, stitched in the 8-millimeter thick armor, illuminated by the Star Shell's burning magnesium. Chang felt less cocooned in safety than he had a moment past.

Sergeant Li began diagnosis of the metal beast's injury. To the left of his own view port, at eye level, was the gas tank. Its tubes ran down to the carburetors through thick rubber hoses. Sergeant Li picked up a big wrench that was sitting between the two pilot chairs and rapped it firmly against the gas tank. It sounded back without an echo. The fuel tank was brimming. He checked the petcock that controlled the fuel, flipping it off and on. It twisted easily back to the 'on' position.

Sergeant Li set the spanner aside and squeezed up out of his seat, following his flashlight through the tight interior to the engine. He checked the carburetors. From the outside, they appeared fine. Then he found it. The engine chokes were engaged. The dead British idiots outside had left the chokes running, cutting the flow of air to the chambers, making the beast run rich with oil, poor with oxygen. Excellent for a cold start, but Li Peng knew that the spark plugs would now be fouled useless, blackened with wet oil.

Sergeant Li opened his rucksack, pulled out a deep-well socket, and set to work on the 6-cylinder Daimler-Knight engine. He unscrewed the tiny knurled nuts which held the wires to the spark plugs, carefully dropping them into his breast pocket for safe keeping. Then he inserted the socket around the plug heads, broke them loose, and spun them free. He wiped each fouled-up plug clean of black, oily residue with his tunic's bottom hem.

When all six were properly cleaned, he inspected them again with the flashlight, running the edge of his shirt sleeve between the spark plug gaps which electrons would jump between, igniting the fuel and air, exploding the pistons into motion, spinning the crank, which created the energy he could harness with the gears to make this cold, dead dragon burst back to life with a roar. He set the plugs back into their holes, screwing them in tightly with his fingers, then he used the socket to get them another quarter turn in. He reset the plug wires and screwed the nuts back on. Then he stood back and wiped his hands clean.

"Alright. We're ready."

Li Peng ducked his head and moved to the large engine crank in front of Number Three and Shen Su. He grasped the crank and tried to turn it. It was stuck tight. He looked up toward Chang and shined his flashlight toward the front controls.

"Chang! Press the foot clutch and shove the gear lever away from you until it stops."

Chang looked down and saw the foot pedal. He reached over with his foot and pressed it gingerly down, then gripped the gear shift. He leaned on it. It slipped out of gear with a *thunk,* sliding into neutral purgatory. *"Yes! It's done, Sergeant Li!"*

Sergeant Li gave the crank a test push and it began to turn. He leaned into it, and it spun once. No response. He let it come to rest, then he spun it again. This time, there was a gentle sputter from the engines; but no life. The third time, she spoke again, and again died away.

Li Peng took a calm breath. He winked at Shen Su. *"Here she goes."*

He spun the crank. The engine bit, the gas vapor exploded in the cylinders, the pistons punched out in sequence, the shaft spun, and the engine roared to life, deafening in the tight cockpit. They could taste a flow of gas and exhaust fumes flooding into the cramped space.

Sergeant Li had to holler to be heard over the engine's din. *"REMEMBER, WHEN YOU HEAR ME BANG WITH THE WRENCH ON THE HULL, WHOEVER IS ON THE SIDE I POINT TO PULLS THEIR LEVER UNTIL I STOP POINTING, YES?"*

Shen Su and Number Three nodded their devout understanding of their duty.

Sergeant Li eased quickly back toward the nose of the tank, disengaging each engine choke lever as he went, not planning to repeat the last occupants' fatal error. He picked up his big wrench and sat into the cockpit seat beside Chang. He engaged the stiff clutch and pulled the gear shifter toward him. Metal ground on metal, then it seated into gear. Sergeant Li released the clutch and the mass of steel, guns, gas, and oil roared ahead with a jolt, metal treads dragging them forward. Sergeant Li banged the hull with his wrench.

From the darkened rear of the tank, Shen Su looked up and saw Sergeant Li silhouetted by the flashlight. He was stabbing his wrench to the right. Shen Su grabbed his gear lever and yanked hard. The tracks on his side of the tank locked up while the tracks on Number Three's side kept spinning, turning the tank sharply right.

Shen Su watched Sergeant Li. When Li Peng's hand dropped, Su pushed his gear lever back forward, grinding it into place as the tracks engaged. Again, the whole tank surged forward with a jolt that made Shen's teeth crack against each other.

Over the deep roar of the Daimler engine, Su heard something else—a high-pitched *PING* as an armor-piercing German reverse round tore through the tank's steel plates, inches from Number Three's head. Number Three cried out as shrapnel from the round sprayed him with tiny, hot shards of steel. He cried out again as a second round went straight through him.

Shen Su grabbed the wounded man and yelled for Sergeant Li, but the noise of the tank, and Li Peng's focus on navigating back to the British lines, made his cries fruitless.

Su grasped Number Three's hand and struggled to assess the damage in the dark tank. He saw that the wound was in the man's belly. The whites of Number Three's eyes were catching enough of the flashlight's beams for Su to see them rolling in his head. The shock of the initial wounding gone, he sucked in a raggedy breath and used it to scream. The keening wail echoed in the tank, singing a horrifying off-key duet with the Daimler-Knight engine.

Su heard the banging of Sergeant Li's wrench on the hull. He looked to the tank's stern and saw Li Peng pointing to the left. Su leaned over his wounded, nameless companion and grabbed the lever, yanking it out of gear. The tank turned five degrees, and Li Peng dropped his hand. Shen Su slid the lever back into gear and they surged forward again, climbing suddenly at an angle. It seemed they had pitched up close to forty-five degrees, and Su had memories of the Atlantic crossing, cresting a wave in the Hell of the ship's hold, then splashing down on the other side. He braced himself, but could not do the same for Number Three. When the tank reached the apex of the British trench line and tipped forward, crashing down onto its belly, Number Three screamed again as they pitched forward, falling out of his seat and slamming Su into the engine block.

Su's ears rang from the hit. He felt blood coming down the back of his head from a cut on the crown. The tank settled onto flat ground and Shen Su heard Sergeant Li banging again, commanding him to turn, but in the cramped space, he was wedged tight between Number Three and the tank's steel floor plates. There was more banging of spanner on hull, then the tank jolted to a halt.

Long seconds passed, and then Chang and Sergeant Li were pulling Number Three off Su. Sergeant Li got Number Three into his seat and tried to assess the wound, while Chang grabbed Shen Su and sat him up.

"Are you shot!? Did they get you!?" Chang asked, breathless.

"No... No. I'm all right." Su pushed himself off the floor and sat back onto the chair.

Chang stared at the bullet holes in the tank armor and the corresponding one in the small of Number Three's back. *"How the hell is this tank a good thing to have if bullets will just go straight through it like a wicker basket?"*

"Only special bullets get through this armor," said Sergeant Li. *"Bullets as likely to blow up the rifle that fires them as they are to hit us. We're okay."*

"Tell that to Number Three. Tell that to the British fellows who are supposed to be piloting this thing," Chang replied.

Sergeant Li eased Number Three back in his seat. The man had passed out cold.

Shen Su wished he could remember the man's name—after all, he was the one who had recruited him for the mission, and now the responsibility for his death seemed to settle onto Shen Su's shoulders, along with the weight of the other four men they had lost.

"Is he dead?" asked Chang.

"Not yet. Will be soon," replied Sergeant Li. *"Shen Su, you gonna have to work both sides until we get back behind the lines, yeah?"*

Shen Su nodded. Sergeant Li led Chang back to the driver's seats and shifted the tank into gear. The engine roared and they jumped forward again, caterpillaring away from the battlefield. Shen watched for Sergeant Li's signal, glancing at Number Three's sagging form, watching the breathing grow weaker by the moment. By the time they reached the rear of the British lines, the breathing had ceased. Number Three's bowels emptied into his trousers, and then he was gone.

♠   ♠   ♠   ♠   ♠

Shen Su stopped in the snow and caught his breath, overwhelmed by the memory of nameless Number Three's death. An exhausted sob burst out of him. As his shaking legs recovered, he reined in the emotion before it could overwhelm him. He heard more howling erupt in the distance. He knew he had to be close now. He set his teeth, leaned forward, and soldiered on.

♠   ♠   ♠   ♠   ♠

CHAPTER ELEVEN

—

BEHEMOTH

Isaiah came hobbling down a snowy incline at a jog, ungainly on his bad ankle. A broad field opened up before him and stretched away, vanishing into the purplish black night and the howling, spinning, tumbling snowfall.

He paused for a breath. His sense of direction had begun to fail, but he pushed forward, faith in his instincts holding fast. He ran through the void of the field with nothing tangible to take bearings on. He felt like a sailor on deck in the mouth of some raging hurricane, and physical exhaustion was bringing him a distinct sense of vertigo.

When large, indistinct shapes materialized out of the night, he slowed. When the forms of neatly ordered black crosses became visible, he stopped and stared hard, thinking he was heading into some kind of graveyard for German war dead.

It took him a long moment to realise that the things before him were snow-covered planes. The top wings of the Albatross D III biplanes, their bodies, and rear wing elevators, were buried in nearly a foot of powder. The black Iron Crosses he had thought represented dead men were paintings on the side of fuselages and rear vertical fins. Isaiah's diagonal approach to the line of aircraft had given the illusion of headstones vanishing into the distance. He could make out at least ten fighter planes, lined up wing-to-wing, disappearing into the night.

With their odd crust, they looked like some museum arrangement of mammoth, extinct, taxidermied corpses, like the ones he had seen in the Museum of Natural History in New York City, lying in state, frozen; vestiges of a world that was now gone. Isaiah briefly lost himself in the memory of his fateful day in that museum, what seemed a lifetime past.

Black Betty came out of the dark, sprinting toward him. Isaiah turned in time to see her coming, but not in time to avoid the impact. His legs swept out from under him and he hit the powder in an explosion of fur and snow.

Black Betty straddled him and licked his face. He swore the big bitch was smiling. Isaiah pushed her away and stood.

"Goddamn, girl, you got to be a little more gentle in your approach. You apt to break me one of these times."

Black Betty let out a gentle huff and stared out into the night.

Isaiah nodded. "Go on. Happy to follow your lead for a bit."

Betty seemed to catch his meaning. She trundled along through the deep snow, Isaiah following. After some fifty yards, she stopped and let him catch her.

When Isaiah reached her side, he found her stalk-still, hackles up, eyes and ears intent on something out there in the dark beyond his senses' ability to perceive. He searched the night and saw nothing. His breath was the only thing he could hear besides the howl of the wind, and he tried to stifle it, paranoid for a split second that it would give away his position. He pushed away the neurosis. Anything close enough to hear his breath would have already slit his throat.

Then Black Betty was on the move. She kept herself low, padding through the snow, stepping fast and calm, on attack bearing, then she leapt forward, bounding full speed. Isaiah stood and ran after her, trying to keep pace, but she moved with grace and power no human could hope to match.

As they ran, Isaiah saw a massive shape rise up out of the gloom. Black Betty tore a path straight toward it. It towered up before them, looking like a dinosaur-age whale's mouth rising out of a frozen ocean. The opening of the massive hangar stretched over one-hundred yards wide and gaped fifty yards high.

As Betty disappeared into it, Isaiah slowed his approach, peering into the depths of the bay. Rafters and beams spider-webbed up, arcing to the ceiling, forming a network of criss-crossing steel to support the vast, snow-covered roof.

As he got closer, he began to make out the rounded contours of the inhabitant zeppelin airship's huge silver nose, staring out at him from her lair.

Suddenly, from the darkness of the hangar, Isaiah saw a flashlight's beams explode on, flashing dull yellow, catching Black Betty in its rays. Her bark echoed hollowly in the gloom, followed by a shriek from the darkness beyond the torch's light. Then Betty collided with the flashlight and sent it spinning away. Isaiah heard the crash of someone hitting the ground followed by a second cry of terror.

Isaiah ran toward the sounds of violence, saber ready, picking his way around and through the massive zeppelin's support beams, until he found Black Betty under the airship's central gondola, pinning a man beneath her. A growl rumbled in her throat as he cried out and fought in vain to push her away. She pressed her chest down onto the man, baring her teeth, flashing them in the darkness, and he stopped fighting, frozen.

Isaiah approached slowly. He picked up the torch and turned it on Betty and her prize. "What you got there, Black Betty? He alive?"

"I'm alive! As God is my witness, I'm bloody alive!" said the man.

"Hm. You wanna keep it that way, I suggest you calm yourself and let me take a look at you, just to make sure you ain't lying."

The man held his hands up. They trembled. "Right. Of course. Right."

Isaiah clicked his tongue. "Come on, girl. Come on." He gently pressed on her flank and Black Betty eased up, taking her weight off the man's torso. She stood over him, hot breath steaming out and hitting his face, bright teeth inches from his neck.

Isaiah ran the flashlight over the man, revealing dirty British fatigues with a lieutenant's badge on the collar and cannonade pins of the Royal Artillery Garrison on his sleeves. There was no blood or sign of mortal wounding on him, and his skin had a fresh red glow to it from the pumping blood and adrenaline coursing through him. If he was not alive, he was hiding it well.

"Let him up, Betty. Let the man up."

Black Betty stepped back, satisfied, and circled out into the hangar, searching the dark for anything else she might find of interest.

"You're not French," the British Artillery lieutenant said.

"I reckon," said Isaiah.

"With the uniform, I thought perhaps you were French-African."

"American."

"American?" The man looked up at Isaiah. "Well, that's not the strangest thing I've heard these days, is it. Be a good lad and turn off that torch. Wouldn't want to invite anything else in here from out there," he said, gazing out of the zeppelin shed into the night.

Isaiah nodded. He flicked the flashlight off.

"Allow my eyes to adjust a moment, then I'll get you to the bunker."

"They got a bunker in here?" asked Isaiah.

"Yes. To house the pilots and air crews, and in the event of shelling or an aerial assault from our lads."

Black Betty circled back and rejoined them.

"Give us a hand, would you?" asked the man.

Isaiah reached out and found the man's hand in the dark. He got a grip and helped him to standing.

"Cheers. Just this way, if you please."

Isaiah and Betty followed the man through the hangar, beneath the zeppelin's silver-grey panels. The airship was as big as any ocean-going vessel Isaiah had ever seen, stretching some one-hundred and fifty meters in length. To witness something of that scale hanging in mid-air over his head was unnerving. He kept an eye on it the whole time, duly impressed. They reached the rear engine room gondola with its huge propeller and Maschinegewehr '08 ports jutting out. Beyond that, the zeppelin's prolate spheroid shape came to its minimus and revealed her wide tail plane and elevators, neatly bisected by a tall vertical fin and guiding rudder.

Another fifty feet brought them to the far end of the hangar. Isaiah made out a line of sandbags that ran along the lip of a short trench.

"Mind the stairs," said the man.

Isaiah came after and found himself stepping down a smooth, poured-concrete stairwell. Black Betty followed just behind him.

"I'll take my torch, if you'd be so kind," said the man. "Not much danger of the buggers catching a glimpse of light while I manage the door."

Isaiah handed him the flashlight. The man clicked it on, lidding the top of it, giving himself just enough beam to illuminate a steel door with a large steel wheel in the center of it. The wheel spun half-a-turn easily and the latch slid free. The Brit opened the door, swinging it wide on oiled hinges, revealing a steep bank of concrete steps that disappeared into blackness. Isaiah hesitated.

"Come on in, lad. Trust me, it feels immensely safer stowed away in there than it does with your derriére in the breeze out here."

Isaiah stepped through the door, followed by Black Betty, who jaunted ahead, down the stairs, disappearing in the blackness.

The artilleryman followed them and spun the internal wheel shut, then bolted the door with a sigh of relief. "Better," he said.

"I suppose," Isaiah replied.

The man turned a ceramic switch. There was a brief hesitation as the current met resistance. Then overhead lightbulbs hummed to life and lit the stairwell with their golden glow.

"Better still, yes?" said the man. He flicked off the flashlight. He was sandy-haired, wearing round spectacles that reflected warm light back to Isaiah and Black Betty.

Isaiah nodded. He figured the fellow to be somewhere in his thirties. He moved with the starched carriage of somebody who came from money, and his accent spoke the same history to Isaiah's ears, but his smile seemed genuine and welcoming.

"I'm Lieutenant Arthur Keith. Royal Artillery Garrison," he said, extending a hand.

"Isaiah Taylor. Was with the Légion Étrangiére."

"Ah, yes. The Foreign Legion. That explains much. Come. Let's get some food in you. How does that sound?"

"Sounds better than the alternative."

As they started down the stairs, he noticed Isaiah's limp. "Oh, good heavens. You've got a nasty one there, eh?"

"I s'pose that's a word for it," Isaiah replied.

"Well, we're in luck then, Mr. Taylor. The Germans have left us plenty of kit to work with. We'll have you right as rain in no time."

"Mm-hm," said Isaiah.

They reached the bottom of the stairs and found a long hallway with doorways off to each side. Black Betty poked her head out of the centermost door. As Arthur led him along, Isaiah glanced into the rooms and saw rows of bunks with random bits of kit and rifles stowed beside them.

"Enlisted men were all on this level. Next one down was Other Ranks and the hospital. Bottom floor is the officers' quarters."

"Three stories down?" asked Isaiah.

"Quite. The Hun is an industrious and fastidious fellow, is he not?"

"I'm guessing it wasn't Huns that dug this motherfucker out."

"Ha! Yes. You are correct. Most likely dug by prisoners-of-war. But they did a dilly of a job with the architecture and the pouring of the concrete."

On the second level, Arthur led him into a spotless infirmary.

"Have a seat and let's get that boot off, eh? See what's what."

Isaiah set the saber down on the cot and sat next to it. Black Betty circled once, then lay on the concrete floor beside him, brown eyes glancing up. Isaiah looked at the caked gore on the boot leather and sighed.

"Let's have it off, Mr. Taylor. Wishing it different than it is will only prolong the suffering," said Arthur.

Isaiah looked up at him, then reached down and slid the knot free. He loosened the entirety of the laces, then pulled the boot off, wincing as its throb knifed through him, vibrating all the way up his leg to his lower back.

"Motherfucker..." Isaiah managed.

"Yes."

Isaiah's sock was saturated with blood.

"Would you like me to remove the puttee and sock?" asked Arthur.

Isaiah nodded. "Yessir, if you would."

Arthur reached out carefully and undid the bloody blue puttee that wrapped Isaiah's calf, unwinding it gently and setting it aside. He rolled the pants leg up and took hold of the top of Isaiah's bloody sock. "Here goes, Mister Taylor. Think of something cheery."

"Nothin' comes to mind."

"Well, think of something uncheery, or just stiffen your lip and muddle through."

Isaiah nodded.

Arthur carefully peeled the sock off until the lion's claw marks began to reveal themselves, fused by coagulated blood to strands of wool and remnants of Caitlin's cotton bandaging.

Arthur winced at the gore. "Well, here goes, lad."

Isiah gripped the steel frame of the cot. Arthur pulled the sock. The wounds gaped, weeping fresh blood as the bandage pulled free.

Isaiah sighed in pain, breathing deep through his nose, trying not to pass out.

"Alright, lad. Alright. Worst is over."

"It ain't." Isaiah studied the ugly wound. "They got some anti-septic and some alcohol?" he asked.

Arthur nodded. "Yes. A full supply of both."

"Needle an' thread?"

"I've no doubt."

"How's your needle point, Mr. Arthur?"

"Passing fair, if I do say so."

"I hope so. 'Cause I don't aim to find out how good your skills with a bone saw are. Fetch up that cleanser, a nip of booze, rummage around and find that needle and thread, then let's get to it."

Ten minutes later, Isaiah was sipping German cognac as Arthur flushed the wound with rubbing alcohol.

Isaiah nearly choked on the cognac. "God-damn."

"Sorry, Mr. Taylor."

"Don't fret. Jus' do what needs doing," Isaiah said through clenched teeth.

Arthur splashed the rubbing alcohol on his hands and scrubbed them together. He gripped the suture needle with a small pair of bright-silver steel forceps and threaded the fine cat gut into the eye.

"Here we go now," Arthur said.

The recall of Aunt Jean going to work on his face flashed through Isaiah's mind, and the warm cognac in his belly helped stir a flush of emotion through him. He quickly reined it in before it could best him.

"Here we go," Isaiah replied.

Arthur sighed, then sunk the curved needle in. He drove the point to the other side of the wound, then drew the needle and thread up and out, pulling the flaps of skin flush together. He pulled the thread all the way through, then tied it into a two-hand square knot. He used a pair of surgical scissors to cut the cat-gut thread, then leaned back to get a clear view, appraising it in the light.

"Right then. Just twenty or thirty more of those and you'll be tip-top," Arthur said.

Half an hour later, it was done. Arthur took a sip of the cognac for himself and let Isaiah close his eyes. Black Betty lay at the foot of the bed and watched him rest.

Arthur took Isaiah's discarded bloody boot and left them dozing in the infirmary.

One flight down, in the officer's quarters, he rummaged through the former occupants' belongings until he had a pair of hand-knit wool socks and a pair of boots that matched Isaiah's size within a centimeter's length. He stopped in the kitchen and put together two plates of pork sausage and bread. When he reached the infirmary, he found Isaiah sitting up, looking at the stitch work on his ankle.

"You ain't a liar. You did some good needle point there," Isaiah said.

Arthur smiled and handed him a plate of food. "We aim to please. You're welcome to sleep a bit, if you like." Arthur looked at Black Betty. "It would seem you have a good friend to guard your slumber."

Arthur set the second plate of sausage in front of her. She sniffed it once, then devoured it.

"Yeah. She's a good girl. But I can't be slumbering," said Isaiah.

Arthur nodded. He sat on the bed and began to wrap Isaiah's ankle in clean white gauze.

Isaiah dug into the plate of food, devouring the bread and spiced bratwurst. "Thanks," he said, through a full mouth.

"You're welcome." Arthur chuckled and nodded. "I was beginning to think that I was the only man left alive on the planet."

"Naw. You ain't. I got some friends out there that was alive last I saw 'em."

"You don't say?"

"Yeah. Came upon you while we was tryin' to run 'em down. How'd you find this place?"

"Ha. 'Find' is not precisely the correct word. The damnable things chased me to it. I was simply running pell-mell from them. When dawn broke on Saturday, I was near spent. As I was coming down the last hillock onto the airfield, I tripped and went down in a heap. As I looked back, the sun came over the horizon and the ones coming after me fell, like sacks of bloody potatoes…" Arthur's eyes were blank, living in the memory. He shook it off and smiled, rueful. "… when they did not stand and come to finish me, I closed my eyes and slept. When I awoke, they were still 'asleep', and I was still alive. I found the zeppelin shed, and this miracle of modern engineering we're in now, and have been hunkered in it ever since."

Isaiah nodded. "Piece of luck, for sure."

Arthur finished tying off the bandage and leaned back, admiring his handiwork and taking a sip of cognac. "Cheers."

Isaiah stripped off his other boot, puttee, and the stinking sock beneath it. He unrolled the fresh wool socks from the tight ball they had been wound up into and took a whiff of the glory of their clean scent, smiling. They were soft, grey merino, long enough to reach the top of his calves.

"Goddamn. Best socks I seen in my life," Isaiah said.

Arthur smiled. "The Germans do know a thing or two about practical luxury."

Isaiah pulled a sock onto his good foot and stretched his toes. Then he pulled on the low-cut hobnail boot.

"How's the fit?" asked Arthur.

"Like a motherfuckin' glove. Thanks."

"I would recommend, that perhaps you ought to let the wound breathe a bit before you put your other sock on. If it gets damp, it'll never seal properly."

"Well, Mister Arthur, I sure wish I could take that advice, but if I don't try'n find my people tonight, I don't reckon I'll ever catch 'em."

"You're going out again? In this storm? That seems rather unwise."

"You're tellin' me."

Isaiah carefully eased the second sock over the bandage, grimacing as it applied pressure to the sutures. A slight sweat broke out on his brow as he pulled the length of the sock past the wounds. He stretched the sock snugly to his knee and wiped his forehead. "They all running south to Verdun. I don't go now, ain't no chance I could run 'em down come the morning."

"These are your compatriots from the Légion?"

"Couple of 'em. The rest we met on the way." Isaiah picked up his plate and continued eating while he related the basic elements of his journey, from Good Friday and the campfire at the abbey to the disaster at the Siegfried Line. When he finished, they sat in silence for a bit while he picked the last crumbs off his plate. When the plate was completely clean and his belly rumbled from its newfound fullness, he spoke. "If I could leave 'em out there with no compunction on it, I prob'ly would. But I got enough in my rear view that gives me a shot of regret now and then. I'll run on south until middle of tomorrow and see if I can find their trail. If I can't, I'll come on back this way, if that'd be alright with you."

Isaiah picked up his bloody puttee and began winding it snugly back around his calf.

"Do any of your German 'acquaintances' speak English?" Arthur asked.

Isaiah nodded. "Old Wolfgang speaks it just 'bout as good as you. And Sergeant Renoir himself speaks as many languages as I ever heard."

"If you're truly bent on heading back out into that mess, perhaps you could make finding Monsieur Renoir and, or, 'Old Wolfgang' a priority," said Arthur.

"Shit. I don't know that I'll find anyone, but I aim to try for all of 'em." He finished winding the puttee around his ankle and tied it off. "Why Sergeant Renoir and Wolfgang in particular?"

"Well, I know it's asking quite a bit, but I've had some time to think these past few days, about what to do, precisely, in the midst of these events, and I believe that if I find someone who speaks German and the King's English, that there is a course of action to be taken."

"What'd you have in mind?"

"I've found what I think to be a crew manual for that damn bloody big balloon that's resting in the shed above us. Unfortunately, it's entirely in German, which I, sadly, did not study a whit of in school. Give me a moment, if you would?"

Isaiah nodded his consent. Arthur stood and hurried out of the room. Isaiah picked up the second boot. He took a moment to prepare, then pressed his wounded foot into it. Even with the low cut, it rubbed against the wounds.

"Fuck."

He slipped it back off and stood, hobbling over to the table that Arthur had found all the medical instruments resting on. He picked up a #10 Brand & Parker scalpel blade and eyed the razor edge.

It sliced as easily through the boot leather as it would living flesh, between the third and fourth shoelace eyelets. Isaiah cut a clean line all the way around the boot until he had fashioned it from a boot into a shoe. He gave the sides a gentle downward arc so that the underside of his ankle bone would not rub raw, then he leaned back and admired his amateur cobbler work. Satisfied, he sat on the cot and eased his foot into the shoe. He laced it up tight, then tested the fit. Not exactly comfortable, but the soft Merino wool muted the pain, and no longer was there stiff leather rubbing against the wounds.

As Isaiah clipped off the excess shoelaces, Arthur reappeared, flush and grinning, holding a thick booklet in his hands. Its cover read:

Besatsungshandbuch
S-Klasse Zeppelin - LZ 91

"That's it?" asked Isaiah.

"Yes. The crew manual, I believe. They were not kind enough to provide an English translation, and German writing always looks like standard gibberish to me."

Isaiah looked it over. "Bee-sat-songs-hand-butch… Yeah, German gibberish for sure. What you want with it?"

Arthur took a controlled breath, keeping his enthusiasm bridled as best he could. "I feel quite certain, that if we could understand the manual, with enough crew, we might take flight."

"In that balloon up yonder?"

"Precisely. The aeroplanes would not get us terribly far."

"Where you aim to fly to?" asked Isaiah.

"Anywhere. With enough supplies, some forethought, you might make it anywhere on the earth. Have you seen these behemoths in the air?"

Isaiah nodded. "To my great motherfuckin' misfortune. They bombed the shit out of us at Liége one night. Flew in low, out' the clouds and fog, gave us hell with MG's and bombs, then turnt tail and flew on outta there. They big, but they sure ain't slow."

"Indeed. Per the manual, I believe the top speed is one-hundred imperial miles per hour."

"Mm-hm. Yeah. That ain't slow for a balloon."

Arthur smiled. "What I've been noodling over, is the idea that, with a crew, it would be possible to fly at a very high ceiling during the night, and during the day we might navigate to the next major thoroughfare for petrol and provisions, then be aloft and travelling before the sun is high. Whereas, here, we may secret ourselves, undiscovered at night, but where can we go from here that we know will be safe and sound once the sun goes down? And what happens when they eventually discover this place and lay siege to it? Curtains, I'm certain."

"Yeah… Curtains for sure." Isaiah considered for a moment, then, "How many crewmen you need for that thing?"

"Well, I would know more specifically with a German translator. From what I can decipher, it looks like a crew of forty is the standard."

Isaiah laughed. "Shit. I ain't got forty. That's a fact."

"Yes, but I believe that number is for a full battle contingent, with multiple men for each station, including bombardiers and machine-gunners, spare electricians, et cetera. I feel certain that we might get by with a third that number. A skeleton crew, as it were."

"Hm. 'Skeleton Crew'. Good name for it…" Isaiah did a quick reckoning of his companions. "If I could gather all of 'em up, that'd put us at twelve."

Isaiah did not factor Donnie into the number, knowing that if he found him, he was definitely going to kill him dead.

"Twelve… Twelve might just get us there," said Arthur.

Isaiah chewed it over for a moment. "They got a armory here?" asked Isaiah.

Arthur nodded. "Yes. Quite the armory indeed."

The armory was back on the top floor. Isaiah cruised the shelves holding a field grey German haversack, impressed. Black Betty heeled beside him, watching as he perused the inventory. There were crate-upon-crate of munitions for the zeppelin's machine guns, a dozen boxed MG '08's, and racks of Mauser 1916s, with loaded 25-round clips by the bushel.

Isaiah picked up a Mauser '16 and looked over the action and the curved cartridge clip, curious. "Ain't no bolt… Looks like a machine gun."

Arthur was leaned against the door frame. "Indeed, but it's not. Semi-automatic, I believe. Their air corpsmen alone carry them. My men…" Arthur had to swallow as he remembered the faces of his men and the end that had taken them. "… My men recovered a pair of those from a fallen fighter craft. They tried to employ them on the front, but the moment they saw some business in the trenches, they seized miserably. I don't believe they do well in the weather. If they did, they'd have made mincemeat of us… Well… we're all being made mincemeat of now, aren't we?"

Isaiah nodded as he took a loaded magazine and slid it into the receiver. "For sure." He pulled the Mauser's action handle back and felt it load a round. "The blowback must load the next round. Like a MG that way," Isaiah said.

"Yes, I believe so. It will not be the most reliable weapon here." Arthur said.

Isaiah shrugged. "If they had a shotgun, I'd grab that up for certain, but they don't. I seen first-hand how a bolt-action rifle does against them motherfuckers.

Doesn't do a god-damn thing, 'cept maybe make 'em mad. Machine guns seem to do enough to slow 'em, but I can't rightly carry one of them MGs with me, and I ain't exactly got a loader, you know? Best I can hope for is a rifle that'll get off enough rounds to take they legs out from under 'em." He looked over the '16. "This'll do the trick, or it won't. Regardless, let's put her on my tab," Isaiah said, shouldering the rifle. He took another half-dozen magazines and dropped them into the haversack.

Near the entryway, he found wooden boxes marked 'Karabingranate '17'. He pulled the lid off, revealing a 10-inch steel cylinder that narrowed on one end, like a big steel funnel. A large, round, threaded nut was on a sleeve at the skinny end. Piled in hay beneath the device were stacks of neatly ordered blackened-steel, puck-shaped discs.

"Hey, Arthur from artillery, this what I think it is?"

"Ah, yes. A grenade launcher."

Isaiah slid the launcher onto the barrel of the Mauser '16 and spun the nut until it was tightly locked onto the end of the barrel. He picked up one of the grenades and popped it into the launcher. He felt the heft of the loaded weapon and tested the aim.

"Take care. I imagine that will kick you like a bloody mule."

Isaiah smiled. "Feel pretty certain that kick'll happen in both directions if I'm forced to use it. Worse for them than it'd be for yours truly."

"Perhaps. But if you dislocate your shoulder, you won't have another opportunity to reload."

"Shit, let's face it, boss. If I'm pulling the trigger on the rifle alone, it's just a matter a' time 'fore they take me. If I have to use this here grenade launcher, I'll just be shooting outta spite, and ain't likely to get a second shot off anyways, discombobulated shoulder, or no."

Arthur's face was grim. "Then let us hope it doesn't come to any shooting."

Isaiah loaded his haversack with a half-dozen rifle grenades, then slung it across his chest, the weight of it resting comfortably against his hip.

♠   ♠   ♠   ♠   ♠

At the bunker's exit door, Arthur handed Isaiah his flashlight and a medical kit.

"You've spare suture needle and thread, rubbing alcohol, and gauze if you need to make any repairs along the way," Arthur said.

Isaiah nodded. "'Preciate it."

Arthur took the brass Cox Arms field compass he had used for ranging his artillery battery's shells onto stout German trenches and fragile German bodies out of his pocket. "Do you know how to use a compass?"

"I reckon," Isaiah replied.

"This is from your people."

"My people?"

"Yes. It's quite a brilliant American invention. The dials are marked with radium paint, so it can be read in the dark. May it see you a safe return."

"Here's hopin'," said Isaiah.

Arthur spun the wheel and pushed the steel door open. Snow continued to tumble down from a black sky.

Isaiah put the Mauser over his shoulder and tightened his grip on the saber. He let his eyes adjust to the gloom, then he and Black Betty climbed the concrete steps. Arthur pulled the door closed after them, entombing them in exterior darkness.

Isaiah heard the wheel spinning the latches closed, followed by the bolt sliding home. At the top step, Isaiah opened the compass. The glow of radioactive radium isotope lit the dial's numbers in an unearthly green. He turned the compass to find north, then took a bearing directly south.

"Alright, Black Betty. Another chance to find Francois and Caitlin. And Renoir and Wolfgang. And the whole goddamn mess of 'em." He looked up at the rear stanchions and elevators of the massive zeppelin's ass end. "And then let's fly the fuck outta this mess with King Arthur down there."

He felt Black Betty's tail wag against his knee. The pair plowed forward on a southerly bearing into the ocean of snow.

After he pushed the slide bolt home, Arthur sat down at the top of the stairs. He put his face in his hands and wept silently. It was the first time tears had flowed since Good Friday. He sucked in a ragged, catching inhale and rocked back-and-forth while the breath choked out of him and hot salty water poured from his exhausted eyes, as if his physiology was attempting to rinse away everything Arthur Keith had witnessed over the past days.

At three-quarters past midnight on Good Saturday Morning, Arthur had been preparing for a midnight sprint to the latrine trench. His dysentery had not been acute enough to deliver him to the solace of a sick bed behind the lines, but it was atrocious enough that he had not excreted anything but liquid for days. He felt in constant, steady danger of soiling himself. When a fellow was twelve days away from a well-earned respite behind the lines, the idea of shitting in his only pants (and underpants) was a terrifying thought.

Just as he was about to excuse himself from the becalmed artillery battery and its BL 60-pounder heavy guns, the telephone rang in the command hut.

The artillery battery itself was on the east side of an elevated ridge. It overlooked the battlefield, but was positioned just below the rise, defilade, thus hidden from view of German ground units and artillery spotters. Each morning before dawn, Arthur and his men used green tarpaulins and long branches of dead beech and ash to camouflage their ordnance, hiding it from the occasional German biplanes that spent their days seeking victims for the corresponding German heavy artillery on the other side of no-man's-land.

Arthur did not consider it his job to rain hell onto German human beings. His job was to blow the matching artillery pieces across the way to smithereens. When he gave the command to 'Fire', he was not sending sixty-pound shells to kill men, he was sending sixty-pound shells to kill machinery. The death of the men, in explosions that turned the steel machines themselves into burning shrapnel which forcefully dismembered nearby human bits (arms and legs and heads and cocks and balls) and immolated any bloody mass that remained, was entirely incidental. At least, that is what Arthur salved his conscience with when he went to sleep at night.

The phone rang again. Arthur bit his tongue and tried to still his clutching belly with his mind.

He lifted the handset. "Hello?"

The switch operator, sitting in a concrete blockhouse three-thousand yards away, was attached to Arthur by an extremely long piece of wire that had been patched nearly every other night when German artillery shells lucked into striking it. The operator asked Arthur to please hold while he connected him to GHQ.

There was a momentary silence, and Arthur's stomach grumbled painfully, then a stentorian voice on the other end of the line passed Arthur fresh targeting coordinates. Apparently, some damnable German Heavies were pounding the hell out of the Sherwood Foresters Infantry, and GHQ wanted those bloody guns silenced statim and without further ado. Would Arthur be so good as to make it so?

"Yes, sir. Of course, sir. Right away, sir," was Arthur's reply.

Arthur hung up the phone and gritted his teeth against his ongoing intestinal distress. He hustled out of the tent and found Sergeant Russell. Russell woke with a start and stood, bleary-eyed, as he digested the information. Arthur cupped his flashlight, then flicked it on, revealing the penciled coordinates of the German battery's current whereabouts.

"Fire Gun One for effect. A single salvo, and we'll see if these numbers are indeed accurate."

"Yes, sir," said Sergeant Russell. He saluted, then went around and roused the rest of his gunnery team.

While Arthur held his guts in, the men hove-to, setting Number One Gun up for range and elevation, repeating the same basic action British gunners had been at from the day the first cannon had been fired at Crécy in 1346, to the hundreds of thousands of times it had been done on land and from the decks of Man-of-War ships ever since. The only differences now being the rifled barrel of the artillery piece, the killing power of the shell's explosive blast, and the fact that no actual 'Fire' was set to a fuse when the order to "FIRE" was given.

Sergeant Russell looked to Arthur.

"Fire for effect, Sergeant," he said. Arthur cupped his ears.

Sergeant Russell called out, "NUMBER ONE GUN. FIRE."

Danny Prince, Number One Gun's trigger man, yanked the cord, the ignition struck, the 60-pound shell flew out of the gun with an earth-shattering BOOM and an explosion of bright white-and-orange light as the barrel kicked back. Then, there was only the ringing in the ears of men already half-deaf from their labour.

Arthur nodded to Sergeant Russell as the hot brass shell was ejected and chucked aside, then, with as much grace as one can, Arthur ran for the latrine trench. He had his belt and buttons undone before he reached the log that hung over the deep stew of feces and urine. Even so, he barely sat onto the tree trunk suspended over the pool when what felt like all of his insides exploded out of him. Arthur's relief was painful.

As he caught his breath, he chuckled to himself, surmising that his own personal artillery battery had just fired for effect. He was extremely grateful that the elevation and trajectory had been spot on and that no misfire had occurred. He wiped himself clean, then buttoned his trousers and headed back up the hill toward the battery.

As he neared his tent, he heard the telephone ringing and hurried in to take the call.

"Hello?" Arthur said.

There was silence on the line.

"I say, Hello? This is Lieutenant Keith, Royal Artillery speaking. Hello?"

There was a pause. Arthur could not say for sure, but it certainly sounded like someone was there on the other end at the blockhouse switch exchange.

"I say, again, Hello? Are you there, Corporal Deavers?... Billy?"

Again, no response, but it was not the dead silence of a cut line.

Then it spoke, in what seemed a thousand voices at once. "THE ANOINTED ANGEL COMES."

The line went dead.

Arthur held the phone to his ear for an excruciating moment of uncertainty and rising fear, then he set the handpiece back into its cradle.

He heard a sudden hullaballoo outside; shouts and cries from his men. His guts cramped again, but he ran for the tent's exit flap.

When Arthur saw what was happening at the battery, he stumbled backward into the woods to hide. His men had been taken.

Everything that happened after the demons lit their bonfire was stuck inside of Arthur Keith, filling his brain and his chest and his empty belly with sounds and images he would never be able to void out of his system.

He watched his friend, Percy Compton, a twenty-year-old loader from Devon—whose stutter was as endearing to the listener as it was frustrating for him—get shoved down and speared. A pair of them held Percy up while a single blow from a sword cut his head half off. He heard the crack of the vertebrae as they pushed his dangling head backward and struck again with the blade to take it cleanly off his shoulders. He watched them twist his arms and legs wide, then hack them free. Then they bisected and butchered the torso.

By then, the bonfire was burning hot. They used the 60-pounder's ramrods to make a spit, then set Percy's meaty remains to roasting over the flames.

While their meal cooked, they spent the interim torturing and maiming the rest of Arthur's gun crew, impaling them on the branches of the dead trees they had used to hide their artillery battery during the day. Then the Imbangala hoisted them high in a wide semi-circle.

As a grey dawn began to lighten the sky, outlining the ring of his men's limp bodies, skewered onto stiff dead trees, Arthur knew he was next. He could not imagine any way to escape his little nest without being seen. His brain could not help repeating his childhood priest's communion pitch, "Truly, truly, I say unto you, unless you eat the flesh of the Son of Man and drink his blood, you have no life in you," and the looping refrain combined with the cannibalistic visuals was driving Arthur insane.

The Imbangala finished the last bits of meat on Percy's blackened ribs and tossed the stripped bones into the fire's coals. They were admiring the skull they had carefully stripped clean of its flesh and tissue, meat and mealy brains, when Arthur made a break for it.

The Imbangala's head man saw him. He cried out to his men. But Arthur's timing had been as impeccable as it was accidental. Had he screwed up his courage to the sticking point two minutes earlier, they would have run him down and killed him without question.

Neither speed nor athleticism had ever been Arthur's strong suit. He was a methodical thinker and planner, so when he took action, it was a physical manifestation of intellectual study. It made him an excellent artilleryman and chess player, but would have made him a profoundly terrible frontline warrior.

But his delay served him well. As the Imbangala ran after Arthur, the sun rose, and they all collapsed in lifeless heaps behind him, their dead bellies paunchy with Percy Compton's charbroiled shanks and flanks, brisket and bottom sirloin, ribs, and bottom round digesting inside them. Arthur did not look back. He ran on until he collapsed.

He hid in the woods that night. From five miles away, he saw his artillery battery explode when Francois escaped the Imbangala himself and blew them sky-high.

Arthur soldiered on in a daze as dawn approached. He did not realize he had passed beyond the German lines until he came over the ridge and saw the vast German Air Corps base with its zeppelin shed below him.

Then he heard it—the sound of men coming for him on the run, and Arthur Keith bolted down the hill, racing toward the dawn, tripping and stumbling, falling and sliding, looking back in terror, and again watching the sun's rise send his pursuers sprawling in lifeless heaps.

And now he was alone again in his bunker. But Isaiah and Black Betty had stumbled into his life and brought him hope. And that was not nothing. He would prepare as if their return was imminent, using his mind's gift for planning and making ready, so that when Isaiah and Betty returned with his air crew, they could move with all haste to depart into the aether.

Robert Burns' poem rang in his ears for a moment. *"The best laid plans of mice and men oft go ugly…"*

Arthur shook his head. Not this time. Not this time. He hoped.

The she-wolf looked over her blood-matted shoulder to see if her little boy was there. He was not. She licked dried gore, last remnants of the day's adventure, off her silver-and-black coat. She had not successfully killed the men, but the anguished screams had their own satisfactions. They may have driven her off for the moment, but she would find them again and finish her work when they let down their guard; of this, she felt certain.

She sniffed the cold air in, seeking scent; something that might entertain her in the meantime. As her brain instantaneously dissected the incoming odors with its hundreds-of-millions of processors, she caught a tender thread she recognized. She recalled the young Irish woman from the woods where she had begun killing men on Good Friday. She imagined how that delicate, pale flesh would taste, how the young woman's dark memories would spark through her mind while she devoured her. The wolf's salivary glands began to shed water into her mouth, wetting her tongue and whetting her appetite.

Then another scent registered. The black man with the bloody ankle. A prime opponent, ripe for the taking, despite the presence of his canine protector. The woman could wait.

She looked back one last time for her young master. He still had not come for her. All in due course. For the time being, she locked on to Isaiah's scent and loped after it, disappearing into the falling snow.

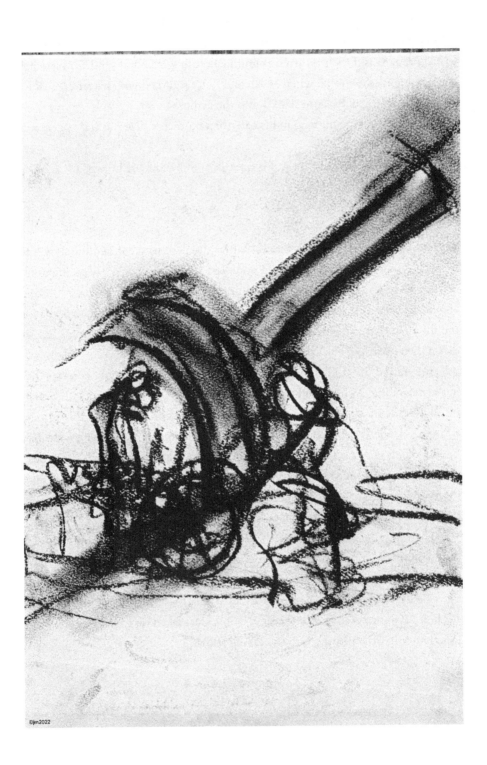

CHAPTER TWELVE

—

SHAME

Finbarr was running out of steam when he and Donnie left the woods near St. Quentin and entered the massive Lafayette Ammunition Dump. The snow-covered steel monsters of Big Bertha and Krupps 150 artillery pieces, birthed and assembled in the black soot and molten steel of Munich and Dresden's forges, reared up before them.

Donnie followed Fin at a jog through the inert heavy guns and into stacks and stands of shells born to explode out of the artillery, destroying anything in their field of fire. The snow crowning them made them seem like jagged teeth of some long-dead Tyrannosaur, sitting erect, yet impotent, in orderly rows.

Donnie's adrenaline was fully depleted. He felt empty and sad. His mind was flashing to all the events of the last few days, from the whorehouse on Good Friday to the abattoir at GHQ, running from the devils on his doomed motorcycle, his near death on the road, and that black boy Isaiah showing up out of the blue and trying to throttle him to death; why, he could not begin to comprehend.

He found his mind reaching further back, trying to understand the cause of all of it, and wondered if the things he, Donald David McMaster, had done might be partly responsible. He knew he made some poor choices throughout his life, but he always made sure to ask the Lord's forgiveness and had been led to believe that was enough. His daddy, Big Don, and his momma, April May, told him time and again that all he had to do was accept Jesus as his Lord and everything would be forgiven. But Donnie never did quite believe it.

"Don't you know he died for your sins?" his momma asked.

"What do you mean, Momma?"

They had been sitting around the fireplace in early December. The toasty hearth burned the chill out of the crisp air. Momma had been knitting. Big Don was sitting in his rocker, drinking still grain alcohol cut with well water.

"Your Lord and Savior, he got himself fixed to that cross so you could have eternal life," Momma said.

Donnie was only five years old at the time, but he still did not want to confess ignorance. His parents set the example from day one. It was not a sin not to know things. The sin was *admitting* to not knowing them. So, he replied, "Un-huh."

"Jesus took the weight of all mankind's sins on his shoulders and let them Romans mightily abuse him, all so you could get saved," Momma said.

Donnie tried to digest that information. He knew the risk he was taking, but, at five, curiosity had not yet been bullied out of him entirely, so he asked, "Do that make any sense, Momma?'

"Course it does, honey. It's in the Bible. 'Course it makes sense."

"But Jesus never knowed me, and he died afore I was ever born, so how'd he know which ones of my sins to forgive?"

"The Lord knows the number of every hair on your head, Donnie."

"… My head?"

"Yes, you silly goose, your head."

Donnie took a long pause. He touched his hair with both hands protectively. "Why's he care about the hair on my head?"

"Well… he don't care about the hair on your head, but he knows the number anyways. He knows everything there is to know about you."

"… Like Santy Claus?" asked Donnie. It was all coming into focus now.

"Sure. Just like Santa Claus."

Donnie mulled that over. "So, I won't get no coal in my stocking?"

"What do you mean, Donnie?" his Momma asked, perplexed.

Donnie was starting to get excited. "If Jesus forgive me all my sins, and Santa Claus is his relation, don't that mean that all my sins is forgiven, and I won't get no coal instead of presents?"

Momma laughed. "Yes, Donnie. That's exackly what that means, baby."

Big Don stirred. "That'll be enougha that talk."

Unfortunately, things had already gone too far for Donnie Junior to set the brakes on his revelation. He finally understood what the point of church was. As long as you went and did what they told you, there was no possibility you would ever awake on Jesus's birthday to find a stocking brimming with dirty coal instead of sugary treats and toys. He stood and whooped, jumping for joy.

He felt Big Don's hand grab his upper arm and squeeze hard enough to make him yelp.

"Boy, you best settle yourself down, or you ain't gonna have to worry about the Lord, you gonna have to worry about the strap."

Donnie settled himself down, right quick. The strap had knocked the tar out of him plenty of times and he would not invite that ordeal if he could help it. He shut his mouth, avoided acknowledging the pain his daddy was causing his scrawny arm, and held tight to his newfound understanding of how Little Lord Jesus worked in mysterious ways.

Accept Jesus. No Coal on Christmas. Hallelujah.

But now, in the Lafayette Artillery Park, in the midst of the raging snowstorm, hunted by dead men who had risen, and having seen people who had actually been crucified, forgiveness and salvation did not seem the most certain outcome. Hellfire, brimstone, and getting thrown in some lake of fire seemed much more likely. To Donnie's brittle mind, as he ran through the snow, away from more crucified men than he had ever imagined possible, it seemed like all the Christmas Coal that had been bought and paid for over the past hundred-thousand years by mankind's sins had finally been delivered, overflowing from five billion stockings, scattering over the entire earth, primed for the torch.

Donnie ran into Finbarr's back and nearly bowled him over. He began to apologize, but when he saw what had stopped Fin in his tracks, he froze, too, stuttering.

Fin turned and shoved past Donnie, who spilled, landing on his bad hip with a yelp of pain.

Fin did not get far. Ten more men stood behind them in bloody uniforms holding sharp weapons. Fin threw down the Mauser, dropped to his knees, and raised his hands in surrender.

The Romans bound Fin and Donnie together and marched them out of the Lafayette Ammunition Dump, up into the woods, following the same trail they had so recently blazed in the snow.

Latin. The voices were all speaking a Latin Fin recognized clearly, though it was coarse and mongrel—the language of Fin's church as spoken by front-line soldiers of the Roman Army when the Gods they prayed to were Jupiter and Juno, Venus and Mars, Mercury and Vulcan, and all the rest of the pantheon; all those great deities stolen from the Greeks and reimagined in Roman form.

Donnie tripped, dragging Fin down with him, and the Romans met them with sharp kicks from the hobnailed boots they inherited with their new bodies.

Donnie and Fin were pulled back to standing.

Fin shot Donnie a look. "Keep your fucken feet, or I'll kill you before these bastards get the chance," he snarled.

Donnie's face trembled and he fought back tears. "I'm sorry. I'm sorry. I'm sorry."

"Keep your 'sorry' to yourself. Just don't fucken fall again, you tit."

Fin was scared now, easily more terrified than he had been in his entire life, but he put on a brave face. He had summoned courage to murder Englishmen on his home soil. He had found it within him to join the British army and serve his enemies so he might turn their own weapons upon them. He survived climbing over sandbags and running straight into German machine-gun fire. He lived through Good Friday's massacre and found the gumption to run from these same monsters after they spent nights torturing and murdering his fellow Irish Fusiliers. And yet, he did not see a way out this time. Exhaustion had him, and the remnants of courage inside him were not bubbling up to seek out an escape.

Fin heard the sounds of axes felling trees, then the Roman patrol pulled he and Donnie McMaster into the field of the crucified. Fin knew the end was before him. His feet stopped working involuntarily when he recognized the man preparing to spike a man's ankles to felled timber.

Before him stood the same one-eyed, kilt-wearing sonofabitch who had accidentally set himself on fire and bought Fin the seconds he needed to make good his escape the night before. Fin did not think fate would lend him the providence of a second miraculous flight to freedom.

♠ ♠ ♠ ♠ ♠

Oberon Junius, the one-eyed Roman in the burnt kilt, slammed the last spike home. The man screamed as it stabbed through his ankles, fastening him to the trunk. Oberon looked back and saw his incoming patrol, with Donnie McMaster and Finbarr Kelly in tow. He waved them on toward the long file of prisoners awaiting a turn to take a ride on a cross of their own.

Oberon stood the sledgehammer in the snow and joined his fellows, who were ready at ropes tied to the cross piece. While six men prepared to guide the base of the cross into its waiting hole, Oberon stood before two teams of ten. He hollered out in Latin. *"Ready... PULL."*

The legionaries pulled the ropes, the crucifix pith slid and angled into the hole before it, the team of six lifted and pushed upward, and the cross, with its now screaming Frenchman, vaulted upward to the sky. It dropped with a satisfying *thunk* into the hole. The men on rope detail held the cross erect while the rest shored up the base with wooden shims, dirt, and clay. Then, men on each side scrambled up the ropes and untied the knots. They dropped the thick hemp down to their fellows, then swung down from their faux tree. On to the next.

Oberon admired the handiwork. Thousands of years prior, when he had been born as Oberon Junius, he helped oversee the crucifixion of two-thousand Jews for General Publius Quinctilius Varus in Jerusalem. And now, after all this time, General Varus had returned to his legions, hell-bent on beating that record. He wanted the number doubled. One-eyed Oberon knew it was not a Centurion's job to question orders. It was a Centurion's job to make his legionaries do their jobs, as ordained by their Gods-appointed commander.

Oberon enjoyed the work. To him, the journey to four thousand crucified men was no different than the journey to two thousand. It was, indeed, a mountainous task, but just as when summiting the Alps, there was no sense looking up at the mountain's peak. The trek could only happen one step at a time. Looked at any other way, it would seem hopeless. They would crucify one man at a time until they reached four thousand. Or forty thousand. Or four hundred thousand. With grit and determination, nothing was impossible.

Oberon was a good manager of men, an excellent overseer; the only problem now was his single eye. It had begun to wear on him. Hammering railroad spikes into men's palms was difficult without depth perception. He had crushed the last man's fingers flat as pancakes on the first swing instead of striking the spike flush, and the imperfection annoyed him. There was a pleasure in hitting just right and driving a spike home with one blow that was spoilt by the need to swing a second time. He was also fairly certain that being one-eyed was the reason he had made the error with the gasoline and lit his kilt on fire the night before, when they were finishing off Fin's band of Irish Fusiliers. It was as embarrassing as it was frustrating. If at all possible, he meant to remedy the situation.

Oberon walked to the prisoners and eyed Donnie McMaster and Finbarr Kelly. He sighed. Poor specimens. Donnie's brutalized body and Fin's missing fingers made them unacceptable vessels, no better than his current one. Oberon scanned the rows of bound men and women with a discerning eye. It was like searching the slave marketplace in Rome for just the right worker. His wife Livia's maxim, delivered whenever she sent him to carry out her bidding while on leave in Rome, followed him now, *"Always pick the right man for the right job."*

His eye settled on two men in particular, a big fellow in the blue wool of the French Army and the brown-skinned Ghurka warrior whose dark eyes stared up at him with contempt. Oberon paused and stared back. He admired the man's fighting spirit. Although he knew he would not inherit it along with the corpse, it was a worthy attribute. Oberon figured that, between the stout Ghurka and the Frenchman, he had two suitable candidates, for certain. Now all he needed was permission to take what he wanted.

Oberon handed his sledgehammer to his adjutant and told him to take a rest. He made one last appraisal of Nepalese Corporal Juddha Jai Pandit and the big Frenchman, then he jogged off into the snowy field.

Juddha Jai watched him go. He did not know what the dead man wanted with him, but whatever it was, he hoped to make him pay a high price for it. Maybe he could take that second eye before they killed him. It would be a small satisfaction, but if that was his final act of defiance, it would do.

156

♠　♠　♠　♠　♠

As Oberon passed through the ranks of trees his legion had killed and turned into torture vessels, he factored out the task still before them. They had mounted nearly a hundred citizens and soldiers between midnight last night and now. At this pace, they would get all of their current prisoners onto trees well before dawn. If they wanted to keep a good, steady workflow, they would need to send out more hunting parties to gather victims.

Oberon found General Varus standing in the center of his field of the crucified, admiring the burgeoning handiwork of his risen legion. Oberon approached with deference and waited.

Varus was enjoying the spectacle. He did not particularly wish to be disturbed. He knew One-eyed Oberon was standing there, looking ridiculous with his singed cock and balls dangling beneath the ruined hem of his burned kilt, that odd-shaped barbarian's blade shoved through his belt, but he also knew that Oberon was an outstanding Centurion who had served him well up until the bitter end in mid-September of 9 A.D.; an end that seemed only hours past.

Varus still felt the sharp, cold steel pressed against his belly, angled up under the ribs, headed for the thick muscle of his heart. When he dropped his weight onto the point, the high-pitched shriek that burst out of him split the evening air. The shame of its femininity was almost as painful as the blade running up into him. His whole body seized and shuddered in pain. He felt hot piss running down his thighs. It was a much worse ending than tradition had taught him it would be.

Mercifully, Varus lost consciousness quickly, well before the Teutonic warriors captured the position, and with it, his head as a trophy. Varus's surviving legionaries were thrown into dried pine cages and burned alive; sacrifices to the woodland Gods the Germans believed had brought them victory over the Roman Standards.

It had been a shameful defeat. Poor leadership had contributed more to the Roman failure than any of the Gods had. When all was said and done, through arrogance, Varus lost 18,000 prime Roman soldiers in less than a week's time. Suicide was the only alternative at that juncture, and ultimately, better than being burned alive with his men. His grandfather, who had ridden against the tyranny of Julius Caesar, only to see his grandson elevated, a favorite of the Emperor, would have been utterly ashamed had Varus returned to Rome alive with his tail between his legs.

And now, Centurion Oberon Junius was a glaring, one-eyed, burnt-scrotum'd reminder of that shame. Without looking at him, Varus raised a casual salute of recognition.

Oberon stepped forward. *"General, we have crucified one hundred and five thus far."*

Varus's nod was nearly imperceptible.

"We have one-hundred, give or take, prisoners left to crucify, then the cupboard will be bare."

Varus gave that information a breath of calculation. *"Leave half your men to crucify the remainder, then take out a century and hunt down more of them. I have made a guarantee of four thousand. So it must be."*

Oberon nodded. *"Yes, sir. There is a city to the south. We will reconnoiter there and see what we can find."*

Varus nodded, dismissing him. Oberon paused. Varus's eyes flitted to him.

"There is another matter, sir. A small one. Of personal nature," Oberon said.

"… Yes?"

"I was thinking… thinking I might take a better body."

Varus's gaze was cold and hard. *"We are Rome. We make do with what we have, and we do not complain of what we have not."*

Oberon flushed with shame. He began to wish he had kept his mouth shut, but now that he had opened it, he knew finishing was the only thing to be done. *"Yes, General. But I was hoping I might simply take one of the prisoners and move into him… I'm not as good to you as I would be with two eyes, sir. It's made me an oaf with my hands."*

Varus considered it as he stared up at the crucified. He turned back to Oberon. *"Do as you see fit. I will trust your judgment. But choose well. We do not have time for foolishness or vanity."*

Oberon bowed, a smile lighting up his disfigured face. He thought perhaps smothering the Ghurka or the Frenchman would be the best way to kill the body while preserving the vessel for his future use. He promised himself he would be neither foolish nor vain in the execution.

When he looked back at Varus to say as much, something strange occurred. Varus looked at him. A bolt of terror surged across his features, eyes rolling. His arms shot out toward Oberon, as if to keep him from falling; his eyes lolled back in his head, revealing bloodshot whites, and then the body Varus had taken over collapsed to the snow, empty.

♠ ♠ ♠ ♠ ♠

Isaiah wondered if there might be more than one wolf out there. The howling was becoming more than a little unnerving, echoing closer and closer each time it cut the night air. He stopped, listening, concentrating, trying to hear past his heartbeat and breath for anything that would reveal his pursuer, but the fallen and falling snow was suffocating any sound that might have reached him.

Black Betty had left his side ten minutes earlier, circling back, searching for danger. His eyes scanned the woods, anticipating that she had not lost the pleasure of catching him by surprise and dumping him in the snow, but the patchwork of drifting flakes and white-coated trees vanished away into darkness, revealing no signs of her.

Another howl, close and clear, sent a shiver through Isaiah. That fucking wolf was near. Isaiah pulled the Red Maiden's saber out and held tight to the leather grip. He turned south and picked up his pace.

Fifty yards on, the woods began to thin. Isaiah slowed his gait. He looked behind him, searching for the wolf, but if she was there, she was still invisible among the trees.

When he turned back, he saw a horse and rider coming down the track toward him. Isaiah slipped behind a beech tree and ducked down. He slid to the edge of the tree and peered out.

The Red Maiden rode Joshua at a walk along the path. Isaiah saw her looking left and right, scanning the woods as she went. She passed his hide and continued another ten paces. Then she stopped, turning in the saddle, looking back, staring right at the tree Isaiah was hidden behind.

Fuck, Isaiah thought.

Gunnhildr turned Joshua's head and brought him back around. She gave a gentle kick to his flanks and he began to sidle toward Isaiah's hiding place.

Isaiah stood the saber in the ground and carefully unslung the Mauser.

Suddenly, Gunnhildr stiffened, almost rising up out of her seat, flinching sharply, as if struck by a javelin. Then Léonie's body went limp and slid from the saddle, coming off fast, landing hard and awkward on the ground. Joshua stopped.

Isaiah's breath caught. There were two possibilities, this woman was playing possum and would be on her feet, steel in his belly the second he revealed himself, or the body had given up the ghost. For now.

Isaiah played the rifle sight through the trees, looking for the wolf. No sign. He glanced back at the Red Maiden, half-expecting to see her standing and running toward him, but she did not move. The war horse stood over her.

"Fuck it," Isaiah said. He put the saber in his belt and took a bead on the fallen woman with the Mauser, easing out from behind the tree and making his way toward her, ready to put a bullet in her head. She lay still, but Isaiah felt more as though he was walking toward a coiled cottonmouth snake than a dead body.

Joshua raised his head as Isaiah approached. Isaiah lifted his left hand, palm open. He reached toward Joshua's reins. He saw steam blow out of Joshua's nostrils. His hand was inches from the reins. A howl split the night. Joshua reared up and kicked his front hooves toward Isaiah, trying to cave in his skull.

Isaiah felt the sharp steel of the horseshoes brush past, millimeters from killing him. He dove back and rolled, spinning himself away into the protective embrace of the trees.

Joshua reared and stamped again, then set himself squarely between Isaiah and his mistress.

Isaiah stood. He circled past the horse and backed his way across the road, expecting the entire time that the horse would bolt and try to run him down, but Joshua held his ground, daring Isaiah to attempt a second approach to his lady fair. He did not.

Isaiah got clear of the road and ran into the woods on the other side. He looked back for Black Betty once, but she was still nowhere to be seen. He turned and disappeared into the trees.

♠   ♠   ♠   ♠   ♠

The Red Maiden had been riding in silent, shamefaced fury when it happened. Her mind was elsewhere, chewing over her failure, or she might have felt it coming. First, the sudden torching of her men in the canal, then the unexpected charge of the British cavalry which stunted the opportunity for a quick end to the ones she hunted. What other unexpected hurdles would rise up in her way? She felt the anger flushing through her. All was chaos now, but that too would pass. She would hunt them all down, one at a time, if she had to, and finish them soundly. She reined Joshua in and slowed him to a walk. She felt his heart thumping and his lungs heaving. She realized if she kept pressing he would go lame, and that would be only add to her list of failures. Patience of the mind was the only remedy, but she was having difficulty mastering her rage.

Although her eyes had been scanning the trees, she was not in the present moment, still seized by anger at her failure. She brought Joshua to a full stop and summoned control. She looked back the way she had come, and sensed something, rather *someone*, hidden in the trees. She flexed her sword hand and led Joshua back around, searching for Isaiah.

Then, suddenly, she felt herself slipping. She lost control. As Léonie's body fell from the saddle, Gunnhildr fell, too; but not toward the ground, away from it, and all went black.

When she came to, she felt on fire. She opened her eyes. The sun bore down hard on her back while the sand of the desert burned her from below. The Crone stood over her. She eclipsed the sun and extended her hand.

"Come, child of Odin. We must have ourselves a chat."

♠   ♠   ♠   ♠   ♠

Inside the roadhouse, Gunnhildr sat at the counter beside the Fat Man, devouring the feast the old woman had placed before her.

The crone was leaning back against the still warm stove, watching with pleasure as Gunnhildr consumed. "You want any more to eat, girl?"

Gunnhildr's mouth was full of the charred rokt fisk. She nodded.

The old woman smiled and cut another steak from the fish. She set it on Gunnhildr's plate and stepped back. "Got to get my hands out the way, or you're like to take a finger with it. Glad to see you've got an appetite, but you ought' take your time. We ain't in no rush here at all. In fact, we waiting for an important arrival, so you might as well just settle in and enjoy your meal."

Gunnhildr nodded and dug into the fish flesh.

The old woman refilled Gunnhildr's water glass and set it on the counter. She stepped back and watched the Norse woman finish her meal and down the water.

When the glass was empty, the old woman spoke again. "You care to tell me how things went from so terribly right to so terribly wrong this evening?"

Gunnhildr looked up, eyes flashing.

"You had 'em on the ropes, ready to knock the poop out of 'em. But almost every single one slipped right through your fingers," said the crone.

A wash of shame flowed through Gunnhildr. A mother's disappointment cut worse than the sharpest blade.

"Uh-oh," said the Fat Man, grinning. "She's playing her ace card on you."

The *SLAP* was like a crack of thunder, and the Fat Man's cheek went bright red, the mark from the old woman's palm stretching from jowly neck to ear.

"You were best keep your jibber-jabber mouth shut tight, Fat Man. Your pieces on the board ain't playing out as you'd've hoped, so if you in the mood for chastisement, save it for your own. There's work to be done, and it ain't getting done, and there's blame enough to go around, an' I sure as Hell won't have you putting that responsibility on this girl. She did her part on Good Friday and I reckon she'll do so again. Now zip your lips unless you want 'em zipped for you."

The Fat Man clenched his jaw.

"Yeah, you keep glaring at me, but you keep that got-damn mouth shut," she said.

He held her gaze, then looked away. She nodded, satisfied, then turned to Gunnhildr. "Alright, girl. Tell me what happened."

Gunnhildr swallowed her shame, then she told the woman of the charge down the hill into the canal, of Ganan's leap, and his triumphant spearing of Halstead, of the moment where her quarry all ran with the certainty they would not run far before death caught them, too, and then of the air exploding into flame, cutting off pursuit.

The old woman thought of Halstead at the gas pump and his refusal to accept his end. She shot a look at the Fat Man, daring him to look up from Henry Ford's insane screed against the Jewish tribe, but he did not take the bait, consciously immersing himself in the pamphlet. She looked back to Gunnhildr, who was staring down at the counter, shamefaced. The Old Woman reached out her gnarled hand and gently lifted Gunnhildr's chin until the Norse woman was looking her in the eye.

"It's all right, girl. It might have felt like this was all going to be a snap when you burned Amiens to ashes, but as you well know, things don't always go to plan. Everybody gets to make their own choices, and sometimes those choices are gon' monkey up the works. We get to make some choices, too." She looked up toward the front door and spoke in Latin. *"Come on in, honey. You're welcome here."*

Gunnhildr looked behind her. A man stood in the door frame, uneasy. His boiled leather breast plate with the Roman Eagle carved across it was bloody and rent with cuts that bled nearly the same color as his scarlet cloak. The scabbard on his hip was empty. His undertunic was stained with dark urine below the waist.

The stunned man reached out and pushed the door open. He stepped through the portal and it slammed behind him.

"General Varus, as I live and breathe. Don't you look a sight, sir. Lord knows you seen better days 'n this one. If you come on in, I promise that you gonna see 'em again. You gonna be squared away right quick, believe you me. Have yourself a bite, refresh yourself with some water. There's work needs to be done, and along with my friend Gunnhildr here, I believe you gon' do it in quite the fashion," said the old woman.

♠   ♠   ♠   ♠   ♠

Oberon Junius stood over Varus's corpse in shock. Perhaps half a minute passed. Then Oberon saw Varus's fists clench, and Varus was returning, flowing back into the corpse, pushing himself up off the ground. Oberon knelt before him as Varus regained his bearings.

"Are you alright, General?"

Varus nodded, swallowing hard. *"Halt the crucifixions."*

"My lord?"

"Halt them for now. We have a new imperative."

Varus explained. Oberon understood.

"Take your new body. Then begin a decimation. We will swell our legions with the living, that the hunt may continue after the dawn. Time is of the essence," said Varus.

Oberon nodded, pleased. Action beat labor any day. Though he had been unwilling to admit it, the work of crucifixion had grown tedious. This new command was much more to his liking. Truly, the Gods were good.

♠   ♠   ♠   ♠   ♠

After the old woman sent Varus on his way with his new mission fixed clearly in his mind, she reached out and took Gunnhildr's hand.

"Come on along with me, girl," she said in Norse.

The old woman led Gunnhildr out onto the back porch to a swing hanging from the rafters. They sat together and looked out at the brutal vista, gently rocking in silence for a time.

"I must admit, I had higher expectations, Gunnhildr. Mayhap too high."

Gunnhildr was silent.

"But now we got old General Varus in the mixture, and I'm wondering if there's any point sending you back at all. He do seem like the kind of man can get a thing done."

Gunnhildr's nod was almost imperceptible. She had been impressed by Varus's bearing, envious of it. She had spent her life fighting for everything she had. Varus had fallen headfirst into a cornucopia at birth, and from what she gathered of the conversation inside, the crone was going to provide him every resource at her disposal in his new life. Gunnhildr had squandered her chance, a third of her army burned to a crisp in the canal not half an hour after she had taken command of them.

"As you heard inside, I'm giving over your army of men to Varus."

Gunnhildr was silent.

"The man's got my confidence now. He made some failures in his life, that's plain as day, but he's got more experience 'n you do at mastering men in large numbers, and experience got to count for somethin', don't you think?"

Gunnhildr could not look at the crone.

"Now don't you get all sour on me. I still aim to put you to use. Here's the question, you still want to keep going? It's entirely up to you."

Gunnhildr did not feel as though this choice was a choice, but the old woman sat and waited for her to respond. She nodded in the affirmative.

"Good. That's what I was hopin' for. Walk with me, child. I got something to show you. A little old gift. I think you gon' like it."

The crone stood and walked into the yard, past the outhouse shack and into the desert. Gunnhildr followed just behind her.

The sun was without mercy. Gunnhildr felt her exposed skin burning, but she kept on without complaint, cresting dunes, then coming down into their troughs, only to find a next wave of sand waiting. It reminded her of storms she had guided her longboat through, in constant danger of the gales taking her mast, or getting caught broadside by a wave that would capsize the longship and take them all under. In those moments, Gunnhildr always recalled her mother's schooling.

Her mother had been sharpening her axe while she queried her eldest child. *"Gunnhildr, if you knew aforehand you could not die in a battle, when the fight began, which way would you run?"*

Gunnhildr, at eight, knew how to answer the question. *"Forward."*

"Yes. Forward. And if you knew aforehand you would be killed in that battle, when the fight began, which way would you run?"

"Forward," Gunnhildr replied, grinning.

"Why?" her mother asked.

"If I am meant to die, I am meant to die. If I am meant to live, I am meant to live. There is no choice. I will go forward and meet my fate with my axe, whatever it be."

Gunnhildr's mother smiled. She had trained her daughter well. It had engrained—there was no other way but 'forward'. Until it got Gunnhildr killed, the lesson served her well and saved her crew many times, whether battling the ocean, or raiding the Irish coasts. So she moved forward now.

When they crested the peak of the next wave of sand, the old woman stopped, hands on hips, and stared into the trough. Gunnhildr reached her side and looked down. At the base of the trench stood a dozen men. Their long beards and braids, their leather armor and scaled-mail coats, their axes, wooden shields painted with the Red Maiden's sigil… Gustafson, and Thorsen, Egillsen, Colborn, and Dag and the rest of her prime raiders stood in the sand staring up at her and the crone in shock.

"Here is my gift to you, child. Your friends come runnin' to your aid. That's what friends are for, ain't it? Due south of you, not too terrible far from where your body is laying, is a little town burned beautifully to cinders 'cept for one little old church. At the top of that little church is that Irish girl and her boon companion, the big African fellow. We almost had him twice

now. Now it's your turn, and I'm hopin' the third time is the charm. I trust it will be. Go forward now, and meet your fate with your axe, whatever it be. Get you that ginger-haired girl. Kill the African with her. Earn the gift I'm giving you by spilling their blood."

Gunnhildr felt the weight of responsibility. She nodded. *"Yes, I will."*

"Remind me again. Which way you gon' run in this battle?"

"Forward... It's the only way."

"Just so."

♠   ♠   ♠   ♠   ♠

Bathsheba was beginning to falter. In the heart of a snow-covered field, Sergeant Tremaine slowed her to a walk, twisted in the saddle, and looked into the darkness and falling snow behind him. Still no sign of the army closing in on him. Had he lost them? Had they chosen to follow and murder his companions instead? More regret for his conscience to meditate on if that was indeed the case. And if they were already dead, reaching the canal and the barge would be a pointless operation. All he wanted to do was kick flanks and gallop, far and fast, but he knew Bathsheba would collapse in the effort, or lead him directly into another gang of these monsters, and that would mean a pointless, pain-filled end for both of them.

Tremaine looked at his wristwatch. The hands told him it was coming on midnight now. Dawn drew closer each second. But death was coming, too. And right now, it felt like death was winning the foot race by a mile.

Bathsheba stopped of her own accord, shocking Darren into the present. She lowered herself to her knees and Tremaine had to slip his boots out of the stirrups and dismount, jumping away as she lowered herself, rolled onto her side, and lay there. Tremaine bent down next to her and felt her breath heaving in her massive chest. She was not dead yet, just spent.

A sound reached him first. He rose and looked back across the snow into the dark woods at the field's edge. They began to flow out of the shadows en masse, fifty yards away, slowing their approach when they saw him marooned in the sea of snow by his exhausted mount.

The first of them stopped twenty yards away. His compatriots formed up next to him as the army of dead behind them filtered out into the field.

So. It would be here, then. He would stand and fight. He would not let them take him alive if it could be helped. He pulled his lance over his shoulder and spun it in his hand, then planted the butt end, making sure the shaft was in easy reach. He unsnapped his holster and drew his revolver. He thumbed the catch and double-checked that the cylinder was fully loaded. It was. He drew his saber and held it in his left hand. Six clean shots, then the lance, then the saber as they closed on him. That would have to be enough.

He let the heaviness of the steel in his hands ground him.

Tremaine felt tears in his eyes. He heard Bathsheba whinny gently behind him.

"It's alright, girl... It's alright."

He was glad he would not have to die with her on his conscience. Charging her into their blades and teeth to be dragged down and devoured would be an unjust ending for the beautiful creature. She had served him well. He hoped she would outlive him, and only wished he had time to pull her bridle and saddle to set her free. He could see no reason why the monsters would kill her after they had dealt with him. But then again, he had not seen the dead men act with anything approaching reason or mercy since Good Friday's massacre began. He hoped they would pass her by and let her live. That was the best he could do.

They kept coming until they were all clear of the trees. There must have been a thousand. There was a breath of stillness, then, as one, they began advancing toward him at a walk.

Tremaine raised his pistol and took careful aim at the foremost man's head. He cocked the hammer. He fired. *BAM!*

The shot flew straight and true. It popped through the dead man's chin. There was a stumble, then the man's feet faltered, and he fell. Then, as if a stone had been heaved into a still pond, echoing out from the fallen man, every single one of the thousand collapsed into the snow.

Tremaine's hand shook. Behind him, Bathsheba twisted her legs beneath her and stood. Tremaine backed away, stunned. The dead men did not move. Darren fumbled his Webley into its holster and sheathed the saber. He grabbed his lance and Bathsheba's reins, then led her away at a jog from the stinking mass of dead men.

When they reached shelter of the woods, he pulled her in and looked past her.

The dead men were moving.

They stood. Their entire mien had changed. Gone was the disordered mob, torn from the bodies they had latched onto. The vessels were filled anew. In place of chaos and fury, crisp martial discipline. There was shouting in Latin, then in moments, they had fallen into strict marching order, four men abreast. When the sergeants called out, they turned south, crisp and rigid, marching in a regimented column at a steady cadence. The Romans Patrick had told him of in the barn had risen from the dead and were on the march, but they were not pursuing Darren. Something else was calling to them.

After the last man disappeared from view, Darren led Bathsheba south for a quarter of an hour, then he stopped and listened for pursuers. Nothing. He patted Bathsheba's neck, then continued on foot for another mile through the snow-covered fields. He had to stop several times to knock down rough-hewn fencing that demarcated ancient property lines so Bathsheba could make her way through, but the rails fell with the same ease the society which invented them had in the preceding days, collapsing into disordered nothingness. All the manmade boundaries that had seemed sacrosanct, that had provided the illusion of clear order, had been revealed as ridiculous. What would ultimately come of that revelation, Darren did not know, but the Djinn was out of the bottle, and shoving it back in did not seem like an option.

A short time later, Darren reached the Somme River, several miles east of the city. He checked his watch. Midnight. It would take an hour, perhaps less to reach the canal and the barge. He fed Bathsheba from his store of grain, then mounted up and rode on.

♠   ♠   ♠   ♠   ♠

When the Red Maiden reawakened in Léonie's body, Joshua leaned down and nuzzled her. She picked up her saber and stood, then grabbed the saddle horn and pulled herself onto Joshua's back.

It took less than ten minutes for her men to find her. She saw the orange glow of torches in the woods, blinking in and out of existence as they passed through the trees, bobbing up and down through the snowfall until they reached her. The dozen of them wore bloody bodies of Australians and Irishmen, Britons and Frenchmen. Gustafson, Thorsen, Egillsen, Colborn, Dag, and all the rest, held torches, trench maces, daggers, officer's sabers and bayonets. If there was to be no Valhalla of endless feasting, with wine flagons and glory to grace their afterlife, they would settle for Ragnarok and a feast of pillage and murder. Either way, the appetites were the same, the only difference being the means of satiation.

She turned Joshua south, following the crone's direction, leading her men on a direct heading for St. Marguerite's holy ground where Caitlin and Francois awaited Adam's return.

©jrn2022

CHAPTER THIRTEEN

—

HELL IS EMPTY

Shen Su stopped and knelt with care. He lowered the gas cans and ducked out from under the ramrod. He cupped a bit of snow and pressed it to the back of his injured neck. The cold was shocking, but it also awakened his mind, which was fatigued in the extreme; nearly as spent as his body. The snow burned at first, but he knew its chill was vital to keep the swelling down, so he summoned a chosen reaction to the sensation. He remembered his father telling him that the first response a human body had to input belonged to the animal brain, but anything after that could be channeled by the human mind. Pain was simply communication. What Shen Su did with that information was entirely up to him.

His neck had stiffened, as he feared it would, and was growing worse by the moment. His head was throbbing, and he realized that despite the cold, he was likely getting dehydrated. He took another handful of snow and bit off a mouthful. He slowly chewed at it, letting it turn to crystal clear water in his mouth, sweet in its coldness. He chose to welcome the sensation. He inhaled the crisp, fresh air. Memories of the sweat and heat, the poisonous stench of the tank's interior—a combination of engine combustion, exhaust, congealed blood, and Number Three's fecal matter—were still fresh in his mind. This misery beat that misery by a mile.

It had been just past midnight on Good Friday when Sergeant Li shifted into neutral and killed the tank's engine. He and Chang stood and moved to the tail of the hot, fume-choked compartment. Sergeant Li opened the hatch at the back left sponson and helped Chang and Su pull Number Three's body out. They laid the bloody, shit-stained dead man on the ground with as much care as they could.

The sounds of the ongoing fight in the trenches echoed to them over the rise, though it seemed to be headed toward a lull.

"Do they always fight this much at night?" asked Chang.

"I don't think so. Germans must be real angry they couldn't steal the dragon," Li Peng said.

"What do we do now?" asked Shen Su.

"Wait for the British to tell us where the dragon goes, then find the truck to take us back to GHQ or walk."

"What about him?" asked Su, looking at Number Three's corpse.

Sergeant Li chewed his lip. *"I think we leave him here. They got plenty of other bodies to bury. One more to throw in the pit won't worry them too much, even if he's a Chinese. I know we're near Arras. I'll write and tell his family where his body got planted."*

They were all shocked out of the moment of reverie as the Hotchkiss MG in the British trenches barked back to life, chattering in bursts. A Star Shell fired from the British Lines exploded above them, and everything was cast in false daylight. The MG kept on as the Star Shell drifted toward earth.

Then suddenly, over the crest of the hill came a stream, then a torrent, of British soldiers racing toward them, terror-stricken, sprinting past the tank and the shocked Chinamen.

"Into the tank! Go!" yelled Sergeant Li.

Chang jumped up into the hatch, disappearing inside. Sergeant Li followed.

Shen Su heard the engine crank, then it roared to life. He watched the panicked British race past. He leapt into the hatch mouth. As he turned to grab the handle to close it, he saw a line of Germans come running over the ridge, chasing the terrified British infantrymen. A pair of them tackled the hindmost man and took him down, mauling him as they went, animalistic. Shen Su gasped in shock.

Su grabbed the handle and began to pull it shut when his eyes were drawn to Number Three. As the tank slipped into gear and roared forward, nearly dumping Su out the rear, and the Star Shell faded to black, Shen Su swore he saw Number Three's eyes fly open.

Then the dragon's treads were spitting mud backward, the horde of Germans was closing on them, and Shen Su was swinging the hatch shut and slamming the latch, sealing them into the belly of their metal beast.

Shen Su staggered into his seat and held on for dear life. He glanced up as he heard Sergeant Li banging the wrench and saw him pointing to the left. Shen grabbed the left-hand lever and yanked it down until he saw Sergeant Li drop his hand to the throttle and roar them forward, again climbing and pitching up, yawing sideways, then finding traction to press on. He could not hear what Sergeant Li was yelling, but it was directed at Chang, then suddenly the whole tank echoed with a new sound as Chang pulled the trigger on the Lewis Machine Gun in front of him. Its staccato roar overwhelmed the Daimler-Knight's cacophony.

The tank ground to a sudden halt, throwing Shen Su forward. This time, he caught himself on the handrails that ran around the engine block. There was the shriek of metal on metal, and then they were going backward. At the sound of Sergeant Li's banging, Shen Su looked up. Sergeant Li was pointing furiously to the right. Su grabbed the lever and the tank spun backward and to the right. Chang stopped firing the MG. When they had gone 180 degrees, Sergeant Li dropped his hand, Shen Su released the lever, the gears ground, and they leapt forward again.

Suddenly, Su heard thumping and pounding on the side of the tank as someone tried to tear the hatch doors off. He heard something above him on the roof, and the realization that he was no longer a member of the Chinese Labour Corps, but a combatant in a war he had only the merest understanding of came over him, and he felt as thoroughly out-matched as his uncles must have when they realized the martial artistry of their fists and feet, their spears and halberds, were no defense against the Lee-Metfords, Lee-Enfields, and Lee 1895 rifles of the Western world's armies.

He saw Sergeant Li directing Chang, who took over with the throttle, pushing them forward. Sergeant Li stood, then moved through the tight compartment and into the side sponson that held the six-pound cannon and the Hotchkiss MG behind it. He put his shoulder against the butt of the Hotchkiss, looked through the targeting slit in the armor, squeezed the trigger, and brass cartridges from its bullet strip began clattering onto the floor as their cargo tore out into no-man's-land.

When Chang screamed, somehow it reached Shen Su's ears. Just as he glanced up, the tank came to a sudden halt as the engine stalled and died.

Shen Su saw Chang lean back in terror, then the tank was being overwhelmed by what seemed an army of boots running on top of it, banging on the roof; a screaming storm aimed down at them in languages Shen Su had never heard. There was the crunch of rending metal as the hot exhaust pipe that ran along the roof was bent up and torn loose, and Shen Su knew the end had come.

As the din grew to a fever pitch, and the sense that they were being dragged down into the earth felt like a physical reality—that the very skin of the metal beast was about to be ripped off its bones so that whatever was outside could come in and devour the soft, warm Chinese men inside it—a new sound joined the terror. It was the ping of machine-gun bullets flying in and stitching the tank from fore to aft.

And then the monsters tearing at the hull were leaping off the tank, running toward whatever fools had decided to challenge them; fools certain that their bullets would vanquish the unarmed men now running at them, violent and deathless, their unfallen numbers overwhelming. The now silent tank sat forgotten for the time-being.

The MG in the distance barked one last time, then ceased. Some screams echoed. Then the battlefield went silent and the only thing Su, Chang, and Li Peng heard was their own breath.

Chang tried to speak. *"Wh-what is happening?—"*

"Shh." Sergeant Li held his finger to his lips.

They all listened, intent. Sergeant Li moved with care to the front of the tank, cupping his flashlight. He stared out through the forward view slit for a few long moments, then he climbed over Chang and went into the right-hand sponson. He looked through the six-pound cannon's gun sights, scanning the terrain, then repeated his search at the Hotchkiss. Satisfied, he waved Chang and Shen Su to him, again putting a finger to his lips, demanding stealth.

Chang and Shen Su joined him as quietly as they could.

"What is happening, Sergeant Li?" Shen Su whispered.

Li Peng whispered back, *"I don't know. We were getting attacked by Germans and British, too—like crazy men gone berserk."* He ran his fingers through his sweaty hair, shaking his head, recalling driving the tank through and over them. *"Here's what we're gonna do. A dumb rabbit in the clover sees the hawk and runs. The hawk sees him move and swoops in for the kill, eh? We're gonna sit here quiet as a smart rabbit and wait for that hawk to fly away, neh? Then we're gonna run. Not another word until the sun comes up and we can get the lay of the land, right? We sit in our chairs and keep our fucking mouths shut tight."*

Shen Su and Chang nodded in agreement. They all eased back through the tank to their respective seats and settled into them. It was nineteen minutes past midnight. Dawn was six hours away.

♠　♠　♠　♠　♠

TAK.

Shen Su startled awake at the sound of a rock jarring against metal. He had been dreaming of his railroad track-laying uncle. He watched him tumble from a tall stanchion into a deep, evergreen-filled gorge, falling hundreds of yards through space, arms pinwheeling in a vain effort to slow his descent, landing hard in a wet concrete footing, then sinking into its depths slowly but surely, until his bald, sun-burnt head disappeared and he was no more, his body now a part of the support for every hurtling rail car that would ever chug across Canada's transcontinental steel tracks.

TAK.

When the next rock struck the tank's left side, Chang and Sergeant Li awoke from their half-doze state, too. A slice of pre-dawn light had begun to peek in through the viewing slits and gun sights. Shen Su made his way silently to the Hotchkiss machine gun on the left side. Sergeant Li reached the six-pounder at the same time. They both looked out onto the battlefield.

Number Three was there.

He stood unsteadily, about twenty yards away, in the mud of no-man's-land. All the blood seemed to have left his body, and now his lower half was crusted in congealed gore that had leaked out of him. Beside him, licking blood out of her fur with a long pink tongue, was a she-wolf, bigger than Shen Su could have ever imagined possible. Number Three patted her head as he bent and dug down in the mud. He found another projectile. He hefted it and launched it at the tank.

TAK.

"What is it?" whispered Zi Chang from behind them.

Shen Su swallowed hard. *"Numb... Number Three."*

Chang's eyes went wide. *"... Alive?"*

Su did not know how to answer that question.

The she-wolf's ears seemed to prick up in the tank's direction. Shen Su and Sergeant Li froze.

"What is it?" Chang whispered again.

Sergeant Li's hand shot up sharply, silencing him.

TAK. Another stone struck the hull. The she-wolf stood. She started toward the tank. Number Three looked after her, curious.

Sergeant Li slid the chamber of the six-pound gun open. He picked up a shell and silently set it into the breach. He ran the chamber closed and felt for the trigger.

The she-wolf paused, sniffing the air, then she trotted off to her right, quickly disappearing from view. Sergeant Li very slowly eased the cannon barrel toward Number Three.

Number Three caught the barrel's gentle movement. He smiled. He took a few steps toward the tank. The first of the sun's rays crested the eastern horizon. Number Three raised his hand to shield his eyes from the blinding light. Then he collapsed.

♠   ♠   ♠   ♠   ♠

They sat quietly for an hour in silent meditation. Then Sergeant Li took a tour of the view slits. The only thing visible besides mud and shell-pocked terrain was Number Three's corpse, face down in the mud.

"What are you looking for?" asked Zi Chang.

"That fucking wolf." Sergeant Li replied. *"I don't see her."*

Satisfied that it had gone, Sergeant Li set all the chokes and went to the starter crank.

"Where are we going?" asked Shen Su.

"As far from here as we can get," Peng said.

"Can't we walk almost as fast as this tank?" asked Zi Chang.

"Maybe. But I'm not walking anywhere that a pack of wolves the size of the one we seen this morning are hunting around in, neh?" Li Peng replied.

That seemed a wise proposition. Li Peng cranked the engine to life, re-set the chokes to 'off' and sat back in the driver's seat.

♠   ♠   ♠   ♠   ♠

They drove the tank all day without seeing a living soul. They found a deserted supply depot in the afternoon where they refueled the dragon and stole as much food, tobacco, and equipment as they could carry. Then they pressed on.

As evening approached, Sergeant Li throttled down. The beast sat idling. He walked through the tank and exited the sponson hatch. A moment passed, then he hopped back in. He put the tank into reverse and had Shen Su spin them forty-five degrees. Then he backed the tank up and over a stream bed and deep into a line of trees. When they reared up against a steep berm, he shifted to neutral and cut the engine.

The Daimler-Knight knocked and pinged for a few moments as it began to cool. Sergeant Li wiped the sweat off his face and sighed deeply before he spoke. *"Okay… Gather branches, leaves, whatever you can find. We gonna try to hide tonight, neh?"*

Su and Chang nodded. They exited the tank on wobbly legs, nearly fainting––the result of uninvited carbon monoxide poisoning. When their oxygen levels improved, they set to work, spending the final hours of sunlight burying the tank in fallen limbs and fresh leaves.

Once it was covered, they climbed back in and choked down hard-tack biscuits. As the sun set, Sergeant Li checked that the hatch openings were all securely latched, then they settled in for the night, huddled in their seats, praying they would remain undiscovered.

The night passed quietly. All three lulled to sleep, exhaustion pulling them down deep.

At around 4 a.m., a British artillery battery exploded in the distance, its dull rumble shocking them all to full wakefulness. They stared out the view slits as the southern sky burned and explosions echoed to them through the trees. The chaos faded away within ten minutes and silence returned.

At daybreak, Sergeant Li quietly exited the tank and surveyed the area. Su and Chang joined him, woozy from lack of sleep.

"Where do you want to go now, Sergeant Li?" asked Chang.

Sergeant Li lit up a cigarette. "Ha! I don't know... I don't fucking know..."

Su and Chang looked at him, not understanding the English.

"Sorry, boys," Peng said. *"We'll have a look around and then decide whether to press on or stay here. Come."*

He led them back down the path the tank had torn as it backed into the woods, then across the small stream and up the opposite bank. They walked another hundred paces west, then Sergeant Li took them in a sweeping 360-degree circle around the berm the tank was nestled into. When they crossed the stream again and approached the tank's tracks from the opposite side, they were content that no one, alive or dead, was in the vicinity.

"Okay, boys. You came to France to labour. We're gonna labour. There are shovels on the tank. Gonna cover up these tracks the best we can and keep burying that tank deep, neh?"

"Sergeant Li?" said Chang.

Sergeant Li looked over at him. *"What?"*

"Is this normal?"

"Is what normal?"

"This. Is this normally how war is?"

"I'm not sure I understand what you're asking me."

"Well, I just wonder if maybe this is how a modern war is, and we haven't seen it, and maybe it just caught us by surprise. Maybe we simply happened to see war at its peak? Maybe we've simply seen and experienced what was breaking the spirits of those white men we seen walking the road, their eyes not seeing the road in front of them anymore?"

Sergeant Li paused, considering. He let out a grim chuckle.

"What is it?" Chang asked.

"I was just thinking, if you're right, probably someone, somewhere would be telling the crazy story of 'the chinks who stole the tank', and maybe they'd be telling it to Warrant Officer Andy. If that was the case, Mr. Andy would most certainly be bright red and splotchy the next time we see him, and I'd have to figure out my explanation for this 'holiday' we're on. I expect he'd get redder and splotchier before he went back to being light pink. That is, if..." Sergeant Li stopped. It looked like he might not begin again.

"If what, Sergeant Li?" asked Chang.

Sergeant Li cleared his throat. *"If the end of the world wasn't upon us."* He let out a deep sigh. *"And as nice as it is to contemplate this as our misunderstanding of events, it doesn't explain our Number Three walking around, throwing rocks, and giggling after we'd all seen him stone dead and on his way to dirt."*

Any hope in Zi Chang for this to be some naive misunderstanding evaporated. *"If this isn't regular war, what is it, Sergeant Li?"*

"HA! You think these stripes on my arm make me enlightened, boy? Your guess is good as mine."

"But you know Europe! You know Canada!... Is this a thing that might be normal here?" Chang's tone was imploring.

Sergeant Li paused, then laughter roared out of him. Su and Chang watched, stunned. Sergeant Li's butt hit the ground and side-splitting laughter nearly choked him. When it ended, he wiped tears from his eyes and looked back up at the two young men. "Holy shit," he said. "You guys still think this is some average occurrence and not the finale of the goddamn world."

The pair just stared at him, uncomprehending, terror tickling their spines. Sergeant Li realized he was their only tether to sanity. He took a breath and rubbed his eyes, then went back to Mandarin. *"Boys, I don't know what's going on, but what seems sensible is to hide here and keep out of the way of it. You're Taoists, right?"*

Su nodded.

Chang shrugged. He wasn't quite sure what he was.

"Then you believe we're living by our choices, making our world whatever it is from those choices, neh?" Li Peng asked.

Su nodded.

"Well, this world we're in right now, it's the world made by what seems like everybody's choices. And maybe we've all been making some bad choices. And maybe this is what comes of all that." He scratched his neck. *"You know anything about the Japanese?"* asked Sergeant Li.

Su and Chang shrugged. Despite never having met anyone who was Japanese, they knew they hated them. That was the extent of their knowledge.

"The Japanese live on a big island. On that island, they're the kings of the world. No one wants to come attack them, neh? Too, too dangerous. Kublai Khan sent two fleets of Mongols to sack those Japanese. Both got sunk to the bottom of the sea by the winds of the Japanese Gods. 'Divine Wind', they call it. Well... we got an island of our own. We got enough biscuits

for days. We got fresh water from this stream. Maybe we're the Japanese hiding in this tank and maybe those guns are our own 'Divine Wind', neh? Blow anyone who comes after us to little bits if they find us?" said Li Peng.

Chang nodded. Su took a quiet breath.

"Worth a try anyway," said Peng. *"Come on."*

They spent most of the morning filling in the tank tracks with mud and leaves. When they got back to the tank, they stopped for a late lunch, then spent the next hours covering the tank in more trees and brush. When they finished, the tank was buried deep against the berm behind it. A close inspection revealed the barrels of the six-pound cannons and the Hotchkiss MGs poking out the sides, but Sergeant Li was content that nightfall would keep them thoroughly camouflaged. Well before sunset, they entombed themselves in the tank's dark belly, gnawing on biscuits, exhausted.

"I'll take first watch," said Sergeant Li. *"Then Shen Su, then Zi Chang. No talking. No noise until sunrise, neh?"*

Shen Su and Chang curled up on the floor of the tank, while Sergeant Li moved to the front. He sat in the hatch above the driver's seat and watched the last rays of sun dapple the clouds. As night fell upon them, he ducked back in and locked it tight.

Each man took his watch in turn while the other pair slumbered. The adrenaline rubbed them raw on their shifts, every sound of the night igniting bursts of fear. Dawn came, mercifully, and Zi Chang let out a sigh. He collapsed into the driver's seat and slept another four hours.

♠   ♠   ♠   ♠   ♠

Morning passed to afternoon in silence, as the three men contemplated the past days.

Before nightfall, Sergeant Li walked to the stream and filled a canteen. His eyes scanned the coming gloom, wondering if the wolf was out there somewhere, but nothing revealed itself.

He returned to the tank and they buttoned it up for a second long, silent night.

♠   ♠   ♠   ♠   ♠

When dawn came again, they opened all the hatches on the tank and let it air out as a cold sun sent splinters of light slicing down through the trees to find them in the glade. Breakfast on the tank's roof seemed to buoy Sergeant Li's spirits.

"Do you know where we are, Sergeant Li?" asked Chang through a mouthful of biscuit.

Li Peng passed Chang his canteen. *"Sort of. Not far from the Belgian frontier, I think. Where we saw the explosions the night before last, that's got to be near the..."* He stopped mid-sentence, raising his hand and pointing.

Shen Su and Chang froze and followed his gaze. A trio of deer, two does and a large buck, had made their way up the grade from the stream. They stared back at the three men sitting on top of their camouflaged tank. Their tails ticked in mild alarm. Then the buck flicked his white tail and the three bolted in unison, their long thin legs revealing unexpected power as a leaping gallop took them into the woods. There was silence, then eight more deer, five youngsters and three yearlings, raced through the glade after their elders, disappearing almost as quickly.

"Well, that's a sign of good luck, for sure!" said Zi Chang.

Sergeant Li took his empty canteen from Chang and shook it. *"Zi Chang. You finished the canteen. The honor of filling it is yours."*

Chang accepted the canteen back, then hopped down off the tank. He looked again in the direction the deer had gone. The forest had embraced them, giving sanctuary that had not existed since the guns began firing in 1914.

As he sauntered toward the creek, Chang heard Sergeant Li and Shen Su talking quietly atop the tank. It seemed a particularly normal morning, the events of Good Friday getting further and further away as their minds tried to heal from the experience. Chang reflected that perhaps his theory was indeed correct, and Li Peng was wrong. Perhaps the last couple of days were normal for the horrors of modern war, and away from the front line and the men prosecuting the conflict, the world had found its way back to a morning of peaceful norms.

Chang reached the stream and knelt beside it. He could not explain Number Three, but he was sure stranger things had happened in the history of the world, and he was going to tell Sergeant Li just that when he got back to the tank. He rinsed out the canteen, then pressed it under the water, letting the air bubble out as water filled the empty vessel anew. He splashed a handful on his face and wiped it away with his shirt sleeve. When he had cleared away the grime and dried sweat, he saw them. He stood and staggered back.

Across the creek, scattering out into the field, were thousands and thousands of dead German men, collapsed in bloody disarray. Zi Chang turned and ran toward the tank, screaming.

♠ ♠ ♠ ♠ ♠

Sergeant Li stood looking out at the bodies as the daylight crested the trees to the east and cast its warm beams across the strewn men. Shen Su and Chang stood behind him, their bodies humming with terror.

Li Peng crossed the stream and walked through the congregation. They watched him kneel and inspect one of the bodies. He looked out and scanned the perimeter. They saw him stiffen, then he stood up and backed away, turning to jog toward his comrades.

"Wh-what is it, Sergeant Li?" asked Zi Chang.

"The wolf. She's in the trees, about a hundred meters to the north. Back to the tank, boys. Back to the tank."

Sergeant Li was measured and calm, but Chang and Su's adrenaline spiked. Their eyes searched the woods to their right for signs of the beast, but if she was there, she was hidden well.

They scrambled into the tank's open hatches and sealed the steel plates behind them.

"What should we do?" asked Su.

Sergeant Li scratched his chin and spat on the deck. "I don't know. There must be four or five thousand men out there. I think if we stay where we are, when the sun sets, these dead men will find us. There's enough of them out there to lift this tank up and roll it onto its head, rip the doors off and slurp us free like oysters from a half-shell."

"M-maybe they were there all along, but we just didn't see them when we arrived..." said Chang.

Sergeant Li smiled, grim. "That's a stupid thought. We walked the entire perimeter before we settled in. It was clear. But I admit, my brain asked the same dumb question before I saw the wolf just now. Some of them dead men are sleeping peacefully in the tracks we laid when we drove in here. It seems we are just three lucky fools that they didn't eat us for dinner last night."

There was silence. Then Shen Su spoke. "Sergeant Li. I know it seems like we are stupid and foolish men. But this is all insanity to us. We've never seen or heard of anything like this, except from stories made to scare children, or in nightmare dreams. And you're the *only one of us who knows anything about this place or these people. And that is why we need you to tell us what to do."*

Sergeant Li nodded. *"Alright. We'll try to get as far as we can from here. Maybe try to find a road, so that our tracks are not so easy to follow, neh? We're gonna need gasoline again soon. I've got a pretty good sense of where two depots are from here, and once we get to the second one, we'll be on a road that should take us toward Paris. We'll take as much gas as we can carry from there and run west until we run dry. Maybe by then we'll have a better idea of what's going on. Agreed?"*

It seemed as reasonable and logical a plan as they could hope for in the chaos they found themselves in.

Sergeant Li cranked the tank to life. The Daimler-Knight roared. He shifted into gear, and they tore free from their temporary home, sending fallen trees and leaves scattering as they lurched forward. When they reached the stream bed, Sergeant Li had Shen Su turn them south. Instead of careening over the fallen men, they bounced and bucked through the stream for half an hour before Sergeant Li guided them out of it and into open fields.

♠　♠　♠　♠　♠

The wolf's howl dragged Shen Su back into the snowy present. She was getting closer. He hefted the gas cans and pressed on.

When he rounded the bend, he recognized the little valley that opened up before him. Ten minutes, perhaps fifteen, and he would be at the tank, sealed up inside it, with enough gas to run from the dead all day long. He leaned forward and plowed ahead.

♠　♠　♠　♠　♠

©m2022

CHAPTER FOURTEEN

—

ALL THE DEVILS ARE HERE

Adam Gillét ran hard, following the indentations Adolf's footprints had left—light grey depressions in a field of white. The cold was a sensation, but there was no suffering from it. He felt blood pumping in the body, and the steady thump of the dead heart pulsing, but any warmth the blood should have caused within him was tepid at best. His leg muscles—rather, Matheus's—flexed and drove him, but fatigue did not register in them, they just kept grinding, effortless, driven by the kick of an eternal piston that needed no explosion to turn its energy into action.

His mind wondered at it all. He did not think that his imagination could conceive of something so huge in scope, but it was possible, and if he was in some sort of fugue state, what was he to do? Force himself to wakefulness? And if he awoke, where would the dream end and life begin? Had there been a Great European War? Was Francois simply a creation of his subconscious mind? Had he even been to Africa? If this was all a dream, perhaps he was still a spoiled child of the French Republic, unaware of the world as it was, poisoned by history books that did not tell the truth, and history teachers who taught history as a monument to men whose greatest achievement was inherent, guiltless violence and abject indifference to cruelty.

He recalled his awe at seeing the pyramids at Giza. In his tent that night, he thought of the thousands of men whose bodies, driven by the bull whip, had been hollowed out by hauling and stacking those massive stones, until their earthly forms collapsed like rag dolls and rotted away in the pitiless Egyptian sun; dead slaves to pitiless Kings and Queens of the Ptolemy line. From the dust, to the lash, back to dust.

No. His imagination could not have invented all of that. Only actual experience could out-teach the comforting lies his nationalist professors had spoon-fed he and his classmates before sending them out into the wide world.

The journey Adam recalled in Africa had been his own 'Road to Damascus'. The scales had fallen from his eyes and he began to see the world as it was instead of as it had been tutored to him. It awakened him to the truth that all empires were gorged to greatness on the fresh blood, gristle, and organ meat of human beings whose only fault was that they stood in the way of progress. Only a fool would believe in the superiority of Europeans after seeing the rest of the world firsthand.

Francois. Adam smiled at the irony of the name. When he awoke in the water of the canal and swam to the mule path, he had every intention of fulfilling her command. Had the woman in the diner sent him to kill anyone but Francois, he wondered if he would simply have done the deed. He killed the two men he found on the way with no compunction whatsoever. Murdering the two quaking German enlisted men—the pair had raped a Belgian farm girl in the early days of the war—brought pleasure and righteous satisfaction. It left him wanting more.

He discovered Francois' trail at the train depot and followed it all the way to the bell tower of the lonely church in Vermand. It was only when Adam found himself stymied by the trapdoor above, separating him from his prey, that he caught the scent and sensation of Francois' warmth just beyond it, and some part of his being fought its way to the surface.

He could not kill the man in the tower above him, regardless of the sins he had committed. He sat down on the landing below Francois, bloody bayonet in hand, and recalled Senegal. In so doing, he found certainty that their time together had not been a dream. It had been, in so many ways, the only chapter in his life in which he had truly been awake and alive. By the time his body collapsed in the morning, reliving their journey had fully reinforced his humanity.

When he awoke at sunset, he knew he could hold fast to his rebellion. If he was to give his soul and body over to something greater than himself, it would not be to erect the crone's monument of blood and bone. If he was to sacrifice himself upon some altar, it would not be one built on humanity's ashes, it would be on an altar of his love for Francois. He knew the crone would make him suffer for it, but he did not care.

And now, running in Adolf's footprints, he knew, to defend Francois he had to kill the Austrian he was hunting. The part of him that was thirsty for blood thrilled at the thought. The old woman awoke the appetite for just this type of deed. Now he would use it to stymie her aims.

Adolf's footprints were fresh. He was close. Adam flexed his cold hand on the bayonet's handle and ran on.

♠ ♠ ♠ ♠ ♠

Rupert Fuchs saw the road he had been searching for open up before him. He stepped out of the field onto it slowly, peering left and right, looking for signs of the dead. There were none. He turned and waved Wolfgang and the others to him. As they came out of the snow-covered crops, he pressed on, turning right, and following the drainage ditch beside the road.

The ghosts of abandoned farmhouses began to appear with regularity, and twenty minutes later, Rupert led the way into the outskirts of St. Quentin, confident. He had wintered there in '15. He knew the terrain as well as he did the streets of Hamburg.

When they arrived at the vast stacks of weaponry at the Lafayette Ammunition Dump, he paused and let the others catch him. They huddled together in the shadows of some thirty-thousand snow-covered, palleted artillery shells, all of which had been bound for Verdun and points east via horse, lorry, and river barge. At the southern end, ranks-upon-ranks of neatly ordered, snow-covered, 42cm Big Bertha Field Howitzers and 150mm towed artillery guns stood. Their barrels jutted up at sharp angles, looking like massive telescopes seeking bloody Mars's angry glow in the night sky.

Rupert knelt and drew a rudimentary map in the snow. *"The city center is just to the south of us, here,"* he indicated. *"We can continue to circle the city by running east, then south, but it will take twice as long to come around to the canal where it meets the Somme River, assuming that is where their boat is."*

Wolfgang translated to Durant.

"The cavalrymen said we should skirt the city," Durant said.

"Oui," said Renoir. "But if we continue in a half-circle around the city itself, we give up any lead we have on our pursuers. And if they were to move straight through St. Quentin, would they not be able to cut us off?"

"Wolfgang? What do you think?" asked Durant.

Wolfgang gathered his thoughts. "The devil we know is behind us. The devil we do not lies in St. Quentin."

"The devils we know are thousands strong. Hunting us. Tell me how whatever lies in St. Quentin could be worse," said Renoir.

Durant caught some of the fire in Wolfgang's glance at Renoir, but ignored it as he considered. Every second they sat unmoving, the hunters pursuing them closed the gap.

"Ask him if there's cover in the city," Durant said.

Wolfgang translated.

Rupert nodded. *"We blew it to rubble when we captured it in 1914 and rubble it remains. It is a 'Cellar City', because the only thing left intact are the cellars. Everyone billeted there is underground. The avenues are clear, of course, for material and troop movement, but the city itself is piles of brick and mortar, shingles and beams. Even the St. Quentin Basilica is near shambles."*

Howling erupted in the distance.

"Oh, Lord…" said James. "Whatever the heck we're gonna do, let's go on and do it."

"I say straight through the city," said Renoir.

Durant nodded. "Wolfgang?"

"Yes. Fine." He looked at Rupert. *"Through the city. We are all in your hands, Sergeant."*

Rupert nodded. He felt the responsibility press on him. *"Good. Good. Quickly then."*

Rupert jogged in the lead, confident of the pathway that would take them to the town center. He had spent many hours of his respites from the front touring the city's remains, imagining how the broad avenues and architecture looked before the ville met its end at the hands of Germany's high-explosive siege. Most of his meanders had eventually led him to where he was taking them now—the juncture where the neatly cut symmetry of Napoleon's St. Quentin Canal met the ranging Somme River's expanse.

The streets were silent. The snow on the cleared avenues showed no footprints or signs of life. The piles of rubble that had been houses and storefronts, banks and schools, haberdasheries and druggist shops, were now misshapen mountains of snow.

Ten minutes later, they approached the city center. Rupert slowed. Some gut instinct whispering to his sapper-wired brain told him to stop. He listened to the voice and signaled the men behind him to halt. Through the darkness, he slipped back to Wolfgang.

"What's the matter?" asked Wolfgang.

"I don't know. Wait here one moment while I go ahead. The city-centre is just before us, and as you can imagine, it is a wide-open plaza. Once we get through there, we can travel on side avenues to the Somme, but I feel it would be prudent to scout it first."

Wolfgang turned to Durant and whispered, "He'll go ahead and scout. He says there is open space ahead he wants to check."

Durant nodded.

"Quickly, sergeant. Let us not waste the time we have gained," said Wolfgang.

Rupert turned and jogged to the corner, then disappeared from view.

James Cox watched him go and looked to Jonah. "Where's that old boy headed now?" he whispered.

Jonah Unger shrugged, uncomprehending.

James felt some panic stirring in him. He looked down and realized he was holding his brother's pocket watch tightly in his hand. The shame of his naked theft of it washed over him. He had mostly forgotten the event. He had even convinced himself at times that it had not occurred, or that Harlan would have wanted him to have it, because what loving older brother would not want to bequeath such a keepsake to their sibling? But in his current state of mind, he had been meditating a lot on sin, in particular, his own sins, and right then, he wished he was a Catholic, because then perhaps he could simply have washed it all away with confessions, and maybe then the demons would not be hunting him, hoping to burn him alive, or worse, nail him up to a cross where he could meditate some more on his sinning ways until he expired like rotten fruit.

Right then, he considered hauling back and heaving the cursed pocket watch into the ruins of St. Quentin. Maybe then he could fool the men hunting him into thinking he had never stolen it in the first place. He clutched the watch, feeling its barely noticeable internal clockwork moving, its mechanical organs, cured by Jonah's deft touch, spinning and turning. But he could not bring himself to follow through on the impulse to rid himself of the proof of his crime.

Instead, he took a glance at its beautiful face, with its glowing radium hands, mocking him with their leisurely pace, telling him he had many, many hours to suffer through before the sun would send its rays over the horizon and save him. He closed the watch and felt the Cox coat-of-arms and the warm sentiment his parents had the horologer etch into the smooth silver. He slipped it inside his pocket and flexed his hands, rubbing them together for warmth, then shoving them under his arms, so he could keep himself from pulling out the watch and checking the time again. Looking at the watch hand's indiscernible movement would only make time's passage drag, and all he wanted now was for time to fly, for dawn to come, and with it a full collapse of the dead.

Then Rupert came running back around the corner and any thoughts of reaching safety vanished.

Rupert's face was white as the snow. He did not slow as he reached them, but whispered, *"Come, Come!"* sharply as he ran past.

None of them hesitated or waited for an explanation. Rupert's terror told them all they needed to know. They ran after him, unquestioning.

♠   ♠   ♠   ♠   ♠

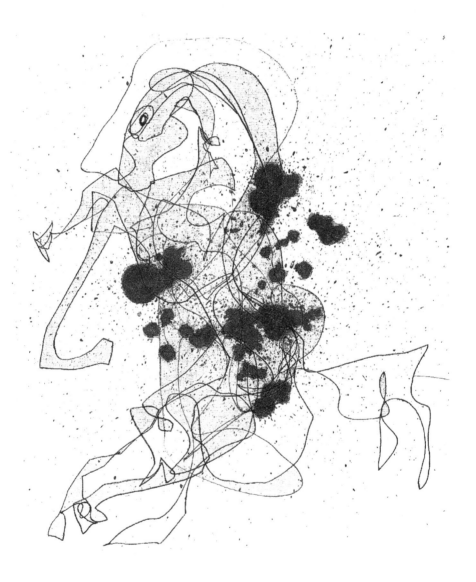

©jm2022

CHAPTER FIFTEEN

—

BLOOD RED BAY

The muffled clip-clop of his horse's hooves on the path had lulled him with their quiet, steady rhythm. Brian Hugh began to nod off, eyes plummeting closed, chin dipping, head lolling, leaning forward in the saddle, when the distant howling shocked him back awake. He sat up and took a long inhale of cold air through his nose and rubbed his eyes. He undid the top buttons of his uniform blouse and let the wind coming off the canal bite into him, but the cobwebs of exhaustion did not clear, and he knew if he stayed mounted now, he would succumb. He scanned the road ahead, the woods running up the canal bank beside him, and the path behind. No signs of pursuit, and wherever the howling canines were, they were not too close. He imagined he would have time to re-mount and ride hard if they made an appearance.

Brian reined in his horse and dismounted. He kicked feeling back into his numb legs and ass, willing blood to flow into them. As the pins-and-needles dissipated, he looked into his mount's eyes. She was a beautiful blood-red bay. When Good Friday fell upon them, his own horse, Gawain, had been cut from under him. Brian had stumbled out of the field and found the bay wandering, with no sign of her rider. She allowed him to take her reins and mount. They had been partnered ever since, but in the madness, he had not thought to name her. He caressed her jaw.

"Alright, love. We'll be at the bloody boat before you know it and there's plenty there for you to eat, I give you my word. Not far now, eh? Not far."

He took a last look at the surrounding terrain, then he pulled his horse's reins and led her onward. Fatigue remained, threatening to entomb him, but Brian forced himself to the exercise of placing one foot in front of the other.

Halfway to the barge, he bent and picked up a handful of snow, then slapped it on his cheeks, forcing himself to keep his eyes open. He knew it was a losing battle. He knelt, trying to reason with himself.

"Look, you dumb twat, if you lay down and fall asleep now, you're most likely going to wake up being skinned, and won't that be a fucking treat after you've kept your sorry self alive for this fucking long. Now WAKE UP! Get back on your fucking feet. Double time to the bloody boat and live to see the fucking dawn. Right?"

He stood, much more slowly than he had any right to, given the dressing down he had just given himself. He adjusted the lance that was strapped across his shoulders and flexed his sword arm. The thought of having to fight anything just now was terrifying. He sheathed his saber and pulled his right leather glove off. He slapped his right cheek as hard as he could. He pulled the glove back on, took a deep breath, then pressed on.

The next hour passed in silence. Brian tried to stay keen, checking for pursuit, scanning the trees for monsters, but his mind was going numb and hallucinatory. Riding alongside Major Danforth and Sergeant Tremaine had kept him sane since Good Friday. The game of slaughtering the risen dead, and even saving the pittance of survivors, had given his own survival purpose and function. But now, detached from any greater circumstance, Brian had lost his rudder. He could not even really remember why getting to the boat was important.

When they found the 38-meter barge floating in the canal, Major Danforth was well-satisfied. She had been some sort of pleasure craft before the war, purchased new at the turn-of-the-century, when Europe sat at peace with itself, like a reformed alcoholic, ready to accept all the hard-earned lessons of the past, primed with a fresh calendar full of opportunity. The slate of history had been wiped clean by the new century's advent. The distinct possibility to fill this next hundred years with profound advancement of the best humanity had to offer lay before them. A bottle of Dom Perignon christened the vessel "Jasmine" on New Year's Day and she sallied forth into the twentieth century.

Alas, humanity could not go a full fifteen years without repeating the mistakes it had made again, and again, and again. So, in September 1914, the Germans took "Jasmine" for their own. She was renamed Vorpostenboote-109 Hans Mauer. The Germans trimmed her in all black and bolted machine-guns to her deck at fore and aft. She ran from the Riqueval Tunnel to the railhead at St. Quentin, into the Somme River, and all the way down to the city of Ham, then back again.

For the majority of men serving aboard V-109, the war had been a pleasure. They kept her deck, machine guns, and engine room in perfect order. Wherever the Captain ordered them, they shepherded their vessel to with speed and grace. To do anything below that standard was to risk being sent straight to the front lines to experience actual war. By 1917, any crew members attracted to that siren song had succumbed. Most recently, three young men had decided that life on a pleasure craft would be more pleasurable if they spent the days sipping on stolen wine. For their sins, they were excommunicated to The Front. After the Captain had them demoted and sent forward with an infantry battalion, all three were killed on their second morning in the line.

The other spur that shuttled men to battle from a peaceful life on the patrol boat was more mundane. It was boredom. Between September 1914 and Good Friday of 1917, a half-dozen young men rotated through, served reasonably well on the pristine luxury craft, then requested transfer to front line battalions. They had not joined the army to experience peace. They joined to test their mettle in battle. They wanted to impress their wives and lovers back home with pretty ribbons and crosses, and tales of glory. They wanted war and all that came with it. To their soon-to-be regret, they got it.

Thus, by Good Friday 1917, the V-109 was piloted entirely by men who had no desire to be anywhere else. Unfortunately, the fact that there was no immediate evidence of blood on their hands did not save them. On Good Friday, when the cadavers of officers bound for Berlin broke out of their caskets in a cattle car that was idling at the St. Quentin train depot, the boatmen aboard the V-109 were some of their first victims. They died, rose up, and scattered into St. Quentin on a killing spree.

Thus, the V-109 was entirely vacant when Major Danforth, Brian Hugh and Darren Tremaine found it.

Major Danforth dismounted and walked the long length of the V-109 while Darren and Brian shared a cigarette.

"What do you think, Sergeant?" asked Brian.

"I'm not sure what the Major has in mind. A river boat excursion, perhaps?" Darren passed the cigarette back to Brian.

Major Danforth opened the doors below the wheelhouse and went below decks. The interior of the barge was spacious enough to accommodate a galley kitchen with bench seating for six and a plentiful store of dry goods. Beyond that, eight hammocks hung with neatly placed footlockers below them against the bulkhead. With the hammocks stowed during the day, the space afforded plenty of room for men on rotational duty during the day to take their ease.

At the stern, he found a pristine and tidy engine room. Not a jot of grease or oil.

Danforth climbed back up on deck and chewed his lip. He opened his cigarette case and pulled one of the last ones out. He lit it with his silver lighter and took a deep drag.

"Gentlemen... I think we've found our way out."

"How do you mean, Major?" asked Brian Hugh.

"Well, Lieutenant, this Péniche is in excellent running order. She's stout and seaworthy. She's got a shallow draft, which means she'll run fast."

"Where shall we run her to, Major?" asked Darren.

"At full steam, if we left at daybreak tomorrow, I reckon we could be in the English Channel before nightfall. Within sight of Dover by dawn the next day. How does that sound, Sergeant?"

Brian and Darren took that in.

"Sounds too good to be true... What if it's in England, too, sir?" asked Darren.

Major Danforth tapped the ash on his cigarette and took another drag. "Well, Sergeant, we shan't know until we know, yes? I, for one, will relish not being trapped behind 'enemy lines'."

"Yes, sir. But playing Devil's Advocate, what if we get trapped on the river and can't reach the channel?" asked Brian Hugh.

"Any choice we make now comes with inherent risk, but I don't see any way that our luck here can possibly hold. Each night, the enemy seems to martial their forces, yes? On Good Friday, what did we see after the first scrum? They separated into groups of three or four. By Saturday, the largest gang was how strong, would you say?"

"A baker's dozen, sir," said Brian.

"Quite right. And then Sunday night?"

"Perhaps one hundred in that orchard, sir."

"Yes. Perhaps twice that. They seem to be coalescing. We cannot, of course, face down two hundred men. If discretion is indeed 'the better part of valor', then I believe we have reached the moment where said 'discretion' is called for. The Charge of the Light Brigade was not a heroic act. It was mass suicide led by a lunatic. I do not intend to follow his example."

Brian and Darren nodded in agreement.

"We'll provision this vessel, then ride back to see if we can round up the threesome we left in that millhouse by the stream, yes? I'd rather a full complement if we're to take her across the Channel."

Five hundred yards southeast of them, they found a stout stone bridge arching over the canal's green span. The road led through the St. Quentin rail yards where German cattle cars awaited plunder. Darren, Brian, and Major Danforth filled a cart with rations and ammunition for the MG '08s. They hitched their unhappy horses to the cart and hauled it all back across the bridge, then north on the mule path to the V-109. It was afternoon before they had it all aboard and stowed.

"Alright, lads. Enjoy the ride tonight. We'll need to cut our horses free tomorrow morning," Danforth said.

Darren Tremaine felt an enormous sadness at the thought of saying farewell to Bathsheba, but he kept it to himself. Major Danforth and Brian Hugh felt the same tug, but survival trumped sentiment.

They ate a late lunch in silence, fed and watered their horses, then rode out on one last patrol, through the empty, rubble-strewn streets of St. Quentin, past a vast German munitions dump, and back through the burned swaths of farmland the retreating German Army had left in their wake.

They found the little millhouse by the wheat field unoccupied. They followed Durant and his company's tracks west as the first flakes of snow began to fall. When the sun began to set, they decided to give up the pursuit and started back south, toward St. Quentin.

Darren felt Bathsheba stiffen under him, sensing it moments before he did, then the distant clatter of machine-gun fire reached them all.

Major Danforth brought his horse around. They listened intently to the rattling echo.

"Christ... He's keeping up a racket. Sounds like he's fighting off a bloody army," said Brian Hugh.

"Alright, lads. Let's go have a look. If we can help, we will. If it's biting off more than we can chew, we'll hold our hand."

They drew their sabers and rode north through the fields. Ten minutes later, they saw the entire eastern horizon blaze orange as the St. Quentin canal burst into flames. Five minutes after that, they were cutting down dead Germans who chased Durant, Rupert, Wolfgang, Renoir, James, and Jonah out of the barbed wire.

Danforth sent Durant and company toward St. Quentin and the V-109, then the horsemen kicked flanks and continued north, searching for the other survivors. They found no one alive.

But the army of dead men chasing Isaiah Taylor found them.

And now, slogging along the mule path in the falling snow, the hopes and dreams of an easy dawn exit from Hell aboard the lovely V-109 seemed a pipe dream to Brian Hugh.

But then, when he looked up from the mule path, the V-109 sat before him in the canal. Her long, flat-black decks and machine guns were now covered in a coat of beautiful white. Brian tied off his horse's reins. He nearly wept with joy as he walked the little gangplank onto the deck. He lifted the lance he had strapped across his shoulder over his head and leaned it against the wheelhouse as he ducked down into the ship's hold. He twisted open a ration tin and devoured the mealy sausages, choking them down with biscuits and water. Then he lay back in a hammock and rested his arm over his face, letting the gentle sway suck him under.

♠ ♠ ♠ ♠ ♠

TAK.

Brian's eyes shot open. He could not tell if the sound of the ricochet had occurred inside his dream, or not. He lay there silent, straining to hear. For a long moment, there was the lap of the canal water, gently rocking the boat, and that was all.

TAK.

This was not a sound inside his head. Something hard had struck one of the glass portholes squarely. Brian sat up. The fog of sleep diminished, but not entirely, making him feel half-drunk. He stood and steadied himself. He held his saber ready and moved to the porthole on the mule path side, peeking out into the night.

TAK.

A stone cracked into the glass, inches from his face. He heard muffled laughter coming from the dark. Whatever was out there knew he was inside. He was being toyed with, like some dumb, broken-backed bird, being teased toward death by a fat and nasty feline.

Brian scanned the night for the source, but he could not see beyond the mule path into the white-covered alleys and alcoves amongst the buildings beyond it. He saw his horse, standing calmly at the other end of the gangplank. His best play was to try to get to her and mount up, then make a run for it. The bridge was not far, and if he could reach it and cross, there was plenty of space beyond it to lose pursuers.

Brian sheathed his saber and eased his way up the steps to the cabin door. He opened it slowly. Snow and cold air gusted in. He stepped out onto the deck, reaching for his lance while he watched the darkness for movement, but there was nothing there; nothing in the shadows. And no lance leaning against the wheelhouse. Cold fear bit hard. He started toward his horse. He saw movement coming down the sloped alley toward the canal. Brian bolted.

He felt the gangplank bouncing under him. He leapt for the saddle horn and swung his right leg up and over, slinging himself into the seat. He reached down to yank the reins free.

His lance struck him under the ribs and speared up into his lungs. Brian slumped to the side and screamed in pain. His feet searched for stirrups they could not find, then the spear was twisted and yanked, pulling him from the saddle. He hit the pavement.

He looked up. He saw the whites of the dead man's eyes framed by red and black skin that had been burned to a deep crisp. He heard dogs barking and coming at a run toward them. He saw the man's face light up in a smile. Then the lance was pulled free and the pain sent Brian Hugh tumbling into a dark well of unconsciousness as his brain tried to protect him from the horrors it knew were coming.

♠   ♠   ♠   ♠   ♠

Little Boy Halstead stood over his victim. He leaned against the bloody nine-foot bamboo lance he had stolen from Brian Hugh and watched the three German Shepherds slow their approach, teeth snarling, sniffing at the fresh bloody scent that was swirling around in the snowy air.

When he saw the four men thundering out of the night behind the dogs, Little Boy Halstead nodded a greeting.

"Well, shoot," said Daddy Cox, "looks like we got beat to the punch on this'n."

Harlan, Sheriff Coombs, and Big Don McMaster joined Daddy Cox. The line of dogs stood between them and Halstead, still growling, uncertain.

Little Boy Halstead extended his hand to the dogs. The German Shepherds slowly advanced, sniffing his burnt flesh. Halstead's corpse reeked of war. He let them take in the scent; gunpowder and iron-rich blood, stale, terror-stoked adrenaline, gasoline and burnt flesh. Satisfied, the German Shepherds let him stroke their soft ears.

"You speak English?" asked Daddy Cox.

"I speak all your languages," said Little Boy Halstead. "Every last one."

Daddy Cox grinned. "Well, alright then." He thrust his chin toward Brian Hugh's slumped body. "That one still alive?"

Little Boy Halstead nodded. "He is."

"We've been throwing a little 'hanging party' up the way a bit. Wonder if we might take this one off your hands, unless, of course, you had plans for him. We've been doing some 'decorating' and we need one more fellow to balance it all out. Wouldn't ask, but we seem to have found all the folks in the area who was still living and breathing. The pickings in this town have gotten pretty slim."

The Little Boy nodded. "Surely. Take him. But have no fear. The others are coming. The 'pickings' in this town will not be 'slim' for long."

And so, Daddy Cox, Harlan, Big Don, and Sheriff Coombs bound Brian Hugh's hands behind his back and hefted him. Little Boy Halstead and the

German Shepherds followed them through the streets of St. Quentin. When they reached the city center and its grand cathedral, Big Don slapped Brian Hugh back to wakefulness. They wrapped a telephone wire noose around his neck, then they strung him up, popping and jerking, gasping and choking, until Brian finally blacked out and came to permanent rest.

♠　♠　♠　♠　♠

©jm2022

CHAPTER SIXTEEN

—

TOURNIQUET

Shen Su paused at the farmyard's threshold. His legs were shaking from fatigue, but he knew Li Peng's dragon was less than one-hundred yards away now, and the only way to reach it was to leave the woods and tramp ahead, naked to any searching eyes, across the open expanse before him. He shook off the fear, bent forward, and began the final slog.

♠   ♠   ♠   ♠   ♠

Just one day past, at mid-morning, to Sergeant Li's quiet delight, they had found the small frontline depot with its stores of food and gasoline. Sergeant Li stuck the gas hose into the tank's bung, hopped down and turned the tap on.

While the gas tank filled, they rummaged through the supplies and found a half-dozen drum magazines for the Lewis Gun. The drums came in pairs of canvas sacks that could be looped behind the neck, dangling the drums on the bearer's chest like some bizarre, massive necklace. Sergeant Li draped a pair over Zi Chang's shoulders.

Chang cupped the heavy drums. *"Biggest, heaviest titties you've ever seen,"* Chang said to Shen Su, laughing.

Sergeant Li rolled his eyes. Su and Chang took the MG drums into the belly of the tank.

Chang stuck his head back out of the sponson. *"Any more metal titties to load, Sergeant Li?"*

Li Peng smiled tightly. *"No more titties. Eat. Piss. We're heading south, full bore, until we find a place to camp for the night. Not gonna stop again."* He inspected the gas flow. As it burbled up and overflowed the bung, he cranked the tap lever, shutting it off. "We should be at the Mirvaux Depot by mid-day tomorrow, then it's a straight shot west to Paris. We'll take that road and get as far from this shit as we can. By tomorrow night, maybe we're clear of it."

Chang looked at him, confused. Sergeant Li realized he had switched back to his native Canada's tongue. He rubbed tired eyes, then repeated it in Mandarin.

As they buttoned up the hatches, the first droplets of rain began plinking down onto the metal roof. The cylinders barked to life and Sergeant Li piloted them south toward Mirvaux and what he hoped would be the final turning point.

The sun had long-since disappeared and rain was falling in heavy sheets when they backed deep into the trees and shut down the engine. They spent half an hour covering the tank as best they could with fallen branches and loose bracken. It was not as quality a camouflage as their last attempt, but with the rainfall, Sergeant Li could not gauge the actual sunset with any accuracy. Better to be hidden decently and locked into the tank, than hidden perfectly, but surprised by nightfall and dead men. They climbed into the tank, soaking wet, but as safe as they could hope to be.

Rain poured down. Lightning flashed through the view slits. Thunder echoed through the hull. In time, the rain's steady rhythm pulled Zi Chang and Shen Su into fitful, exhausted, nightmaring sleep.

The first watch passed slowly. Sergeant Li went in and out, pinching himself and flicking the tip of his tongue along the roof of his mouth, just enough to tickle his eyes back open. He yawned and stretched, and felt his head nod backward toward the chair, but as it did, he heard a sound and wrenched his neck up, suddenly wide, wide awake. He leaned forward silently, peering through the view slit, looking for movement in the darkness beyond the tree limbs that covered the tank.

The rain had passed, and now the full moon shone down, lighting the black woods in bright slashes of white. Some fifty yards distant, out of the blackness, Sergeant Li saw someone coming. Li Peng's fingers clutched the handgrip and trigger housing of the Lewis Gun.

A man in filthy British khaki stumbled into the clearing and paused, staring back the way he had come, breathless, searching the forest behind him for pursuit.

Sergeant Li saw more motion, predatory, through the trees. The moon caught a naked man's white skin, a hunter carrying a long spear, circling behind unsuspecting Dr. Halstead.

Sergeant Li put the MG's bead on the man with the spear. His index finger touched the trigger.

The naked spearman raised the weapon and threw, striking Dr. Halstead in the back, sending him screaming to the forest floor. Before Li Peng could make the trigger pull, the naked man was on his prey, wrenching the spear out, burying its point in the ground, then binding and dragging Halstead away into the woods.

Long moments passed in silence.

Li Peng's finger left the trigger. He sat back from the view slit, squeezed his eyes shut, shoved his knuckles into his forehead, and wholeheartedly wished he could awaken from this goddamn nightmare.

Dawn came, crisp and cold. As the sun struck the tank, Li Peng honestly did not know if he dreamed the spearing of Dr. Halstead by Harry Fucking Moss, or actually witnessed it. He decided it did not matter. Su spun the starter. Li Peng dropped the tank into gear and drove them onward.

By mid-day, the sky was crystalline blue, the vista unmarred by clouds. Despite the roar of the tank and the clatter of its spinning tracks, there was beauty to be seen. Li Peng had Su and Chang open the rear hatches and he flipped the forward view port armor up so that cold, fresh air would flow through the tank. They drove for two more hours before he shifted into neutral and let the beast settle to a stop. The silence when the engine shut down was stunning. Peng rubbed tired eyes and yawned.

Zi Chang stood and stretched as best he could. He looked into the little cage where the carrier pigeon was nestled away. He broke off a piece of stale biscuit and passed it through the bars to her. She pecked at it and swallowed it down. Chang smiled.

"Are we stopping for the day?" Chang asked.

"No. Just a toilet break and a bite of food. I want to reach the Mirvaux depot before nightfall," Peng replied. He gave a solid thump to the gas tank with his steel spanner. The hollow echo told him she was still at least half full. *"I figure we can get there without a problem. We'll hunker near Mirvaux for the night, then cut west to Paris."*

Chang grabbed a roll of toilet paper and led the way out of the tank, followed by Su. Li Peng took a stale biscuit from the tin and followed after them.

The crisp air felt good after the stagnant, oily reek of the tank's interior.

Chang walked around to the side of the tank. He unbuttoned his trousers and squatted, holding the steel tank tread for balance. The tremendous fart that came out of him made Li Peng and Shen Su laugh as they urinated on trees.

"That's a lot of wind for such a little fellow," said Sergeant Li.

"Just be grateful I didn't do it in the tank," replied Chang. He unspooled some toilet paper and wiped himself clean. *"You'd have both needed gas masks for certain."*

Li Peng and Shen Su buttoned up.

"Anyone need toilet paper?" asked Chang.

"I wish," Peng said. *"Those biscuits have my guts seized up tight."*

Su nodded. *"Same here."*

Chang tucked the paper roll under his arm and peed on a sapling in front of him. Su was already stepping into the rear sponson when it happened.

The wolf was a strobe of silver and black. Her open mouth flashed razor teeth, bright white, and shining pink gums. The teeth hit Chang's side and sent him tumbling. Dark urine sprayed into the air and the toilet paper roll flew away, spinning into the aether, its long tail following, like some forlorn comet.

Chang's scream was a high-pitched shrieking wail. The she-wolf shook him, and bit in again as he punched at her head and tried to kick himself free. Her teeth caught his forearm, savaging it, and when she bit again, her rear carnassial and molars broke it cleanly with a loud *POP* that sent Zi Chang into shock.

Li Peng's boot caught the she-wolf under the ribs, and she stiffened, but did not release Zi Chang. He kicked her again with all his strength.

The she-wolf dropped Chang's broken body and lunged for Sergeant Li. He jumped backward, but she already had her teeth sunk into his calf. She locked her grip and dragged him along with her, pulling him away from the tank, past the shaking, bloody body of little Zi Chang.

Sergeant Li screamed in pain and tried to grab hold of the sapling Chang had been pissing on, but the she-wolf was too strong. She dug in her back legs and yanked him along after her, shredding tissue and tendon, hitting tibia and fibula bones, sending deep waves of pain rumbling and rushing through Peng's system.

The roar of the Hotchkiss machine gun caught her by surprise. The she-wolf dropped Peng's wrecked leg and bolted as hot metal exploded out of the dragon's side, splintering the trees and cutting the air around her, whistling past her sensitive ears and soiling her nose with its poisonous lead fumes. She danced backward and spun away, vanishing into the forest as Su held the trigger down, spraying rounds after her through half-closed eyes.

Su released the trigger. The ringing in his ears was all he heard at first. Then the sounds of Zi Chang wailing reached him in the tank's cockpit. Su let go of the machine gun and ran for the rear exit.

Li Peng was hauling himself through the muck, dragging his dead leg behind him, back toward the tank, as Su dropped out of the hatch.

Su ran to Zi Chang's side. The horror of the open wounds on his torso and arm froze him for half a second, then he remembered that the fucking she-wolf was still out there, close at hand, blood-thirsty, and he shut off his gut-churning response to the gore. He cradled Chang and hefted his fragile little body, then ran with it to the tank. He lifted him into the left hatch as gently as he could, pushing him through, easing him into its belly, then he slammed the door and turned back for Sergeant Li.

His eyes searched the woods for the silver coat of the wolf as he knelt and got a shoulder under Li Peng's arm, then he stood and pulled him up, half dragging him, lurching back toward the sanctuary of the tank. At the open right hatch, he jumped up, then turned back to pull Li Peng after him.

Su saw her streaking out of the timber. He yanked Li Peng with all his strength. Peng shrieked in pain, tumbling past Su and crashing to the floor of the tank. Su had no time to regret that he was the cause. He grabbed the hatch door handle and yanked it shut just as the she-wolf leapt. She hit the steel hatch full speed with her head. Su jammed the latch down. He looked across the tank. The hatch he pulled Zi Chang in through was open half an inch. Su jumped up, stumbling across the tank bay. He grabbed the handle, slammed it shut, and punched the latch down before the wolf-bitch could paw it open and fight her way in to finish them all.

Su's breath was coming too fast. He shut his mouth, trying to stop the hyperventilation and bring his heart back into something resembling control. He looked at his wounded companions. Zi Chang was half-conscious. He began to moan. The sound was like ice water poured down his back, bracing Su back into the present.

Li Peng's eyes glared fiercely in the darkened tank as he pushed himself to sitting and looked at his ruined leg draining blood onto the tank's floor plates. He undid his belt and pulled it free, then slid it under his hamstring. He pulled the free end through the buckle and yanked it as tight as he could.

Peng nodded toward Chang. *"You've got to try to stop his bleeding... Use your belt to tie off that arm of his and then we can take a look at his belly."*

Su nodded. He felt his brain go numb, refusing to respond to all the hellish input in front of him. He unbuckled his belt and slid it out of its loops, then he set to trying the impossible.

As he tied off the leather tourniquet on Zi Chang's arm, Shen Su was glad of the numbness his brain had given him. He let it spread and armor him against his circumstances, then he set to work on the other impossibilities before him.

When Su bound Li Peng's tattered leg, Peng passed out without a sound. Whatever scream had wanted to pour out over his vocal folds never found purchase, exiting as a silent exhale. For a moment, Su thought Li Peng had expired, but then he saw his belly moving up and down easily, as breath continued in and out through his slack mouth.

He finished binding strips of wool torn from Sergeant Li's shirt around the congealing wounds. He leaned back when he finished and shuddered at the ugly job he had done. It looked better than it did when he began, but remained a horror all the same. At least it was clean. Thankfully, the medical kit in the tank's belly had been replete with hypochlorite. He poured it liberally on both men's wounds.

Su moved to the other side of the tank where Zi Chang's tiny broken body lay. Chang was still unconscious, shrouded in a wool army blanket, breathing shallowly. Su had never seen anyone so pale, but he was glad Chang was still breathing. The wounds were bad, but the wolf had not gotten her teeth through his belly to organ meat, and Su hoped Chang's shock would pass. The arm was beyond Su's ability to save. The tourniquet had kept most of the blood inside his body, but the arm would be the sacrifice. Su knew it would have to come off at some point. He said a quiet prayer that he would not have to be the one to put a saw to it.

"*Shen Su…*" The sound of his own name startled him. On the opposite side of the engine compartment, Sergeant Li was sitting up, staring at his ruined leg.

"*Yes, Sergeant?*"

"*… Is Zi Chang alive?*"

Su nodded as he squeezed behind the engine and stood over Peng. "*Yes, Sergeant. Barely. But alive, yes.*"

Su saw that Li Peng was breathing shallowly through his nose, trying to control his response to the pain.

"*Help me to the driver's seat… We must get to the depot at Mirvaux and try to cover as much ground as possible before nightfall.*"

"*You can drive?*"

"*I only need one leg for the clutch and brake, and I need you to steer at the back. I can't very well move from side to side to clutch the tracks to turn us, neh?*"

Su nodded. He took Sergeant Li's hands and helped him to his feet as gently as possible, then he supported him as he fumbled his way forward.

A lance of pain stabbed through Peng as he sat into the cockpit seat.

"*Crank the engine,*" Li Peng mustered.

Su nodded. He headed to the back of the tank and spun the starter. The Daimler-Knight barked in response. Sergeant Li dropped it into gear. They ground forward, pressing on toward the hope of Mirvaux.

The sun was a few hours from the horizon and unexpected snow was already coming down when they came upon the little vale that the Mirvaux depot had been hidden in. It was not hard to find now. The entire thing was on fire. Sooty grey ash from the blaze mixed in with the white flakes and returned to earth.

Shen Su thought Sergeant Li might well give up then. When he reached the front seat and stared out at the billowing black smoke with its heart of orange flame, devouring the depot and pouring into the forest around it, he was ready for the end.

Li Peng was slumped in the driver's seat, looking down at his ruined leg. He reached up without looking and turned the engine kill switch. The engine died away, then the only sound was the crackling of the fire's consumption. Peng searched out his wrench and tapped the gas tank. It rang back hollowly. He had gauged the beast's range of travel correctly. She would be dry as a sun-bleached bone within ten miles.

The question was on the tip of Su's tongue when Li Peng answered it.

"Okay... We need to find a place to park for the night where these flames won't catch us. And we need gas. And it looks like we won't be getting any of that here." His laugh was mirthless. *"Is Chang still alive?"*

Shen Su glanced back. The little fellow's breath rose and fell beneath the olive wool blanket. *"Yes."*

"Well, that's something. I'm not sure what will happen if he dies in the middle of the night. Probably wake up like Number Three and let the wolf in for her supper."

Su took that in silently.

"Eat some biscuits. You're going to need your strength. Finally gonna put your strong back to work, young man," said Li Peng.

They continued south through the falling snow until the sun began to set. Li Peng pulled into the farmyard. He shifted into reverse and backed up beside the broken-down barn with the last fumes in the gas tank. The beast idled high for a time, then shuddered and death-rattled of its own accord, starved of petrol.

Peng sketched out to Shen Su the path to the only possible stores of gas he knew of. It was a meandering journey, but Su had a clear picture of Li Peng's mental map.

He set out into the falling snow at a quick pace. It took him an hour to reach his destination. He found the British petrol stores a mile beyond the empty front line trenches. In the heavy snow and darkness, burdened by the weight of the gas cans, it took Su twice as long to make the return trip.

♠   ♠   ♠   ♠   ♠

And now, Shen Su stood before the silent, snow-shrouded tank. The gas cans sat in the snow behind him. There was no need to pour the stinking tonic in until the dawn broke, and he did not have the strength to carry them another yard.

The gusting winds had drifted snow up to the top of the tracks, making the tank all but invisible in the dark, sidled up against the broken barn. It looked like a poorly designed rhomboid-shaped outbuilding, covered in snow, the guns pointing out of its midsection seemed merely broken branches of some dead tree.

Keeping Zi Chang alive had been the first impossible thing he attempted that day. Running on foot through the woods in search of gas-o-line was the second. Fighting his way through the snowfall to bring it to his dying friends would likely be the last.

Su stumbled stiffly toward the rear sponson hatch. As he approached it, the numbness held him, even now. Su briefly wondered if real feeling would ever return. He thought it might be best if it did not.

He searched the dark woods behind him for the wolf, but she was not there. Nothing but blowing snow. He looked toward the tank.

"*Sergeant Li?...*"

There was no reply. Shen Su felt a chill run through him. Had he come all this way only to find them dead? And if they had died, what would that mean for him?

When he reached the door in the sponson, he paused, listening for signs of life. There were none. He reached out for the handle, grasped it in weak hands, and pulled. It did not budge. He knocked on it.

"*Sergeant Li?...*"

He heard the latch scrape, metal on metal, then the steel plate swung open on its hinges and Zi Chang's pale face was dead center in the hatch frame. He sat back without a word and made room for Shen Su, who tumbled up and in, then shut the door on the world beyond it, latching the night's horrors out, interring himself in the beast.

CHAPTER SEVENTEEN

—

PAX ROMANA

Adolf ran full tilt. He imagined the heavy steel of Francois' cutlass striking him in the back. He shot a look over his shoulder for death that he knew was coming. His front foot slid over a snow-slicked root, and he tripped and fell, arms pinwheeling to try to catch his fall, then he was on his way headfirst over a grade, slipping and falling, rolling and tumbling to a painful halt at the bottom of the gulley.

When Adolf opened his eyes, he saw a pair of boots inches away from him. He heard the owner of the boots laughing. Adolf rolled onto his side and had to cover his eyes from the bright glare of a burning torch as the man knelt beside him and poked a trench dagger's point under his chin. Then rough hands grabbed Adolf and hauled him to standing.

The man with the torch gave him a once-over. "*Bind him,*" he said in Latin.

The two men holding him began to yank his arms behind his back and Adolf cried out in pain, "*Please! Please don't hurt me!*"

The Romans laughed. They had heard that phrase a lot over the past few days.

♠ ♠ ♠ ♠ ♠

So close. He had been so close to capturing Adolf himself. Raised in the French Catholic practice, Adam Gillét understood Latin well. He watched and listened from the woods as thirty men from Oberon Junius's cohort marched away on a southerly bearing with Adolf in tow. When the last man in the Roman column had gone, he slid over the embankment into the gully and fell in behind them. He increased his pace until the rear guard was in sight.

When the Sergeant at the rear looked over his shoulder and saw Adam, he was surprised for a moment.

"Aye. Pick up your pace or I'll have you whipped."

"Yes, domine." Adam nodded and fell in, joining the dead centuria's crisp marching order. When he had the opportunity to strike Adolf, he would take it. Until then, he would bide his time amongst his fellow dead men, enduring with patience, shifting to full-throttle action to end the man when he could.

♠ ♠ ♠ ♠ ♠

Caitlin watched Francois, uncertain how to proceed. His cutlass lay before him on the bell tower's stone floor. He was kneeling, eyes shut tight, hands clasped, gently rocking himself. She heard him speaking low in an admixture of Arabic and Wolof, and though she understood neither language, she recognized desperate prayer when she heard it. She stepped back and let him be. Whatever he was suffering through had cut him off at the knees.

Caitlin walked to the rampart. She shook her head. This was insanity. She figured she had gone 'round the bend. She was likely in some padded room in a mental hospital, sedated for her own safety. Just as likely, she had taken a fall from her father's old mare and landed on her head. Now she lay in a hospital bed in Kildare, comatose and approaching death one hour at a time. The last two years had all been a literal nightmare instead of a figurative one, and the last few days were just a culmination of an insane story her subconscious had built up, imaginary brick by imaginary brick. And all of it was built on the fundamentally ridiculous notion that a war had erupted in Europe entirely by accident. Some Serbian boy had murdered an Austro-Hungarian Archduke and his wife, and that had triggered a slow-going Armageddon. Her mind must have decided that was too ridiculous a story to believe, so it conjured up this truly insane final chapter. Maybe when the end of the story came she would snap out of her slobbering, straight-jacketed mental stupor, or awake from her paralytic coma and everything would go back to normal. She closed her eyes and prayed that she would open them and find herself in some white hospital, mental or otherwise, instead of a white Hell. When she opened them, nothing had changed.

She pushed aside her fantasy. She was not dying. She was not insane. It was the world that had died and lost its mind, not her. She was just along for the ride. She leaned Isaiah's shotgun against the battlement and hugged herself for warmth, stamping blood into her feet. She looked at the boots Isaiah had taken from the dead German boy and given to her, and was grateful for the deed. She knew she never would have climbed out of the canal Hell in her Adelaides with their damnable heels. Between the shotgun and the boots, Isaiah had proven himself a good friend, perhaps the best she had ever known.

She looked out into the night, wondering if he had somehow made an escape, too.

The wind that had been gale force at times since the sun set had calmed. She saw the snow-covered ruins of Vermand and the fields and woodland to the northwest which they had come through.

When she first saw the tiny orange globes dancing through the woods, she thought she was witnessing some imaginary will-o'-the-wisps. Then she realized they were torches.

"Oh, Christ… Francois! We have to go." She grabbed the shotgun and ran to his side. "They're coming."

Francois picked up his cutlass and stood. Caitlin pulled him with her to the wall and pointed. "You see? There."

Francois saw the distant torches flickering as they moved through the trees. He watched the lights for a long moment.

A shiver of fear shot through Caitlin. "This is the only building standing for a mile in any direction. You're mad if you think they won't come have a look. And if that German boy is leading them, they'll come straight here." Caitlin reached out and touched his forearm. "Francois, I know you want to wait for your friend. And if you want to die in this church, there's nothing I can do to stop it. But I won't sit here for whatever's coming. Please, for mercy' sake, we have to go."

♠   ♠   ♠   ♠   ♠

Caitlin led the way. The road took them south for more than a mile and ran through the burned-out hamlet of Attilly. It ran west for another quarter mile from there, cutting a path through thick woods, heavy with snow. Caitlin slowed her pace as they came out of the shroud of darkness the trees provided into open farmland coated in white. She did not know where to go from there.

Then a sound reached them. Directly ahead, the distant clatter of a machine gun.

She looked to Francois. "What should we do?"

Francois knew that if their comrades were alive, they were likely at the epicenter of the guns. He pictured Renoir and Isaiah, perhaps Wolfgang and the little Jewish fellow at the trigger of a machine gun, and Francois wanted to run to them, to die alongside them. Had he been alone, he would have.

"Anything out here that heard that will go in that direction. If you would live, we must choose another way," he said.

Caitlin nodded. A machine-gun's bark might hold off the enemy for a time, but it definitely would draw every roaming dead man within range of its siren call, and there were not enough bullets in the world to stop that tide.

Caitlin took Francois' arm and pulled him off the road. They ran south across the field through the thick snow. By the time they reached the far side and slipped through the slats of a rough-hewn fence, the machine gun had gone silent; whatever hope the man behind the trigger had of fighting off what had come for him evaporated into thin air.

♠   ♠   ♠   ♠   ♠

©jm2022

CHAPTER EIGHTEEN

—

BASILICA

Rupert was near tears. His chest burned from the cold air. He could barely catch his breath. But he kept running. A glance over his shoulder told him that the only ones giving chase for the moment were his companions. He knew that would not last. Once they saw his footprints at the Basilica, or the dogs caught his scent, the dead would follow.

When Rupert ventured ahead to scout the city center, he had come south out of the Rue de Labon and slipped into the plaza on the north side of the massive gothic cathedral. All he could make out in the swirling snow were the outlines of the St. Quentin Basilica's façade. He knew it was in ruins. Long range artillery shells and bombs dropped from biplanes had set fire to its roof and turned the masonry to rubble in places. He had seen all the resulting destruction first-hand, but the snowfall disguised the damage, and in the dark of night, it seemed the medieval wonder had been miraculously restored to its former glory. If the sun rose in a blue sky the next morning, he imagined it revealing a gleaming, perfect snow cathedral.

He had moved east, then south past the towering entry way. The doors were gone, and the tall portals stood like black eye sockets in some massive alien skull.

Rupert hugged the side of the building as he rounded the corner. His height was all that kept him from running face-first into the pair of boots that dangled above him, six feet off the ground.

Rupert stared up at the size eleven boots and the dead man wearing them. The rope the man was strung from disappeared up into falling snow. Rupert stopped in his tracks, shaken. Ahead of him he could see, suspended from the finials lining the roof between the bell tower and the narthex, five more dead men, lynched and hung up to adorn the cathedral in an orderly line.

He saw movement in the plaza about two-hundred feet away, just beyond the sixth hung man. Rupert froze, then ducked back into the shadows. Four men stood in the dark, staring up at the roof, holding a slumped British cavalryman between them. Three big German Shepherds prowled around them through the snow.

While Rupert watched, a rope fell from the roof above and hit the ground. The slack end followed a moment later. He heard one of the three men yell out, "That'll do! Now come on down and join the party, Sheriff Coombs!"

Rupert looked up and saw the dark outline of a man perched on the roof high above waving down to the hanging party. He turned and made his way along the roof line toward the widow's walk that would take him into the basilica.

One of the hangmen stepped forward and picked up the hemp. Practised hands looped it and began twisting it around into a hangman's knot.

As Rupert watched, the other three men dragged Brian Hugh forward. They spoke English with an American twang and laughed as they dropped the loop over his head, then the man who had done the hangman's knot pulled in the slack and yanked the noose taut. The others seized hold of the long tail with him, and all three yanked the ensnared man up into the air. Brian's cavalry boots kicked and lashed out as the dead men strained against his weight, forcing him to defy gravity.

Rupert heard one of the men say, "Come on, Harlan, put your back into it, son. One, two, three—"

There was a vicious yank and Brian Hugh shot up another four feet, kicked out weakly, and went still, going limp as the hangmen tied off the rope, leaving him dangling, slowly oscillating toward stillness, like some fleshy pendulum.

Rupert slid back, deep into the shadows of the bell tower. He heard the man coming from behind him. Rupert ducked silently into the corner of the stone façade and willed himself to be invisible. He saw the man plainly when he came around the last corner. Rupert was close enough to make out the rank on his lapels. The body had been that of a German Lieutenant in life. He was certain the man would turn and see him. But he did not. He turned the corner and loped toward the hanging party with a lop-sided grin. Rupert kept himself contained. He imagined the dead Lieutenant's companions turning about to see their friend as he came around the bend. He knew that if he slipped away too soon, they would see him as he fled. He also knew that if they decided to come back in this direction, they could not miss him when they turned the corner. He silently counted off the seconds he imagined it would take for the dead man to reach his party, then he risked all.

At the edge of the basilica, he glanced once toward the dead men as the Lieutenant joined them. Rupert ducked low and slipped around to the front of the cathedral, turned the bend, passed the entryway, then bolted, racing toward the intersection, rounding onto the Rue De Labon and toward his waiting compatriots.

Durant, James, Jonah, Wolfgang, and Renoir felt his terror, heard his urging "Come. *Come!*" and ran after in his wake.

♠ ♠ ♠ ♠ ♠

Rupert led them back north at a dead run until they reached Boulevard Richelieu, named for His Bloody Red Eminence, Cardinal Richelieu—the priest who slaughtered and neutered his Huguenot Protestant enemies and manipulated the Thirty Years' War to bring France to the penultimate ranks of European power; all the time shoring up France's burgeoning dominance of the Canadian wilds, thus assuring French Catholicism's powerful influence there in the centuries to come, as the savages were tamed and the land was exploited to its full potential.

Rupert took them at a steady jog along Richelieu's road; eyes constantly mindful of the avenue ahead, scanning the boulevard and its cross streets for any sign of more hunting parties, and looking back to make certain that the only men running in his footprints were still among the living.

When they reached the roundabout at Place Longueville, he ran them straight through it and southeast onto Boulevard Henri Martin. After several hundred yards, he stopped at the sharp corner where Rue De La Pomme Rouge joined the boulevard. He knelt there, breath heaving, while the rest of his companions caught up.

Wolfgang was the first to join him, with Durant and Renoir not far behind. Jonah was next, with James just after.

"What did you see?" asked Wolfgang.

When Rupert got his breathing back under control, he told Wolfgang what he had witnessed in the Basilica's plaza. *"Five men. Three dogs. They were hanging men and women from the basilica's roof."*

"Christ... Did they see you?" asked Wolfgang.

"No," Rupert said. *"I don't think so."*

Wolfgang relayed the information to the others in English. James blanched at the images Wolfgang conveyed.

Durant nodded, subdued. He knew that five dead men were as likely to be the end of them as five thousand.

Wolfgang looked to Durant. "What do you want to do?"

"How far to the river?" asked Durant.

Wolfgang passed the question to Rupert.

"Less than half a mile," Rupert replied.

"He says, not far, half a mile, less," said Wolfgang.

"Okay," Durant said. "We keep heading for the canal, but let's slow down enough to see any trouble coming before we run straight into it."

Wolfgang told Rupert, who nodded, ashamed, considering it dumb luck that he had not run them straight into an encounter. He looked back up the boulevard once, then he led them across the street at a steady, calm pace, eyes searching the road for predators hidden in the night.

♠   ♠   ♠   ♠   ♠

Chapter nineteen

—

LOTS

Donnie and Finbarr huddled on the ground at the tail end of the long chain of prisoners, all leashed tightly to each other by telephone wire. Finbarr was lashed at the wrists to the brown Ghurka, Juddha Jai Pandit. Donnie sat just behind them at the very end of the line.

Donnie veered close to weeping again, but he bit back the tears. His Poppa would be so ashamed if he saw his soft son now. Big Don had done everything he could to guarantee that his namesake would not be some lily-livered pansy. He had given him plenty of the rod and the belt, more than enough, he hoped, to guarantee a strong man as his heir. The sad truth was, the rod is what spoiled the child. But the rod was much easier to wield than grace or forgiveness and ten times faster in effect than patient reasoning. Donnie's father absorbed many beatings from his own papa and did not feel at all ruint by them. So, he passed the beatings on down the line to his son, ruining his boy as his own father had ruined him.

Finbarr Kelly escaped the majority of his own father's beatings. Old Man Kelly was a keen puncher in his prime, but by the time Finbarr reached the age of rebellion, Old Man Kelly was a drunk, not fast enough to catch his son and whup him. The majority of Fin's damage came at the hands of nuns and vicars. Fin looked down at his mangled appendages. The throb from where his fingers had gone missing reminded him of the mighty rappings those lost knuckles had taken from sisters, enthusiastically forcing him to learn his ABC's so he could ingest the bible. He would gladly take a thousand strikes from a ruler now if he could swap them for his lost digits.

"Wh-whatta you think's gonna ha-happen to us?" stuttered Donnie.

Fin shot him a look. He did not care even the slightest bit what was going to happen to Donnie.

"They ain't just m-mindless m-monsters," Donnie whispered. "I hear them talking to each other, just like p-p-people, but I don't get a lick of what they're saying, do you?"

"Latin," muttered Fin.

"Wh-what?" asked Donnie.

"Latin, you dumb fucker. They're speakin' fucken Latin."

Donnie did not know if 'Latin' was one of the many countries he had never heard of. He guessed it must be. He wanted to kick himself for not paying better attention in school.

"Can you speak it?" asked Donnie.

Fin looked at him. "What?"

"Latten. Do you speak the Latten language?" asked Donnie.

"I know it from church is all. I can't fucken speak it past a prayer and some fucken hymns," Fin said.

"M-maybe you could sing one of them hymns, and then maybe they'd think you're with 'em and you could at least get us some kind of chance."

Fin's glare told Donnie to shut his mouth.

Donnie shuddered. He wanted to shut up, but could not help himself. "P-please! I don't want to get set up on no cross like Jesus. That sun's coming up at some point. If we can keep alive 'til then, we got a whole day to figure some kind of way out of this. P-p-please, let's try something," Donnie begged.

Fin shook his head. "Shut your fucken mouth. You want a way out of this, sing your own fucken hymn, stand up and dance a fucken jig for 'em. Do whatever you fucken want but leave me out of it."

Donnie was stunned by the reproach. He realized then that he was truly all alone in this world. He looked up at the line of crucifixions, vanishing away into the snow and night, and the tears his father tried mightily to beat out of him fell. "Lord have mercy... Lord have mercy..."

Donnie saw the lights of torches coming through the snow-shrouded woods.

What came next would have little in the way of mercy in it.

Out of the gloom came thirty men of the 1st Centuria of Oberon's Cohort. They marched past the prisoners at a steady tramp into the field. At the rear, two legionaries pulled a German corporal along and dumped him on the ground behind Donnie, Fin, and Juddha Jai.

They took the end of the wire linked to Donnie's hands and bound the German fast to it.

Donnie recognized Adolf before Fin did. "Hey..." he whispered, "You're the blind fellow, right? You was in the tunnel. Can you see now?... Did you see where anybody else got to? Was you alone when they found you?"

Adolf gazed at him. The voice was familiar, but this was the first he had actually seen Donnie's face. It was not a face that inspired hope. Adolf turned his glazed eyes away and muttered, "Kein Englisch... Kein Englisch."

♠   ♠   ♠   ♠   ♠

Oberon Junius arrived at the batch of prisoners at the same time his returning patrol finished binding Adolf to Donnie McMaster. It only took one glance at the new arrival for him to dismiss the weakling corporal.

Oberon walked past Donnie and Finbarr, who was staring at the ground, devoutly praying that the one-eyed man would not recognize him, but Oberon paid no attention to Fin. He was intent on choosing his future home. His good eye went back and forth between Juddha Jai Pandit and the Frenchman. The Frenchman's size was appealing, but he experienced the wiry strength of the Ghurka firsthand when they captured him, so it remained a pure toss-up. Oberon assessed Juddha one last time, then dismissed him as an option. The Frenchman's intimidating mass won the day. Strength of body would be a better aid than strength of spirit.

Oberon gave a nod toward the Frenchman. A pair of legionaries grabbed hold of the big man. They cut him loose and tied Juddha Jai to the man ahead of him, then they dragged the Frenchman forward and shoved him to his knees, holding him fast.

Oberon planned to make the most of this vessel, so he walked around behind him and wrapped his thick arm around the man's neck. He grabbed hold of his own wrist and used it as a lever to choke and choke and choke until the Frenchman stopped fighting and passed out. Even then, Oberon did not let go. He collapsed on top of the man and held his grip for another minute, just to be sure, choking the life from him, carefully, casually, cruelly.

Juddha Jai watched the man who held his Khukuri commit the act. Rage burned inside him. Juddha Jai swore he would find a way to lay waste to Oberon Junius before they nailed him up to a tree. But it was an impotent threat. Just how impotent became apparent in the moments after the murder was over and done.

The Frenchman's body went still. Much to Oberon's disappointment, it soiled itself. That would have to be sorted out. Yet Oberon's spirits remained high. He knew the way was clear. When he was certain that death had the Frenchman, he let go of the chokehold, then stood and released his own spirit's hold on the one-eyed, scrotum-singed Scotsman.

While Juddha Jai, Donnie, Adolf, and Finbarr watched, the body hit the snow. The kilt blew open and stayed that way. The dead man's bare ass shone upward for the entire world to see.

Oberon Junius's life force fought its way out, exiting his nose and mouth, coalescing, then slithering across the cold ground to the still-warm, facedown Frenchman. It snaked beneath him and found his nose and throat, pouring up into the cavities, filling his lungs, kick-starting his stilled heart.

Oberon opened his eyes, and the world was in full three-dimensionality again. He sat up and brushed the snow off his thighs, nodding to himself, pleased as punch. He would never take two eyes for granted again.

Donnie was crying out loud now, horror stricken at witnessing the theft, uncertain if the French soldier's end had been better or worse than what awaited him.

Oberon picked up the Khukuri blade and spat on the one-eyed corpse, satisfied.

Now he was ready.

Oberon turned to his adjutant, Dominicus, a squat, former Scottish sergeant, who had, in his own ancient life, been Oberon's Pilus Posterior in General Varus's Roman Legions.

"We halt the crucifixions now. The General has need of these men." Oberon said.

"Yes, sir," Dominicus replied.

"Get them all into line on their knees. Time for a decimation."

In short order, Dominicus and his cohort had torches lit and were kicking and pushing all the prisoners onto their knees in a vast semi-circle. Beyond the circle of torches, the crucifixions ranged off into the snow and howling darkness.

Oberon Junius began at one end of the arced line of prisoners and counted off ten men. "Unus, duo, três, quattor, quinque, sex, septem, octo, novem, decem."

While Dominicus cut the wire that bound the ten men together, Oberon stood back and bellowed to the prisoners, "Latina? Latina? Qui loquitur lingua Romanis fecit audire?"

Fin was on his knees next to Donnie, Adolf, and Juddha Jai. Donnie looked over at him, but Fin refused to connect. Fin understood Oberon's question, and yes, he understood plenty of Latin, but he had learned in the infantry that only a dim-witted fool volunteers for anything.

Oberon tossed the Khukuri back and forth from one hand to the other, enjoying the balance and heft, excited that it was about to get wet.

"Last tempus... Qui loquitor lingua Romanis fecit audire?" asked Oberon.

A trembling pair of bound hands rose from near the center of the semi-circle. "I do, sir. I speak Latin. Et Latine loquimir."

Oberon nodded, and Dominicus walked to the man. He clipped the wire that held him and pulled the rail-thin Irish priest to his feet. Father Michael O'Toole had never quite filled out his British Army uniform. Even before the stress and horror of war cost him fifteen pounds he could not spare, the smallest jacket available hung loose about his shoulders. The collar of his order was an inch too wide at the neck, and his uniform tunic made him look like a skinny child outfitted in his father's suit coat.

"You speak Latin?" Oberon asked.

"Yes, sir. It is the language of my faith."

"You speak the languages of these men and women?" Oberon said, gesturing broadly to the prisoners with his blade.

"*Yes, sir,*" Michael said. His French was excellent and his German had improved immensely during the course of the war as he extended his ministry to German prisoners.

"*You will translate what I say,*" said Oberon.

"*Y-yes, sir. I will.*"

Oberon nodded. Dominicus grabbed Father Michael and pulled him along to the center of the semi-circle.

Oberon gave a wave to his men, and they separated the first ten prisoners from the rest, corralling them into the middle, where Michael and Oberon waited.

Dominicus had a grey porcelain jar under his arm. He conferred briefly with Oberon who nodded, then elbowed Michael.

"*You will tell them what I speak,*" Oberon said.

"*Yes, sir,*" Father Michael replied.

As Oberon spoke, Father O'Toole translated as best he could. "There will be... a lottery... Each man will draw a lot. Nine men's lots will be red... One man's lot will be white... The man with the white lot will be freed." He repeated it in French, then again in broken German.

Dominicus, lottery jar in hand, stood before the ten men who had been separated out.

"*Tell them to take their lot, but do not look at it or show it to anyone. They will all reveal their lots as one,*" Oberon said.

Michael translated.

In succession, each of the ten men's shaking hands, still numb from the tight binding, reached blindly into the depths of the jar and took a scrap of fabric, holding their fate hidden in clenched fists while Dominicus walked in front of them.

When the jar was empty, Dominicus stood back. Oberon grinned. Gambling had always brought him a thrill. Throwing dice and tossing bones with his legions over casks of wine had been one of his greatest illicit pleasures in life, and although he was not a player in this particular lottery, it brought him a jolt of joyful anticipation all the same.

Oberon raised his hand. "*Tell them to reveal their lots when I lower my fist.*"

Michael passed it on in three languages. Oberon took one more moment, hand hanging in the air, building anticipation, then he dropped his fist. The ten men opened their hands and looked at the future before them, spelled out in their palms with crumpled fabric remnants lit by the legion's torches.

A dashing German Air Corps Commander, Hermann Goering, held the sole white scrap of cloth. His hand shook and his throat was raw from tonsillitis that had sent him to the comfort of a field hospital. He had been recuperating there when Good Friday came, so when he claimed his unexpected victory, it was in a weak, rasping, raw voice. "Ich habe es. Ich habe das weisse tuch…" He held the white fabric high.

Before the war, Hermann had been in the infantry. He was strikingly handsome and strong, the cream of the German pre-war machine. Hermann had shown the initiative to start up a Bicyclist Corps in the Alsace-Lorraine, taking his men on long rides through the rolling countryside in short pants and combat boots. He used those rides to build their morale, discipline, physique, and endurance. When the war came, he pressed his joyful, obedient, handsome, strapping young men to the front, where they sacrificed their physically fit selves gladly for their courageous leader, earning him an Iron Cross, Second Class with their actions.

In the aftermath of his first combat, when his entire peloton was killed in action, Hermann found himself secretly despondent and more than a bit broken by the violence of the experience, despite the dapper Iron Cross the Crown Prince pinned on him. He went to the Field Hospital and diagnosed himself with Rheumatoid Arthritis. Seeing as how he outranked the chief medical officer, his affliction kept him off the battlefield for the time being. He silently prayed the war might end before someone decided he was not truly sick anywhere but in his head and kicked his ass end back to The Front.

One lovely afternoon during his long recuperation, a dear friend from home paid a visit and told of the joys to be found in the blossoming German Air Corps. On canvas wings with machine guns at your fingertips—that was the way to fight a war, not tooth-and-nail in the mud.

Hermann did not need much convincing. The doctors had begun making noises about his impending release back to the infantry. He applied for an immediate transfer to the Air Corps. It was swiftly rejected. There was a long waiting list for the nascent Air Force and Hermann was at the tail end of it. Many miserable German gentleman-warriors had watched the Fokkers and Albatross biplanes humming overhead, buzzing free through the breeze like Valkyries. The planes struck envy in the hearts of men stuck fighting the French and British to a standstill in the trenches, knee-deep in mud and guts. Those with connections fought to the front of the line and escaped into the sky. No space remained for sad sack Hermann Goering.

But Hermann refused to stay deterred by rejection. The maxim 'Who Dares Wins' stuck in his mind. So, daring Hermann wrote out and signed his own transfer papers into the Air Corps and sauntered away from infantry life for good. And there, above the fray in the great blue yonder, he found the joy of war returning, as he swooped down and loosed Hell on men still mired in the trenches.

Unfortunately, all that joy abruptly vanished when he found his airship machine-gunned out of the sky by a pair of French Sopwith biplanes.

Hermann limped away from the crash landing and was given an Iron Cross, First Class for his efforts. But Hermann was done with flying. As soon as he recovered from his wounds and was sent back to his unit, he curiously developed a damnable case of tonsillitis, and had his chief medical officer ground him and send him to an aid facility far behind the front lines. He had been enjoying recovery at a converted estate outside St. Quentin, while trying to figure a way to make his grounding permanent without seeming a coward, when Good Friday washed through the hospital and found him taken prisoner by dead men.

Just hours before, he had accepted the fate of crucifixion that lay before him. But now, sitting in his palm was glorious freedom. He held the white fabric aloft and rasped out again, triumphant, "Ich habe es. Ich habe das weisse tuch!"

The rest of the men in his tenth stared at the red cloth fates in their hands, the taste of hope turning to sharp bile.

Dominicus pulled Herr Goering out of the line and brought him to Oberon. Oberon took the white fabric from Goering's hand and dropped it back into Dominicus's jar. Dominicus walked the line of the other nine and accepted their damning red scraps of cloth back.

Oberon turned to Father Michael. *"Tell him to kneel."*

"Er bettet dich zu knien," Michael said.

Hermann nodded and knelt in the snow. Oberon stepped forward and thrust with the Khukuri, driving it into Hermann's belly, twisting, then ripping it back out. Hermann shrieked and fell on his side, holding his guts in, his moan of pain barely audible through his tonsillitis-ravaged throat.

Father Michael was very concerned that his translation had been faulty. He stepped back involuntarily, but Oberon grabbed him by one frail arm and held him close.

Nine of Oberon's men stepped toward the other lottery contestants. They put bayonets into their hands and stood back.

Oberon's grip on Michael tightened. He nodded toward the nine. *"Tell them that they must use their knives to free this man."*

"Wh-what?" stuttered Michael.

"Debent liberado eum."

Michael translated. "Y-you m-must f-f-free him."

The nine men stood there, bayonets in hands, surrounded by dead Roman legionaries, and they understood, but they did not want to understand.

Oberon nodded to Dominicus. Dominicus grabbed the first man in the line, a young British corporal, Charlie Haversham, lately of Devonshire, and pulled him toward Goering.

"How do you say 'et liberado eum vivere' in your tongue?" Oberon asked Michael.

"Free him… and live," Michael replied.

Oberon nodded to Dominicus again. Dominicus took Corporal Haversham's bayonet hand and pointed it toward Hermann.

"Free. Him. And Live," said Oberon in broken English.

Corporal Haversham understood. He had been through a thorough schooling in use of the bayonet in basic training. He had honed his technique on straw dummies and mastered it there, as his Sergeant taught him the art of making the 'killing face'—teeth bared, mouth open wide and screaming, face flushed red, tendon cords in the neck flexed to bulging as one shoved the bayonet home, twisted it sharply, then yanked it free.

He had murdered hundreds of straw dummies before he came to France and applied his technique on a random German fellow he met in the no-man's-land scrum. Practise makes perfect. The boy had died in agony, his wail precisely an octave higher than Corporal Haversham's battle cry, creating a harmony that haunted Haversham's dreams. Before tonight, he had done it to a half-dozen more German gents—stab, twist, yank—and to be fair, the men he had killed would have been just as happy to do it to him, but even that righteousness was not enough to force the echo of that first boy's high tenor out of Charlie's memory.

Haversham looked at poor Hermann. He leaned on the training his drill sergeant had imbued in him through relentless repetition. He breathed deep. He put on his 'killing face'. His face reddened as his war cry bellowed. He stabbed Hermann Goering in the ribs, twisted the bayonet, then yanked it free in a spatter of hot red.

The Roman Legion cheered.

Oberon let go of Michael and grabbed Haversham, pulling him into a bear hug. He kissed him on the forehead, released him and stood back, smiling. Then he spoke the Roman Legion Sacramentum as Father Michael stumbled through a translation.

"Step forward, and swear by the gods of Rome, the heads of your ancestors... and your own honor... an unbreakable oath that you will follow your commander wherever he may lead... You will obey orders enthusiastically and without question...You relinquish the protection of Roman law and accept the power of your commander to put you to death without trial for disobedience... You promise to serve under the standards of Rome faithfully, even at the cost of your life... Swear it."

Oberon looked in Charlie's eyes. Charlie glanced at Oberon's Khukuri, still dark with Hermann's innards.

"I swear..." Charlie said.

Oberon nodded and continued in Latin, then looked to Father Michael.

Father Michael spat out the translation, "You are now a soldier of Rome..."

At this, the surrounding legion of dead men erupted again in cheers. Oberon good-naturedly pushed Corporal Haversham, newly-minted Roman Auxiliary Soldier, toward his men and turned to the other eight holding bayonets in their hands.

Clear understanding of the choice that lay before them began to dawn. Oberon pointed his Khukuri at Hermann, whose throat was bleating like some mortally wounded farm animal.

"Libera. Eum," Oberon said.

There was no need for translation.

The eight men surged forward and shoved their bayonets into Hermann Goering. When they stood back, Hermann was a sack of guts in a wash of red snow, and they were living men, reborn and welcomed into a New Roman Army.

Goering's body was left empty where it fell.

Dominicus counted off the next ten men, cut them free, pulled them forward, and the lottery began again.

♠   ♠   ♠   ♠   ♠

When they got to the last ten prisoners, there were nine dead men in a red slush of snow alongside Hermann. Eighty-one new-minted members of the Roman Auxiliary, holding freshly-blooded bayonets and trench daggers in their hands, stood in formation behind them.

Dominicus and Father Michael approached with the lottery jar. Six men took their lots before they reached Juddha Jai, Finbarr, Donnie, and Adolf.

Juddha Jai locked eyes with Dominicus. Defiant.

Dominicus did not flinch from the gaze. He spoke Latin.

Father Michael translated. "He says you must take a piece of fabric to determine your fate."

Juddha Jai's eyes never left Dominicus. He reached in and took a lot. Juddha did not particularly want to die, but he definitely did not aim to live as part of some reborn Roman Legion Auxiliary. (The irony that he had served enthusiastically as a member of a different empire's Auxiliary Army nearly two-thousand years after the Roman one died off did not occur to him at the moment.) His only hope now, was that these monsters would place a sharp implement into his hands so he could bury it deep in one of the beasts before he died.

Finbarr was next. He said his prayers silently and plunged his good hand into the jar. He fished through four different bits of fabric before choosing his lot and clenching it in his palm.

Donnie bit back tears and stuck his trembling hand in the jar. "Oh, dear Lord, dear Lord, dear Lord…" He closed his fingers around a piece of fabric and pulled it back out, fist squeezed tight around his fate.

Adolf was numb. His opportunity at glory had come and gone. He had failed to kill Caitlin and Francois as he was ordered, and now his fate had arrived. He closed his eyes, prayed for divine intervention, reached into the jar and took his lot in hand.

The ten of them stood there waiting, eyes darting around the group, heady with adrenaline, more awake than they had been in days, as they walked the razor edge, death on one side and life on the other, uncertain if they would be stabbing or bleeding when the revelation came.

Oberon raised his fist. It hung there, lit by the torch's flickering warmth, snow falling heavy around it, then Oberon dropped his fist and they all revealed their palms, peeling back their fingers to see what the fates had brought them.

Donnie was the only one who cried out in joy. "Yes!" A red scrap of fabric sat in his hand.

Adolf let out a shuddering sigh of relief when he saw red fabric resting in his fingers.

Juddha Jai looked down and saw the same flash of red in his own palm. He would have the chance to make one strike. Dominicus was closest, but Oberon would be the prize. Savaging the body he had watched the dead man steal with such joy would be a measure of vengeance. If he could take back the Khukuri the monster had dishonored with his butchery of the unarmed German and use it once or twice before they overwhelmed him, even better.

Finbarr stared at his palm. His hand was shaking. White cotton sat there, sentencing him to death. He snapped his fingers back around it and looked up. But it was too late. Dominicus had seen the flash of white. Before Finbarr could move, Dominicus's hands shot out and grabbed him by the jacket. He yanked Fin toward him and twisted his hips, throwing Finbarr past him into the snow, landing him in front of his fellow lottery competitors.

Armed legionaries pushed forward from the other side, completing a circle around Finbarr's sprawled body.

Donnie stared down at his companion. He knew he could stab Fin. He felt the same as he had at the lynching his uncle took him to when he turned eighteen. He had not wanted to be the first man to hurt the black fellow, but being fourth or fifth did not seem nearly as bad. Yes, he could most certainly stab Fin. But he fervently hoped he would not have to go first.

On Dominicus's word, Legionaries began handing bayonets to Donnie, Adolf, Juddha, and the other lucky six. When all of them were suitably armed, the Romans stood back and watched.

Finbarr knelt, weeping, shaking, in a state. "No, no, no, no…" He tried to make eye contact with Donnie, but Donnie only stared beyond him into the falling snow.

Oberon entered the ring and looked down at Fin. He scanned over the nine with bayonets. Juddha Jai caught his eye. He saw a flash of contained ferocity, Juddha's defiance unmitigated by Oberon's merciful lottery, and now holding a trench dagger in his hand. That one would have to be watched, and most likely put down. Oberon stored it in his mental notebook and returned to the task at hand. He looked at Fin and made a quick appraisal.

He turned toward Father Michael and spat out in Latin as he gestured to Finbarr, "Libera eum."

"NO! Et loqui Latin! Et loqui Latin! Qui interpretari!" Fin yelled.

Oberon smiled down at Fin, shrieking up at him in desperate Latin. Oberon looked at scrawny Father Michael, then down at the Irish man. He knelt next to Fin, Khukuri to his neck. *"You speak Latin?"*

"Yes!... Yes. I can!" He spat out the Lord's Prayer as quickly as he could, "Pater noster, qui es in caelis, sanctificetur nomen tuum. Adveniat regnum tuum. Fiat voluntas tua, sicut in caelo et in terra. Panem nostrum quotidianum da nobis hodie, et dimitte nobis debita nostra sicut et nos dimittimus debitoribus nostris. Et ne nos inducas in tentationem, sed libera nos a malo. Amen!"

There was a moment of silence when he finished.

"I learned it when a boy I was. In church," said Fin.

Oberon grinned at the bad grammar. *"And you'll serve with honor in my legion? You'll translate for your fellows?"*

Fin did not understand everything Oberon had said, but he understood 'serve' and 'honorem', so he nodded his head fervently and said "Yes, sir! Yes, domine!"

Oberon plucked the white fabric out of Fin's hand and stood. He looked across the circle at Donnie, Juddha Jai, and Adolf.

Donnie was a mess, but Oberon could see a born follower as easily as Finbarr had. Once bound to him, he would be loyal to a fault.

If he brought Juddha Jai to heel, he would be a good warrior, and Oberon had brought greater men than Juddha into the Roman Legion and broken them to his will. If he could not break him, he would kill him. Until then, he had potential value.

But Adolf was a weakling. Oberon had no use for weaklings, especially weaklings that would chafe against the bit. He balled up the bit of white cotton and tossed it in Adolf's direction. *"That one. Free that one."*

Adolf tried to take a step back, but strong hands had him. He shrieked in terror as Oberon smiled, but suddenly Adolf saw Oberon's eyes glaze over, as if he had gone into some sort of stupor, jaw hanging slack, body's tension all gone, meat and bones standing there, balanced precariously, about to collapse. Adolf watched fat snowflakes land on the dead man's eyelashes and sit there. Just as Adolf thought the body would collapse, the eyes blinked, and the snowflakes fell away. Focus returned to the eyes, and he gave Adolf a second look.

"Please! I'll do anything! I know where some more are hiding! I can take you there!" Adolf cried out.

"Stop," Oberon said to his men. *"Not this one. He means something to somebody."*

Oberon turned from Adolf and looked at Juddha Jai in the torchlight. *"That one. Kill the brown one."*

There was a moment's hesitation before Father Michael translated, but Juddha Jai knew what was coming.

Father Michael raised a bony finger, pointed it in Juddha's direction and said, "He says free that one."

Juddha slashed out with his trench dagger, driving Donnie, Adolf, and the legionaries holding him, toward Finbarr and Oberon. Juddha spun with the cut and used its momentum to plant his foot and explode away, powerful legs weaned on the Himalayan snowpack and tundra carrying him into the dark woods.

Fin felt rough hands grab him by the collar and drag him up to standing.

Oberon's hot breath hit him in the face. *"If you would live, bring me that one's head. If you fail, I will find you and strip your flesh and the flesh of every one of these with you an inch at a time. Go. Prove yourself."*

Fin felt Juddha's Khukuri's handle shoved into his good hand, then Oberon pushed him away.

Fin glanced at the broad, angled blade shining in the torchlight. He looked at the trail Juddha left in the snowpack and the eight men who had been ready to murder him just moments before.

"He says we bring him that brown bastard's head, or he'll kill us all." Fin looked at Donnie. "Get a torch."

Donnie did not move.

Fin held up the Khukuri, "IF YOU WANT TO FUCKEN LIVE, GRAB A BLOODY TORCH AND COME ON!"

Donnie reached out and accepted one of the oil-soaked torches from Dominicus. The other seven men took torches from the dead men, then Fin led them at a run, in desperate pursuit of Juddha Jai.

Oberon and Dominicus watched the bobbing globes of fire disappear into the snowy woods. He silently rooted for Finbarr's victory. He hoped for the return of the Khukuri. That had been a gamble, but he wanted to give his fighting dog as much of an advantage as he could. The thrill of the game buzzed inside him. In a different age, he and Dr. Halstead would have been good friends at the dog fights. Whether in ancient Rome or modern Perth, the men drawn to that world were cut from the same cloth.

"Do you think they'll bring him back?" asked Dominicus.

Oberon shrugged. *"I don't know. But I'll wager two months of salt and gold that they do. And if they do not, we'll round them all back up and make an example for the rest on the cost of failure."*

Dominicus nodded. *"I'll take your wager."*

Oberon smiled. *"And you'll lose it. Put five legionaries with each of our auxiliary squadrons, then send them out to hunt. We'll put them to the test now, then decide which ones to execute before dawn and which ones to keep."*

"Yes, sir." Dominicus gave a slight bow at the waist, then went to incorporate his dead men amongst the living recruits.

As Dominicus shouted out to his sergeants, Oberon thought he heard something. He turned toward the woods and listened intently.

A machine gun barked again in the distance, then went silent.

♠   ♠   ♠   ♠   ♠

Adam Gillét watched the decimation. He saw Adolf singled out for execution, and for a brief moment, the responsibility of killing him to protect Francois was taken off his shoulders. Then some divine intervention turned Oberon's gaze on Juddha Jai, and chaos erupted when he ran. Adam watched Finbarr, Adolf, Donnie, and the others disappear with torches and blades, hunting the Ghurka. Adam slipped away from the legion and into the trees, cutting an arc through the snow until he saw the torches ahead of him, then he accelerated in pursuit of Corporal Hitler, knowing this would be his last, best chance to kill the man.

♠   ♠   ♠   ♠   ♠

Darren Tremaine walked Bathsheba along the railroad running beside the canal that served as the southern boundary of St. Quentin. He passed the rail yard, now blanketed in snow, where he, Brian Hugh, and Major Danforth had gathered the stores for the V-109 barge just that morning under a cold, clear, blue sky. It seemed a lifetime ago. A hundred yards past it, he saw the old stone bridge arcing over the canal and its mule paths.

When Darren reached the bridge way, he mounted Bathsheba, settling onto the cold leather of her saddle. Suddenly, the hairs on the back of his neck rose up sharp as the rattle of a machine-gun echoed in the distance. Darren listened intently. There was a second burst, then nothing. Signs of life out there. And where there was life there was certain to be death.

He kicked Bathsheba to a trot and rode across the bridge to the St. Quentin side of the canal. He turned east at the first intersection. He knew he was less than five hundred yards from the barge.

He patted Bathsheba's neck. "Come on, girl, not far, not far now. Get me to that bloody boat and you'll have earned your freedom in spades."

♠   ♠   ♠   ♠   ♠

CHAPTER TWENTY

—

BAM-BA-LAM

Black Betty lay in wait for her prey. The fallen snow on her coat blended her seamlessly into the darkness beside the silver bark of the fallen tree. It did not take long for her breath to calm, and when he passed by her hiding place, she was as near to invisible as she could be.

She hit the man in the hamstring, sinking her teeth deep into his dead flesh and tearing through the taut tendons behind his knee. He tried to turn on his good leg and slash her with his bayonet, but she leapt up, catching his wrist and putting all two-hundred pounds of her weight into it as she locked on. He fell, twisting over her back. The wrist bones cracked, and the bayonet disappeared in the snow. Betty released the mauled hand and went for the neck to finish him. He ducked his chin, and his face was caught in her teeth instead. She savaged it, then snapped her teeth lower, getting his whole jawbone in her mouth and crushing until it shattered into bits. One more vicious surge and she had the whole of his neck. She shook and bit until the vertebrae snapped and the body lost all animation. She gave it one last shake to be certain, then left the useless body in a heap, disappearing into the woods, hunting the other two that were seeking Isaiah, as yet unaware they had gone from predator to prey.

She found the second one following the false path she had laid, neck bent, absorbed in the act of tracking. She smashed into his knees from the side, tearing the ligaments cleanly. As he fell, he stabbed with his bayonet and struck her side, but it was not a clean blow. As he pulled his arm back to thrust again, she lunged, catching him at the elbow and shaking his arm back and forth until her teeth hit bone with a satisfying crunch. He tried to stretch for his fallen bayonet with his good hand, but she grabbed him by the neck and clamped on, squeezing until she heard the bones go CRACK. She left the paralyzed dead man face down in the snow and loped into the night.

Her inherited skill on the battlefield had not failed her. One man to go. It took her an hour to find him. She followed her own tracks, which she had left in wide loops leading away from Isaiah.

She tested the wind and caught the scent of burned flesh and oil that she remembered from the canal, but it was distant for now. She smelled horses, too, but again, not close enough to cause her concern. When she finally came across her third victim's scent, a spark of worry struck her. The dead man had left her trail and zeroed in on Isaiah's. In the hour she had spent tracking him, anything might have happened. She abandoned patience and ran.

He turned when he heard her coming. As she leapt, his bayonet stabbed out; but her recall of the Colosseum served her well. Instead of trying for the kill, her aim was for the tender fingers holding the blade. She knew her victim's teeth and claws could not match hers; if she separated him from his weapon, all that stood between her and ending him was time.

The bayonet hit her neck, spiking through her thick hackles. She yelped in surprise but did not slow. Her teeth hit his knuckles in almost the same instant, and she bit down hard. She felt the thumb come free cleanly in her molars. She twisted her head sharply. The pain of the bayonet's stab shot through her, but she held fast, closing her grip, feeling his pinky and ring fingers tear loose, then she let go and shook her head.

The dead man managed a step back, maimed hand dangling, then he surged forward. Betty lunged to meet him and caught him in the side. Instead of locking her grip, she snapped, twisted, and tore, snapped, twisted, and tore. When he tried to fend her off, she grabbed his forearm and locked, dropped her weight and pulled him down, applying all of her jaw strength until she felt both wrist bones dislocate. The arm went limp and Betty released, snapping up for his neck, digging in her teeth, and locking; shaking, savaging him, the hot blood from her neck wound mixing with his until he went limp as a rag doll, connection lost. Betty dropped him.

She shook her coat free of snow and blood, then she trundled along, following Isaiah's trail, tail wagging.

Intent on reuniting with her friend, she never heard it coming.

♠   ♠   ♠   ♠   ♠

Isaiah approached the dilapidated barnyard slowly. The snow-covered house and adjacent barn's roofs were sagging. The windows were all dark, and the front door had been broken off its hinges a long time past.

A howl split the night. Isaiah shot a look back. That one was close at hand, perhaps within one hundred yards. Isaiah fought the impulse to drop the cavalry sword and bring the Mauser and its grenades to bear. One trigger pull was likely to bring everything within a mile down on top of him. He weighed his options and looked at his sword. It strained credulity to think he could fight off a full-grown wolf with the dull saber.

"Fuck it. Done runnin' from your howlin' ass."

He slid the saber into his belt and unshouldered the Mauser. He checked the grenade's seating in the launcher, then flicked the safety off. He set the rifle butt to his shoulder and leaned into it, hoping he could offset what figured to be a violent kickback when he fired. He moved like a predator now instead of prey, heading back the way he had come, searching the woods for the monster hunting him.

He stepped with care, retracing his path, figuring whatever was after him was following those same footprints in his direction. Perhaps he could catch the wolf believing its supper was still running scared and beat it to the punch. And perhaps this was where it would all end.

He traversed fifty yards, then he caught sight of the big, dark canine mass sitting in his wake. He brought the bead of the Mauser up smoothly and took careful aim, continuing a slow, steady approach. If he failed to kill the wolf, he would have her to worry about, plus every dead motherfucker in a square mile. The last thing he wanted to do with his one shot was have it go wide.

His finger pressed the trigger, his shoulder prepared for the agony of a bad kick, he clenched his teeth together and started to squeeze. Then he realized that the thing laying in the trail was no wolf.

It was Black Betty.

Isaiah ran to her side. She was breathing shallowly, huffing through her nostrils. He saw her brown eyes looking up at him, and a nearly silent whine came out of her. He knelt by her and touched her side. His hand came away, warm and wet with blood.

"Aw, fuck… Fuck…" he said. His insides stirred with a pain as sharp as whatever had savaged the mastiff.

Isaiah looked up from Black Betty and scanned the surrounding trees. Whatever had done this was not visible.

"How bad you hurt, girl?"

She let out another small whine as his hands gently probed the wounds.

"Fuck…"

Isaiah set the Mauser down and fumbled Arthur's flashlight out. He carefully cupped the end and flicked it on. It flashed dully through his fingers as he did a quick appraisal of her injuries, then as quickly as he turned it on, he shut it off.

Isaiah took a breath. It was not good. That was certain. She had wounds to her face and neck, an ear torn pretty badly. The thing had gone for her eyes, but it seemed not to have taken either of them. The real concern was the slash in her side. There was no safe way to determine how deep it had gone—if it had reached organs or cut through muscle tissue; if it was mortal, or not.

The howl that broke the silent snowfall cut the night, painfully loud. Isaiah's eyes shot up, searching the night for the wolf, but still, she was nowhere to be seen. He wondered if she might be watching him from cover, gloating—her trap set and sprung, the only thing left, the joy of watching him suffer through the death of his companion; then she would come for him.

He looked down at Black Betty. He would not leave her to the mercy of the wolves and whatever else was out there. He spun the round nut on the grenade launcher and removed it from the Mauser, dropping the launcher and its load into his haversack. He thumbed the safety off, stood, and raised the rifle, taking a bead on Black Betty's forehead. Her chestnut eyes gazed up at him from the dark, and he fought tears that welled in him, drowning his vision; choking back the cry that wanted to come out of his throat.

Isaiah swung the Mauser over his shoulder. She was a big girl, but maybe he could carry her, at least as far as the farmyard, and maybe there he could inspect her thoroughly and try to bandage her up with the medical kit Arthur had pieced together in the zeppelin bunker. Or maybe he would make some kind of stand there and they could die together. Anything would be better than killing her himself.

He got his arms under her and tried to lift. Nothing doing. Two hundred pounds of dead weight was beyond his capacity to drag.

Isaiah sat back. He pulled the rifle off his shoulder and reversed it, so that the butt end was up, the barrel pointed down. He eased Betty over onto her side, ignoring the quiet yelp she made, then he furiously dug the snow out from beneath her belly. He scanned the woods again, then turned around and leaned back against her bloody ribs. He got his left arm between her forelegs and his right arm between her back legs, wrapping her torso around his neck. He linked his forearms tightly, then twisted up and to his left, swinging her hindquarters onto his shoulder. He used the momentum to swing her whole body over the top of him as he spun onto his knees. He took a deep breath, then used every muscle fiber in his legs and back to press up to standing.

His first step nearly slipped and took them both back down, but he was able to stagger forward and use his momentum to stave off disaster. He turned toward the deserted homestead, bent forward, and plowed through the snow toward it, certain that at any moment, the wolf would strike from the darkness and finish them both.

♠   ♠   ♠   ♠   ♠

Black Betty had been hustling along on Isaiah's path. The wound on the back of her neck hurt, but the dead man's stab had not succeeded in slicing muscle or reaching bone, so although it bled freely, she was unconcerned. The thrill of her victories flowed through her and she was excited to see her companion, to feel his pride in her. Then she would lick her wounds before returning to the task of seeking out his pursuers and ending them.

The she-wolf struck from behind. Betty felt the teeth sink into her hip, then her legs were out from under her. She twisted sharply, snapping her teeth on a mouthful of air as the wolf danced away.

Betty searched the trees, but the wolf had vanished back into the canopy. She moved gingerly as she spun, not wanting to test the rear leg with weight just yet. She knew that if she fell, the wolf would be on her in an instant. She stretched the leg and let her growl thunder in her chest and throat, teeth bared, as she searched for the wolf's scent. To her relief, she could move the leg. If the wolf had succeeded in cutting the tendons that ran down her hamstring, the combat would have been as good as over. For now, the only thing she was losing was blood. She settled her weight back evenly on all four legs and waited for the wolf to make the next move.

The silver beast stepped out of the darkness. Betty's teeth bared. She lunged forward and the she-wolf met her charge. Their teeth cracked against each other, then they were both snapping and biting, dodging by millimeters and snapping again, each of them trying to find purchase and rend.

The wolf caught Betty's ear and bit through the soft skin. She twisted her head and tore the ear badly, then tried to get a hold on Betty's face.

Black Betty yanked her injured ear free from the wolf's mouth, spattering the snow with blood. She saw the teeth coming for her eyes, and ducked under the wolf's attack, seizing hold of the silver scruff and sinking her canines into the fur, trying to find flesh and arteries beneath it, but the thick layers of skin and fur were all she could damage. Her teeth finally got to blood, but Betty knew it was not a mortal hold. She released and tried to get a second strike, but her enemy was too fast, and Betty felt her entire face engulfed in the wolf's mouth. Serrated teeth and stabbing canines tore in and tried to lock.

Betty snapped and bit hard. She felt flesh, hot and soft between her teeth. She locked onto it and shook her head with all her strength. The wolf's tongue tore and split. Betty heard the thing yelp and then her own head was out and free. For a moment, she was blinded by her own blood. She lunged and snapped, but hit only empty air. She felt teeth catch her in the side, and she doubled over, trying to use her paws to slash and shove the wolf away, but the wolf was enraged now, berserk, trying to gut her.

Betty yelped from the pain. She felt her end coming as the wolf worked to drive sharp canines into her soft belly meat.

Betty lashed out, desperate, but this time, instead of snapping on air, she felt the wolf's foreleg engulfed in her mouth. Her molars locked on and she squeezed tight and twisted. She felt the bone breaking and the wolf released her hold, yelping and wrenching her wounded leg free.

Black Betty kicked her weakening hindquarters and stood on shaking legs, turning with the wolf as it circled her on three legs, looking for the kill strike, her silver coat wet with blood.

Betty knew she was badly hurt. But she would not submit and hope for mercy. She knew if she turned cur and showed her belly, the monster she was fighting would not let her live on in shame. She would sink those fangs into her stomach and devour her hot innards while she still lived.

The she-wolf circled and circled, bleeding from her neck and face, holding the injured foreleg off the ground, useless. The opening for a kill strike did not come. She stopped, bared her teeth, then turned and hobbled away into the woods.

Black Betty waited a long time before limping after Isaiah. She made it half-a-mile before she collapsed. She took in a deep breath and howled for her friend to come rescue her. When she opened her eyes again, he was there; love, horror, and pity in his eyes as he knelt down and tried to save her.

CHAPTER TWENTY-ONE
—
ST. QUENTIN

Shen Su collapsed back against the tank's bulkhead. In the sanctuary of the locked down tank, he gulped water and stale ration bread. He looked to his left, where Zi Chang sat, eyes closed, breathing shallowly. In the flashlight's beams, across the tank in the machine-gun and cannon bay, he saw Li Peng's dazed eyes staring blankly. The tattered remnants of his torn leg were elevated, resting on the central engine.

"*How are you, Sergeant Li?*" asked Su.

Li Peng shrugged. "*I don't know... Dying, maybe. And you?*"

"*The same,*" Su replied.

Li Peng laughed quietly, not wanting to disturb Zi Chang. "*My mother used to say 'we die a little every day'. I think she thought that perspective would help my brothers and I embrace life a bit more.*"

"*Did you?*" Su asked.

Li Peng shrugged. "*I don't know. All I know is that if I was dying a little yesterday, I'm dying a lot today.*"

"*Yes.*" Su finished the ration bread and took a last swallow of water. He leaned forward and stretched his aching neck.

"How much gas did you bring?" asked Peng.

"Four cans' worth," Su replied.

Peng mulled the math in his head. *"We'll need more than that, but hopefully that'll get us to another cache. What did you see on the road?"*

There was a brief silence. Shen Su did not particularly care to revisit it, nor did he want to put it into words that would remove any doubt whether it was true or not. Finally, he spoke. *"You know the ranks and ranks of dead men we saw where we camped?"*

Li Peng nodded.

"I think I saw them again. But this time they weren't dead."

He told Peng about the horde of dead men chasing the three British horsemen.

Peng closed his eyes. "Fucking nightmare," he said in English. He opened his eyes and looked up at Su. He repeated it in Mandarin.

Su was quiet then for a long time. Finally, he spoke. *"What should we do, Sergeant?"* asked Su.

Li Peng shrugged. *"Sleep. Hope to wake up. Pray that Zi Chang doesn't die in the night."*

"Not dead yet, Sergeant Li," said Chang in a weak and guttered voice. *"Not yet."*

Shen Su leaned over and held the canteen up. *"You want some water, Chang?"*

Chang nodded. His face had a dull sheen to it, waxy from the dried tears and adrenal sweat that came with the pain and horror of the she-wolf's attack.

Shen Su held the canteen to Chang's lips and let him take a mouthful. Chang coughed quietly, but kept the water in.

"How are you feeling?" asked Su.

Chang smiled weakly. *"We'll see."*

Su nodded. *"Yes."*

"Been trying to figure out how our 'philosophical farmer' would manage to look at me and find the possible good in it," said Chang.

"I'm sure he would find a way," Su replied.

"Maybe. Or maybe he would say, 'What we 'see' is that you are well and truly fucked, young Zi Chang. No two ways about it."

Shen Su had no answer.

Chang lay back. *"Listen, my friend… I don't want to be whatever Number Three is now. I don't want someone else getting in my body and using it to kill you. Before that happens, throw me out and run me over with this fucking tank. Once I'm dead, I want to stay that way forever."*

Shen Su nodded, unable to find any words. When he opened his mouth to speak, a sharp "SHH," came from Sergeant Li. He was staring out of the Lewis Machine Gun slit at the front of the tank.

"Someone is coming," whispered Li Peng.

Shen Su left the canteen with Zi Chang and eased his way forward to the driver's seat.

Li Peng set his shoulder to the Lewis gun and leaned into the butt. He stared through the sights and brought them to bear on his target.

Isaiah Taylor staggered into the snow-covered farmyard, the mass of Black Betty hanging limply over his shoulders.

Peng's finger settled onto the trigger. Shen Su's hand touched his forearm.

"Wait," Su whispered.

♠ ♠ ♠ ♠ ♠

Isaiah turned and looked back to the tree line. He had not seen the wolf yet, but he felt her coming. He looked across the yard to the house and considered trying to get inside, but it seemed more likely to be a place he would be trapped than a place he could defend. Here, in the center of the yard, where he could see the wolf bitch coming and maybe get off a shot, was the only spot he could make a stand. He lowered himself to his knees and let Black Betty slide down with a whimper.

He searched the trees as he unslung the Mauser '16. He pulled the grenade launcher back out of the haversack. Shaking, freezing hands fitted the cold steel tube back onto the barrel. He twisted the lock nut tight, then fumbled in the bag for a grenade. He found a blackened-steel puck. Numb fingers took it out and slid it into the barrel, where it settled into place with a faint 'click'.

He flicked the safety off and nestled the Mauser against his shoulder. He stood and scanned the trees again, turning a full 360 degrees, past the barn and the farmhouse, half-certain that the second his back turned she would be on him.

♠　♠　♠　♠　♠

In the tank, breathless, Su and Peng watched the man set down his wounded dog and search the trees while he loaded his grenade launcher.

Peng kept him in the machine-gun reticle, ready to fire at the first sign the man had seen the snow-camouflaged tank.

As the man turned a slow circle, rifle at his shoulder, searching for his enemies, Su and Peng saw her coming. As the man faced the farmhouse, her massive silver and black form limped out of the woods behind him, silent, heading for his back.

Shen Su wanted to scream. Li Peng hesitated. The black man heard the she-wolf coming, he started to turn, too late.

Peng opened fire.

♠　♠　♠　♠　♠

Bullets ripped the air. Isaiah felt their heat burn past him. Instinct sent him sprawling flat as the Lewis Gun roared. He saw the she-wolf dance back, hit by the fire. A spray of blood scattered into falling snow, then she was spinning away, running into cover of the trees.

The MG stopped. Isaiah looked back. He saw the hidden tank now, nestled against the barn, shrouded in snow. A moment passed, then a hatch opened in the roof and a figure rose out of it.

"Holy shit," said Isaiah.

Shen Su hopped down from the hull. He approached slowly. When Su spoke, it sounded like a question, but Isaiah did not understand a word.

"Sorry, pal. Whatever you're asking, I can't give an answer," Isaiah said.

Su looked back toward the tank and shrugged. Then a voice spoke in English from the confines of the machine.

"He asked if you're alive or dead," said Li Peng.

"Shit... Good question. Pretty sure I'm alive. For the minute anyway, and glad of it," said Isaiah.

"Are you wounded?" Peng asked.

Isaiah shook his head. "No. Banged up, but nothing life-threatening, if that's what you're asking. I figure that fuckin' wolf woulda liked to change that."

"Yes… She would've."

"Obliged for you pulling that trigger, but I reckon it's gonna bring the rest of those motherfuckers this way in a hurry."

There was a moment's silence from the tank. "That does seem likely," Peng replied.

There was a flurry of Chinese from the tank. Then the Chinese man in the yard held out his hand to Isaiah.

"That is Shen Su," said the man in the tank. "If you'll help him put petrol in our dragon, we'll make a run for it."

"You got room for my dog up in there?" asked Isaiah.

"Is he alive?" Li Peng asked.

"She." Isaiah slung the Mauser over his shoulder. He knelt by Black Betty and searched for her eyes. She whined gently. "Yeah. She's alive. The second she ain't, I'll part company with you all and hunt that fuckin' wolf down myself."

There was another flurry of Chinese from the tank, then Shen Su bent down and got his arms under Black Betty's hips. Isaiah dug under her chest and together they lifted and hauled her across the barnyard to the side of the tank. The rear hatch in the sponson opened and a flashlight beam lit the entryway.

Shen Su and Isaiah hefted Black Betty into the opening, then Isaiah climbed up and pulled her the rest of the way in, settling her on the walkway, the Daimler-Knight crankcase on her left and the Hotchkiss Machine Gun and 6-lb cannon on her right.

Shen Su ducked back out into the night as Isaiah stood. He looked at the badly wounded little Chinese man who let them into the tank, then beyond him, to Li Peng behind the Lewis Gun.

"I'm Peng," said Sergeant Li.

"Y'all look a sight," Isaiah replied.

"That wolf took a turn with us," said Li Peng.

Isaiah looked at Peng and Chang's bandaged wounds. "I'll say. Tell you what, if we get through this night, I know a place we could go that's got a full-stocked hospital."

"*If*… There is a lot of power in that very tiny word," Peng said.

"For sure," said Isaiah.

"Can you help Shen Su with the petrol?" Li Peng asked.

"Yessir." Isaiah nodded.

He stepped past Betty and hopped out of the rear. When he glanced back into the tank, he saw Zi Chang carefully hold a canteen out to Black Betty with his good hand. He saw Betty's tongue lick at the water. Hope.

"Hope in one hand. Shit in the other. See which one fills up first."

Isaiah's father's voice echoed. He searched the woods for the wolf while he jogged around to where Shen Su was hefting petrol cans onto the top of the vehicle.

Su climbed onto the tank's roof and searched out the bung port, twisted off the cap, and began dumping his hard-earned gallons of gasoline into the bone-dry tank. Isaiah hefted the last two gas cans, then climbed up himself. He unslung the Mauser and watched the woods while the dragon choked down as much gasoline as she could swallow.

They were coming. Isaiah knew it in his bones. The machine gun's rattle could not help but summon the beasts. The only questions were how fast they would arrive, and how many would be in the pack when they came.

Something warm and wet hit the top of his head. Isaiah looked up and another fat drop of hot rain struck his cheek. There was a distant roll of thunder, then the last falling snow was chased down by incoming rain.

By the time he and Shen Su got back into the tank and latched it shut, rain was pouring, striking loudly on the tank's steel hull. It sounded like a Mississippi midsummer downpour hitting the corrugated tin roof of his family's home, the precedent for a massive hurricane spinning up from the Gulf of Mexico to lay waste to everything in its path.

Shen Su cranked the engine and reset the chokes as The Dragon stuttered, coughed, and roared to life. Li Peng shifted into gear and the beast leapt forward, tracks driving through deep snow that was quickly dissipating into watery slush. They rolled south onto the road, headed directly for St. Quentin.

♠　♠　♠　♠　♠

North of him, somewhere in the wooded distance, Darren Tremaine heard Li Peng's burst of machine-gun fire. It rattled a second time, then went silent. Then the hush of rain began to roll over him, pelting down into the snow-covered streets of St. Quentin. Darren looked up as the warm water began to come in earnest, quickly saturating him.

He heard a steady clop of hooves resounding through the streets toward him. He reined Bathsheba in and squinted through the curtain of falling water as Brian Hugh's riderless horse trotted into the roundabout ahead of him.

Darren spurred Bathsheba, cantering her into the intersection. Brian's bay stopped and stood on tenterhooks as Bathsheba carefully approached. The horses greeted each other, care-filled, and Darren was able to lean over Bathsheba's neck and get hold of the bay's dangling reins.

He looked north, in the direction from which Brian's horse had come. Around a bend, fifty yards distant, he saw men coming toward him on the run. Darren dropped the bay's reins and angled slightly to his left, giving himself a broad range of attack. He raised his saber, ready to strike.

♠   ♠   ♠   ♠   ♠

Rupert Fuchs heard the crackle of the machine gun. He slowed, listening, trying to get a bearing on where precisely the sound came from, but after the second salvo died away there was nothing. Wolfgang, Durant, and the others caught him. They, too, had heard the rattle of the MG.

"Lewis gun," said Renoir.

Wolfgang nodded. "Yes."

Rupert looked at Wolfgang, questioning. *"Our compatriots?"* he asked.

The warm rain began spitting down.

Wolfgang shook his head. *"It doesn't matter. We must keep going. Whoever that is, we cannot help them anymore than they can help us. One machine gun won't stop what's coming."*

Rupert nodded. The MG fire had come from somewhere to the northwest. Rupert realized it was a self-centered inclination, but he fervently hoped the sound would pull the hangmen and the German Shepherds in that direction. At least the man who had pulled that trigger was armed, which was more than Rupert could say for himself. He looked back up the snowy avenue for the dead men and their dogs, but saw no sign of them. He quickened his pace, leading Durant's band south. He knew the canal was close.

As the hot rain began to come down in sheets, Rupert saw the trail on the ground ahead of him revealed—fresh hoofprints, darkening as water filled the depressions the hooves had stamped in the snow.

Rupert waved Wolfgang to him and pointed them out. *"A horse! Perhaps we are close to the boat."*

Durant, Renoir, Jonah, and James caught them.

"What is it?" Durant asked.

"A horse," Wolfgang replied. "Our saviors from the Siegfried Line?"

"Maybe. Maybe not. Do they lead to the canal?" asked Durant.

Wolfgang translated for Rupert.

The little sapper nodded. "Ja. Ja."

The sharp report of dogs barking in the distance sent a cold razor of terror up Rupert's spine.

"Oh, shoot… Oh, Lord… Them hounds you saw are comin'…" said James Cox.

Rupert did not need to be told what to do. He ran, following the hoofprints south. The canal was near. He had no idea if it offered sanctuary or not, but as long as he had two feet and a destination he would run. His legs propelled him toward the final roundabout that he knew would take them to the waterfront itself. They were closer than he had thought.

As he entered the intersection, he caught sight of a horseman in the dark, rising up before him, saber cocked above his head. Rupert tripped, sliding to a stop in the melting snow, hands held up to ward off the coming blow.

"WAIT!" Wolfgang cried out. "We are with you! We are with you! You told us to come here!"

Darren Tremaine held his hand as he studied the men before him.

Durant, Jonah, James, and Renoir came running into the intersection behind Wolfgang and Rupert and stopped, breathless.

Darren lowered his guard. "You all made it through?" he asked.

"Yes," Durant said. "There were others with us at the tunnel, but we haven't seen them since then. Don't know if they got through or not."

Darren nodded and lowered his saber. "The barge is not far. You're being pursued?"

Durant stepped forward. "Yes."

The sounds of the dogs barking echoed again.

"How many?" Darren asked.

"Five men. Three dogs," said Wolfgang.

Darren considered it. Five men was a lot to tackle on his own. "Did you see another cavalryman?" He pointed toward Brian's mount. "The man riding this horse?"

Rupert recognized the word 'cavalryman', he turned to Wolfgang. *"A kavallerie man? Yes. I saw one."*

Wolfgang nodded. "He says he saw one."

"Where?" asked Darren.

"Dead... At the Basilica... They hung him." Rupert said.

Wolfgang's translation cut Darren deep. "Jesus wept... Right. The canal is two blocks south. The barge should be just there. Loose the starboard bow line and the breast lines, get the boiler running, and prepare to cut the stern free."

Durant nodded.

"Go," Tremaine said. "And be ready to run by the time I reach you. I can't fight five men and three dogs, but I'll try to run them in the opposite direction, then turn and meet you at the barge."

"To the canal," Wolfgang told Rupert.

Rupert Fuchs needed no more direction than that. He ran. The others followed.

Darren looked at Brian's horse. He settled Bathsheba, then quickly dismounted and approached the bay. It only took a moment to throw the flap over the saddle and unbuckle the billets from the girth. He pushed the saddle up and over. The shining leather and wool blanket splashed into the slush. Darren undid the throat latch buckles and pulled off the crown and bridle, dropping them alongside the saddle. The big horse shied away, then turned and ran, disappearing into the rain, her sleek coat lit by a burst of lightning. Then she was gone.

Rain poured down. The cobblestones were quickly clearing as the snowmelt joined the rain, turning the streets into a canal of their own. Darren climbed onto Bathsheba's back and turned her toward the coming dogs and dead men.

"Last run, girl. Last run. Get me through this and you'll be free and clear to join your mate. 'Death or Glory', eh?"

Darren tightened his grip on her reins, then kicked her flanks, charging toward the dogs and whatever was coming with them.

♠   ♠   ♠   ♠   ♠

At the Basilica, the German Shepherds had been the first to catch Rupert's scent. It overwhelmed the sharp bite of adrenaline and blood left in the air by the hanged men. The little sapper's warmth and lividity beckoned them.

Little Boy Halstead stood over the footprints in the snow holding his broken spear in one hand and Brian Hugh's long bamboo lance in the other. Harlan, Daddy Cox, Sheriff Coombs, and Big Don McMaster joined him.

Little Boy Halstead gave the dogs their command. "Seek."

The three leapt forward, running in Rupert's steps. Halstead and the others followed fast behind them.

When they discovered Rupert's tracks joining a host of others and realized there were at least five more men with him, they were filled with joy. Six more bodies adorning the Basilica would bring perfect balance to their work of art.

They heard the distant roar of Peng's MG, but it was not close enough to draw their focus from the task at hand. The warm rain began coming down. It seemed the exact temperature of human innards. Their palates slobbered at the thought of running down the men ahead of them and hanging them high.

♠   ♠   ♠   ♠   ♠

Darren Tremaine rode hard, saber stretched out before him, horse and rider moving as one. He saw the dogs first, when a steady pulse of lightning lit the flooded cobblestones. The three German Shepherds, vulpine, splashed toward him, sending sprays of water in their wake as the rain rushed down from above. Another flash, and he saw Dr. Halstead's burnt flesh and sharp spears, and the four men running just behind him, screaming for blood as they came.

Darren balanced himself with his knees and thighs as Bathsheba galloped for him one last time. They blew past the dogs, who tried to nip and turn Bathsheba, but she listened to Darren's intent and pressed on toward the real danger. His knees guided her on an attack bearing that would keep Halstead and his spears on her right.

The lightning and thunder were now a steady strobe and roar. The charging dead men faltered in their pace as the horse's true power revealed itself in galloping strides.

Darren raised the saber overhead, ignored the sharp lance points, and slashed down toward Halstead. He felt the saber bite flesh, then he was swinging it up and over his head, cutting through the rainfall, high in the saddle, coming over and down again in rhythm and finding Big Don McMaster's German body. The blow struck hard, sending Big Don face-first, skittering into the overflowing gutter.

Darren reined in Bathsheba and she wheeled effortlessly, facing the way they had come, eyes rolling with her own adrenal surge. More lightning lit the street. The five dead men were not giving chase. The two he had struck were both back on their feet and running after Durant and his companions.

Darren slid his saber into its sheathe and pulled the lance off his back. He spurred Bathsheba, and she charged after them. Darren rode like a knight in tourney, lance tucked under his arm, tight to his side. He aimed it at Big Don's back and rode him down. It speared straight through. The lance head and more than two feet of bamboo burst through his chest. Big Don grabbed hold of the shaft protruding from his sternum with both hands as he fell, wrenching it out of Darren's grasp, nearly pulling him off Bathsheba's back in the process.

Darren reined in and reached for his saber hilt, guiding Bathsheba back toward the downed man. He drew the saber and readied to finish Big Don.

The broken lance that cut down Philip Halstead hit Darren Tremaine in the kidney. He screamed.

Bathsheba felt his pain and terror. She bolted as he slumped forward in the saddle, holding tight to her mane with both hands.

Darren stayed in the saddle, forcing himself not to black out from the pain. He looked back. They had turned. They were running in Bathsheba's trail. They smelled Darren's blood now and wanted it. The other living men would wait.

Darren leaned forward, slumped over the spearhead that was sticking out of his belly, holding tight to the saddle horn as Bathsheba ran.

♠   ♠   ♠   ♠   ♠

SPQR

CHAPTER TWENTY-TWO

—

THE 13TH

Oberon Junius looked up as the sound vibrated through the air to him, muffled by falling snow. It was so familiar, its cadence and lyrics burned into his mind by tens of thousands of hours marching the Roman road, that he thought it must be his imagination at first.

"*We're men of the thirteenth,*
Rome's legions win the day,
We'll fuck your mothers, and all of the others, Piss off, clear out of the way,
You've heard the trumpet sound, the infantry advance,
Soldiers of Rome, we'll burn your home,
Our Standards in your arse…"

Then they came into view, more than three-thousand dead men, crisp in formation, six abreast on a Roman road all these men had marched upon before. They did not carry the Eagles, they had no shields or pilum, but Oberon recognized the pride stock of his 13th Legion pouring out into the field and heard the Centurions calling out, *"TARDA… AD DEXTRAM—DEPONE!*
AD SENESTRAM—DEPONE!"

The ranks behind the first began to wheel to both sides and deploy, until what seemed to Oberon's experienced eye, six full cohorts of the dead were ordered to parade rest in front of him.

"AD LAXARE!" screamed a Centurion.

There was absolute stillness. The only sounds, falling snow and burning torches.

The living men who had just been made members of the Auxiliary stood together, fear trembling through them.

Then, out of the darkness, emerging from the rows of crucified men behind Oberon, General Varus rode. He guided his horse to the center of the army, in between Oberon's men with their huddled, living-and-breathing Auxiliary, and the vast, rigid ranks of reinforcements the old woman had blessed him with, as promised.

Varus's voice echoed out, *"MEN OF THE 13TH, THE GODS HAVE SENT YOU TO ME, REBORN. YOU MADE YOUR OATH TO ME IN LIFE. YOU MADE YOUR OATH TO ROME. YOU LIVED BY THAT WORD OF HONOR AND DIED BY IT. YOU LIVE AGAIN NOW TO FULFILL THAT PROMISE."*

As he spoke, warm droplets of rain started falling. Varus looked up as it began to overtake the snow and pour down into the field.

"YOU SEE? EVEN THE SKIES ARE WEEPING WITH JOY THAT YOU HAVE RISEN! GIFTED BY THE GODS WITH A SECOND LIFE, YOU WILL NOT DIE A SECOND TIME. ALL THAT I ASK, IS ALL YOU HAVE TO GIVE."

From the ranks, someone yelled "FOR VARUS!", and the chant began, "VA-RUS! VA-RUS! VA-RUS! VA-RUS! VA-RUS!"

General Varus reveled in it, touched by ecstasy. The feel of the warm rain made him recall the beach at Anzio, the summer's hot rainstorms that came with sheet lightning he watched with his father from the comfort of their villa, as the bolts savaged the dark-blue Tyrrhenian Sea beyond the surf.

Varus raised his hand, and the chanting ceased. They settled obediently into silence. Then, the rattle of Li Peng's machine gun reached them. Varus looked to Oberon.

Oberon Junius had heard it, too. It was difficult to get a direct bearing on its location, but he knew it was somewhere to the east.

"Centurion, what is that?" asked Varus.

"I don't know, sir. But I expect we can face it, whatever in the Hells it is," Oberon replied.

Varus smiled. *"And so, it begins."* He turned to the risen men of the 13th Legion. *"WE GO FORTH NOW, LEGION. CONQUERING AND TO CONQUER!"*

There was a roar of approval, then in unison, thousands of dead men's voices cried out, *"VICTORY FOR ROME! VICTORY FOR VARUS!"*

Oberon barked out to Dominicus, *"Marching order. The whole legion and the auxiliary with them. Let's find out if our new recruits will spill blood for Rome."*

Dominicus shouted out to his sergeants, and they fell in, the dead Romans pulling the living contingent of Auxiliaries into line with them.

The war machinery began to turn in earnest. Oberon's cohort led, calling out the cadence, as the reborn 13th Legion heaved into formation and marched through the field, a living juggernaut of the dead and living, plowing toward the city of St. Quentin at a steady tramp, while the rain poured down upon them, its warm shower washing the dried blood from them, cleansing their sins, creating a blank canvas upon which they might paint sins entirely anew.

♠ ♠ ♠ ♠ ♠

Juddha Jai heard the familiar sound of a Lewis Gun barking. He paused for half a breath and reoriented toward the sound, accelerating, heart pounding, legs churning through the snow. A glance over his shoulder revealed torches in the woods; Finbarr, Adolf, Donnie, and the rest running in his trail. He lifted his knees and sprinted ahead as the rainfall caught up to him.

♠ ♠ ♠ ♠ ♠

Finbarr led Adolf, Donnie, and the other six men in their squadron at a steady jog. Their torches lit Juddha Jai's footprints. Fin paused when the machine gun erupted in the distance, but not for long. For now, the MG fire had nothing to do with him. There was only the task at hand.

Run down the Ghurka.

Take his head off.

Bring it to the Roman and buy passage to the dawn.

Then, come morning, when the sun rose up Godlike and struck the Romans down as if it was Apollo himself, Fin would make a break for it. Until then, there was only the task at hand.

The rain began. Fin saw Juddha Jai's footprints starting to vanish in the slush. Losing Juddha Jai would mean losing everything. Fin leaned forward and ran.

♠ ♠ ♠ ♠ ♠

Adolf was just behind Finbarr, ecstatic. His certain death followed close by miraculous mercy had triggered a flush of chemicals that had him high-as-a-kite, spinning and twisting in the aether as it tried to take wing, fighting the string that tethered it to some stupid, gleeful child's wrist.

The image stuck with Adolf, and he wanted to yank that little bastard off the ground by the string and listen to him scream and wail as he pulled him up, up, up into the raging storm; higher and higher off the ground until the bit of twisted cotton filament could take no more and snapped, dropping the brat down, down, down; his shriek like nails on a chalkboard until he hit, dashed on the rocks, irretrievably broken. Adolf laughed out loud at the image. Adolf did not take pleasure in much, but schadenfreude was part of his birthright, and his father's beatings and mother's disappointment had made sadism his one true joy. He watched the other torches bouncing along through the woods, held by Donnie McMaster and the others, and he let out a whoop of joy.

Donnie McMaster looked over at Adolf and let out a rebel yell of his own, infected by Adolf's enthusiasm. The pain in his hip was gone. He, too, felt the immaculate pleasure of having survived, of being resurrected now as part of something much bigger than himself, and he was thrilled. He did not care what he had to do. He had been taken in and given life, accepted into something larger, grander, and more powerful than he would ever be as an individual. He would gladly do whatever it took to remain there.

♠ ♠ ♠ ♠ ♠

Adam Gillét ran through the darkness thirty yards behind Fin, Adolf, Donnie and the rest of their little lynch mob. He had witnessed Oberon's condemnation of Adolf and was satisfied that would be the end of him, but then some divine communication had occurred, and the death sentence had been revoked. He did not know for certain that murdering Adolf would offer any real protection to Francois, but he would do what he could, while he could. He had this moment, and nothing beyond it held much promise. He knew when dawn came, he would slip away from Matheus's flesh. A knot of fear in his stomach told him that the old woman would not allow him to come forth again. When the sun rose, she would be waiting, and her revenge for his betrayal would be swift and sure, brutal and eternal. If he did not kill Adolf now, he never would. If he did not find Francois again tonight, he would not see him again. The rain began to fall. He accelerated, closing the gap with Adolf Hitler.

♠　♠　♠　♠　♠

Juddha Jai slipped in the melting snow. He slid down the grade on his backside, but kept his momentum going and rose out of it, propelling himself forward. The sound of the Lewis Gun was his lodestar. He had spent hours-upon-hours training, carrying, cleaning, firing, and killing with his own Lewis MG, and the roar and clatter were as comforting a thing as he could imagine right now. He knew he was fixed on the direction the sound came from and hoped he would not run past its position now that it had ceased fire.

The rain was coming down full bore, harder and harder, and as the snow began to vanish and stream away into the gullies and ditches, the night took on a green-black cast without the bright reflection of the snow's white blanket.

Juddha came out of the woods and splashed through fast-moving, knee-high water in a drainage ditch. He climbed up onto the cambered dirt road beyond it and ran. The MG had to be close.

Then he slowed. He smelled it. Exhaust. It was dampened by the rain, but the scent of burnt fuel was unmistakable. The road arced from eastward bound to due south, and as he jogged around the bend he saw it ahead of him, a metal beast one hundred yards distant, its steel tracks tearing a path through the mud, its engine belching smoke out of the broken exhaust pipe that ran out of its roof. Juddha found his last burst of energy and accelerated.

♠   ♠   ♠   ♠   ♠

Finbarr saw the fast-flowing drainage ditch appear in front of him and tried to clear its flow in one leap. His foot slipped on the far side and he fell into the ditch, nearly losing hold of the Khukuri. His wounded hand caught his fall. He nearly choked on the muddy water as he cried out in pain. Somehow, he clung to the Khukuri and jumped up, clambering over the bank and onto the road, forcing away the pain, his only desire now, a violent end for Juddha Jai.

Adolf and Donnie were not far behind. They were slower getting through the fast-rising water, their guttering torches barely holding a flame in the downpour.

Donnie was first onto the far bank. He tucked his dagger into his belt, reached out to Adolf, and pulled him up onto the road.

The six men behind them were doggedly pressing the pace. Adolf ran after Finbarr while Donnie stayed and helped the others up as they came. The last man got to the road's edge and Donnie reached out for him. He grasped the cold hand of Matheus Nilsen's walking corpse. Donnie felt death in the grip and wanted to let go, but the dead man held tight and pulled himself up into the dying flare of Donnie's torchlight.

Donnie made eye contact with Matheus and wished he had not. Without a word, Adam Gillét, in Matheus Nilsen's corpse, ran after Adolf and the pack.

Donnie turned and hustled after him. He drew his trench dagger, clenching it and the torch as he ran. The enthusiasm that had flowed through him had been quenched by the dead man's touch. He felt no need to catch his fellows. Let them engage the Ghurka and behead him. Donnie would arrive just in time to stand witness, and thus not have to partake in the slaughter. On top of relieving him of responsibility for killing the man, being last to the fight would guarantee that he would not be the first to die. That was more than enough for Donnie.

♠   ♠   ♠   ♠   ♠

Shen Su heard a thump on the roof. He let out a yell of warning that reached Isaiah and Li Peng at the front of the tank. They looked back. In the glow of the flashlight, they saw Shen Su pointing at the ceiling.

"It's on the roof! Something's on the roof!" Shen Su hollered.

Zi Chang lay beside Black Betty in the right-hand gun sponson. He was staring up, terrified, as something moved above him toward the front of the tank.

Li Peng released the accelerator and the metal treads ground to a halt. Over the sound of the engine's idle hum, they heard the boot steps coming forward, then there was a hammering at the ceiling hatch and a cry of "HELP! HELP! LET ME IN!"

Isaiah and Li Peng shared a glance. There was nothing said. Isaiah gave the Lewis Gun a twist and pulled it free from the gun port. He leaned back and aimed the MG upward at the hatch. Li Peng turned the latch. He pointed his flashlight at the steel plate as it was pulled open. Rain poured in. A thoroughly drenched, dark-brown face stared down Isaiah's barrel at them.

"Please… Let me in. They are coming," said Juddha Jai Pandit.

♠　♠　♠　♠　♠

Li Peng plowed the tank along the road, through the ruins of St. Quentin, the Daimler-Knight engine roaring.

Isaiah knelt next to Juddha Jai in the sponson. Juddha was bent forward, elbows on knees, beneath the six-pound cannon, catching his breath. Zi Chang passed his canteen to Isaiah, who handed it to Juddha Jai. Juddha took a deep swallow and gave a nod of gratitude.

"HOW MANY?" Isaiah hollered over the engine.

"HUNDREDS," Juddha Jai replied. "Bloody hundreds of them…"

"HOW CLOSE?"

"CLOSE. I DON'T KNOW HOW CLOSE, BUT CERTAINLY CLOSE."

Isaiah turned the flashlight toward Black Betty. She lay on her side, her coat a bloody mess, but he saw her brown eyes looking his way. Still alive. For now.

Isaiah gave her a gentle caress, then eased his way forward and sat back into the co-pilot seat.

"How many did he say?" Li Peng asked.

Isaiah shook his head. "Too fucking many." He scanned the tank with the flashlight. He saw the burlap sacks that held pairs of Lewis Gun drums. Above them, hanging in a holster was a Verey-Light flare gun and a box of 12-gauge magnesium shells.

"How close are they?" Li Peng asked.

Isaiah unholstered the Verey-Light and grabbed the box of shells. "About to find out."

In front of the tank, there was a huge flash of lightning. Isaiah and Peng saw the wide span ahead of them, roiling water spraying up on either side, all caught in the bright white strobe of plasma.

The St. Quentin Canal. A stone bridge arching over its breadth.

"Well, shit… That ain't bad news. Long as there ain't a hundred setting on the far side, we might keep 'em off-a us," said Isaiah. He turned back to Juddha Jai. "HEY. YOU RATED ON A LEWIS GUN?"

Juddha Jai nodded. Isaiah grabbed a pair of ammunition drums and passed them to Juddha. Juddha slung them around his neck. Isaiah followed the drums with the Lewis Gun itself.

"COME ON. WE'RE ABOUT TO EARN OUR SPOT IN THIS MOTHERFUCKER," said Isaiah.

Isaiah dumped the box of flare shells into his haversack and picked up the Mauser grenade launcher. He unlatched the roof hatch and pushed it open on its steel hinge. Rain rushed in. Isaiah followed his Mauser up into it, disappearing through the black rectangle. Juddha Jai passed the Lewis Gun to him, then followed.

The hatch slammed shut and Li Peng gassed the tank toward the bridge that spanned the St. Quentin Canal. Lightning flashed again, and through the view port he saw the roar of whitewater where the sudden influx of snowmelt and downpour had swollen the canal high over its banks and was striking the bridge in a violent torrent, spraying up and over its side where the cutwaters met the support arches, and onto the roadway itself.

The bridge was only fifty yards away, but as the tank crept toward it, slow and steady, it felt like a thousand miles.

♠   ♠   ♠   ♠   ♠

The sky over Isaiah and Juddha Jai was something out of a nightmare. Above the downpour, the towering clouds strobed with internal lightning bursts revealing massive, tumbling, grey-and-white structures. Sudden, terrifying, silver veins of lightning stuttered back and forth between the thunderheads. A bright bolt ripped down through the sky and into the ruins of St. Quentin with a crack that rivaled any heavy artillery. Its echo shook the air.

"Fuck," Isaiah said, as he pictured the next strike hitting the steel tank's hull full-on and flash-frying all of them.

The rain was near blinding. Isaiah imagined this was what it would feel like to round Cape Horn on some Spanish man-of-war, mainsail blown full, sheets overhauled.

He moved carefully along the centerline of the tank, hyper-aware of the massive treads grinding forward on either side of him. Slipping and falling, getting an appendage caught up in the steel treads, was a certain way to a violent end. He could picture the tread seizing his boot, yanking him forward, dragging him the length of the tank, then pulling him down and under, only to come back up again at the rear, a raw, meaty mess.

Juddha Jai came just behind him with the Lewis Gun.

Isaiah reached the ass end of the tank. Sitting on stanchions, across the width of the tank, was a wooden unditching beam. Isaiah settled behind it as Juddha joined him. Isaiah shielded the rain with his hand, staring back into the storm. He saw them. It looked like a handful of fireflies, bobbing through the black night, barely glowing in the rain. Isaiah knew they were torches borne by men on the run.

Juddha rested the Lewis Gun bipod on the wooden beam and checked the action. He took a bead on the torches.

"HOLD ON A MINUTE. GONNA GIVE THESE MOTHERFUCKERS SOMETHING TO THINK ABOUT."

Juddha nodded.

Isaiah unslung the Mauser. He leaned it against his shoulder and sighted over the grenade launcher. He thought about Arthur's advice on the kickback. Fuck. He slid the butt end under his arm and set it against the lip of the rear roof hatch.

He aimed toward the middle of the flickering orange globes and pulled the trigger. *BAM!*

The bullet spun through the rifled barrel. It struck the grenade dead center and kicked back hard, slamming painfully up into Isaiah's armpit as it drove the metal puck out of the launcher.

The grenade hurtled back through the rain, arcing gently as it began to shed momentum, pulled by gravity back toward the earth. When it struck in the midst of the men hunting Juddha Jai, it exploded in a sudden, violent, orange burst of shrapnel.

♠   ♠   ♠   ♠   ♠

One moment Finbarr was running flat out. The next he was face down in saturated mud, spitting gritty dirt and rainwater, ears ringing from the explosion.

He looked behind him and saw a torch lying on the cobblestones, sputtering out to blackness. Lightning struck somewhere close by, and he felt the vibration of the thunder shudder through him. The flash lit up his companions. The image only lasted a quarter second, but it stayed in his mind. Adolf was huddled in a ball behind Finbarr, screaming. Fin could not tell if he had been hit. Six of his men were definitely dead. Mouths and eyes open and frozen, bright blood where their bodies caught shrapnel that might otherwise have found Finbarr. At the rear of the strewn bodies, Donnie was on his hands and knees, forehead pressed against the ground.

Fin looked ahead to where he had last seen the tank. He saw a thick muzzle flash. Time stood still, then a magnesium flare burst in the air and showered burning silver down onto him. He saw another muzzle flash from the tank. He heard the bullets cut the surrounding air, then the sound of the Lewis Gun roaring in Juddha's hands brought Fin fully back to the here-and-now.

Fin dove into the drainage ditch beside the road and was immediately yanked downstream by its rip, as the flooding ditch tried to pull him under. He reached out instinctively with his ruined hand and screeched in pain when the nerves reminded him there was nothing remaining but raw stumps where fingers had been. He managed one deep breath, which pulled in nearly as much rain as air, then the current dragged him under and bounced him along the drainage ditch toward the canal, bridge, and tank. Fin desperately wanted to cough the rainwater out, but he knew from his brother's tutelage in Kildare's canals that the moment you created a vacuum, water would try to fill it, and once your lungs were topped with liquid, you were good as dead.

He spun his body so his legs were ahead of him. He dug his heels into slick mud, slowing his momentum, then pushed himself up, breaching the surface. He managed to get half a breath in, nearly choked on it as he stifled a coughing fit, then his feet lost purchase and he was dragged under again.

His rear end and lower back bounced off something jagged, but he kept his scream inside his head. He stabbed out with the Khukuri and dug it into the clay, holding fast to the hilt as it found purchase. Fin pulled with all the remaining strength he had. His body stretched long, sucked by the flow of water. He twisted over and dug his toes into the clay, then, half a step at a time, he fought his way back toward the Khukuri handle he had imbedded into the bank.

When he reached it, he stood, yanking the blade out of the ground and dragging himself out of the central torrent, fighting up the side of the culvert and onto the berm above it. He fell forward into the road.

He saw the tank, twenty yards from him, a third of the way across the bridge, spitting bullets back toward his men. Fin dodged the rounds and lost the Khukuri as he scrambled back into a narrow sanctuary against the bridge's parapet. He lay on his side, pressed against the cold, wet, stone wall, coughing, weeping, staring up at sheets of rain and a strobing sky, all hope lost.

When Isaiah's grenade detonated, Donnie McMaster's decision was made for him. He had been comfortably running, last in line, just behind Adam. He heard the tank's engine and wondered what the heck it was. He had seen plenty of new-fangled gas-powered vehicles in his brief lifetime and had developed a love for all things mechanized by internal combustion, but this was the loudest one he ever heard.

Lightning flashed, revealing the rear end of the green metal monster and its fast-spinning steel treads. Donnie's breath caught. He wondered what goddarn good a bayonet would do against something like that, and his wondering mind slowed his pace. The seven men who had been just barely ahead of him quickly gained ground on Fin and Adolf, and Donnie found himself slowing to a jog, far at the tail of the ragged column.

Dumb fucking luck was, again, Donnie McMaster's finest pal. Isaiah's grenade went off at dead center of the group. Donnie skidded to the pavement. The six men in the middle were killed instantly. Matheus Nilsen's corpse, directly in front of Donnie, and the men just behind Adolf and Fin took shrapnel in their fronts and backs, respectively, and went down hard.

Donnie was completely untouched. He sat up, in shock, checking his chest for blood, blinking in the rain. He saw the flare explode above Fin and watched the Irishman slide off the road, disappearing under a torrent of white and brown water, dragged off down the ditch toward the canal. He saw Adolf on the ground, weeping. Then machine-gun bullets were skipping in as fast as the rain.

Untouched Donnie wanted to remain 'untouched'. He dragged himself up and across the road, stumbling to his feet. Another flare burst above them. Adolf's rolling eyes caught his, and then they were both up and running for the cover of a side street that angled northeast, away from the tank and its murderous roar.

♠   ♠   ♠   ♠   ♠

Donnie ran through the pouring rain, leaving the dead, the tank, and the machine-gun bullets behind, feet pounding on slick cobblestones.

After what felt like a mile, but was more likely a quarter of that distance, he slowed, wincing on his bad hip, winded. All adrenaline gone, the pain had returned, and he was ready to surrender. He bent at the waist and tried to catch his breath as Adolf caught him.

Adolf's breath was heaving, too. He squatted and planted his palms on the cobbles. He wanted to weep again, but he imagined what his father would say and choked the rest of his tears back down.

"Did… Did anybody else make it?" Donnie stammered.

Adolf did not understand a word Donnie had uttered. "Kein Englisch! VERSTEHEN SIE? KEIN ENGLISCH!" Adolf screamed.

Donnie shot him a sharp look. He did not like anyone to scream at him, no matter what language they were speaking. There was a long moment of silence between them. Rain poured. Thunder rumbled. Then the Lewis Gun began barking again, echoing through the streets. Donnie and Adolf straightened as one and ran, pressing on in the opposite direction of the gunfire.

♠   ♠   ♠   ♠   ♠

Adam Gillét felt the stab and heat of the shrapnel balls as they burrowed and burned into his dead skin. He slipped on the cobbles and went down hard.

It took him a moment to process the injury, and he felt like he was standing on the lip of a bottomless chasm, preparing to lean out over it until he reached a point of no return, then he would be falling, swan-diving into it, rocketing downward until his momentum reached a feverish pitch and he began to burn alive, losing his hair and eyelashes, his eyelids peeling back and giving up their precious orbs, his skin charring and stripping away, his extremities following, arms and legs blackened nub ends, as the friction of his skin against air turned him into a screaming, white-hot ball of plasma.

Adam's eyes shot open. Not yet. A flare burst, then the Lewis Gun began chattering from the tank. He scanned the wreckage of Finbarr's squadron. Adam saw Finbarr stumble and drop into the ditch. The torrent sucked him under and away, vacuuming him toward the bridge and the flooding canal. The two men who had borne the brunt of the shrapnel were ruined, legs hanging on by a thread, one completely severed by the combination of ballistic metal balls and TNT. The other men Isaiah's grenade struck were bleeding out into the gutters, adding to the deluge that was trying to drown Finbarr Kelly.

He saw Adolf and Donnie stand and dodge into the cross street to escape the MG fire.

Adam pressed the wet cobbles and stood. As he began to run, an MG round smacked him in the thigh, knocking his legs out from under him. Adam pushed himself up again. There was no pain, but he could tell that something in his hamstring had been severed by the bullet. When he got to his feet and fought toward the side street, his gait was an awkward limp. He bent forward and ran as fast as his broken body could carry him, in desperate pursuit of Adolf and Donnie.

♠ ♠ ♠ ♠ ♠

As the tank's treads spun them across the bridge, Juddha Jai checked his fire. Isaiah reloaded the Verey-Light and shot another flare toward the men they had killed. He shielded his eyes, but even under the flare's glow, with the sheet of rain and the distance, it was hard to discern whether or not any of them were still moving.

The tank roared across the bridge, tearing up the stone roadway as it went.

Isaiah leaned over to Juddha. "BACK IN A MINUTE," he yelled.

Juddha Jai nodded and kept his focus on the path behind them.

Isaiah slung the Mauser and stuck the Verey-light pistol in his belt. He half stood and crept back toward the nose of the tank.

Lightning flashed and struck nearby. The *BOOM* of its thunder crack vibrated through him and he smelled its bittersweet ozone scent in the air. He wondered if getting struck by lightning killed you so quick that you did not feel anything. He had seen men shot straight through the brain pan with beatific looks on their dead faces; they never saw death coming and never knew she had paid a call. Isaiah thought lightning might do the same. He could definitely think of worse ways to go.

More lightning flashed. Below the bridge span he saw what should have been calm water in a perfectly ordered canal instead flowing at frighteningly violent speed, high above the manmade banks. At the cutwaters, spray exploded up and over the tank. Isaiah wondered how long the bridge would hold. He imagined the span suddenly collapsing out from under the tank's tonnage and sucking them all under. All things considered, a lightning strike would be the more merciful way to go.

Isaiah reached the forward hatch and pulled it open. He slid in and shut the hatch plate.

"We got all the ones I could see," Isaiah said.

Li Peng nodded, pale in the beam of the flashlight, eyes intent on the dark road ahead. He had looked down into the flooded canal. He felt the bridge's give as they crossed and imagined its collapse as Isaiah had. When they rolled onto solid ground on the far side, Peng realized he had been holding his breath nearly the entire time. He clutched, braked, and released the accelerator, then shifted into neutral.

"Where now?" asked Peng.

Isaiah mulled it a moment. "Y'all got plenty of rounds for them big guns?"

Peng nodded. "A full compliment."

"Let's put those motherfuckers to use, then. That canal's a goddamn flood and worse by the minute. Ain't a swimmer alive or dead that could stroke across. We drop that bridge, we maybe buy some time."

Peng nodded. He clutched and shifted, then banged hard on the tank hull with his wrench. Shen Su pulled his lever. The tank began to spin in a tight circle.

Isaiah glanced down at Black Betty and Zi Chang. Both seemed to be hanging on. It may have been by a thread, but the thread had not yet been cut. Isaiah opened the hatch and pulled himself back up into the dark rain.

Peng finished the one-eighty. The dragon's artillery guns aimed directly back at the span it had just slogged across.

♠　♠　♠　♠　♠

Donnie and Adolf covered another half block, then slowed to a spent walk. Donnie's mind was fractured. He did not know what to do. One simple job. All they had needed to do was catch the darkie, kill him, bring back the head, and they would have all gotten to keep on living. It could not have been a simpler lifesaving chore and they had failed. And now that Finbarr was gone, how would they explain the failure to the Romans? Donnie knew the price of failure. They were definitely going to crucify his mother's only son. He swallowed hard and started to cry. He did not think there was any way Adolf would notice in the darkness and rain.

He blinked away the tears, and in that instant, he was blindsided, struck squarely in the ribs. His feet spun out from beneath him, and he hit the street with a grunt of pain. He rolled over onto his back and shrieked, trying to push the man on top of him away.

Lightning burst above them and Donnie ceased struggling when he saw the face of the little German Sapper.

Rupert Fuchs stared down at Donnie, as surprised to be on top of the American dispatch rider as Donnie was to be on the ground.

More running footsteps echoed off the wet pavement. Donnie looked up as lightning forked across the sky. Durant was first to enter the square. Wolfgang, Jonah, Renoir, and James Cox followed.

Another jagged burst lit the intersection again.

"Holy Crow!... Donnie?!" cried James Cox.

♠　♠　♠　♠　♠

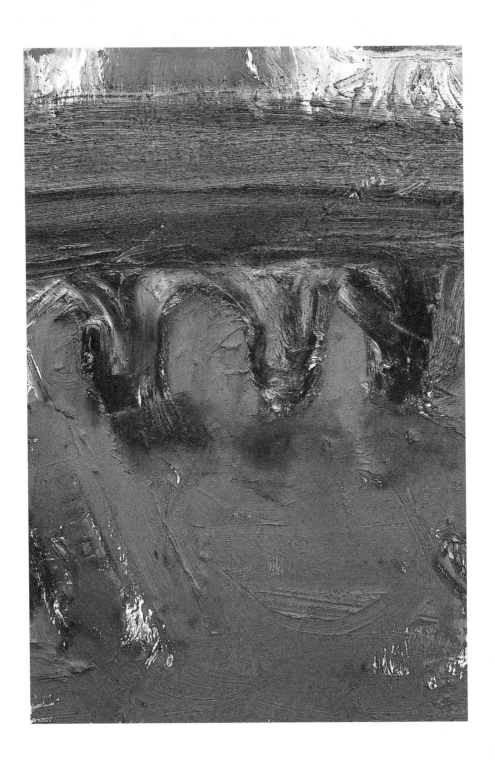

CHAPTER TWENTY-THREE

THE BRIDGE

Hot rain fell, loudly striking the canopy of trees, spattering down onto Caitlin. When it hit her, her first thought was that it was blood. She wiped her face and it came away clean. Not haemoglobin, just rain. She stopped and caught her breath. She stared up as the water poured down, saturating the snow on the branches and sending balls of slush and ice plummeting to the earth.

She looked back as Francois caught her. A dozen torches entered the field behind them, following a woman on horseback, no more than two-hundred yards away.

Caitlin grabbed Francois and pulled him along. She had to shout over the downpour. "Come on! The rain will ruin our tracks. If we can lose them now, they won't be able to find us in this mess without bloodhounds!"

Francois nodded. Here was hope. Caitlin took his hand and ran south.

The storm of lightning above them, crackling in the air, seemed to build in the clouds as it danced and growled inside them, spreading out in overlapping staccatos, then alternating between pulling bolts upward from the ground, and hurling them back to the earth with vicious cracks.

The Lafayette Artillery Dump opened up before them, its big guns and ordnance gleaming in the fresh wash of water that stripped them of their snowy cover.

Caitlin and Francois ran along the pathway that cut through the stacks. For a brief moment, Francois recalled his time with the Imbangala, and the massive firestorm he had unleashed with the grenades in his haversack. He imagined the 30,000 shells here detonating as one. There was enough TNT in the piles and rows to destroy a city, but he had no means to begin the ignition. Attempting to harness one of the artillery pieces would take half-a-day, and at this point, he did not believe they had half-a-minute to spare; the dozen chasing them with torches were on foot, but he had seen the woman on horseback, and recognized her from the Riqueval Canal. He could imagine the ending already. The rider would run them down. The dozen would feast on whatever remained.

They exited the ammunition park at a dead sprint. Then they heard it. The hollow *BAM!* of Isaiah's grenade exploding. A long moment passed, then there was a Lewis Gun's thunder.

"THIS WAY!" Francois yelled. He squeezed Caitlin's hand and led her south, changing course and running toward the gunfire.

They covered a thousand yards, then they heard the clatter of hooves coming. Caitlin pulled Francois' arm and he followed her as she cut right, leading him into a tight alleyway. The rain poured off the eaves of roofs left in shambles by the German invaders. Caitlin and Francois froze and watched the alley's mouth. The rider cantered past, a tympani of steel-shod hooves smacking cobblestones. Caitlin grabbed Francois and led him, tearing away down the dark alley.

A burst of lightning revealed a lane ahead opening up. As they neared the intersection, another strike lit the swollen, raging water of the canal right before them, running high above its containment and onto the adjacent path.

The mule path was already half-flooded. As they came out onto it, more lightning played across the sky, revealing pieces of the street itself, undermined by the violent wash of water, already sagging and being sucked into a canal that had not been built to withstand a surge of this magnitude.

The resounding roar of the MG drew their eyes. Less than a hundred yards east of them, lightning illuminated arches supporting a stone bridge, the wet, dark-green steel of the tank rolling across it, and the silhouette of the MG's trigger man, perched atop its rear, firing in bursts back across the span.

Caitlin took one look back down the alley. She saw the woman on horseback turn into it and begin to gallop toward them.

"COME ON!" she yelled.

Caitlin let go of Francois' arm and ran, sprinting toward the bridge with Francois just behind her.

Chunks of the mule path collapsed and fell away into the burgeoning flash flood. The water roaring past and the crashing thunder drowned the MG's report, but Caitlin still saw intermittent muzzle flashes as the tank reached the other side. Its treads locked. There was a pause, then it spun in a circle, until it was facing back the way it had come.

As they reached the stone stairway that climbed up to the bridge, Caitlin shot a glance back. The woman on horseback had slowed, moving with care on the collapsing road. A lightning burst showed the dozen men behind her running in her horse's wake. Caitlin put her head down and surged up the steps, arms pumping, breath heaving.

She heard the flood of water before she saw it. The drainage ditch that nearly killed Finbarr had been a gutter only twenty minutes past. Now it was a growing eight-foot-wide span of white water, racing alongside the road toward the bridge, blasting its flow down into the canal. Caitlin hesitated, but Francois grabbed her hand.

"COME."

He stepped into the water. It nearly ripped his legs out from under him, but he found a piece of cobblestone in the mud and planted his foot on it. He put both hands on Caitlin's waist, then twisted and hefted her, throwing her across, where she tumbled onto the roadway.

"GO," he said.

Then Francois stepped back out of the drainage ditch and drew his cutlass, turning to face the Red Maiden and her men as they climbed the stairs toward him.

♠ ♠ ♠ ♠ ♠

Isaiah was behind the trigger of the left-hand 6-pound artillery cannon. Juddha Jai was stationed across the tank from him at the cannon on the right.

"Aim for the cutwaters!" yelled Isaiah.

Juddha Jai nodded. He squeezed the trigger and the entire tank shook and ached from the deafening *BOOOM!*

The shell exploded in a gout of orange flame, striking the bridge, sending shards of stone scattering down into the canal. While Juddha Jai ratcheted the brass out and slid another into the breach, Isaiah took careful aim at the center of the span with his own cannon. His finger settled on the trigger and he steeled himself for the report. A massive bolt of lightning lit the night.

Isaiah saw them.

Caitlin stood on the far side of the bridge, looking back to where Francois, cutlass drawn, had placed himself in front of a woman on horseback and her tribe.

"Fuck…" said Isaiah.

Before Isaiah could yell out, Juddha Jai pulled his trigger a second time, and his cannonade hit the cutwater again, ripping a piece of the center arch away.

"HOLD ON! HOLD ON!" Isaiah yelled.

Juddha Jai barely heard him, but he glanced over and held his trigger.

"My friends! They're out there! Wait 'til I get them across!"

"What?" asked Juddha.

"Two of my friends, they're on the other side. Hold up a second!" hollered Isaiah.

"Quickly!" yelled Li Peng.

Isaiah grabbed the flare gun and the Mauser. He spun the grenade launcher off the rifle's barrel, shoved open the hatch, and leapt up and out into the rain.

Finbarr Kelly lay in the shelter of the bridge's parapet, huddled in a ball, barely hidden from view of the tank. He heard the explosions and felt the bridge shudder from Juddha Jai's assault. The guns went silent. Fin knew he had to get up and run, but he imagined the machine gun finding him the second he rose and cutting him down. Then he imagined escaping from the tank's fire only to walk into the arms of the Romans, empty-handed and proven useless. He would be crucified, and more, before dawn. Lying on the bridge until the tank took the choice away from him did not seem like the worst possible option.

Fin looked back as lightning rent the sky. He was shocked. Caitlin O'Leary was not twenty feet away from him, easing slowly onto the bridge, staring back the way she had come.

Suddenly, *POP!* A Verey-Light flare burst above her, bathing all in silvery magnesium light.

Caitlin spun toward the flare. She saw the flash of the Khukuri blade laying on the wet cobblestones where Fin had dropped it. She reached down and grabbed the heavy knife, holding it in front of her, warding whatever was coming out of the darkness over the bridge toward her.

Fin's mind—so elementally gifted at cold calculation—did the math. Perhaps he could return to the Romans less than empty-handed. Perhaps the gift of Cait would be enough to purchase his life.

"CAITLIN!" he yelled.

She saw him, soaked and dirty, feral and bloody; she shied back.

"It's me, Cait! It's Fin!" He stood and ran to her, slowing as he approached, hands up, offering peace.

"Fin?"

"Aye!" He tried to give her his most charming smile, but with his hollow cheeks and sunken eyes, there was little charm to be had. "Come with me! Those devils in that bloody tank will blow you to bits! I know a safe place!" He grabbed her hand and pulled her toward him. He felt her resistance. He knew he could overcome it by force if he had to. "Come on, girl. It's me!"

"Francois! We have to try to save him!"

Fin looked at the flooding mule path. He saw the clash of blades and heard the cries as Francois fought the demons. Fin nodded. "Give me the knife!"

Caitlin held the Khukuri out and Fin ripped it from her hand. He shoved it in his belt then wrapped his hand firmly around her wrist.

"You've got to come with me, Cait. I know a safe place!" Fin said.

There was a roar of gunfire, and Fin dodged back to the parapet, dragging Caitlin down with him. When they looked for the source, they saw a man coming across the bridge, firing from the shoulder, past Fin and Caitlin.

In the glow of the falling flare, Caitlin recognized Isaiah Taylor's scarred face, moving with determination, loosing rounds toward the scrum of battle on the stone stairway behind her.

ALL THE DEVILS ARE HERE

♠ ♠ ♠ ♠ ♠

The Red Maiden waved Egil and Colburn up the steps. *"Take him,"* she commanded.

They had not taken anyone in some eleven-hundred years. The hunger to fight the man before them made their mouths water.

Francois stood his ground. As the first of the Vikings charged, he thrust his cutlass toward the man's face. The blade sunk into Colburn's cheek and was out again in a flash, slashing into his sword arm and nearly severing it. Egil slowed his approach as Colburn backed away, switching his infantry saber to his left hand.

As Colburn shrieked his battle cry and charged back up the stairs, Isaiah's flare exploded above them, bathing them all in its white fire.

Francois' blade slashed Colburn across the belly and knocked his sword aside. As they crashed into each other, Francois twisted his hips, throwing Colburn past him, into the rushing water of the ditch. The torrent yanked him under, sucking him away, throwing him over the side of the ditch and into the canal. The rip of the water pulled him down and he vanished beneath it.

Francois spun back toward Egil, who was coming fast. He caught the first blade and turned it aside with a clash of steel, then something sharp stabbed out and he felt a dagger's point strike his hip bone. Before he could stab again, Francois punched his pommel into Egil's mouth, cracking teeth and jawbone. He pushed the Viking backward, barely escaping the dagger's second thrust, and swung down with his cutlass. The razor-sharp blade plowed halfway through Egil's neck. Francois wrenched the cutlass free and shoved Egil again, sending him tumbling down the steps toward his fellows.

Francois eased up, testing the strength of his injured hip. He watched the Red Maiden's men, spreading out to hit him en masse. Francois took a calming breath and flexed his sword hand. He would not go down alone.

Suddenly, the Red Maiden's mount, Joshua, shrieked and reared up as Isaiah's bullets zipped through the air, striking him in the chest and neck, immediately followed by the semi-automatic rifle's report. Joshua let out a keening whinny of pain, eyes rolling. The Red Maiden tried to hold on, but he bucked again and threw her off, forehooves kicking wildly into the band of men around him. When Joshua reared again, his back legs slipped out from under him and he collapsed sideways into the rushing canal, dragged downstream and under, disappearing in the roiling spray.

♠ ♠ ♠ ♠ ♠

Isaiah pulled the Mauser's trigger, but there was no report. He ejected the cartridge magazine and grabbed a replacement from his haversack as he stalked forward.

Lightning struck, and he saw the Red Maiden and her men, peppered by his first fusillade, shoring up their ranks and advancing up the stairs toward Francois.

Isaiah saw Fin and Caitlin huddled by the bridge. "HEY! GET TO THE TANK! WE'RE GONNA BLOW THIS BRIDGE TO SHIT!" he yelled.

He slid the magazine home and wriggled the bolt, but it did not want to slide. Arthur Keith's warning about the Mauser's poor quality in service echoed in Isaiah's head. He muscled it, and the bolt slid, bringing a round into the firing chamber.

"GO ON!" Isaiah ran past Fin and Caitlin, rifle raised, trying to separate his targets from Francois. He opened fire again, sending rapid-fire rounds spinning past Francois, into the Vikings.

Isaiah glanced back and saw Fin holding fast to Caitlin, setting her between them.

"No!" said Fin. "There's a safe place on this side! If you follow me, I'll take you!"

Isaiah shook his head. "Ain't a safe place nowhere close on this side of the river! Get to the tank!"

Isaiah turned to the mule path and emptied the magazine across the flooded ditch. "Francois! Get across! Get across!" he yelled, but Francois could not respond or disengage, he was fighting for his life.

Isaiah ejected the spent magazine and reached for a replacement, pulling it from his haversack and shoving it home. He forced the slide again and brought it up. He fired once, then the rifle seized. "FUCK!"

Isaiah heard Caitlin cry out. He turned. The Khukuri was cutting the air, singing toward his head. He raised the Mauser an inch, and it caught the blade squarely on the steel receiver. The blow knocked him sideways, and he fell to the street, scrambling to bring the barrel back up before Fin swung a second time.

"NO!" screamed Caitlin. She tried to grab Fin's arm, but he threw his elbow back, catching her squarely in the face. The impact sent stars shooting through her vision as she went tumbling to the pavement. She tasted the warm, salty wet of her own blood pouring from her nose and mixing with the rain as she fought her way up to her knees, trying not to pass out.

When Fin turned back toward Isaiah, he found him back on his feet. The Mauser was pointed directly at his face. "You a dead man, motherfucker."

Isaiah worked the bolt once. He squeezed the trigger. Nothing. Fin charged, Khukuri raised. Isaiah swung with the barrel of the rifle and caught Fin under the chin, but then the Irishman was on him, tackling him, trying to bring down the Khukuri, screaming bloody murder.

Isaiah dropped the rifle and grabbed Fin, pulling him close, spinning toward the bridge's parapet, rolling hard, so that Fin's left arm was pinned against the stone wall, stopping him from bringing the blade to bear. Isaiah seized Fin's wrist, wrenching, trying to twist the blade out of it.

Isaiah's other hand found Fin's right forearm. He worked his way down it to the hand. He touched the edge of the dirty bandages. He caught hold of the bloody, splintered nubs that had been Fin's fingers before the machine-gun ruined them. He grabbed hold and twisted them back as far as he could. Fin's shriek was ear-shattering. He dropped the Khukuri and tried to get hold of Isaiah's hand, anything to stop the surge of pain.

Isaiah saw Fin rear back his head, then he was coming in a rush, bringing his forehead down into Isaiah's face as hard as he could.

The force of the strike was brutal. Isaiah lost his grip on Fin. He swung his elbows together and locked them in front of his face, trying to fend off a second hit.

When the second blow did not come, Isaiah looked up. He saw Fin's pale, pain-ravaged face in the dying flare light. He saw the Irishman's gaze shift to the distance, and a smile twisted his lips. Isaiah saw the Khukuri blade catch light as it cut the air. It hit and embedded halfway through Finbarr Kelly's skull. He crashed to the bridge in a dead heap.

Caitlin stood over them in shock. The bloody Khukuri fell from her hand.

Fin lay still for a long second.

Then Finbarr Kelly's body twitched and twisted and wrenched itself up off the ground. Fin turned on Caitlin, screaming, and charged. She slipped away from his ruined hand, but he grabbed hold of her hair with his left and began pulling her to him.

POP! A blinding magnesium flare lanced up and struck Fin's right cheek. The white burning mass stuck, setting flesh on fire, melting skin and eyeball and nose cartilage. Finbarr dropped Caitlin and took two steps back, then the flare exploded, and the burning elemental metal enveloped Fin's entire head in a halo of whiter-than-white fire. He stumbled back again.

Isaiah's kick took him the rest of the way. Fin crashed backward over the parapet and hit the water. The burning magnesium submerged, but the fire did not douse it. The flames kept on, jumping and dancing underwater, as Fin's corpse was ripped under the bridge and dragged downstream.

Isaiah felt a flush of exhaustion. The effects of Fin's head butt throbbed in his skull.

Francois.

The thought of his friend brought him back. He ejected the empty flare shell and reloaded. His eyes sought the Khukuri blade and found it. He grabbed it and ran for the overflowing drainage ditch.

But there was no one there. Across the now twelve-foot-wide flow of whitewater, there were two ruined dead men at the top of the stairs, savaged past use by Francois' cutlass. But of Francois and the Red Maiden, and all the rest of her men, there was no sign.

Isaiah backed away. Something drew his eye to the road that ran from St. Quentin to the bridge. Movement in the dark, one-hundred yards away. He aimed the flare gun and fired.

POP! It exploded above the first rigid ranks of thousands of dead Romans marching toward them in lockstep. At their head was a man on horseback. They were in no hurry, coming down the street at a steady, perfect cadence through the pouring rain under the glaring magnesium's light.

"Holy shit…" said Isaiah. He took Caitlin's hand. "RUN! *RUN!*"

Together, they sprinted across the bridge toward the tank.

When they reached the far side, Isaiah set his hands and helped Caitlin onto the tank's hull.

Isaiah scrambled up after her and pounded on the hatch. "HIT THAT BRIDGE!" He turned to Caitlin. "Cover your ears!"

She cupped her hands over them just in time. Both six-pounders unleashed eardrum shattering salvoes that struck the bridge span dead center. There was a two count, then the guns fired again, and then again. Large chunks of rock and pavement crashed into the water. But the bridge held. The masons who laid its foundation one-hundred years prior would have been proud.

Isaiah saw the Roman column moving toward the mouth of the bridge, steady on, undeterred by the cannon fire. He grabbed Caitlin's arm and led her to the top hatch. He pulled it open and eased her down and in.

As he dropped his legs over the lip to follow, he noticed something in the air and paused. At first, it was more a feeling than a sound, vibrating through him, but then the tank's hull picked it up and began to vibrate along with the air. It sounded like some thousand-voiced choir building from a *sshhh* to a scream. Isaiah looked east.

In the lightning's flash he saw a huge surge of water tumbling toward them through the canal, ripping away toe-paths and building foundations as it came, pushing a tonnage of debris before it, led by the black hull of a German Army barge.

BA-BAMM!

The twin cannons fired again, striking the bridge. Isaiah realized it did not matter. He dropped down into the tank. The stench of cordite and gunpowder, gasoline fumes, and dried blood was like a punch in the teeth.

"FLOOD'S COMING! WE GOT TO MOVE!" Isaiah hollered.

Li Peng was taking a shell from Shen Su and reloading when Isaiah reached the deck. His ears were still ringing from the shot, so he was not sure what Isaiah had said.

"What?" Peng asked.

"WE'VE GOT TO MOVE! FLASH FLOOD!" Isaiah yelled.

"Oh Christ..." Peng processed the implications, he limped to the driver's seat. He clutched and shoved the gear into reverse. With a sudden jolt, he accelerated, and they lurched in reverse, away from the bridge.

The surge of water struck the tank in the nose with the force of a massive fist, knocking them sideways. Caitlin, Isaiah, and Juddha Jai went crashing to the deck as the water tried to flip them.

Shen Su held fast to the cannon as they pitched and yawed. The horror of the Atlantic crossing came back in no uncertain terms. That he could survive that peril only to be drowned in some lowly canal seemed ridiculous. He looked to Zi Chang, who, miraculously, had achieved an even paler complexion than before. He clung to the wounded mastiff with his good arm. The tank pitched forward again as its tracks flailed in soft mud, and water began pouring through the front view ports and Lewis Gun sight, dousing Sergeant Li.

Suddenly, the treads found purchase. The tank leapt backward, slamming Li Peng into the console with a cry, but he held the accelerator firmly. The Daimler-Knight roared and the tank ground up the bank. It reached a forty-five-degree angle, then dropped, engine screaming, pulling them up and out of the flood's wrath.

As the treads found solid earth, grinding them away from the flood, Li Peng looked back to Shen Su with a ragged, grim-faced smile. *"Saved by a Dragon, neh?"*

Shen Su nodded, breathless.

"Get back to the gears for me. I need your help steering," said Li Peng.

Shen Su let go of the cannon and scrambled his way through the packed tank, past the ginger-haired woman and the scar-faced black man, past the black-haired fellow with brown skin and sharp eyes, past dear Zi Chang who was almost certainly dying, and the massive bloody mastiff beside him, who likely was, too, but had offered her warmth as comfort to the little Chinese fellow, regardless of her pain.

Shen Su settled in at the gears. The tank came to a stop. Li Peng struck the right side of the hull with the wrench. Su pulled the lever and the tank spun one-hundred-eighty degrees. Li Peng waved him off and Su released the track into gear. Then they were plowing forward into the storm. The Romans, the canal, and the hell of St. Quentin left further behind them with every passing second.

♠   ♠   ♠   ♠   ♠

When the German Army barge struck the bridge cutwaters, the boat splintered. The rush of water sent the remains crashing up and over the bridge parapet. The damage from the 6-pound guns had no real effect, but where mankind's savagery had failed, nature's would not. The crush of water and debris exploded the spandrel walls, parapets, and roadway. The arches and cutwaters collapsed and were dragged and tumbled downstream like toys kicked by some giant child in a temper fit. It grabbed the stone foundations and tore them out of the mud. Within moments, it was as though Napoleon's masons and labourers had never composed the perfect symmetry of the span. It might as well never have been.

General Varus watched in awe as the flood dismantled the bridge. His horse danced back, terrified, and he yanked the reins, pulling him all the way around in time to see the road leading to the bridge, its foundations undermined by the sudden current, collapsing into the wash.

Panicked, with his entire army now at his back, Varus shrieked at Oberon Junius. *"TURN THEM! TURN THEM!"*

Oberon Junius bellowed for the men to come about, and his Sergeants echoed the cry over the water's roar, but Varus could not contain himself. He turned the gelding and kicked his flanks, charging through his men, turning what might have been an orderly retreat into chaos and confusion.

Oberon watched Varus disappear, racing his horse over and through his own men. He shook his head, disgusted. He looked back across the canal and saw the metal turtle, half-submerged, going under. Suddenly, it found purchase, driving backward, then plowing up and out of the canal. He watched it disappear over the ridge.

"It may not be this night, but we'll run you down soon enough, and, metal turtle or no, we'll bring you low," Oberon thought. *"Yes, indeed."*

He turned back to his army, for the truth was these men belonged to him and always had. There would always be 'Caesars', bestriding the world with their grand schemes, but when it came to turning those schemes into reality, it was the men on the ground who counted—the reliable workmen who made things happen—not the grand men whose whims set the horror shows in motion. He hollered out to his sergeants, and in short order had his army turned away from the flood. They fell into crisp marching order and began a steady tramp out of St. Quentin.

Oberon ordered two squadrons out of the column and sent them scurrying east and west in search of a crossing. He knew well that the scope of the force would now become a hindrance. Once a juggernaut this size began to roll, it was difficult to turn. Plans had to be made, decisions set in stone, then action could be called for. Until then, patience, as painful as it was, was everything.

CHAPTER TWENTY-FOUR

—

V-109

"**H**oly Crow!"

James Cox reached down and grabbed Donnie's hand. "Come on, Donnie! We're gonna be okay! There's a boat waiting for us!" he said.

James and Rupert helped Donnie to his feet. Lightning stuttered, illuminating Adolf in the shadows behind Donnie, shaking and uncertain.

"Hey!" James said. "Whatta you know? You're that blind fellow!" He looked back at Donnie. "Did you all see anybody else on the way?"

Donnie shook his head. "No. Didn't see no one else."

Durant, Wolfgang, Jonah, and Renoir came around the corner, running through the downpour. They pulled up short when they saw Donnie and Adolf.

In the distance, the Lewis Gun started barking again. Durant guessed it could not be more than four or five hundred yards away.

"What's happening back there?" Durant asked Donnie.

Donnie stammered, "I—I don't know. I don't know what's happening back that way. They's a big truck with guns, that's all I know, I swear!"

Durant sensed there was more to the story, but there was no time. "Let's go," he said. Then he was leading the way through the flooded street, toward the canal.

Lightning cracked, revealing the last hundred yards, and Durant saw the water from the avenue pouring over the mule path into the overflowing canal. Not far now. Not far.

♠   ♠   ♠   ♠   ♠

Adam Gillét watched from the shadows as Adolf ran onward with the band of living men. As they gathered and ran toward the canal with Donnie and Adolf in their midst, Adam limped after them. He cursed his luck. He did not see a way to get to Adolf without killing the others or being cut down by them, but as long as he killed Adolf, it did not matter what became of him. He would find the moment to make his strike, then come what may. He gave up hope of seeing Francois again. Adolf's murder was all the farewell present he could hope to give.

♠   ♠   ♠   ♠   ♠

Darren Tremaine knew he was dying. Bathsheba had slowed to a steady canter. Every step she took racked his body with pain. Nausea flushed through him. He looked at his blood-soaked belly and saw the spear head poking out. Three feet of shaft was sticking out of his back. He vomited. Then he blacked out and slid from the saddle, splashing into the melted slush. His blood flowed with the water, down the gentle grade and into the canal.

Bathsheba stood over Darren until the German Shepherds found them. She stamped and danced away as they growled and barked at her, then she turned, her hooves clip-clopping away into the night before Little Boy Halstead, Harlan, Daddy Cox, Sheriff Coombs, and Big Don McMaster joined the dogs.

Halstead twisted his spear out of Darren and shook the blood off it, letting the rain wash the remainders away.

"Well, shit," said Daddy Cox. "Was hoping we could add this one to our gallows, too, but he is doornail dead. Shame."

"He gonna wake up?" Sheriff Coombs asked Halstead.

Halstead bent down. He rolled Darren's body over. The cavalryman had passed, that was certain. His eyes were open and rolled back, jaw slack, face shining pale-white when lightning flashed, but there was no sign the vessel would fill and rise again.

The Lewis Gun raging in the distance cut through the night.

"Well, boys," Daddy laughed. "Maybe the hanging party ain't over just yet after all."

"No," said Little Boy Halstead. "It has only just begun." He stood and led the way.

♠ ♠ ♠ ♠ ♠

Durant reached the rushing canal first. The black, hundred-foot long V-109 barge sat low in the water. The sluice flowed past, splashing up onto her deck. The mule path was already submerged. They had to fight through the canal's knee-deep current to cover the last forty yards to the bow of the boat.

The barge strained at the taut ropes cleating it to the dock. Durant grabbed the bowsprit and pulled himself onto the deck. Wolfgang followed, then he and Durant helped Rupert, Jonah, James, Donnie, Renoir, and Adolf up after them.

Durant turned to Wolfgang, "Get the engine running. I'll release the bow line."

Wolfgang nodded.

They heard staccato rifle fire downstream.

"Whatever that is," said Wolfgang, "once we are under way, we will be traveling straight toward it. How long?" Wolfgang asked.

"What do you mean?" said Durant.

"How long do we give the cavalrymen?"

Durant stared into the night for a long moment. "Get the boiler lit. Once we've got steam, we're cutting loose. We'll give them until then."

Durant jumped back off the deck, sloshing through the water to the bow. He followed the line down to a concrete dock submerged under three feet of black flood water.

Wolfgang grabbed Rupert. *"Can you get the boiler lit?"*

"Yes," Rupert replied.

"Go."

Rupert headed for the rear of the boat and the raised cockpit that sat beyond midships. Wolfgang saw the little sapper flashlight that hung from Rupert's neck light up as he pulled the chain, then the light disappeared down into the darkened galley, its dull glow vanishing into the belly of the boat, as Rupert headed for the engine room.

Wolfgang turned to Jonah. *"Check the machine guns at fore and aft. See that they are functional."*

"Yes, Captain," Jonah Unger said. He headed for the MG '08 that was bolted to the deck at the front of the boat.

Adolf started after Rupert, toward the cover of the galley, but Wolfgang grabbed him. *"No. He can manage it. Give me your bayonet."* Wolfgang held out his hand.

Adolf's look of anger at the request was lit by a burst of lightning. He shied away from Wolfgang's touch.

"Corporal, your bayonet," Wolfgang repeated.

Whatever resistance Adolf felt, he choked down. He held out the bayonet the dead Romans had pressed into his hand and Wolfgang took it.

"Help Corporal Unger with the MGs," Wolfgang said.

Adolf chafed under the command. He wanted his bayonet back. He wanted to get out of the rain below decks with Rupert Fuchs. He wanted to kill Wolfgang and Jonah Unger and all the rest of them. But he bowed under Wolfgang's gaze and silently followed Jonah up to the front gun.

Wolfgang looked to the two Americans, James and Donnie.

"Wh-what do you want us to do?" asked James Cox.

"You keep watch at the front." Wolfgang looked at Donnie, standing soaked and forlorn next to James. "You,—" Donnie looked up. "You keep watch at the rear. Call out if you see anything coming."

James patted Donnie's shoulder in what he hoped was a reassuring fashion, then he went forward over the slick black deck and stood behind Adolf and Jonah Unger, who had already begun an appraisal of the machine gun's working order.

Donnie hesitated, then limped past Wolfgang toward the stern, staring back into the pitch-black rain. The dead men were coming. When they caught him again, they would not hesitate to punish him for his failure. He felt certain of one thing—his own doom.

Wolfgang looked at Renoir. For a second, he saw his brother's death through Renoir's eyes again—Sebastian's head, skull splintering from the sniper shot, the pink spray of misted brains and blood, the collapse of dead muscle and bones, useless organs and fat, wrapped snugly in German Field Grey wool. He felt his body hum at the image, then he tucked it away again. Now was not the time.

"I'll cut the breast lines from bow to stern. You get the stern warp line ready to cast off," Wolfgang said.

Renoir nodded. "Oui."

Wolfgang headed for midships and jumped down into thigh-deep water on the mule path, while Renoir followed Donnie toward the stern, searching out the rearmost warp line.

At the bow of the boat, Durant strained at the rope that held the V-109 in a tight embrace to the foremost steel cleat. The wet rope was impossible to move. It had been tied off loosely when the water was a foot below the mule path, but with the flood of rain and melted snow pushing the water four feet higher, it was now taut as a steel cable. The cleat hitch knot itself was pulled mercilessly tight.

Behind him, Wolfgang found the first of three breast lines that cinched the middle of the boat to the dock. He felt his way down until he found the cleat, but just as Durant had, he saw that pulling the knot free was an impossible task.

"It's no good," Durant yelled over the downpour. "We have to cut them loose."

"Yes! I understand. I'll cut the breast lines first."

"Right!" Durant replied.

Wolfgang set the serrated edge of Adolf's bayonet against the wet rope and began sawing. The strands began to fall away, and in half a minute, the breast line's final threads tore apart. He fought the current, splashing through it until he reached the stay rope at midships. He cut into it as quickly as he could, sawing away at rigid, wet hemp.

At the rear of the boat, Donnie knelt by the stern machine gun, staring into the night, not really seeing anything but his own impending murder, certain he was helpless to stop it.

Renoir joined Donnie and found the stern line running from the boat to its dock cleat. He slid past Donnie and hopped onto the flooded dock, following the rope down. It led him underwater. He tried to keep his face out of the black canal flow but could not reach the rope's tail. He ducked under for a half a second, but the memory of drowning was like an electrified fence and it sent him back up, hyperventilating. He worked to calm himself. He was not buried under rocks. He was not traveling in memory to the murder of his prostitutes and the revenge he had taken for them. He had a simple task to accomplish that might save his life. He breathed deep and submerged, blind in the blackness, feeling desperately for the rope that would set them free.

Wolfgang felt the midship breast line split. He pushed through the rising water to the last breast line and cut into it.

In the distance, louder than the thunder, the sound of the six-pound artillery guns in the tank, firing point blank, echoed up the canal to them. Wolfgang redoubled his efforts, leaning forward, putting all his weight into driving the blade of the bayonet through the rope that had them trapped on the dock.

Lightning flashed, and he saw Renoir explode up out of the water, heaving in air. He wiped the water out of his eyes and looked back to Wolfgang.

"I have the rope," Renoir yelled, "but she is seized to the cleat. We'll have to cut it."

"I know," Wolfgang shouted over the downpour and the guns. "We need to cut the bow line first, then I'll bring you the bayonet."

Renoir nodded. Lightning struck. Wolfgang and Renoir saw Bathsheba coming down the path toward them, stepping high through the flood. They saw the whites of the horse's eyes rolling in terror as she moved past them, riderless.

Renoir shook his head. "Our cavalryman… We cannot wait for him."

Wolfgang nodded. He followed the horse the length of the boat to Durant, rushing through the water with the bayonet.

Jonah and Adolf were halfway to Donnie at the rear machine gun when Bathsheba and Wolfgang splashed past on the mule path.

James Cox watched in horror as the shell-shocked horse cantered past Durant. When Bathsheba reached the avenue that ran to the canal, she turned into it. With a powerful burst, she leapt from the flooded mule path and disappeared into St. Quentin's blackened streets.

"Here!" Wolfgang yelled, as he handed Durant the bayonet. "Hurry!"

Durant grabbed the blade and cut into the rope, sawing desperately.

"We should not wait to cut the rear line." Wolfgang said.

Durant nodded. "If the rider's not here before we cut the stern warp, he's not coming!"

On the V-109 deck, Rupert came up from below decks and stumbled to the bow, hollering down to Wolfgang, *"The boiler is lit! But we won't have power for some time!"*

"We'll ride the current until we do!" Wolfgang replied. *"Get to the wheel and be ready to steer us!"*

Rupert nodded and headed for the con.

Durant was halfway through the bow line when they heard yelling from the rear of the boat. Then the machine gun erupted in a roar of fire.

♠   ♠   ♠   ♠   ♠

Rupert reached the steps that led to the wheelhouse and yelled to Jonah who was kneeling at the rear machine-gun beside Donnie and Adolf, *"Make ready! As soon as the stern line is cut, we are going!"*

"Yes, Sergeant!" Jonah replied.

Rupert climbed the stairs and took the wheel.

Adolf stood behind Donnie, both men hovering over Jonah Unger as he inspected the rear MG.

Jonah opened the MG '08 receiver and pointed toward the ammunition box. "Gib me die munitionsgürtel."

Donnie heard the stream of German and, remarkably, understood precisely what the Jewish fellow was asking for. He opened the ammo can and felt for the end of the cloth belt filled with brass, lead, and white powder. He passed the belt to Jonah, who dropped it into the teeth of the MG and snapped the receiver closed. He moved the well-oiled gun back-and-forth on its tripod, testing the sweep. He was pleased to see it had been well maintained.

Lightning flashed. Jonah Unger looked up. He saw the beasts splashing down the mule path toward Renoir. He cried out to the Belgian, "HUNDE! *HUNDE!!!"*

Renoir looked back. Three massive German Shepherds, pushed by the current, surged through water up to their necks, raging toward the Belgian.

Renoir stepped backward. His foot caught on the cleat, and before the first dog leapt, he was already falling, tripping backward over the rope. It saved his life. The foremost German Shepherd's teeth snapped air where Renoir's face had been a millisecond before.

Renoir felt the dog coming down with him, and he shoved into its soft belly, throwing it past him, down the mule path, driven by its own momentum. Renoir's back hit the water and he disappeared into it. He heard the water-dampened roar of Jonah triggering the machine gun.

♠   ♠   ♠   ♠   ♠

Wolfgang saw Renoir disappear under water. The German Shepherd splashed down. When it came back up, it was plowing toward Wolfgang and Durant, teeth flashing.

Wolfgang set his feet as the dog tore through the water. It leapt and struck. Wolfgang grabbed for its hackles and felt sharp canines ripping into his forearms, stabbing with its muzzle, trying to find purchase on arteries or anywhere that delicate organ meats sat waiting. Wolfgang fell back, fighting desperately to keep the beast from getting past his arms to his head and neck.

Then Durant was there, and Wolfgang heard the dog yelp as the bayonet stabbed into it, again and again. It tried to turn its teeth on Durant, but the blade came up under its chin and Durant shoved and twisted the dog away, then drove all his weight down, pressing the steel point through the base of the skull, up into the dog's brains. The Shepherd went limp and Durant released. He twisted and pulled, yanking the bayonet out.

The MG kept chattering at the rear of the barge.

Durant grabbed Wolfgang by the shoulder. "Are you alright?"

"Yes! Cut the line!"

Durant found the bow rope and felt for the notch he had already sawed halfway through. He slid the bayonet into it and ran its bloody teeth back and forth furiously. The rope split in two and went slack.

The rushing canal caught the head of the boat and slammed the nose of the V-109 into the canal pilings. The steel deck rail bobbed up and caught Durant in the hip, knocking him to his knees on the streaming mule path. The current grabbed him and tried to pull him away, but Durant found purchase and stumbled to his feet. He fought past Wolfgang as the water surged, struggling toward Renoir and the last rope at the stern.

"GET ON BOARD, I'LL CUT THE REAR WARP LINE!" Durant yelled.

Wolfgang nodded and tried to stand, but he had to stop halfway, catching his breath. His left arm was bleeding badly and throbbing. He flexed his forearm and found that the muscles would all contract. The attack had not rent tendons or muscle. He hoped the dog's teeth had not severed a vein.

♠ ♠ ♠ ♠ ♠

As Renoir sat up and sucked in air, the MG's sound vibrated through him. The stutter of muzzle flash lit the canal along with staccato lightning from the sky. A bracing roll of thunder drowned the MG's bark. The two German Shepherds caught in Jonah's field of fire danced and yelped as bullets tore through them.

Donnie guided the cloth bullet belt smoothly out of the feed tray up to Jonah's waiting MG. Jonah released the trigger. When lightning flashed again, it showed the current catching the dead dogs and pulling them out into the canal, past the boat and into the night.

Durant reached Renoir and helped him up.

"Give me the bayonet! I'll cut the line!" Renoir hollered.

Durant nodded. He handed him the bayonet and stumbled to the edge of the boat, reaching for the railing.

Renoir grabbed the final rope and sliced into it.

♠ ♠ ♠ ♠ ♠

While Jonah's bullets ripped through the thick fur and skin of the dogs, on the far side of the boat, Little Boy Halstead pulled his blackened body out of the canal and onto the vessel's deck.

Harlan, Daddy Cox, Sheriff Coombs and Big Don McMaster came after him. The five of them had slipped into the canal and let the fast-moving flow take them underwater to the boat. They latched on and eased their way to midships, on the canal side, waiting patiently for the German Shepherds to draw the attention of the men on deck. When the MG lit into the dogs, they followed Halstead silently up onto the barge.

♠ ♠ ♠ ♠ ♠

Adolf was backing away from the roaring machine gun. He glanced to where Rupert was making ready in the wheelhouse. He looked at the stairs that led to the safety of the hold below, but before he could escape down them, Little Boy Halstead grabbed him and dragged him back behind the cover of the wheelhouse, pulling him close. Adolf felt cold spittle hitting his face with the rain as Little Boy Halstead spoke.

"Your debt is not paid, boy. You owe the Fat Man." Little Boy Halstead pointed toward Jonah Unger. *"Start with the boy who is killing my dogs."*

"No... I—I have no weapons," Adolf stammered.

"With your hands then. We are done with your excuses."

Adolf swallowed hard. *"Yes, yes... I will."*

Little Boy Halstead released him. Adolf stood. He took a halting breath and then, before fear could stop him, he started across the deck to where Jonah and Donnie were firing at the German Shepherds.

The machine gun quit. There was a second of breathless silence. Jonah searched through the rain for more targets.

Adolf reached out for Jonah, hands shaking. He lunged, wrapped his arm around the young man's neck and yanked him backward, choking him. They hit the deck, flailing.

Donnie cried out in surprise as Adolf seized Jonah. Then Big Don had his son, squeezing his neck, vise-like, smothering his mouth with his hand, stifling his cry of alarm.

Big Don whispered harshly as he dragged his son away from Adolf's attempted murder, "SHH. Shut your mouth, boy. Shut your goddamn trap. Papa's here now."

Donnie knew his father's voice when he heard it. He shook with terror. He took heed.

Donnie saw a tick of movement, then Little Boy Halstead ran past them, spear in hand. Just as Durant pulled himself on deck, Little Boy Halstead struck, smashing into him, tackling him backward off the boat.

"Follow my lead, sonny," said Big Don.

"Yes, sir. Yes, papa!" Donnie squealed.

Big Don released Donnie. His son watched the big German body his papa was in run across the deck of the boat, striding past Adolf and Jonah Unger. Then Big Don leapt. He seemed to hang in the air, then his body slammed down onto Renoir, who was bent at the waist, furiously sawing through the last line linking them to the dock. They disappeared into the black water.

Donnie stumbled across the deck, climbed over the rail, and followed his father.

JEFFREY PIERCE

♠   ♠   ♠   ♠   ♠

Renoir never sensed them coming. The rope was nearly cut through when he
was blindsided. He dropped the bayonet as he pushed himself back up, but then
punches were raining down on him. He felt a brutal strike to his skull, behind
his right ear.

Then they were savaging him with their fists, snapping at him with their
teeth, shoving him under water and holding him there, sending punches down
into the blackness aimed at his kidneys, forcing him to suck canal water down
into his lungs. They held Renoir there until he gave up, ceasing all struggle,
folding into the tender mercy of deep, dark oblivion.

♠   ♠   ♠   ♠   ♠

In the wheelhouse, Rupert had been making the boat ready when it began. All
that remained was to cast off. In the light of his sapper flashlight, he saw the
pressure gauge needle starting to climb as the coal burning in the boiler room
began to build steam. He turned the wheel and felt the rudder moving smoothly
in response. When he heard Jonah Unger yelling "HUNDE! *HUNDE!*" he
turned and saw the machine gun erupt, lighting into the German Shepherds.

"Shit…"

He looked to the bow, where James Cox was watching Wolfgang and Durant
fight the first hound. Lightning ripped the sky and Rupert saw Durant savage
the thing with the bayonet. Durant stood and stumbled backward then grabbed
Wolfgang and pulled him up. Rupert could not tell how badly Wolfgang had
been hurt, but it seemed like they had the moment of breath they needed to cut
free of the dock and get under way. He saw Durant slice the bow line and get
knocked sideways, then he was helping Wolfgang along. The machine gun went
silent. While Wolfgang struggled toward the side of the boat, Durant splashed
along to Renoir at the stern line and passed him the bayonet.

Rupert looked back toward the stern MG. Lightning struck. He saw Adolf
choking the life out of Jonah Unger. He saw dark forms running across the deck
toward Durant and Renoir. Rupert raced down the steps, yelling at the top of his
lungs.

301

James Cox watched in horror, helpless, as Durant and Wolfgang fought the German Shepherd. He forced himself toward the railing and saw Durant shoving the blade home and finishing the dog. Gunfire roared from the stern. He saw Durant cut the line and run through the water toward the stern as the machine gun silenced. Wolfgang was bleeding badly from the dog bites. James stretched out his hand to help him board.

"Come on, Mr. Strathmann! I got you!"

Wolfgang reached out for him. James saw Wolfgang's eyes go wide. Then movement flashed past James, and Wolfgang disappeared under a pair of punching, kicking, raging dead men.

"NO!" James yelled. He started forward, ready to leap to Wolfgang's aid, but strong hands grabbed the nape of his shirt and shoulder. He spun backwards, felt his legs catch on his attacker's hip, then he was falling, hitting the deck, head hammering down and bouncing off it. He blacked out for a millisecond, then came to. He rolled onto his side, trying to stand, but his legs would not listen. Then something grabbed him by the collar and smashed him down onto his back, straddling him, trapping his arms by his sides. He tried to yell out, but his voice box was not reconnected to his brain's impulses. Then the thing was ripping open James's coat and pulling his pocket watch out. He smelled rank dead breath as the thing on top of him leaned in.

"Hey there, baby brother. Had to go and filch my watch, didn't you?" Harlan Cox asked.

James Cox flinched at the sound of his brother's voice.

"Don't you remember mama always saying, 'it's what you do when no one's a-watching that reveals your character?' You remember that?"

James did. But now Harlan had his trachea in his hand and was squeezing the cartilage. Even if he had a reasonable reply, he could not have offered it.

"You know what the Good Book says for thieves, baby brother? It says we cut off your hands. So, I suppose that's where your punishment oughta begin. Let's kick off there and see what comes next."

Harlan's father and Sheriff Coombs were disappearing with Wolfgang Strathmann in tow, pulling his limp body down the path, ready for the hangman, but Harlan was utterly serious about a different path for his brother. Slow, steady, cruel, meticulously violent, then buried alive; the exact same style of death that had taken Harlan's life. Harlan Cox was ready to bathe in his brother's blood.

Harlan stood and hauled James to his feet. He dragged him across the deck and threw his sibling overboard, splashing onto the mule path.

♠   ♠   ♠   ♠   ♠

Adolf had Jonah Unger's neck cinched tight. He was squeezing with all of his might. Jonah felt the throb of his own pulse in his neck dwindling, even as his heart tried to pump blood faster and faster. He sucked in a breath of air, reached out, then jammed his sharp elbow back into Adolf's testicles.

Adolf screamed in pain, and his grip loosened. Jonah shot the elbow again, then Adolf was pushing him away, trying to save himself from another strike. Jonah fought to catch his breath and stand, but he could not make it past his knees. He looked up and saw the little sapper, Rupert Fuchs, leaping down the wheelhouse steps, then he was standing between them, the little round flashlight around his neck lighting up Adolf's anguished face. Rupert held a short ratchet blade in his hands.

"What are you doing?! What are you doing?!" Jonah heard Rupert yell at Adolf.

Adolf charged. The little sapper did not flinch, he met the attack and stabbed upward into Adolf's belly. Corporal Hitler shrieked. Rupert pulled the knife out and slashed at him. Adolf stumbled backward, hands trying to ward off the attack, naked palms taking a raking cut that splayed them open, scattering blood into the rain. Adolf's calves hit the deck rail and he tripped backward out of the boat.

♠   ♠   ♠   ♠   ♠

Rupert saw Adolf disappear. Beyond him, lit by his dying flashlight, he saw the horribly blackened flesh of Halstead's naked back rise out of the flooded path. The spear in Halstead's hand cocked back to strike the man below him. Rupert Fuchs did not hesitate. He dropped his knife and jumped, reaching for the spear shaft, strong hands closing around it as his body crashed into Halstead's corpse.

The spear ripped free from Halstead's grasp.

Little Boy Halstead roared. He had been one thrust from the joy of ending Durant and spoiling the entire game. He turned to destroy whoever had done it.

His own spear shot straight up, through his open, screaming mouth. The leaf of the steel blade went through his soft palate. Rupert's legs drove him up, sending the blade shearing through Halstead's brain stem and vertebrae. Halstead's corpse went limp. The dead weight nearly yanked the spear out of Rupert's hands, but Rupert tore it free. The corpse dropped into the water. It bobbed up, then floated away down the rushing mule path.

Rupert yanked the chain on his flashlight. He reached down into the water and found Durant. He pulled him to his feet, then dragged him, coughing and spitting, to the side of the boat. He helped Durant get his hands wrapped around the wet steel of the deck railing, then Rupert turned to where Renoir had been assaulted by Big Don and his boy, Donnie Junior. They were gone.

Rupert pulled the chain again and looked to the front of the craft. Another burst of lightning seared the night, and he saw James Cox being hefted off the boat onto the mule path. The man who had thrown him stood on the bow, triumphant. He glared back toward Rupert's dull yellow flashlight. Of Wolfgang, Daddy Cox, and Sheriff Coombs, there was no sign.

Suddenly, the rear rope Renoir had savaged to threads split in two. The stern of the boat caught the current's energy, and it tore away from the dock, dragging Durant out into the flow, hanging by his fingers from the railing. The front of the boat slammed into the pilings and stuck, while the ass end careened out into the ever-widening canal. Rupert considered an impossible leap, but knew his legs would fail him. He saw the bow held up on the pilings. He ran toward it, spear raised.

♠   ♠   ♠   ♠   ♠

As James Cox surfaced and stood, in the flare of lightning, he watched Halstead's limp corpse float past. He looked up at Harlan and began backing away on shaking legs. He saw Harlan glance up the canal toward the little sapper's beam of light. Then the boat was yanked into the current as the rope fibers gave. When the bow hit the pilings and caught, Harlan's boots slipped on the deck and he stumbled overboard.

James dodged back as the boat thrust toward him. He felt his brother's hand brush his chest as he hit the water beside him. Adrenaline saved James. It sent a pulse through his legs and he flew, knees high, legs striding through the water. He scrambled out of its flow into the mouth of the avenue Darren Tremaine's horse had escaped up. He surged out of the canal water and ran after Bathsheba, faster than he could ever have imagined possible, desperation spurring every step, every burning breath, every impossibly fast contraction of his little heart, as he vanished into the dark streets of St. Quentin.

♠   ♠   ♠   ♠   ♠

Rupert Fuchs was splashing toward the bow of the boat as it began to grind against the concrete and pull away from the dock pilings. He saw James Cox rise and run. He saw the dead man stand and turn after James.

Rupert raised the spear. When his left foot stepped forward again, he turned his hips and let the spear fly. It impaled Harlan Cox through the back and sent him stumbling forward, tripping, and falling facedown into the canal.

Rupert did not miss a step. He saw the boat sliding out of reach. He leapt. His chest struck the railing full-force and his arms wrapped over it. He held on, despite the pain, as the boat pulled away and began to move down the canal at a forty-five-degree angle. Rupert threw his leg over the railing and pulled himself onboard.

Jonah Unger saw Durant slipping from the railing. He grabbed Durant's forearms and leaned back, straining with all his weight to drag him onto the V-109 as it broke free and began to glide, off angle, down the swollen canal. As the front end broke free and careened away, the backside of the boat caught more of the canal's energy and began to expand its angle.

With one last surge, Jonah pulled Durant up and over the railing and both men fell onto the deck beside the machine gun.

Durant tried to stand. He could not. He could barely breathe. He was certain his ribs had broken when he landed on the mule path. "The rudder… turn the rudder, or we'll get stuck sideways…"

Jonah did not understand a word of it. Durant passed out.

The rear of the V-109 swung out, wider and wider toward perpendicular. Rupert limped along the deck, fighting through fatigue, desperate to reach the wheelhouse before they turned completely sideways. He felt the rear of the boat strike the mule path on the south side of the canal. He heard it grinding against steel and concrete. The front of the boat struck the north mule path, and suddenly they were slammed to a stop, lodged sideways in the canal. Water began rushing up and over the deck. By the time Rupert reached the wheelhouse, it was pouring down the stairs into the ship's hold.

"*SHIT!*" Rupert yelled.

Jonah Unger was next to the machine gun beside Durant's inert form, trying desperately to keep him above water.

As Rupert knelt beside them, he felt it coming. He looked back and heard the rushing roar before the lightning could illuminate it.

"*Holy mother of Christ...*"

One hundred yards away, closing steady, a mountainous wave of black water and debris roared and tumbled down the canal toward them.

♠   ♠   ♠   ♠   ♠

At the concrete wall on the distant side of the Riqueval Tunnel, when the rain began, the snow melt and fresh rainwater gathered quickly. Within minutes, the gorge beyond the Riqueval Tunnel had completely drowned the tunnel mouth. It poured through the machine-gun slits and murder holes, then the force ripped the door off its hinges and water poured into the tunnel. The first pieces of concrete failed, then the entire wall exploded inward, followed by a wave of water moving with incredible speed. It smashed through the Peniche barges inside the tunnel like toys, dragging their flotsam onward, guns and gas and aeroplane parts all crashing through barriers and shorting out the overhead lights as the water reached the ceiling.

When the water's flow hit the exit six kilometers away, it exploded into the canal like a fire hose. It unmoored the three barges there and threw them south. It took hold of the hundreds of burned bodies on the shore and dragged them pell-mell along with it, gaining speed and power as the water's volume doubled and tripled in size, destroying everything in its path.

Rupert Fuchs was the first to hear it coming.

♠   ♠   ♠   ♠   ♠

"*Come on! COME ON!*" Rupert yelled.

He grabbed one of Durant's arms and Jonah took the other. They could no longer see the coming wave, but they heard it. They hauled Durant to the stern and threw him over, then leaped down beside him. They grabbed hold of him again and dragged him, clambering desperately up the steep, soaked bank of the canal. As they reached the peak, the wall of water struck the V-109, lifting and throwing it down the canal like a child's bath toy, all the care and dedication its sailors had poured into it sundered in a breath.

Rupert and Jonah were hit by the spray and knocked over. The water tried to pull Durant's body away, but they held fast to his wrists and hauled him out of the flood.

On top of the berm, Jonah collapsed back on the wet grass, breath heaving. In the distance, he heard six-pound artillery cannons giving their all. Then the guns went silent. There was only the sound of the rushing flood. He sat up beside Rupert and looked down at Durant.

"Is he alive?" Jonah asked.

Rupert leaned over Durant's chest and listened. He nodded. *"I think so."*

Jonah looked across the flood of water toward St. Quentin. *"They got them all… James… Sergeant Renoir. Captain Strathmann… the other American…"*

"Yes."

"And Adolf… He tried to kill me!"

"Yes," Rupert replied.

"Thank you, Sergeant… You saved my life."

Rupert nodded. He patted Jonah's shoulder.

Durant began to stir.

"How are you, Lieutenant?" asked Rupert.

Durant understood 'Lieutenant', but that was all. He forced himself to sit up. He looked down at the surging floodwaters.

Rupert shook his head. "Das boot ist weg. Unsere freunde." Rupert stood and held out his hands to Durant and Jonah. "Komme. Wir müssen gehen."

"Where will we go?" Jonah asked.

Rupert shrugged. *"Anywhere but here. Yes?"*

Rupert reached out. Durant and Jonah took his hands. He helped them up to unsteady feet, then they followed the little sapper as he led them over the berm, heading south into black rain.

White lightning split the sky. Thunder boomed and rolled. As the lightning faded, the dark night swallowed them whole.

♠ ♠ ♠ ♠ ♠

EPILOGUE

—

SINS OF THE FATHER

James Cox flew up the street through the pouring rain, his strength birthed out of pure terror. If the devils wanted him tonight, they would have to cut him down as he ran.

Lightning sliced the sky, its thunder shaking through the street, concurrent with the flash. James flinched sideways, but kept on, galvanized. The searing whiteness had revealed salvation. He would not be denied.

Bathsheba stood frozen in the middle of the intersection ahead, terrified, eyes rolling. James slowed as he approached. Her reins dangled before her. James knew his brother must be coming, but he did not look back. If he saw Harlan tearing through the streets after him, his own fear would spook the horse and he would die. He ignored Bathsheba's front hooves and the damage she would do to his head if she reared and lashed out. He reached out trembling fingers and grasped hold of the wet leather reins. He could feel her tension building, ready to explode. He eased to her side, grasped the pommel, slid a foot into the stirrup, and leapt into the saddle. Bathsheba let him guide her head around, then he kicked her flanks. She heeded the command, eager, charging away through the streets of St. Quentin.

James never looked back.

♠ ♠ ♠ ♠ ♠

When Renoir opened his eyes, lightning flashed. He saw Donnie McMaster dragging him by one arm and a big dead German sergeant hauling him by the other. He felt the back of his boots juddering as he was pulled across the cobblestones.

He heard Donnie ask the dead German, "Where we takin' him, papa?"

The dead German grinned. "Case you ain't heard, hangin' party ain't over yet, sonny. Not by a damn sight."

Then Renoir flickered out.

♠ ♠ ♠ ♠ ♠

Wolfgang opened his eyes when the rope around his neck cinched an inch tighter. His hands were bound in front of him with telephone wire. The fingers had begun to numb from lack of blood flow. He felt his legs dragging behind him, ankles also strapped tightly together. He looked up through pelting rain and saw the silhouettes of the men carrying him, backlit by stuttering lightning, as they hauled him toward the towering St. Quentin Basilica. He saw Sergeant Renoir, hanging limp in the arms of two other men. Then they stopped. Wolfgang felt the hold on his underarms release and he hit the ground full force. The back of his head bounced off stone and the wind was knocked out of him. He grunted in pain and rolled onto his side. When he opened his eyes and looked up, he saw a dozen dead men coming out of a shadowed alleyway.

Daddy Cox, Sheriff Coombs, Donnie McMaster, and Big Don stood over their pair of prisoners as the men approached. Donnie peed in his pants. He knew the Romans had come for him.

"How do, fellows?" asked Daddy Cox.

The leader of the squadron stepped forward. "Da nobis captivum."

Latin was not in Daddy Cox's bailiwick. He shrugged. "Didn't catch a lick of that, boy. You're gonna have to speak the English."

The dead man turned to his fellow Romans. *"Take him."*

The squadron stepped forward. Daddy did not require a common language to understand what would happen if he resisted. He knew when he was outmatched. Daddy stepped back and released his hold on Wolfgang's leash.

"Easy there, fellas, we don't want no trouble," he said.

The Romans grabbed Wolfgang and pulled him up. Four of them hefted Renoir's limp form, then they disappeared with the pair into the rain, leaving Daddy, Sheriff Coombs, Donnie, and his father behind.

Daddy looked at Coombs. "Well, shit… What in the hell you think that's about?"

For his own part, Donnie McMaster would have jumped for joy if he had the energy. That the Romans had not exacted immediate, violent retribution upon him for failing to bring them the Ghurka seemed like a gift from God in Heaven. He would not take this second chance for granted. He swore to Jesus he would never do any bad deeds ever again.

♠   ♠   ♠   ♠   ♠

The Red Maiden led her depleted pack of warriors through the streets of St. Quentin, chewing on the bitterness of her setback. In a shocking turn of events, the African had murdered five of her raiders before they took him down. Between the surging water, the metal beast spitting fire, and the man who shot her horse out from under her, walking away from the assault with the African in tow was a victory, albeit a lukewarm one. The failure to kill the Irish woman galled but could not be helped. Caitlin would have to wait.

In the near distance, she heard the echo of the tank's guns firing on the bridge and was glad she had not tried to charge into them. Then the roar of the water overwhelmed the roar of the tank. She looked back down the avenue and saw the black wall of water crash through the canal, destroying everything in its path. She was grateful for the instinct that told her to run and the humility to listen to that urging. She recalled raiding an Irish coastal village. They had sacked and raped the town. They might just as easily have sat back and feasted, but the same voice in her head told her to take to the waves. Her raiding party had barely hoisted anchor when the mounted knights came galloping across the sandy beach toward them. Her men sunk their oars deep and were out of range of the longbows within minutes. Gunnhildr knew that if the chainmail-clad men had caught them feasting, or on the sand, they would have ridden them down, one and all, without breaking a sweat.

She looked back at Francois. Four of her men held him, one on each arm and leg, while a fifth kneed him in the ribs every time he tried to fight his way loose.

When she looked forward, she saw a broad avenue opening ahead of them. It was filled with men standing in rank and file, guttering torches in their hands.

Gunnhildr pulled up short. Her men followed suit.

Oberon Junius strode down the avenue toward them, followed by his army.

♠　♠　♠　♠　♠

Adolf stumbled along through the pouring rain, weeping. He saw blood pouring from his slashed palms, spattering down into the flooded streets when lightning cut the sky. He hugged his midsection with his forearms. He could not distinguish blood from wet wool, but his belly stung sharply from Rupert's stab and he was certain he was dying. He fell to his knees in despair. He shut his eyes.

SLAP!

Adolf saw stars as the open hand struck his cheek. Adolf's eyes shot open, and he found himself kneeling in sand. The bright desert sun was half-blinding. He looked down at his hands. They were unmarred, as was his belly. He looked up and the hand that slapped him swung again, splitting his lip and making his ears ring.

As he blinked away tears, he realized that the man with the close-cropped hair, imperial handlebar mustaches and ice-blue, dead eyes striking the blows was his papa, Alois.

Alois grabbed his only son by his collars and pulled his face up. *"This man tells me you have not held up your end of the bargain,"* Alois said.

Adolf could smell the dark beer on his father's breath and taste it in the spittle that hit his face. He looked across the parched backyard of the diner to the Fat Man who leaned casually against the building, enjoying the shade the rear porch awning cast into the sun-baked yard, his girth seeming to hold up the building as much as it held up him.

"How can you bring such shame on me?"

Alois struck his son again.

♠   ♠   ♠   ♠   ♠

Adam saw Adolf collapsed in the street, lit by a lightning strike. He gripped his bayonet and broke into a jog toward him.

♠   ♠   ♠   ♠   ♠

Isaiah pressed the heels of his palms against his eyes. The roar of the tank vibrated through the whole of his body. The heat after the snow and the downpour felt like a blessing, even with the stench of the burning gasoline. He could imagine letting it lull him to sleep and awakening with the dawn, wedged between Caitlin and the Chinaman, Black Betty at his feet. But he knew if he slept where his dreams were likely to take him. He forced his eyes back open.

"HEY," he hollered to Li Peng. Peng looked back over his shoulder. "HOLD UP FOR A MINUTE," Isaiah said.

Peng decelerated and the tank sat at idle.

Isaiah stood and came to the front of the tank. "Say, Sergeant, how'd you feel about making a loan of that Lewis Gun to me for the night?"

Peng cut the engine and the tank died. Caitlin looked up at Isaiah.

"What are you doing, Isaiah?" Caitlin asked.

"Only thing I can. Last I seen of Francois, he was living. Until I seen him dead with my own eyes, I got to assume that's still the case. If I leave him behind now, I ain't ever gonna be able to leave him behind, you know what I mean?"

Five minutes later, the agreement was in place. Isaiah shook hands with Li Peng, then he looked back to Caitlin. "Hey. Keep that girl alive for me if you can."

Caitlin stroked Black Betty's scruff and nodded. "I will."

Then Isaiah and Juddha Jai Pandit climbed out of the tank and jogged into the diminishing rain toward St. Quentin's overflowing canal. In moments, the black mist embraced them and they vanished into its bosom.

♠   ♠   ♠   ♠   ♠

ABOUT THE AUTHOR

Jeffrey Pierce is an actor and writer. He has appeared in over 140 episodes of television and streaming series, most recently in HBO MAX's adaptation of *The Last of Us*, Amazon Prime's detective series *Bosch,* and the Hulu series *Castle Rock* from Stephen King and J.J. Abrams. He has also had the pleasure of acting in some of the top video games of the past decade, most recently starring in *Call of Duty:WWII* and *The Last of Us Part II*.

ABOUT THE ARTWORK

Jai Mitchell is self-taught. He found his gift as part of his own journey to health and well-being through art therapy. You can see more of his work at https://www.artjaigantic.com. For information on purchasing any of the art in The Reckoning Series, contact: alijayart@gmail.com or go to: https://store.alijayfineart.com

NOTE FROM THE AUTHOR

Word-of-mouth is crucial for any author to succeed. If you enjoyed *The Reckoning: All The Devils Are Here*, please leave a review online—anywhere you are able. Even if it's just a sentence or two. It would make all the difference and would be very much appreciated.

Thanks!
Jeffrey Pierce

We hope you enjoyed reading this title from:

Subscribe to our mailing list – *The Rosevine* – and receive **FREE** books, daily deals, and stay current with news about upcoming releases and our hottest authors.
Scan the QR code below to sign up.

Already a subscriber? Please accept a sincere thank you for being a fan of Black Rose Writing authors.

View other Black Rose Writing titles at
www.blackrosewriting.com/books and use promo code
PRINT to receive a **20% discount** when purchasing.

Made in the USA
Monee, IL
15 December 2023

49237116R00194